# THE TRIAL OF FALLEN ANGELS

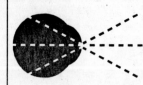

This Large Print Book carries the
Seal of Approval of N.A.V.H.

# THE TRIAL OF FALLEN ANGELS

## JAMES KIMMEL, JR.

**WHEELER PUBLISHING**

*A part of Gale, Cengage Learning*

GALE
CENGAGE Learning

Detroit • New York • San Francisco • New Haven, Conn • Waterville, Maine • London

**GALE**
CENGAGE Learning·

Copyright © 2012 by James Kimmel, Jr.

Portions of this book were previously published under the title *Forgiving Ararat*.

The Author's Note has been adapted with permission from *Suing for Peace*, by James Kimmel, Jr., the second edition of which will be released as *Legal Advice for the Soul*.

Wheeler Publishing, a part of Gale, Cengage Learning.

Wheeler Publishing Large Print Hardcover.

The text of this Large Print edition is unabridged.

Other aspects of the book may vary from the original edition.

Set in 16 pt. Plantin.

LIBRARY OF CONGRESS CATALOGING-IN-PUBLICATION DATA

Kimmel, James P.
  The trial of fallen angels / by James Kimmel, Jr.
    pages ; cm. — (Wheeler Publishing large print hardcover)
  ISBN 978-1-4104-5529-1 (hardcover) — ISBN 1-4104-5529-7 (hardcover) 1.
  Future life—Fiction. 2. Women lawyers—Fiction. 3. Large type books. I. Title.
  PS3611.I466T75 2013
  813'.6—dc23                                    2012042934

Published in 2013 by arrangement with Amy Einhorn Books, a member of G.P. Putnam's Sons, a member of Penguin Group (USA) Inc.

Printed in Mexico
1 2 3 4 5 6 7 17 16 15 14 13

*For John, Leo, Franz,*
*Charles, Herman, and Emily,*
*who came before*

*That* art thou . . .

"I think it well you follow me and I will be your guide and lead you forth through an eternal place. There you shall see the ancient spirits tried."

— DANTE, *The Inferno*

*I do not remember anymore.*

*Were my eyes blue like the sky or brown like fresh-tilled earth? Did my hair curl into giggles around my chin or drape over my shoulders in a frown? Was my skin light or dark? Was my body heavy or lean? Did I wear tailored silks or rough cotton and flax?*

*I do not remember. I remember that I was a woman, which is more than mere recollection of womb and bosom. And for a moment, I remembered all my moments in linear time, which began with womb and bosom and ended there too. But these are fading away now, discarded ballast from a ship emerged from the storm. I do not mourn the loss of any of these, nor am I any longer capable of mourning.*

*I was named Brek Abigail Cuttler. I have just learned that what is is what I knew once as a young child and glimpsed twice in twilight as an adult. I have chosen what is from what is not. And I will always be.*

11

■ ■ ■ ■

# PART I

■ ■ ■ ■

# 1

I arrived at Shemaya Station after my heart stopped beating and all activity in my brain irreversibly ceased.

This is the medical definition of death, although both the living and, I assure you, the dead, resent its finality. There's always cause for hope, people argue, and sometimes miracles. Even after death. I've discovered, for example, that if a miracle fails at the final moment to keep you alive, there's still the possibility one will come along later, at the Final Judgment, to keep you from spending the rest of eternity wanting others dead.

I didn't know I had died when I arrived at Shemaya Station, nor did I have any reason to suspect such a thing. Nobody announces that your life's over when it is. As far as I was concerned, my heart was still beating and my brain still functioning; the only hint that something out of the ordinary had hap-

15

pened was that I had no idea where I was or how I'd gotten there. I simply found myself alone on a wooden bench in a deserted urban train station with a high arched dome of corroded girders and trusses and broken glass panels filthy with soot. I had no memory of a train ride, no memory of a destination. A dimly lit board in the middle of the waiting area showed arrival times but no departures, and I assumed, as most who come here do, that the board was broken or there were problems with the outbound tracks.

I sat and stared at the board, waiting for it to flash some piece of information that would give me a clue about where I was or at least where I was going. When the board refused to divulge anything further, I stood and gazed down the tracks, as anxious passengers do, hoping to see some movement or a flicker of light in the distance. The rails vanished into utter darkness, either a tunnel or a black starless night, I could not tell which. I glanced back at the board again and then, forlornly, around the station: ten tracks and ten platforms, all vacant; ticket counter, newsstand, waiting area, shoe shine, all empty. The building was completely quiet: no announcements over the loudspeakers; no whistles blowing, brake shoes screeching, or air compressors shrieking; no conductors shouting, passengers complaining, or panhandling musicians playing. Not even the sound of a janitor sweeping in a far corner of the building.

I sat back down on the bench and noticed I was wearing a black silk skirted suit. The sight of this suit made me feel a little safer. I had been a lawyer during my life, and lawyers always wear suits to feel less vulnerable. This particular suit was my favorite because it made me feel the most confident and least apologetic as a young woman when I entered the courtroom. I smoothed the skirt on my lap, admiring the weight and rich texture of the fabric and the way it glided over my stockings. It really was a beautiful suit — a suit that attracted glances from colleagues, opposing counsel, and even men on the street. It was a suit that said I was a lawyer to be taken seriously. The best part of all was that I had found it on a clearance rack at an outlet store — a power suit *and* a bargain. I loved that suit.

So there I was, sitting all alone on a bench in this deserted train station, infatuated with my black silk suit, when I noticed some small stains on the lapel of my jacket. The stains were crusty and yellowish-white, and I assumed I had probably spilled cappuccino on myself earlier in the day. It was one of my favorite drinks. I scratched at the stains with the edge of a polished but chipped fingernail, expecting the aroma of coffee to be released; but a very different scent floated into my consciousness instead: baby formula.

*Baby formula? Do I have a child . . . ? Yes, of course . . . a child . . . a baby daughter . . . I remember now. But what's her name? I think it begins with an S . . . Susan, Sharon, Samantha, Stephanie, Sarah . . . Sarah? Oh, yes, Sarah.*

But try as I might, I couldn't remember anything about Sarah's face or hair, or the way she giggled or cried, or the smell of her skin, or the way she might have squirmed when I held her. I remembered only that a child had grown inside of me, had become part of me, and then had left to join the world around me — where I could see her and touch her but not protect her the way I did when she was inside me. And yet, even though I couldn't remember anything about my own daughter except her name, I wasn't bothered by this in the least. Sitting there on the bench in Shemaya Station, I was far more worried about the stains on my jacket — terrified somebody would see what I had allowed to happen to my favorite "I belong" black silk suit.

I scraped more vigorously at the stains. When they wouldn't go away, I lapped at my fingertips to moisten them. But instead of disappearing, the stains grew larger and changed in color from yellowish white to deep wine red.

*The dye's beginning to run . . . that's why the suit was on the clearance rack.*

But the stains started behaving differently too. They liquefied, sending crimson streaks down my jacket, skirt, and legs. This fascinated me. I dabbed my fingers in the red fluid, tentatively at first, like a child given a jar of paint, then with growing confidence, drawing two little stick figures with it beside me on the bench — a mother and her young daughter. The liquid felt warm and viscous and tasted pleasantly salty when I put a finger to my tongue. A pool of it gathered on the concrete floor of the station, and I slipped off my heels and tapped my toes in it, lost in the creamy sensation.

In the middle of all this, an old man walked up to my bench and sat down beside me.

"Welcome to Shemaya," he said. "My name is Luas."

Luas had moist, gray eyes, as if he was always thinking something poignant, and an

19

annotated, gentle sort of frog's face, flabby and wise like a worn book. The face seemed familiar, and after a moment I recognized it as the face of my mentor, the senior lawyer who had hired me out of law school.

*Now what was his name . . . ? Oh yes, Bill, Bill Gwynne. But the old man sitting next to me said his name was Luas, not Bill.*

Luas welcomes everybody to Shemaya. He appears differently to each of us, and to each in his own way. He might be an auto mechanic or a teacher to one, a father or a preacher to another, or maybe a madman or all of these combined. In Shemaya, we dress one another up to be exactly whom we expect to see. For me, Luas was a composite of the three older men I had adored during my life: he wore a white shirt with a tweed blazer that smelled of rum pipe tobacco, the way my Grandpa Cuttler's clothes smelled; and, as I said, he had Bill Gwynne's flabby face; and when I showed him my feet and my left hand, all covered in red, helpless like a little girl playing in her spaghetti, he flashed my Pop Pop Bellini's knowing smile as if to say: *Yes, my granddaughter, I see; I see what you're afraid to see, but I'll pretend not to have noticed.*

"Come along, Brek," Luas said. "Let's get you cleaned up."

*How did he know my name?*

I looked down again, but now my clothes were gone — my black silk suit and cream-colored silk blouse, my bra, panties, stockings, and shoes. They had never been there, actually. There had been only the idea of clothes, as I was only an idea, defined by who I'd insisted on being during the nearly thirty-one years of my life. Only my body remained, naked and covered with blood. I knew now the red liquid was blood, and that it was my blood, because it was spurting through three small holes in my chest, and because it felt warm and precious the way only blood feels. Suddenly my perspective shifted, and it seemed as though I was watching it all from the opposite bench.

*Who is this woman? I wondered. Why doesn't she put her fingers in the holes and stop the bleeding? Why doesn't she call out for help? She's so young and pretty, she must have so much to live for. But just look at her sit there — she does nothing but watch, and she feels nothing but pity: pity for the platelets clotting too late, pity for the parts of her body that had once been the whole. And there — see how her brain flickers, losing reasoning first, then consciousness. Listen. The roar of nothingness fills her ears.*

Luas removed his jacket and wrapped it

around my shoulders. I was crying now, and he hugged me like the granddaughter I might have been. I was crying because I remembered a past that existed before Shemaya Station and Luas, before the baby-formula stains and the blood. I remembered my eyes, Irish green like my father's, and my hair, long, thick, Italian black like my mother's. I remembered the empty right sleeves of my clothes: pinned back, folded over, sewn shut. I remembered people wondering — I could see it in their faces — what an eight-year-old girl could have done to deserve all those empty right sleeves? I remembered wanting to tell them, to remind them, that God punishes children for the sins of their parents.

Yes, for one brief and unbearable moment, I remembered many things when I arrived at Shemaya Station. I remembered crayfish dying in the sun and the cruelty of injustice. I remembered the stench of decaying mushrooms and the impossibility of forgiveness. I remembered the conveyor chain on my grandfather's manure spreader amputating my right forearm from my elbow and flinging it into the field with the rest of the muck. I remembered the angelic face of my daughter, Sarah, just ten months old, young and fresh and precious. I remembered formula dripping from her bottle down the empty right sleeve of my suit and the pinch of guilt for leaving her at the day care that morning and the punch of guilt for feeling relieved. I remembered dust on law books and the bitter taste of coffee. I remembered telling my husband I loved him and knowing I did. I remembered picking up my daughter at the end of the day and her squeals of delight when she saw me, and my squeals of delight when I saw her. I remembered singing "Hot Tea and Bees Honey" to her on the way home and wondering what my husband had made for dinner, because he always makes dinner on Fridays. Most of all, I remembered how comfortable life had become for me . . . and that I would do anything . . . give anything . . . *stop at nothing* . . . to make it last.

And then my memories vanished, as if a plug had been pulled. There was just baby formula turned to blood, everywhere now, all over my face, neck, and stomach, streaming down my elbow and wrist, streaming down the stump of my right arm, turning red my legs and feet and toes, washing away my life and spilling it onto Luas, painting us together in an embrace, soaking through his jacket and shirt, spreading across his face, pooling onto the floor, and clotting

23

into ugly red crumbs around the edges.

This is how I arrived at Shemaya Station when I died.

And somewhere in the universe, God sighed.

# 2

Luas led me from the train station to a house not far away. We followed a dirt path through a wood, across a pasture, a garden, an apron of lawn. The city I'd imagined beyond the walls of Shemaya Station didn't exist. We were in the country now.

The sky as we walked was moonless, dark violet, and iridescent like a pane of stained glass. Luas led me on in silence, supporting me when I stumbled. I was still stunned. Every few yards the weather raged between the extremes of hot and cold, wet and dry, as if even the heavens were stunned too. I felt no physical pain. In an obscure corner of memory my torso throbbed and my nerves shrieked — but these were distant sensations, recollections more than feelings. My skin felt stiff as I moved, encrusted with dried blood.

The house to which Luas led me had a broad porch with a white balustrade and wide green steps. An octagonal lamp hung from the ceiling, projecting blocks of light onto the lawn. The house reminded me of my great-grandparents' home along the Brandywine River in northern Delaware, with the same threatening Victorian turret and gables and pretty scrollwork along the eaves and trim, like so many large homes built in the 1920s. Everything about it was permanent and massive, a bulwark against fate and time: the heavy red brick and fieldstone, the slate roof, the tall windows and ceilings, the thick porch columns and solid brass doorknobs.

On the porch stood an old woman waving excitedly in our direction. Luas squeezed my hand and stiffened to help me up the steps.

"Our guest has finally arrived, Sophia," he announced.

They exchanged polite hugs the way older couples tend to do, and I braced myself for the old woman's screams when she realized her husband had brought home a nude woman half his age and covered in blood. But for all the scandal and gore of my appearance, you'd have thought this was the condition in which all her guests arrived. She rushed forward and wrapped herself around me, carelessly staining her blue chamois dress with my blood before peeling herself just far enough away to see my face and caress my cheeks.

"Thank you, thank you, Luas," she said, breathlessly, almost crying.

Luas winked at me and walked back down the steps into the darkness from which we'd come, leaving a trail of bloody shoe prints.

*They're obviously mad,* I thought.

Sophia had an ethnic face, Mediterranean and expressive and proud, with an angular forehead and thin lips. Her tarnished silver hair coiled into a bun, and she spoke with an Italian accent.

"Oh, Brek," she whispered. "My precious, precious child."

"Nana?"

The word exhaled from my lungs with a whimper, accompanied by the recollection of an old photograph, the face of my great-grandmother Sophia Bellini, my Nana. She'd died from a stroke when I was four years old.

"Yes, child, oh yes," she said.

My earliest memory was from her funeral. I'd thrown a tantrum when my mother made me kiss Nana Bellini good-bye in the open coffin. I remembered the slap of my mother's hand across my face, and that Nana's eyes did not open, and that her smile, serene and insane, did not change.

"Nana?"

"Yes, child," she said again, squeezing me close. "Welcome home."

I grinned and pushed myself away.

There comes a moment in every nightmare when disbelief can no longer be suspended and one must choose between waking or allowing the drama to play on, comforted by the thought that it is, after all, only a dream.

I stepped around Nana, the illusion, and ran my fingers along the white column at the top of the steps. Sure enough, there were my initials — B. A. C. — carved with an eight-penny nail one August afternoon when I sat on the porch drinking iced tea and wondering whether summer would ever end and middle school would finally begin. The scent of mothballs and garlic wafting from the kitchen was as distinct to my grandparents' home as the scent of lilacs to late spring. The screen door chirped twice as it had always done, and our family pictures were arranged on the dry sink in the hall.

"I'm dreaming," I said to Nana. "What an odd dream."

A smile crossed her face, the same knowing smile that had crossed Luas's in the

28

train shed, as if to say: *Yes, my great-granddaughter, I understand. You're not ready to accept your own death yet, so we must pretend.*

"Is it a lovely dream?" she asked.

"No. It's a scary one, Nana," I said. "I'm dead in it and you . . . you're here, but you're dead too."

"But isn't that a lovely dream, dear?" she asked. "To know that death isn't the end of everything?"

"Yes, that is lovely," I said. "I'll try to remember it when I wake up, and I'll try to remember you too. I can never seem to remember your face, Nana; I was too young when you died."

Nana smiled at me, amused.

I yawned and stretched. "My, this is such a long dream," I said. "I feel like I've been dreaming all night. But that's a good thing. It means I'm sleeping well. I'm so tired, Nana. I want to sleep some more, but I don't want to be scared. I want this to be a nice dream now. Can we make it a nice dream so I won't have to wake up and chase you away?"

"Yes, dear," Nana said, hugging me again. "We can make this a nice dream. We can make this the nicest dream you've ever had."

She led me upstairs without another word,

drew me a bath in the claw-footed iron tub off the main hall, and hung a thick terry-cloth robe from the door. The dream was improving already. Before leaving me to soak, she paused to look at the stump of my right arm. I smiled, as I always did when someone noticed the amputation, to put her at ease. She kissed my forehead and closed the door.

Although the bleeding had stopped, I had to flush red water from the tub and refill it twice. There were three holes in my chest: one in my sternum and two through my left breast. I fingered each hole indifferently, as though I were merely touching a blemish. I could feel the soft tissue inside — torn, fatty, and swollen — and jagged edges of broken bone.

After my bath, I wrapped myself in the robe Nana left for me behind the door and crept through the second floor of the old house, resurrecting memories both pleasant and sad. There was the happy photograph in the master bedroom of Nana and Great-grandpa Frank posing before the Teatro alla Scala on their thirtieth wedding anniversary. My mother told me that one month later, Great-grandpa Frank confessed to having escorted his mistress to the very same opera house while on a business trip to Milan.

Nana somehow overcame her humiliation and anger and offered him the forgiveness he sought. In return, on the wall between the windows, Great-grandpa Frank hung a large crucifix with a large Christ, whose mournful eyes watched over his side of the bed as a reminder. A heart attack took him the following year.

My grandparents moved into the house after Nana's death and their belongings now filled the room, but the crucifix remained: alert, watchful, reminding. It was really their house I remembered, not Nana's. Beneath the cross stood a small bookcase filled with hardbound volumes by Locke, Jefferson, and Oliver Wendell Holmes, and lesser treatises on contracts and procedure. They were my grandfather's law books, and after the accident with my arm and the lawsuit that followed, I began to look upon their impressive leather bindings and heft with a sort of reverence and awe. The pursuit of justice seemed to me a more noble and honest religion than the one I heard preached each Sunday in church.

Next door, my uncle Anthony's room was a time capsule sealed in 1968, the year after Nana died. In some of the black-and-white photographs on the walls he's slumped against a howitzer, the strain of fear and fatigue twisting his face into a haunted smile. Dog tags and a crucifix with the right arm broken off hang from a chain around his neck. The only color photograph in the room was taken two years prior to these. In this photograph, First Lieutenant Anthony Bellini stands gallant and brave in full dress uniform next to an American flag. My grandparents kept this picture on the dresser beside the dog tags, the broken crucifix, and the sad blue triangle of cloth presented to them at Uncle Anthony's funeral. I loved that broken crucifix. Jesus was missing the same arm as me, and when I touched it, I believed he somehow understood. I didn't remember Uncle Anthony; he was sent to Vietnam soon after I was born. When I asked about him I was told only that he was a hero.

The bedroom across the hall belonged first to my grandfather's brother, Gus, and, next, to Uncle Alex before he himself shipped out to Vietnam two years after Uncle Anthony. Uncle Alex returned in one piece from the war, though, so my grand-parents had no need to create a second shrine. Instead, they used the room to store broken chairs, boxes, and clutter that couldn't find a home in the rest of the house.

My mother was the oldest of the three Bellini children. After she married, her room became the guest room, but they kept her things. The bed was white, with a dingy canopy I detested. A pair of ragged old dolls sat glumly against the pillows, yearning for affection and needing a bath. The lacy curtains she had sewn from an old table-cloth decorated the windows, and at the foot of the bed sat a pine hope chest filled with silly letters and pleated skirts and photographs of horses and kittens. It was a little girl's room, and, in many ways, my mother remained a little girl all her life. Her room was way up high in the turret, where a princess would sleep — an oval-shaped refuge protected from robbers and dragons, with small windows facing the front and side of the house. Mom and I lived here for an entire year after she divorced my father. I slept next to her every night in the same bed. We ate popcorn and read books, and sometimes she cried herself to sleep. I was the grown-up in that bed, and this made me feel safe. Grown-ups were always safe. She had nursed me back to health after the accident with my arm, and I was happy to repay the favor. I couldn't replace my father any more than she could regrow my arm, but somehow we helped each other heal from our wounds. We were never close the way some mothers and daughters become, but we loved and understood each other as only a mother and daughter can.

After my bath, I had intended to dress and go back downstairs to talk to Nana, but I suddenly felt drowsy and weak, as though I were descending within my dream into a deeper level of sleep. I succumbed to the urge, sliding in with the dolls beneath the crisp cotton ticking of my mother's bed and turning out the white unicorn lamp. I fell fast asleep. During this sleep, I began dreaming of my last day on earth.

# 3

It's early morning and I'm nursing Sarah in bed with the television on. We're watching Bo, in his first month as the new anchorman of the Channel 10 *Morning News,* trying to make chitchat with Piper Jackson, Channel 10's incredibly dull but incredibly beautiful new weather girl. Regardless of atmospheric conditions, Piper's tight skirts and blouses guarantee fair skies and high pressure. Bo and Piper make a picture-perfect couple on the set and smiling down together from the slick, new highway billboards that have already helped increase ratings for the show. I seethe with jealousy every morning — until Piper opens her mouth. Today, while talking with Bo about a tsunami that has just devastated the northern coast of Japan, she mispronounces it "samurai" and speculates that this must be how Japanese warriors got their name. Bo cringes.

"It's pronounced 'sue-*na*-me,' Piper," he says.

Piper looks bewildered, like a puppy being scolded for peeing on a rug.

"What is?" she asks.

"The Japanese word for tidal wave."

"Oops," she replies airily, her strawberry red lips ripening from scolded-girl pout into naughty-girl smile. "Well, I guess that explains why they call Japanese warriors tsunamis."

The cameraman knows exactly what to do. The shot widens to take in Piper's low-cut top and admittedly impressive cleavage. You can almost hear the spontaneous applause of men all over central Pennsylvania and the spontaneous groans of their wives, girlfriends, and mothers. I pleaded with Bo to stick to reporting the news, but Piper and her breasts were bigger and better than the news.

Sarah finishes nursing, oblivious to TV ratings, perfectly content to see a miniature of her father talking from a box on the dresser no matter what he says. Sometimes she tries to talk back, as though they're having a conversation.

I shower quickly, planning as I scrub where to pick up with the summary judgment motion I'd been working on and sticking my head out to be sure Sarah's still on the bed. When the network news replaces her daddy at seven, we switch to Big Bird, and I finish applying my makeup and put on my cream silk blouse and black silk suit. I carry Sarah into the nursery and change her diaper, dressing her in a light cotton jumper before switching to pants and a sweatshirt after remembering Piper's warning that a cold front will be moving through late in the day. Sarah's hands swing over her head and she stares at them in astonishment, as though she's seeing them for the first time, a pair of birds from nowhere, soaring and swooning to the music whispering through her tiny mind. With all my might I try to store this moment away — the wide fascination of her eyes and the delicate contractions of her fingers, the sunlight that celebrates her revelation, the polished perfection of skin on her belly — all locked up in my memory like a jewel in a safe-deposit box to be taken out later and adored.

I drive Sarah to a day care operated by Juniata College as a teaching practicum. It's an excellent facility, bright, cheery, and clean, with energetic professors and students eager to try the latest methods and techniques for developing infant minds. The classes are small and Sarah never lacks for stimulation or attention. She's always laughing and playing, and her pediatrician says her verbal and cognitive skills are advanced for her age. When I visit during the day, I'm convinced she's better off here than if I cared for her at home. But when I kiss her good-bye in the morning and she waves her little hands and looks after me with those sad brown eyes, I wonder whether I'm fooling myself — or whether I'm worse off even if she isn't.

While I'm unbuckling her from her car seat, she flips her bottle upside down and seems to deliberately squirt formula on the lapel of my jacket.

"Hey, stop that!" I say, pretending to be angry. "Nobody messes on Mommy's favorite suit, not even a cutie like you."

I reach the office by eight-thirty and wave to frog-faced Bill Gwynne, who's already on the phone with a client and whose desk, restored to order by his secretary last evening, is already a mess. Our offices occupy a historic red-brick row house next to the county courthouse in Huntingdon, Pennsylvania, used first as a blacksmith's shop at the time the town was founded in the late 1700s. I toss my briefcase and purse into my office on the second floor and fix a cup of cappuccino, using a canning jar and microwave to froth the milk. Cup in hand, I head up to our small law library on the third floor, where I continue the legal research I've been working on for the past four weeks, trying to come up with a defense that will allow our very wealthy and very lucrative client, Alan Fleming, to avoid repaying the $500,000 he borrowed from a bank. This might seem like a fool's errand, if not a little unscrupulous, but it's actually my favorite part of legal practice: the intellectual challenge of winning a case that most lawyers would, and should, lose, by uncovering an overlooked fact or finding a forgotten law.

This particular morning, the blind lady of justice bestows upon me a generous gift in the form of a little-known banking regulation from the Great Depression called Regulation U, which forbids banks from making loans to purchase stocks if other stocks are pledged as collateral but worth less than fifty percent of the loan. The regulation was intended to prevent stock market crashes from taking the banking system down with them, but it catches my eye because Alan purchased stocks with the loan he'd defaulted on and, as I recall, pledged other stocks worth only thirty-five percent of the loan. If the bank knew this, then it violated the regulation and would be barred from suing Alan to recover the debt. We would win the case on a technicality.

I race back down to my office for the transcript of the deposition I took of the bank's loan officer, Jorge Mijares, to see whether he knew that Alan intended to use the loan to buy stocks. The transcript comprises several hundred pages of testimony given under oath before a court reporter with each line of testimony numbered for easy reference. Scanning through it, I recall how, like most of the male witnesses I had confronted during my short legal career, Jorge Mijares had refused to take me seriously because I was a young woman. I used this to my advantage. I had discovered that rather than resent and resist the arrogance of men like this, I could more easily defeat them by flirting with them and using their prejudices against them. Their unbounded conceit inevitably led them to become distracted and careless — and to say more on the record than they intended.

On page 155 of the transcript, I locate the testimony I was hoping for — the testimony that destroys the bank's case. I'm thrilled. I take the transcript and the regulation over to Bill's office and lay them on the last open patch of mahogany on his desk. He's buried in a file and doesn't look up as he speaks.

"Yes?" he grunts.

Bill's always irritable in the morning, and this morning even more so because he's preparing for hearings in two cases at once. His eyes dart from file to file, fingers snapping at the papers. He's wearing a conservative gray suit and matching vest, white shirt, and maroon tie. He's old school and never takes off his jacket in the office, even in the middle of the summer.

"Read it," I say proudly.

"Why?"

"Because it's how we're going to win a case we're supposed to lose."

He glances at the regulation. "What's this got to do with anything?"

"Mijares testified he knew Alan was using the loan to buy stocks. But he didn't post the collateral required by the regulation. The loan's void and unenforceable as a matter of law. We win."

Bill snatches the transcript from the desk. There's silence as he reads the testimony, then he starts laughing. "Jorge got a little carried away with himself, didn't he?"

"He likes to think that he's very charming," I reply.

Bill puts down the transcript, picks up the

41

regulation, and reads it. "He won't be so charming when he finds out you outfoxed him," he says. "I'm glad to see you know how to handle men like that. Jorge's father would be disappointed if he read this. He was a professor of archaeology at Juniata College, very well-mannered and cultured. He hired me to represent the grape growers in the cyanide case. Wealthy family. The Mijares still own vineyards in Chile."

"Wow, you handled that case too?" I say, always amazed at Bill's remarkable legal career. I was in college during the public scare over red Chilean table grapes being laced with cyanide. When the news stories broke warning people not to eat them, my dorm roommate promptly started buying them and snacking on them by the bunches. She hated red grapes but her boyfriend had just broken up with her. She said she didn't have the courage to slit her own wrists and figured grapes would be the easier way to go.

Bill nods.

"But I thought you only represented plaintiffs back then, not defendants."

"The growers were the plaintiffs," Bill replies. "There was no cyanide. The scare was a hoax, but hundreds of Chilean farmers lost everything — thousands of tons of fruit were embargoed and destroyed. We sued the government to lift the embargo, and we sued the insurers to pay the claims. And, yes, we won."

Outside the window beside Bill's desk, the morning sun strikes the bright yellow fall leaves of a maple tree, making the tree appear as though it has burst into flames. A small sparrow lands on a branch, risking immolation.

"I hope we win another one," I say.

Bill doesn't respond and an awkward silence follows. I realize I'm rubbing the stump of my right arm and he's watching me. The bird in the maple flies away, having survived the inferno.

"When can you finish the brief?" he asks.

"Rough draft by Tuesday."

He puts down the regulation and starts in on one of the files in front of him. "I'll be in court all afternoon and then I have a board meeting," he says. "Have a nice weekend."

"Thanks. You too." I gather my materials and get up to leave but Bill stops me.

"It's a creative argument, Brek," he says without looking up. "Few lawyers would have thought of it."

"Thanks."

I turn to leave but hesitate. I'm gratified by the rare compliment but suddenly remorseful about the outcome. "So, Alan Fleming keeps five hundred thousand dollars that don't belong to him because of a technicality?"

Bill sighs disappointedly. "Yes," he says, "and with any luck this afternoon I'll put an arsonist back on the street because of a technicality. But next week I'll have an innocent man freed on the same technicality, and a legal technicality will win an injunction against the landfill that's discharging dioxin and killing all the bass in Raystown Lake. You can't have one without the other, Brek. Justice wears a blindfold because she isn't supposed to see who's loading the scales."

# 4

I leave Bill at his desk and return to my office. From my window, I can see the Juniata River dappled with reflections of scarlet and jasmine leaves on the trees, each a unique frame of autumn.

*Bill's right,* I think. *I've done nothing wrong defending my client on a legal technicality. In fact, I've done my job perfectly and the system is working exactly as designed, which is more than can be said for the system that allows someone like Piper Jackson to do weather forecasts.* Which reminds me to telephone Bo at the studio.

"Hi," he says. "I was just getting ready to call you."

I yawn rather loudly and unexpectedly. "Wow," I say, "sorry about that. It's been a long morning . . . So what's the latest from the wires? Did they ever catch that samurai warrior who attacked the northern coast of Japan? I heard he did a lot of damage."

"Very funny," he says.

"Sounds like he really *saké*d the coast."

Bo groans. "I've heard that one three times already this morning — all from women. You people can be so jealous and mean. How did Sarah's drop-off go?"

*"You people?"* I protest. "Jealous and mean? The woman's a babbling idiot. How can you stand her?"

Bo hesitates, pretending he's trying hard to find a reason. I know he likes her even though she's an embarrassment. Finally he says, as though helpless before an irresistible force, "Well, she does have beautiful . . . weather forecasts."

"You're a pig, Boaz," I respond. He hates it when I call him by his actual first name. His parents named him Boaz after King David's great-grandfather and the American soldier who rescued his mother's family from the Nazis during World War II. "Sarah was fine," I say. "She spilled formula on my suit."

"She loves doing that," Bo replies. "I'm on my way to Harrisburg. Harlan Hurley is being sentenced this afternoon. They want me to cover it since I broke the story."

My secretary, Barbara, sticks her head in to tell me Alan Fleming's on the line. I ask her to take a message. "When will you be home?"

"Six-thirty or seven unless things get crazy," Bo answers. "I should still be able to fix dinner."

"What are we having?"

"Any requests?"

I start writing an outline of the arguments for Alan's summary judgment brief on a legal pad and don't hear Bo's question.

"Hello?" he says. "Food? Any ideas? I can tell you're working on something."

"What? Yeah . . . the brief in the Fleming case. Sorry, I just came up with a new genius defense. Even Bill was impressed. No, I can't think of anything for dinner, whatever you want."

"I hear Hurley's skinhead buddies will be protesting at the courthouse. Did you shave your head this morning?"

"No," I reply, "but I'm very cute bald. You've seen my baby pictures."

"You know," Bo says, baiting me because Bill and I are members of the American Civil Liberties Union, "I value free speech as much as the next guy, particularly because I'm a reporter, but rallies advocating the oppression and destruction of ethnic groups go a little too far, don't you think? Why should they have the right to use public property to incite hatred and violence?"

I lose my train of thought and have to go back to the top of the outline.

"Really, I want to know," Bo presses. "How can you defend them?"

This is an argument we've had a hundred times. "Who decides what speech is okay and what speech isn't?" I automatically respond. "It's fascinating how you liberal Jews suddenly get all conservative when the subject is anti-Semitism. You can't have it both ways, Bo. Using your theory, Jews should be banned from demonstrating in favor of Israel because Israel oppresses the Palestinians. Your mother lived through the Holocaust and even she thinks anti-Semites have the right to express themselves. Maybe you should listen to her once in a while."

"My mother's biased," Bo replies. "And crazy. You're not even Jewish, but she runs around telling everybody at the synagogue that you're a better Jew than me because you went to Rosh Hashanah and Yom Kippur services with her this year. Do you have any idea how difficult you're making life for me?"

"So I like challah bread," I say.

"Hurley's not just any fringe anti-Semite with a big mouth, you know?" Bo persists.

"He was the financial controller of a public school district and diverted nearly one hundred thousand dollars from their curriculum and textbook budget to his white supremacist group to produce a documentary claiming the Holocaust was a hoax."

Here we go, all over again. I swear I've heard this all before. "Yes, that's outrageous," I say. "But he's not going to jail for denying the Holocaust. Denying the death of six million people might be offensive, but it's still free speech. He's being sentenced for misappropriating school funds, period."

"Let me finish," Bo insists. "We keep digging up more. You're gonna love this. Turns out that Hurley's white supremacist group, Die Elf, also received funding from Amina Rabun before she died, and probably even afterward. Apparently her nephew or something is a member. I think his name is Ott Bowles. Did you ever run across him during the lawsuit?"

Now I see where all this is leading. It's not just about white supremacists; it's personal. "No, I've never heard of him. But you've got to stop right there, Bo. We sued Amina Rabun and we won. The case is over. She paid your mother restitution for the property the Rabuns stole from your mother's family in Germany during the war. Her father and uncle were Nazis. It's hardly a surprise that she or her nephew would be involved with Die Elf. If you turn this story about Hurley into a personal vendetta against the Rabuns, you're going to lose all credibility as a reporter. You've got to let it go. Hurley was caught stealing school district money and now he's going to jail for it. Justice has been served. End of story."

"Hey, lighten up," Bo responds. "I only mentioned the connection between Rabun and Die Elf because I thought you would be interested since you knew her. I have no intention of reporting any of that. I agree with you, it's totally irrelevant." He lowers his voice to almost a whisper. "But here's what is relevant. Promise you won't say anything to anybody. None of this is public yet."

"Okay."

"You know this Samar Mansour character, the guy Die Elf was paying to make the documentary?"

"Yes."

"Well, Bobby just found out that Mansour dropped out of Juniata College a couple of years ago and went to Lebanon. Although Mansour was born and raised here, apparently his father was a Palestinian refugee after Israel won the 1948 Arab-

Israeli War. We have sources who say Mansour trained with Hezbollah, the Islamic terrorist group. That means Hurley wasn't only using school district funds to support Holocaust revisionism, he was supporting terrorism. That's more than just free speech. This might be the first documented case of white supremacists joining forces with Islamic extremists."

"Okay, that's pretty disturbing —"

"Yeah, it is. But that's not all. One of our sources just told us that Die Elf has a weapons cache on their compound outside Huntingdon. Assault rifles, grenade launchers, machine guns, ammonium nitrate and diesel fuel for bombs — everything a well-prepared terrorist organization needs. He said he'll let Bobby and me film it after Hurley is locked up safe and sound today. We're going to take them down, Brek. Not just Hurley but the entire organization. I'll bet CNN puts me on live during prime time for an entire week. This is the kind of story that could get me back to New York."

I start to worry. This is the part of Bo's job that I hate. He is Jewish and yet he spent months undercover with his producer, Bobby Wilson, infiltrating a white supremacist group. He could have been killed — and still could be if he keeps chasing them. I

51

want Bo to leave them alone. I'd rather have him flirting with Piper Jackson on the set of the local news every morning than risking his life doing investigative reports to get a shot with the national networks.

"Why can't somebody else do this?" I ask. "You have no idea what kind of risks you're taking. These people are crazy."

"There's nothing to worry about," Bo replies. "They wouldn't dare touch me. The FBI's watching everything they do now."

"But how do you know it's not a setup? Desperate people do desperate things, Bo. And revenge has a way of drowning out rational thought, not that these are rational people to begin with. You said so yourself, they're terrorists. They don't care whether they get killed as long as they take a bunch of people with them. You already broke the main story. If the FBI is watching them, then you've got to tell the FBI and let them handle it. They're the experts. You're just a reporter, remember? You don't even know how to shoot a gun."

"Everything's fine, Brek," Bo says condescendingly. "I'm sorry I even brought it up."

He always does this, belittle my concerns. It infuriates me. I say nothing.

"What's the matter?" Bo asks.

"It's not only your decision," I say, trying

to keep my voice down so my secretary doesn't overhear our argument. "If you were single, things would be different and you could do whatever you want. But you have a wife and a daughter now, Bo. What about us? You're not only putting yourself at risk, you're putting Sarah and me at risk too."

Bo muffles the phone. I hear someone talking to him in the background, then he comes back on. "Sorry," he says, "the crew's waiting in the van. I've got to get to Harrisburg."

"Please be careful, okay?" I reply. "And we're not through talking about this. I really think you should turn everything over to the FBI."

"Okay, I'll be careful," he says. "And we can talk about it tonight. When do you think you'll finish up today?"

"Around six."

"That's pushing it kind of close with the day care, isn't it? Even with two salaries I don't know how much longer we can afford the five-dollar-a-minute penalty for picking Sarah up late. At some point, they're going to kick her out, and then what will we do?"

He was right. We were already running a $500 tab in late penalties for the year, and the director had begun warning us in increasingly blunt terms that the time-out

53

chair for adults means "out" — for good.

"Don't worry about it," I say. "I'll be there on time."

"Okay. Bye. I love you," he says.

I'm still nervous. "Be careful, Bo."

"I promise."

"Okay. I love you too. Bye."

I hang up and look at the photograph on my shelf of Bo and me at his sister Lisa's wedding. He's wearing a yarmulke and looks so sweet and happy. I fell in love with Bo Wolfson for all the best reasons — because he was incredibly handsome, wonderful, sensitive, caring, a man who made me feel special, loved, and complete, and who even accepted my disability as a charming attribute rather than a cause for fear and revulsion.

But Bo's religion made the package for me irresistible. Although I was a Catholic girl raised in a community of fundamentalist Protestants, Bo's Jewish heritage, with its stories of struggle and heroism and promise of being chosen by God, glittered like an exotic jewel. My parents were disappointed, but I had had a lifelong quarrel with Christianity. Jesus' teaching of turning the other cheek, which, to me, formed the bedrock of the religion, made no sense in a world filled with warfare and violence, a world filled with people like Harlan Hurley, a world that allowed an eight-year-old girl to lose her right arm.

I focus now on the yarmulke Bo wears in the photograph, but this universal symbol of Judaism suddenly recalls for me, as a Gentile, not the blessings of a chosen relationship with God but the suffering and sacrifice of five thousand years of tragedy. A chill runs up my spine as I think of Harlan Hurley and Die Elf trying to reignite the hatred of the Nazis and, perhaps, the incinerators. I imagine how it would feel to be hunted and murdered across the centuries. Am I brave enough to bear that burden? Do I want it for my daughter?

In my ignorance, I had actually assumed Rosh Hashanah, the Jewish New Year, would be a festive and gay celebration, like New Year's Day. But it turned out to be just the opposite — brooding and ominous, the day God judges the lives we've lived during the previous year. The shofar blasts, calling the congregation to worship inside the synagogue, were terrifying — the voice of God condemning the entire human race. But the liturgy for the day, the Musaf Tefillah, had the effect of reaffirming my belief that God and justice are inseparable and one. Maybe by being a lawyer trained in pursuing justice I had joined the Chosen and found an inside track on redemption. At nightfall on Yom Kippur I wondered whether my name was sealed in the Book of Life or the Book of Death.

I return to my summary judgment brief, working through lunch and stopping only when I realize I have ten minutes to get to the day care and avoid the dreaded five-dollar-per-minute fine. When I arrive, Sarah is the last child there, gumming a Nilla Wafer into a sticky brown paste around her mouth while watching a videotape of Barney the Dinosaur. The shame of being the last mother to pick up her child almost spoils my joy at seeing her. Sarah is covered with dull red paint stains, all over her little sweatshirt and sweatpants, hands, neck, and face. She toddles toward me as fast as she can, arms outstretched, smiling and cooing. I kneel down. Miss Erin, the day-care intern from the college, grins.

"Hi, baby girl," I say to Sarah, sweeping her up into my arm and kissing her face, inhaling the sweetness of her hair. I look up at Miss Erin. "How was she today?"

"Great," Miss Erin says. "She's been a very good girl."

Miss Erin is a junior at the college and

has definitely found her calling. She looks like a cartoon come to life, with two small black dots for eyes, thin sticks for arms and legs, and freckled cheeks framed by long ropes of braided orange hair. She *loves* little kids, and they love her.

"Sorry about the mess," Miss Erin says. "I'm going to miss her so much. She was my favorite."

"Are you leaving?" I ask, assuming from her response that she won't be seeing Sarah again.

"Well, I am going home for the night," she replies, puzzled by my question.

"But when you just said you were going to miss her and she was your favorite . . . I guess you meant for the weekend."

Miss Erin looks at me strangely and gives Sarah a kiss. "Good-bye, sweetie," she says. "I love you."

Sarah gives Miss Erin a peck on the cheek.

"Thanks for taking good care of her," I say, grabbing Sarah's bag of nearly empty milk bottles and art projects and glancing over her activity sheet for the day. "Have a nice weekend."

I carry Sarah out to the car, buckle her in, and slip a cassette of "Hot Tea and Bees Honey" into the tape player. As we drive away, I glance at her in the rearview mirror and ask her how her day went. She pretends to answer with cooing and babbling sounds.

We stop at a convenience store on the way home to buy milk. The parking lot is empty. An autumn breeze freshens the car when I open the door. It's not even six-thirty yet, but it's already dark as midnight. I unbuckle Sarah from her car seat. She reaches for my hair and I tease her by tilting away. She giggles, exposing a single tooth. Her hair falls into her eyes, dark and full of curls like her daddy's. Carrying her across the parking lot, I'm humming the song we had been listening to on the cassette.

We enter the store and head for the dairy case in the back. I have to juggle her with one arm as I pick up a half-gallon of milk. We turn and head back toward the counter through the pastry aisle. Sarah reaches out with her tiny hand and knocks a row of cupcakes onto the floor. As I stoop to pick them up, the overpowering smell of decaying mushrooms fills the air. *How strange,* I think. I turn to locate the source but, suddenly, find myself back at Shemaya Station, on the bench beneath the rusting steel dome. Sarah's gone. And I'm sitting next to Luas, covered in my own blood.

# 5

Dead people doubt the irrevocability of their own deaths. We either don't believe we're dead or we try to find a way to reverse it. We learn to accept death only gradually, at our own pace and on our own terms. But this creates confusion because we extend the torn fragments of our lives into the open wound of the afterlife, grafting the two together. For sensitive souls — the souls of saints and poets who lived their lives in the knowledge that truth exists only in the spiritual world — the transition to Shemaya might seem perfectly seamless and immediate. But for the rest of us, including people like me, who placed their faith in logic and reason and what could be measured with instruments and seen with our own two eyes, the transition from life to death takes much longer. We resist, deny, and explain away our mortality at every turn. Thus, the very first thing we forget when we die is how it happened. Or, more accurately, this is the very first thing we choose not to remember, because to remember such a momentous event is to concede the inconceivable.

The next morning, which was my first morning in Shemaya, I awoke to the smell of coffee and cinnamon. These were the aromas I'd become accustomed to on Saturday mornings during my life, and as far as I was concerned this was just another Saturday morning. Bo would get up early for a jog and bring breakfast home from the bakery, slipping quietly out of the house and returning with a bag full of sticky buns and other goodies. I loved him for this. While he was gone, it was my privilege and vice to linger in bed with my eyes closed, drowsy, warm, and contented beneath the covers.

That morning in Shemaya, I lingered in bed just this way, in the blissful state on the border of sleep, unable to discern the meaning of the bizarre dreams about the train station, Luas, and my great-grandmother, trying to commit them to memory before they dissolved into the noise and distractions of a new day. *What was it she said that I wanted to remember . . . ?* I'd forgotten already. Dreams can be elusive that way. The house was quiet, Sarah still asleep. The surreal images from the night and the possibilities of the day floated through my mind like fireflies, and I chased after some and let others get away. It would be a beautiful autumn weekend. Friends had invited us on a hike up Tussey Mountain and later to an apple orchard for cider and a hayride. Sarah would fall asleep in her backpack to the rhythm of Bo's steps. There were leaves to rake, floors to vacuum, and groceries to buy. And I'd have to return to the office for a few hours on Sunday to work on my brief.

Lying there in bed, I considered the possibility that I might just be turning into a good lawyer after all. What a wonderful feeling to wake up to. I pushed back the covers and opened my eyes . . .

There was blood everywhere, all over the sheets and my body.

I screamed and jumped out of bed, banging my head against a post that didn't belong in my bedroom — the white post of my mother's canopy bed in my grandparents' house in Delaware.

*Oh, how clever,* I thought, rubbing my head and trying to calm myself down. *I've awakened from my second dream but not the first.*

I peeked out the window facing the front of the house. Only a dream could explain what I saw. Half of my grandparents' estate glowed golden, orange, and umber in the fading colors of autumn, while the other half shimmered in the fluorescent greens and pastels of spring. Sunflowers wilted and pumpkins ripened at one end of the garden as daffodils and tulips blossomed at the other. Red squirrels gathered acorns among robins searching for earthworms. Two flocks of noisy Canada geese flew by overhead, one going south and the other north, separated by a dissonant zone in between where a fierce winter blizzard exhausted itself beneath a scorching August sun. I marveled at the merging seasons, struck by the enormity of their compression in space and time. It explained the hot and cold, wet and dry I'd experienced walking up to the house with Luas the night before.

Nana must have heard my scream. She entered the room without knocking, dressed in her pajamas and a flower-print bathrobe.

"Are you okay, dear?" she asked with concern in her voice.

"It isn't real," I said calmly, pointing out the bedroom window. "It's scripted and mechanical . . . a dream . . . like you."

Nana opened the window, allowing the conflicting scents and temperatures outside to flood into the room in equal and opposite waves.

"But it's not a dream, dear," she corrected me, dusting small mounds of yellow tree pollen and powdery white snow from the windowsill. "During your life you only dreamed of being awake." She started making the bed, ignoring the fact that the sheets were soaked with blood. Pulling the comforter taut, she said, "Let's go downstairs and have breakfast. I made carrot muffins just the way you like. We can go on that hike up Tussey Mountain later today. I know you were looking forward to it."

I watched her, amused by the dream. "But it isn't morning and I'm not awake yet," I insisted. "If I were awake, you'd be gone, so I think we'd better change the subject." Nana placed her hand on my arm, an old woman's hand, wrinkled and rough against my skin. She was trying to convince me that I wasn't dreaming. The effect was authentic, but I wasn't impressed. "Dead people don't talk," I said. "And they don't have eyes to see each other or bodies to touch."

She squeezed my arm. "That's true, dear," she said. "But it's easier now for you to think of death that way. You aren't ready yet to let go of life."

"But I'm not dead," I said. "Look —"

I jumped up and down, doing a little jig in the bedroom and waving my arm around to prove it.

Nana indulged me with a smile. "Your mother shouldn't have slapped you like that," she said. "I would have been scared too. I can't imagine what she was thinking, making a four-year-old kiss an old dead woman."

I looked at her in sheer horror. This was one of those nightmare moments just before waking when the thing you've been dreading is about to happen and you know you're powerless to stop it, the moment that produces maximum terror, causing you to scream out in the middle of the night. Which is exactly what I did.

I ran down the stairs, shouting "Nooooo!" at the top of my lungs. Through the kitchen and out the back door I ran, past the sink cluttered with baking dishes and the table with the plate of fresh carrot muffins. I stopped on the back porch and closed my eyes, hoping it would all go away.

I imagined reaching across the bed for Bo and finding his hip with his boxer shorts bunched up, and his legs, warm and downy, pulled up to his chest. I nuzzled close, contouring my body to his, the way a river conforms to the shape of its bank, defining itself by what it is not. His skin smelled masculine and strong, and his whiskers

thrilled my arm when it brushed his chin. I
kissed him on the back of the neck and
adjusted my breath to the gradual expansion and contraction of his chest. He stirred
and smacked his lips softly. It must have
been two or three in the morning because I
swore I could hear the faint laughter of the
college students who lived on our street
returning home from their Friday-night parties. But when I opened my eyes to see the
clock on the dresser, I found myself still
standing on Nana's back porch in Delaware,
with the seasons, and my sanity, colliding.

"Bo! Bo!" I yelled.

"Brek, honey, it's okay," Nana called from
the kitchen. "I'm right here."

"Bo! Hold me! Hold me!"

But I couldn't feel him anymore.

I leaped from the porch and raced around
the house, hoping a sudden burst of exertion would jar me awake. Through winter,
summer, spring, and fall I ran, past the oak
with the tractor-tire swing, around the
garden simultaneously leafy and barren,
through beds of tulips dripping with dew
and chrysanthemums covered with snow. I
tripped over the hump of a root and landed
facedown on the soft needles, my robe
spread out around me like the wings of a
fallen dove. I stayed there for a moment,

catching my breath, inhaling the sweet pine scent and searching for answers — logical, material answers. *What is happening to me? Why can't I wake myself up?* It was the most terrifying dream I'd ever had.

I stood up, brushed the needles from my robe, and looked around. To my surprise, I saw my car parked behind the rhododendrons. Suddenly the magical light retreated, taking with it the idea that this was all a dream, as if reason itself had been a passenger trapped in the car, waiting to be released by my glance. *Hot and cold, night terrors, hallucinations . . . a fever? Yes, of course! A fever would explain everything that has been happening to me!* I even remembered not feeling well on Friday and wondering whether I was catching a cold, that my skin had felt cool and damp. I gazed around the lawn again and up at the house. I looked down at my legs and feet and flexed my left hand. Everything was right where it was supposed to be, and everything worked as it was supposed to work. Only the seasons were out of place, and that surely could be the result of a fever.

*I must have driven to my grandparents' house in some sort of delirium and collapsed.*

Nana was gone when I went back inside. The dishes in the sink were put away, the counter cleaned. A thin film of dust coated everything, as though it hadn't been used in weeks. The oven was cool. Not even the aroma of the muffins lingered in the air.

*I'm making it all up after all. I really am at my grandparents' house in Delaware.*

I ran upstairs to the bathroom and looked at myself in the mirror. There was my black hair, intact but disheveled, and ashen skin and bloodshot eyes. Carefully, gingerly, using my fingertips, I pulled open my robe. The holes in my chest and the red stains were gone. I laughed ruefully for having even looked. I took the mercury thermometer from the medicine cabinet and slipped it under my tongue; it read 106, confirming my self-diagnosis. I obviously needed to get to a doctor, but equally obvious: *I am alive!*

I went into my grandparents' room and phoned home but got the answering machine.

"Bo, it's me," I said. "Are you there? Bo? I don't know what's happened . . . I think I'm really sick. I've got a fever and I guess I blacked out. I'm all the way down in Delaware at my grandparents' house. I don't know how I got here; I can't remember anything after picking up Sarah at the day care yesterday. Oh, God, I hope she's all right. She's not here with me, nobody's here . . . I'm so sorry. She must be starving. There's formula in the cupboard and extra diapers in the basement . . . I don't know whether to come home or try to see a doctor here . . . I think I'm feeling a little better, so maybe I'll try to make it home and see how I do. I can always turn around. Okay . . . I'll be there in a few hours. Give Sarah a big hug and kiss for me . . . I love you guys. Bye."

I found my clothes piled beside the guest-room bed, my black silk suit with formula stains (no blood) on the lapel, my blouse, stockings, underwear, and shoes. And there was my purse with my wallet and keys. I dressed quickly and left a note for my grandparents that I'd been there and would explain later.

# 6

The fall sun warmed the interior of my car, dry-roasting the confetti of autumn leaves on the hood even as budding trees and blooming crocuses swelled at the opposite end of the driveway. Between them, a snowstorm melted into the sultry vapors of a midsummer day. I must have contracted some sort of rare tropical disease like dengue fever. Whatever it was, it was better than being dead.

I inserted the key into the ignition and held my breath, still not certain my fever had broken and worried there might be more surprises in store. The engine roared to life. "Thank God!" I said aloud to myself. My car had always been my sanctuary, the one place in the world where, despite a missing arm, I was equal to everyone else and in control. I didn't have special license plates, and I didn't park in the special places close to stores, but my car was in all other respects a vehicle for the handicapped. My parents gave it to me for my high school graduation, and Grandpa Cuttler made the necessary alterations himself in the toolshed beside his barn. He bolted a rotating aluminum knob to the steering wheel so I could turn it with one hand and moved the ignition switch and stereo to the left side of the column. Extenders on the shifter, wiper stalk, and heating controls enabled me to operate them with the stump of my right arm. I refused to wear a prosthesis, but I wasn't ashamed to drive one. The day they surprised me with it was among the happiest days of my life, and theirs as well. The car purchased for me the independence I'd dreamed of and for them a penance for the sin of my disfigurement at such an early age.

I took a deep breath and nudged the shifter into gear. The car accelerated forward smoothly, and I actually enjoyed negotiating my way through the fluctuating seasons, blasting through the alternating bands of rain, slush, snow, and dry pavement. The drive from northern Wilmington to our home in Huntingdon took about three hours. I tried to remember my trip down to Delaware from Huntingdon the night before — what I'd seen, what I'd been thinking, what I'd been listening to on the radio. I couldn't recall anything. This worried me because I'd always had an excellent memory. I remembered the first chapters of the novels I read as a teenager and the holdings of the Supreme Court decisions I read as a law student; I remembered the lyrics to old TV theme songs and all the birthdays in my husband's family to three degrees of consanguinity. But I couldn't remember anything after picking up Sarah yesterday at the day care and stopping by the convenience store on the way home.

The gas gauge indicated the tank was full when I left Delaware. It didn't move the entire drive home. Strange, but no more so than anything else that had been happening to me. The trip was otherwise uneventful. The typical number of cars and trucks occupied the highway and did the typical things cars and trucks do. The landscape, sky, road signs, buildings, and billboards looked as they had always looked, except everything was wrapped in variegated bands of winter, summer, spring, and fall. The mountains crawled along the banks of the Juniata River like gigantic striped caterpillars, their deciduous forests alternately ablaze in reds, oranges, and yellows; snow-covered and white; just budding and speckled green; then lush with deep leafy jade.

Gorgeous. Another pleasant but unexpected aspect of the drive was the serendipitous way the radio stations seemed to play the music I wanted to hear, when I wanted to hear it, without any DJs or commercial interruptions.

All in all, things were looking brighter for me with every mile, and I believed an end to my misery was near. But as I turned toward Huntingdon on Route 522, an anxious feeling overcame me that washed my optimism away. I began to worry about the nature of my illness and what it might mean. *Maybe I have a brain tumor,* I worried. *Or maybe my hallucination of being dead is a premonition of the real event to come.* Bellini women from my great-great-grandmother on down swore they were visited by an angel in the middle of the night to prepare them before somebody close was about to die. *Was Nana Bellini that angel, coming to prepare me for my own death?*

Suddenly the possibility of a terminal illness was more unbearable than the possibility of already being dead. I imagined receiving the news from the doctor and falling to pieces, then telling Bo and holding Sarah close, knowing I wouldn't see her grow up. Who would braid her hair, or make her Halloween costumes, or teach her to bake cookies? Who would introduce her to Louisa May Alcott and Harper Lee, or take her camping or to the ballet, or comfort her through puberty and adolescence? Who, but her own mother, could convince her that there's nothing in life that she, as a girl, or a woman, couldn't do? I was nearly hysterical by the time I turned down our street.

Bo's car was parked in front of the house, and I screeched to a stop and ran inside. Everything looked as I'd left it Friday morning. But no one was there. Bo's cereal bowl with a puddle of milk in the bottom sat on the coffee table next to the unread back sections of *The New York Times.* Bagel crumbs and empty jars of strained peaches and pears cluttered the kitchen counter; the food bowl of our black Labrador retriever, Macy, was half full, but she didn't bark when I entered and was nowhere to be found. Our bed was still unmade, and the romper I'd decided not to dress Sarah in was still draped over the rail of her crib. I checked the garage and found the jogging stroller, so they couldn't be out for a run. There was no note by the phone. I went back outside and looked around the house and in the garage. Nobody. The entire neighborhood was deserted.

We lived on a Lilliputian street in Huntingdon near Juniata College with small brick homes dwarfed by old sycamore trees shaped like giant broccoli. Having been born and raised in Brooklyn, Bo insisted on living in a town with a college. It was his only hope of transitioning from Manhattan to Appalachia. His dream was to be a reporter and news anchor in New York City, but the television stations there told him he needed small-market experience before they would even consider looking at his audition tape. This disappointed and terrified him. He thought of small-market television as a forsaken third world of vacuum tubes and static that existed somewhere between the Hudson River and the Hollywood Hills.

Applying to Channel 10 in Altoona had been my idea, actually. It was one of the stations I had grown up with on visits to my Cuttler grandparents' farm, one of only two stations with VHF transmitters strong enough to reach the antenna strapped to the brick chimney on their house. Altoona was just about as small-market as you could get. Schools and businesses in central Pennsylvania close for the first day of buck-hunting season, and, in contrast to the skyscrapers of Manhattan, grain silos and coal tipples are the tallest man-made structures. When Bo got the job, I called Bill Gwynne, the lawyer in Huntingdon who had represented me and my family after the accident with my arm. Although Huntingdon was even deeper in the middle of nowhere than Altoona, Bill was considered one of the top trial lawyers in the state, and he happened to need an associate. The timing and location seemed just right for me, almost destiny.

I heard music playing in the house next to ours and went over, hoping to find somebody who might have seen Bo and Sarah. Nobody answered the door when I knocked. I pounded on the front doors of all the houses on our street: some with frosted windows, the sidewalks in front covered with slush and snow, and others baking in the afternoon heat. Nobody answered, and I started to panic. I ran over to Washington Street. The hoagie shop and bookstore were open but empty — no customers or employees. The entire commercial district was strangely silent except for the occasional sound of passing cars and buses. I ran down the sidewalk past bicycles chained to parking meters and cars parked at the curb, looking in the doors of vacant shops and cafés for any sign of life. It made no sense. This was the busiest part of town on a

Saturday in the fall. I eventually ran out to a line of cars queued at the stoplight to ask if anybody knew what was going on, but as I approached and peered in the windows, I saw no drivers or passengers in any of them. Even so, when the light turned green, they revved their engines and proceeded on their way down the street in the normal flow of Saturday traffic.

A tormented howl suddenly shattered the eerie silence of the street. I looked around to see where it was coming from and discovered it was coming from *me.* It was the sound of madness. I made a wild dash through the cafés and shops, throwing things from tables and shelves, smashing dishes and glasses. I wanted someone, anyone, to come and restrain me. When no one appeared, I tore out into the middle of the street without looking, daring the cars to hit me. On cue, they screeched and smoked to a halt.

"Where is everybody?" I screamed at the top of my lungs. "Why won't somebody help me?"

I climbed onto the roof of one of the cars to get a better view and watched in disbelief as traffic backed up in both directions through the changing seasons. Some cars had their windows down, some up, wipers and lights on and off. Two police cruisers raced to the scene, red and blue lights flashing and sirens blaring, but no officers emerged. The cruisers just pointed menacingly at me.

I broke down sobbing on the roof of the car. There was nothing left to do. I'd been frightened this badly only once before, as a child in the emergency room of Tyrone Hospital when the attendants laid me on a gurney and placed my severed forearm inside a lunch cooler beside me. I had been amazingly calm until that point. I believed my Grandpa Cuttler when he promised me in his pickup truck as he raced me to the hospital that if I kept my eyes closed everything would be all right. But then they started wheeling me down the hall, and I saw the anguish on his face and tears pouring down his cheeks. The gurney crashed through the swinging doors and deposited me into the nightmarish hell of an operating room. I was crazed with terror. They slashed away my clothes, stabbed needles into my veins, and removed my severed arm from the cooler and held it up to the light like a wild-game trophy. The arm didn't seem real at first: the skin was slimy and dishwater gray, the white elbow bone protruding from the end, tinged with smears of cow manure and blood, the fingers — my fingers — gnarled into a grotesque fist. I fought the nurses until they forced an anesthesia mask over my mouth and I lost consciousness.

Losing consciousness . . . This was all I hoped for now, howling on top of the idling car in the middle of gridlocked Washington Street. But it wasn't to be. I stayed on top of the car that first afternoon in Shemaya until the sun overhead divided itself into four different suns, one for each season, each sun setting over the mountaintop at different points and different times, torching the sky into a blaze of pink and gold flames. Inconsolable, I crawled down from the car and walked back home. The traffic jam cleared as the cars continued on their way to nowhere.

When I reached our house, I heard a voice.

"I'm sorry, child," Nana Bellini said. She was sitting in the rocker on our front porch, enjoying the beautiful evening as though she'd just stopped by for dinner. I was certain now that I'd be locked up soon and sedated. I was obviously insane. I talked to her while I waited to be taken away.

"How was your drive?" I said, adopting her *Everything's normal and we're all happy to be here* attitude.

"We're not there, dear," she said.

"We're not where?"

"Do you remember when you were a little girl and your bedroom turned into a palace and knights rode beneath your windows on great white horses?"

"Who are you?"

"Remember, child? You pretended to lounge in long flowing gowns, dreaming of the prince in the next castle. You created a world within the world that had been created for you. You painted its skies, constructed its walls, and filled its spaces. Like a tiny goddess, you caused a land to exist with nothing more than your mind. But as you grew older, you found the existing structures of time and space more convincing and put aside your own power to create in favor of the creations of others. But the power to create wasn't lost, Brek. It can never be lost. It's natural at first for you to re-create the places that have been dear to you."

"Where's my husband and my daughter?" I demanded. "Where is everybody?"

Nana smiled — that patient, knowing smile of hers and Luas's, as if to say: *Yes, my great-granddaughter, reach now, reach for the answers.*

"We're not there anymore, child," she

said. "It was a wonderful illusion, but it's gone. You've returned home. You won't see them again until they come home too. Free will is absolute. We can't direct the movement of consciousness from realm to realm —"

She was scaring me again. "Leave me alone!" I shouted. I ran back down the walk toward my car.

"Wait, child," she said. "Where are you going?"

I didn't know where. I just knew I had to find Bo and Sarah. I had to get help. Maybe it wasn't Saturday, maybe it was still Friday and I could pick Sarah up from day care and start all over. *It's all just a dream,* I kept telling myself, *just a bad dream; you have a fever and you're sick.* I climbed into my car and started the engine.

Nana called out to me: "What would the day care look like?"

As soon as I thought about it, I was there. The house vanished, and with it my car, the trees, the street, the entire neighborhood. The rough brick wall of our neighbor's house was transformed into the day care's smooth white wall decorated with paper blue whales that Sarah and the other children had painted with Miss Erin's help. Bright, freshly vacuumed play rugs now covered what had been the lawn. The cubby I'd crammed with fresh crib sheets, diapers, and wipes on Friday morning stood where the passenger seat of my car had been. Colorful plastic preschool toys were stacked neatly near the curb. A craft table with boxes of Popsicle sticks, bottles of glue, and reams of colored construction paper emerged from the porch steps. The scent of baby powder and diaper rash ointment filled the air. But there was no laughter in the day care, no squeals or cries. Not a child. Not a teacher. Not a sound.

Nana stood in the doorway, watching me explore the space, searching for the wizard behind the curtain.

The next thought that came into my mind was the set of the morning news where Bo had tried to banter with Piper Jackson. As quickly as the memory arose, the wall of colored whales metamorphosed into the sunrise mural that served as a backdrop for the newscasters. Studio cameras stood where the cribs had been, and lighting racks dangled from the ceiling. But like my neighborhood and the day care, the set was deserted.

I thought of my law office next. My desk, computer, files, bookshelves, treatises, diplomas, and pictures of Bo and Sarah surrounded me instantly. Then came Stan's Delicatessen on Penn Street and my Bellini grandparents' beach house in Rehoboth Beach, followed by my Cuttler grandparents' barn and my bed in the physical therapy ward at Children's Hospital of Philadelphia, where I watched Bobby Hamilton, with both arms amputated, learn to tie his shoes with a long crochet hook in his mouth. I revisited the cinder track behind my high school, where I'd won several races against two-armed opponents and amazed myself and the small crowds. I sat at the bar at Smokey Joe's on Fortieth Street near the University of Pennsylvania in Philadelphia, where I had danced the night away with my girlfriends during law school. I knelt before the altar at Old Swedes' Church, where my best friend, Karen Busfield, who had become an Episcopal priest, asked whether I would pledge my troth to Boaz Wolfson before God and pronounced us husband and wife. I wept in the delivery room at Wilmington Hospital, where my mother had given birth to me, and then again at Blair Memorial Hospital in Huntingdon, where I'd given birth to Sarah and Bo's tears dropped onto my lips.

Each room and space from my past came as fast as I thought of it, as though I were plunging down a shaft cored through the center of my life.

I went back to linger, walking the sands of the Delaware shore, climbing the haymow in my grandfather's barn, pulling on the Nautilus machine that strengthened my left arm to do the work of my right. I revisited not only the locations but the reality, every detail: the sinewy saltiness of Stan's corned beef, the burning smoke and stale beer of Smokey Joe's, the warm rain on our wedding day, the cold stirrups of the delivery-room bed. Nana accompanied me, but did not interfere. Her fascination with how I had lived my life nearly equaled my fascination with the power to re-create it. But the exertion of doing all this exhausted me, and soon portions of one space began blurring into others. The images, the realities, congealed into a single nonsensical mass that finally ground to a halt under its own weight.

Everything went blank. And then it filled with an indescribable light that seemed to emanate from nowhere and everywhere. Through this light Nana extended her hand to me in a gesture of love, smothering the blaze of fear that had nearly consumed me.

"You're dead, child," she said. "But your life has just begun."

# PART II

# 7

"You are not prepared for what you would see. So we must limit what you will see, which is only possible, Brek Abigail Cuttler, because you insist upon what you believe is your sight to see."

Luas spoke these words while placing a felt blindfold over my eyes in the vestibule leading back into Shemaya Station. He was like my father on my wedding day at the rear of the church before giving me away, ironic and wistful, lowering the veil over my face before escorting me into the unknown. He wore the identical gray suit, vest, shirt, and tie Bill Gwynne had been wearing at the office the last day I saw him. The resemblance between Luas and Bill was uncanny, as was his resemblance to both of my grandfathers. He sometimes seemed to be all three men at once, shifting physical features like a hologram. For my part, I looked as fresh and presentable as I did on my wedding day. Nana had fussed over me all morning in a mother-of-the-bride sort of way, making certain my hair and makeup looked just so. But instead of a wedding dress, I wore my black silk suit, from which she had managed to remove the baby formula and the blood.

The suit had become my uniform in Shemaya: the garment that represented my identity, the proof that I had lived a life, and, most important, the symbol and reminder to myself that I fully intended to return to that life. Because I did not, could not, and would not accept the possibility of my death.

It has been said that the first stage of grieving is denial, the essential survival mechanism that protects survivors from the enormity of the loss they have just sustained and that enables them to go on. This is no less true of the dead grieving for themselves and those they left behind. Nana and Luas wanted me to accept it, but I was willing to do no more than humor them and bide my time until I was cured of whatever disease had seized control of my mind.

This strategy helped me cope and kept me sane — yes, one can go insane in the afterlife. But it did nothing to quench the desperate longing I felt for Sarah, which at every moment threatened to consume me and drive me over the edge, whether I was dead or alive. *Where is she?* I worried incessantly. *Who is taking care of her?* Bo was a great daddy and knew what to do, but he wasn't me. He didn't wake up three extra times during the night to pull up the covers she had kicked off. He didn't know the difference between her cries of hunger, dirty diapers, tummy aches, and boredom. He hadn't memorized the telephone numbers for the pediatrician and the poison control center. He didn't read the ingredients and nutritional value of everything she ate or study the pharmacological insert sheets and drug-interaction and side-effect warnings of every medicine she took. He didn't fawn over the toddler outfits in department stores and make sure she was the most adorable child at the day care. And he didn't take time every weekend to record in her baby book all the milestones of her life and what a beautiful little girl she was becoming.

Oh, how I ached to hold her, to feel her heart pounding and her chest rising and falling, my precious, beautiful brown-eyed girl. My determination to see her again kept me going. I would do everything asked of me to get back to my daughter, my husband, my home, and my life. I willingly conspired with Nana and Luas in the fantasy that I was in heaven while secretly knowing it was just that — a fantasy, an hallucination — and I would be with them soon.

Nana had explained that I would be spending the day with Luas but gave no hint of where we would be going or what we would be doing. It would be my first day away from her since arriving in Shemaya. While primping my hair in the bedroom mirror before leaving her house in Delaware, I asked her if Luas was my great-grandfather Frank, whom I had never met.

"No, no," she said in her Italian accent, amused by the suggestion. "Luas isn't your great-grandfather, dear. Frank has already moved on. Luas is the High Jurisconsult of Shemaya."

"What does that mean?" I asked. "High Jurisconsult?"

"It means he's the chief lawyer here."

"But I thought we were in heaven," I said, not quite sarcastically, instantly aware of the contradiction and smiling inwardly. "Why would anybody need lawyers in paradise?"

Nana looked surprised. "You don't think God would allow souls to face the Final Judgment alone, do you? Even murderers on earth have a lawyer to represent them, and the outcomes of those trials are only temporary. The stakes are higher here, dear. All of eternity."

I was speechless.

"Luas will explain everything," Nana assured me. "But let me tell you a little secret. He needs your help. Don't let him know I told you."

"He needs *my* help?" I said. "I'm the one who needs help."

"Yes, dear," she said, "and by helping Luas you'll be helping yourself."

"What exactly does he need my help with?"

Nana paused for a moment and looked at me in the mirror. "He wants to leave Shemaya but he can't find the way out. It happens to almost everybody. Shemaya isn't what it appears to be. In fact, it's the exact opposite. Try to remember that. It's as easy to get lost here as it is on earth. But it's actually easier here to find your way back home. That's what people don't understand. It happens automatically, when you're ready."

"Ready for what?" I asked.

"Ready to move on, dear," Nana said.

I was confused. "I thought you just told me that Luas wanted to leave?"

"Oh, he does, very much," Nana said. "But he isn't ready and so he remains. Only

91

he can choose."

"How long has he been here?" I asked.

Nana thought for a moment. "I think it's been about two thousand years, dear," she said. She smiled and put down the hairbrush. "Come along now, it's time to go see him. He can explain how Shemaya works better than me. His job is to train the new presenters. I only know how to help them leave."

Luas continued his instructions to me in the vestibule: "The train station is crowded now with new arrivals," he said. "You will hear nothing, but you will feel them brushing against you. Make no attempt to reach out to them, and do not, under any circumstances, remove the blindfold. The entrance to the Courtroom is at the opposite end of the station. We'll be going straight through. Are you ready?"

The blindfold was tied tight around my head, and I was growing increasingly nervous. "Why can't I see them?" I asked. "And what do you mean, 'Courtroom'?"

"I'll explain later," he said, tugging at the blindfold knot one last time to be certain it was tight. "If we don't get going, we'll miss the trial. Can you see?"

"No."

"Then you're ready. Follow me."

He grasped my left elbow and urged me forward, his body stiffening against the weight of the doors. Entering the station, I immediately sensed a great throng of people milling about in ghostly silence. What I thought were bodies began brushing against my hips and shoulders, but heeding Luas's warning, I made no attempt to reach out to them. Even so, halfway through I could no longer resist the temptation to peek beneath the blindfold.

What I saw is difficult to describe.

The train station was filled not with people's bodies but rather with their *memories*. Thousands of glittering spheres floated in midair about the train station like stars in the nighttime sky. A person's entire lifetime of thoughts, sensations, images, and emotions filled each sphere, flashing and arcing inside like brightly colored bolts of electricity. These were raw memories, not the sanitized recollections we tell one another over cups of coffee or even the more honest accounts we record in our secret diaries, but life itself as experienced and remembered by those who lived it. By looking at a sphere, I came into direct contact with the memories inside without the protective filter of another person's mind, which made the memories seem as though they were *mine.*

Suddenly, like an actor at an award show watching scenes spliced together from a lifetime of films, I found myself reliving the experiences of people whom I had never known but who seemed in a very real sense to be *me.* One moment I'm working a sewing machine in a sweatshop in Saipan, then I look at another sphere and I'm climbing the catwalk of a grain silo in Kansas City. I look at yet another sphere and I'm careening through the streets of Baghdad in the back of a taxicab, then tending the helm of a trawler in stormy seas off Newfoundland, strolling the rows of a vineyard in Australia, driving a front-end loader from a mine shaft in Siberia, severing the head of a Tutsi boy with a machete in Rwanda, kissing the neck of a lover in Montreal. I was more than mere spectator to these events. My fingers cramped as the fabric slid beneath the needle, I choked on clouds of dust billowing over the dry wheat, my body leaned as we swerved to avoid a pedestrian crossing the street, I barked orders to my crew on deck and saw the fear in their eyes as the waves crested the bow, I felt the warm spray of blood as I thrust the machete again into the convulsing corpse, and I whispered softly while indulging the desires of my lover. Alien memories coursed through me as though I were emerging from multiple lifetimes of amnesia, leaving me confused and lost. Unable to stand any more, I pulled the blindfold back down over my eyes. Luas led me on until finally we passed out of the station.

"Are you all right?" he asked as the doors slammed shut behind us.

I was unable to respond; my body trembled.

"Here," he said, "you can remove the blindfold. Sit."

We were in a remote, vacant corridor of the train station now and sat down together on a bench. Luas brushed away the hair that had fallen into my eyes and smiled. "I knew you would peek," he said. "You're not one to obey rules, even when they benefit you." He gazed back toward the doors through which we had just emerged. "You see them for who they are, Brek Abigail Cuttler. You have the gift."

I was barely able to understand his words. It was as though I'd been raised on a desert island without music, books, television, or maps and suddenly been given a glimpse of the world. I wanted to see more. I needed to see more. I got up from the bench and turned toward the doors.

"Not yet," Luas warned. "It's too soon. You're not ready."

I grasped the door handle.

"No, Brek." Luas spoke sternly. "You must do exactly as I say or you will lose who you are. Do you understand?"

"Who am I, Luas?" I said, confused and lost. "Or, should I say, who was I?" I pulled on the door.

Luas tugged on the empty right sleeve of my suit jacket, causing me to turn toward him.

"You did it on purpose," he said, indicating the empty sleeve. "Quite bold, actually. Why, there isn't a child who hasn't comforted herself to sleep knowing that if pushed too far she could simply deny her parents what they treasure most of all. Children play the same dangerous game adults play on the tips of ballistic missiles, but unlike adults most children recognize the futility of trying to win by losing. Not you, Brek Cuttler. No, you heard your grandfather's instruction to stand clear of the conveyor chain as an invitation to trade a pound of your own flesh for the pleasure of the pain on your parents' faces and the sorrow in their voices."

I was stunned. My darkest secret. His tactic was instantly effective. I remembered now who *I* was, and that my life was very different from the lives of the souls in the train shed.

"How did you know?" I asked.

"Oh, I know many things about you, Brek Cuttler," Luas said.

"Then you should know they were getting a divorce," I said, "and that my mother was an alcoholic and my father hit her and he . . . You should know I thought I'd only get a cut when I reached into the machine, not that I would lose my arm. I just wanted them to listen. Can you understand that? I just wanted them to stay together. Is that too much for a child to ask?"

I glared at Luas as if he were my own father. Luas was silent.

"You have no right to judge me," I said. "I've been punished my entire life for the sin of trying to keep my parents together. I've more than paid for my crime, if you can call wanting a family a crime. You know all my secrets, is that right? Do you know about the phantom pains, when you think your arm is hurting even though you don't have an arm? Do you know what it's like not being able to hug another human being because you're missing an arm to hug them back? Do you know about bathing, dressing, eating, and sleeping with only one hand, and about the jeers of children and the cruelty of adults? Do you know about the awkwardness of every new meeting? Do you know about clothes with useless right sleeves?"

"All that was forgiven long ago," Luas replied.

"Forgiven? Really? I don't remember forgiving anybody."

"Please, Brek," he said, "sit down."

I released the door and sat back down with him on the bench. Two sculptures had been chiseled into the stone wall opposite the bench. One was of a Buddhist temple in the foothills of Tibet and the other of a synagogue in the foothills of Mount Sinai. Luas noticed me looking at them. They seemed out of place in a train station.

"Have you heard of the Book of Life and the Book of Death?" he asked.

I nodded.

"They don't exist," he said.

I exhaled in relief, prematurely.

"God doesn't maintain them. We do. Each one of us. A record of every thought, word, and deed in our lives. The storage is quite perfect, actually. It's the recall that's incomplete. Not that this is a defect. Important reasons exist for narrowing the field. Forgetting traumatic events helps one cope, and there's the exquisitely practical need to discard portions of an ever-growing body of experiences to avoid being consumed by them. Memory isn't the defective tape recording you've been led to believe. It's the tape player itself, playing back the tracks of music we select — and sometimes those we don't. Replayed on the right machine — a high-quality machine — the music can be reproduced with great fidelity and precision, nearly as perfect as when it was first created."

Although hewn from solid rock, the stone reliefs on the wall metamorphosed as Luas spoke, reworking themselves into brooding animations of viscous stone. Two elevated thrones surrounded by great mounds of crumpled scrolls replaced the temple and the synagogue. In front of the thrones queued long lines of people, naked, their faces erased from their egg-shaped bald heads. Thin, fat, young, old, male, female, tall, small, each person carried a scroll, some bulging and heavy and others compact and light. Upon the thrones sat identical orbs like the sun with rays emanating in all directions. At the foot of the thrones stood a robed soul who received the scroll from the next person in line and appeared to read aloud as the parchment unspooled. When the end was reached, the scrolls were cast by the readers onto the mounds and the bearers disappeared without direction or trace, replaced by the next in line for whom the process was repeated. Luas paused to watch the somber procession.

"You've been given the privilege, and the responsibility, of replaying the tape for others," he said.

"I don't understand."

"That is what we do here, Brek," Luas explained. "It's why we've been brought to Shemaya, to read and dissect the record of life and plead to the Creator the imperfect case of the created, as oil and canvas would, if they could, explain to the artist flaws of texture and color, or as string and bow would, if they could, explain to the composer disturbances of pitch and tone. We've been appointed to tell the other side of the story, Brek — to explain their fears and regrets, their complicity and victimization, their greed and sacrifice. We're here to make sure justice is served at the Final Judgment."

Luas's words should have literally put the fear of God in me, but, as I said earlier, I hadn't accepted my death at this point. To the contrary, I'd been waiting and watching for an opening to rejoin the life I once led.

Yet what Luas said was so outrageous that my earlier thoughts of fever and illness turned into the possibility that I might have been involved in a terrible accident and suffered a serious brain injury.

*Maybe I was in a car crash, or fell off a cliff during the hike up Tussey Mountain. Maybe this is what a coma is like. Maybe when Nana was dressing me before entering the train station, she was really my nurse preparing me for surgery and Luas is my neurosurgeon. Maybe the blindfold he lowered over my eyes is an oxygen mask to keep me alive.*

I clung to these hopes now as Luas explained things, terrifying things, I could neither comprehend nor accept — things that could not be so unless I was, in fact, dead.

"Okay," I said, playing along, afraid that if I let him know I was on to him he might make a mistake during the operation and either kill me or leave me a vegetable. "So you're my lawyer and you're trying to help me avoid being sent to hell for sticking my hand in the manure spreader, is that right? Can't you get me a plea bargain or something? Credit for time served?"

"Hardly." Luas laughed. "Why did God promise not to flood the earth again?"

A puzzled expression flashed across my face.

"Oh, come now," Luas said. He removed a pipe and a pouch of tobacco from his jacket pocket and packed the bowl as he spoke. "Surely you know the story. Things only got worse after the fiasco in Eden. Cain murdered Abel, and later one of his children murdered a young child. Humans began mating with beasts and engaging in every sort of debauchery. God was furious — and rightly so. He decided to destroy the lot of us as justice demands, but when the flood waters receded, He felt remorse. Imagine that, Brek. God regrets what God has done. Remarkable, isn't it? He makes us a promise: 'I'll never do it again,' He says, and He drapes rainbows from the clouds as a reminder. First He decides that extermination of the human race is the final solution — to borrow an ugly phrase — but as soon as He's driven humanity to the brink, all is forgiven and our survival is guaranteed, even if we return to our wicked ways. Why the change of heart? Why even spare Noah in the first place?"

"I guess because Noah was the only one who obeyed," I said.

Luas paused to strike a match and light his pipe. "Correct," he said, "and if Noah had disobeyed?"

"He would have been killed with the others."

"Correct again," Luas said between puffs. "Divine justice. But what explains God's last-second change of heart about the rest of us? It's because of this astounding about-face that beyond those doors at the end of the corridor, inside the Courtroom, there will be argument for many souls today that they have a place in the Light and, for those same souls, the Dark. They'll learn their fates today and greet their eternities. You see, Brek, every birth of a human being is a potential crime and a pending trial. It's the Courtroom, not a pot of gold, that sits at the end of God's rainbows. God promised us those rainbows would guarantee a place for man in the world of sun and clouds, but He said nothing about the worlds to come."

Luas rose from the bench and gestured for me to follow him down the corridor.

"Of course," he continued, puffing on his pipe, "we do not deal here with bodhisattvas or saints, caitiffs or fiends. The conclusions for them are foregone, the judgments obvious and unassailable. Our concern in the Courtroom is for the rest of humanity — the good people who sometimes cheat, the bad who sometimes do good, the billions who failed to sacrifice everything to become priests or prophets but resisted the temptation to become demons or demigods. We put on no false airs here. We do not ask whether there has been renunciation for the Hindu, awakening for the Buddhist, reckoning for the Muslim, salvation for the Christian, or atonement for the Jew. These are mere obfuscations of Divine Law. There is only one question to be answered during the Final Judgment of every human soul, and it is the same question that concerned God before the Great Flood: What does justice demand?"

We stopped in front of the doors.

"Accounts rich and grave are reconciled beyond these doors, Brek Cuttler," Luas said. "Could you speak honestly of yourself there? Could you damn yourself if damning is what you deserved, setting aside fear and hatred for truth? Could you stand before the Creator of energy, space, and time and save yourself? Could you pass through those doors, knowing your experience of eternity would be forever shaped by what you said and left unsaid? Could you explain what, during your entire life, defied explanation?"

I began to panic. I couldn't have made up these words if my brain had been knocked around inside my skull during a car accident or falling off a cliff. And I couldn't have made up the memories I experienced passing through the train shed either — they were too vivid, too exotic, too real. The possibility of my own death was becoming more and more inescapable.

"You're taking me to be judged, then?" I said, backing away. "I really am going to hell for putting my arm in a manure spreader?"

"Judged? You? Of course not!" Luas said, genuinely surprised by my question. "I told you all that was forgiven long ago. I'm taking you to receive your heavenly reward, Brek, not to send you to hell. You've always hoped and prayed you would come here. Shemaya has been the motive behind your every decision and the basis of your every interaction from the moment when you realized you suffered after the loss of your arm, not because you would never again be able to dangle from monkey bars or swing a softball bat or play a violin but because it was unjust that millions of other girls could."

Luas paused a moment to gauge my reaction and puff on his pipe. I kept my distance, convinced that I was about to be condemned.

"A member of the bar, not the clergy, offered you justice after the accident, isn't that right?" he continued. "You discovered at an early age that the legal system provides the redemption religion can no longer afford, and that lawyers are the true priests and judges the true prophets. You craved justice more than anything else in your life. And so on the day your childhood friend, Karen Busfield, told you she was accepted into a seminary to become an Episcopal priest, you were filled with despair, not joy. You were already in law school by then. Do you remember how you mocked her? You said: 'When a child with bruises on her body reveals to you her father did it, Karen, what will you do? Tell her to pray and put it in God's hands? And when she says she's been praying every night for ten years but the beatings still continue, what will you say then? God's hands can't be bothered with children, Karen. If you really want to save people's souls from sin — not just the sin of hating others and themselves but the sin of hating the God who breathed life into them and then abandoned them — you won't pray for them, Karen. You'll give them one of my business cards and tell them to call me.' "

I stared at Luas, trying to understand how he could possibly know all these things.

"And do you remember Karen's reply?" Luas went on. "She said you didn't let her finish. She was planning to join the Air Force, like her father, and become a military chaplain. 'The Air Force doesn't call lawyers when somebody misbehaves, Brek,' she said. 'They drop bombs on them. Now *that's* justice.' And you said to her: 'They'll never take you, Karen. They'll see right through you.'"

Luas stopped to puff on his pipe.

"You understood the great truth of life, Brek Cuttler," he continued. "You understood that the pursuit of justice is the purest form of religion and the highest human aspiration. You became a disciple of justice. Now the time has come for you to receive your reward. You've been chosen to join the elite lawyers of Shemaya who defend souls at the Final Judgment. I was being facetious when I asked you if you could defend yourself in the Courtroom. That always gets the attention of new arrivals. No, the only question now is whether you can walk through those doors if *someone else* depends upon what you say and leave unsaid. If you speak for humanity, not yourself. But this question was answered about you long ago, was it not? My job is not to assess your fitness but to show you the way."

Luas emptied his pipe into an ashtray on the wall, then slipped his hand into his vest pocket and removed a golden key from which dangled a sparkling Magen David, the crescent moon of Islam, figures of Shiva and the Buddha, the yin and yang, and a crucifix. "This is yours," he said, handing me the key. "It's the key to the Courtroom."

I refused to take it.

"Go on," Luas insisted. "This isn't the time for fear and indecision. You've been waiting for God to smite the evil and reward the righteous since you were eleven years old and you put those boys on trial for murdering crayfish. How wonderful! To you, even crayfish deserved justice! Rejoice, Brek Abigail Cuttler! Your prayers have been answered! There *is* justice after all! Finally, praise God, justice!"

# 8

Behind my best friend Karen Busfield's house, beyond the ash piles left over from the old coal furnaces and a small abandoned building, glistened the wide pleasant stream known as the Little Juniata River. The Little Juniata flows north out of the Allegheny Mountains, draining the small creeks and springs that bless the hills and valleys with life, then due south when it reaches Tyrone, Pennsylvania, where my father's family, the Cuttlers, who were simple farmers, are from. When the Little Juniata reaches Huntingdon, it spills into the big Juniata River, which is a big river only once every twenty years during a hurricane and at other times is just normal-sized, not wide, not deep, and not fast. The big Juniata River continues south until it empties into the Susquehanna River at Clarks Ferry near Harrisburg, and the Susquehanna, which is a big river all year round, continues south until it reaches Havre de Grace, Maryland, where it flows into the Chesapeake Bay. There is a marina there, where my mother's family, the Bellinis, who were more wealthy and better educated than the Cuttlers, docked their sailboat. And so it was that my father's and mother's families were connected in this way, by the rivers, long before my parents met. I remember being astonished when I discovered this relationship on a map, like suddenly recognizing the shape of a connect-the-dots rabbit. I wondered about its meaning, and, like an astrologer searching for signs in the heavens, I began reading all kinds of maps for signs of what my future might bring. After that, when I waded into the Little Juniata River or sailed the Chesapeake Bay with my grandparents, I could not resist wondering where the water had come from and where it was going and whose lives it would bring together.

The Little Juniata River is shallow in midsummer and has a limestone bottom of slippery, moss-covered river rocks. Karen and I could walk for miles through its knee-deep, clear waters wearing cutoff shorts and old sneakers, stumbling, sliding, drenching ourselves, and laughing merrily. We carried our lunches with us and ate along its banks, pretending to be early explorers charting the river for the first time. The aboriginal tribes we encountered, which is to say the boys from the different neighborhoods along the river, tracked our movements warily, as if we really were from a faraway land.

Girls never played in the river, but Karen and I weren't like most girls — not because we were more tomboyish or brave, but because we saw the world differently. For example, we thought the river was interesting and full of possibilities, which most girls did not, and we believed we had equal right with the boys to play in it, which most girls would not. Ours was a difference of curiosity and perspective.

One hot July afternoon, while Karen and I were exploring the river, we shocked ourselves and the boys by catching crayfish with our own bare hands — no easy feat for a girl with only one arm. Little Juniata River crayfish are difficult to catch. Like handicapped girls, they're timid little creatures, seemingly aware of their vulnerability and embarrassed by their own bizarre bodies. You must approach them from behind without casting a shadow, while they're sunning themselves in shallow waters on the mossy green river rocks they try so hard to imitate. They dart backward when frightened, vanishing in a cloud of silt into the nearest crevice. You must be fast, and you must grab them by the large middle shell to avoid their sharp pincers — like lifting a snarling cat by the scruff of its neck. Held this way, they're perfectly harmless. But make a mistake, and they'll give you a painful snip and you'll drop them back into the water.

Karen and I proudly waved our crayfish high in the air that afternoon, cheering and hollering with the excitement of biologists discovering a new species. We examined them up close, noticing how their tails curled into a ball to shield their soft underbellies and their pincers strained to reach back over their heads to nip at our fingers. We stroked their antennae and clicked our fingernails against their hard shells. And finally we returned them to the river, worried they wouldn't survive if we kept them out too long.

There isn't much more you can do with a crayfish. You might shake it in the face of a boy to make him wince, but you could embarrass him this way only once, and the consequences for the crayfish were dire. When the boys saw we were still alive after handling the nasty things, they bravely attacked the river and a fierce competition set

in. Soon buckets were filled with crayfish
and records were made of who caught the
most and the biggest. This is where the
minds of girls and boys turn in opposite
directions. Karen and I were content to
study the crayfish for a minute or two and
set them free. The boys, on the other hand,
weren't satisfied until they'd tortured and
murdered the lot of them. Their buckets
became killing grounds.

Karen and I were horrified. We pleaded
with the boys to end the competition and
spare the crayfish. We tried to wrestle the
buckets away, but the boys were too strong.
We threw rocks at them and called them
names. We even threatened to kiss them if
they refused to stop — but it was no use.

Even though we couldn't liberate the
crayfish, I was determined to bring the boys
to justice for their crimes. So I established a
courtroom of rocks and logs along the
riverbank and held trials. I knew just how
to do it. My Pop Pop Bellini was a lawyer,
and I had seen him, valiant and righteous,
cross-examining witnesses. I myself had
testified in court about the accident with
my arm. So I appointed myself lead prosecutor and told Karen she could be the
judge and the jury. To my shock and dismay,
Karen betrayed both the crayfish and me by

refusing to participate, claiming that punishing the boys wouldn't do any good. I thought she was sweet on one of them, probably Lenny Basilio, who kept running up to show her his crayfish. Even the boys doubted Karen's motives, but to their credit they knew they'd done wrong. They'd gotten bored with the killing and thought trials might be fun.

Since Karen wouldn't help, the boys offered to sit as the jury for one another, promising to listen impartially to the evidence and render a fair verdict. I was against this, but Karen, relishing her role as spoiler, reminded me that a jury is supposed to be composed of the defendant's peers, leaving me no choice but to agree. I would be both prosecutor and judge, and Karen would sit by and watch.

I put Lenny Basilio on trial first to spite her. Lenny was the weakest and most sensitive boy of the group, the one always being pushed around. He was also the nicest. He'd been afraid at first to catch the crayfish and had to be teased by the others into doing it, but once he got started he became very efficient and caught the largest crayfish of the day — a wise old granddaddy of a crustacean the size of a small baby lobster. Although by far the biggest and most powerful crayfish in his collection, it was too heavy and slow to defend itself against the younger ones and became the first casualty in Lenny's bucket. Lenny looked genuinely remorseful when the big crayfish died. I knew he'd be easy to convict for the murder.

I called him to the witness stand — a flat piece of river rock resting on a platform of sticks — and told him to raise his right hand. We recognized no right against self-incrimination along the banks of the Little Juniata River. All defendants were forced to testify.

"Do you swear to tell the whole truth, Lenny Basilio, so help you God?" I said.

Lenny shrugged his shoulders and sat down.

I placed his bucket before him, filled with fetid crayfish parts. "Did you put these crayfish in this bucket?"

Lenny looked into the pail and then over at his buddies.

"Remember, Lenny," I warned him, "you're under oath. You'll be struck dead by a bolt of lightning if you lie."

Lenny let out a whine. "But the crayfish pinched me first!"

"Yes or no?" I said. "Did you fill this bucket with crayfish?"

"Yes."

"That's right, you did. And after you filled it, you stirred it up so the crayfish would snap at each other, didn't you?"

Before Lenny could answer, I dredged through the water and pulled out the lifeless granddaddy crayfish, already turning white in the heat like a steamed jumbo shrimp. Its right pincer had been amputated, just like my right arm. I showed the crayfish to the jury and made them take a good long look at it. Although a few of them snickered and made coarse jokes, the expressions on most of their faces suggested that even they were appalled and saddened by what had happened. Then I showed it defiantly to Karen, who shook her head silently. I turned back to Lenny.

"You did this, didn't you, Lenny Basilio?" I said. "You killed it. You took it out of the river and put it in your bucket and killed it."

"But I didn't mean to," Lenny pleaded. He looked like he was about to cry.

I dropped the crayfish into the bucket and turned toward the jury in disgust. "The prosecution rests."

"Guilty! Guilty!" the boys all cheered.

"Just a minute," I said sagely. "You've got to vote on it to make it official. We have to take a poll. John Gaines, what say you?" I spoke the way the courtroom tipstaff had spoken while polling the jury during my trial.

John Gaines glared at Lenny. "Guilty," he said, leaning forward and baring his teeth for effect. "Guilty as sin."

"Mike Kelly, what say you?"

"Guilty!" he said with enthusiasm.

"Okay," I said. "Robby Temin, what say you?"

Robby looked sympathetically at Lenny. "Guilty," he whispered.

"Jimmy Reece?"

Jimmy threw a rock at Lenny and laughed. "Guilty . . . and he's a crybaby too!"

The boys all laughed.

I slid behind the judge's bench and banged a stone against the river rock. "Order in the court!" I hollered. "Order in the court!" The boys became silent instantly. I was impressed with my newfound power.

"Wally Miller, what say you?"

Wally glared back at me, full of insolence and venom. He was the biggest and meanest boy, the bully of the Juniata River. Everybody was afraid of Wally Miller, including me. He had a permanent look of malice about him and a well-earned reputation of quasi-criminal behavior.

"Not guilty," he said, keeping his eyes

fixed on me.

My jaw dropped. Before I could protest, the other boys chimed in: "What? Not guilty? No way! He's as guilty as the devil!"

Wally held up his hand to silence them. "I said, not guilty," he insisted.

Lenny Basilio's face brightened. By some miracle, Wally the bully had actually come to his rescue. It must have been a first. With a warm smile of gratitude and friendship, Lenny virtually danced over to Wally to thank him. But as soon as Lenny got there, Wally cocked his arm and thumped Lenny hard in the chest with the heel of his hand, knocking him to the ground. He leered at the other boys. "Just kidding," he said. "Guilty. Guilty as hell! Let's hang him!"

The boys broke into a riot of cheers. "Guilty! Guilty as hell! Hang him! Let's hang Lenny!"

Lenny scrambled to his feet and backed away. He looked hurt and terrified. Tears spouted from his eyes.

I slammed the river rocks together. "Order! Order!" I said. "Order, or I'll hold you all in contempt and end this trial right now!"

The boys quieted down, and I turned to Lenny. He looked at me desperately, but I felt no sympathy for him. I was still thinking about what he'd done to the crayfish.

"Lenny Basilio," I said gravely, "you've been found guilty of murdering crayfish."

Lenny hung his head low.

"Murder is the most serious crime there is," I continued, "but we can't hang you, because there's no death penalty on the Juniata River."

Lenny perked up, but the boys started booing and hissing.

I slammed the rocks together again. "Order!"

"We can't hang you, Lenny," I said, "but you've got to be punished . . ." I thought for a moment of what his punishment should be. I looked down at the bucket and then out at the river. "You took the crayfish out of the river where they lived and put them on the land where they died. Justice demands an eye for an eye and a tooth for a tooth. As the judge of this court, I hereby sentence you, Lenny Basilio, to be taken from the land where you live and spend the rest of your life in the river."

"Throw Lenny in the river! Throw Lenny in the river!" the boys cheered.

Lenny tried to run, but they caught him and dragged him kicking and screaming into the river. He struggled for a while but finally gave up. After dunking him several times, the boys returned to the riverbank, leaving

Lenny standing in the middle of the river, looking pitiful, dripping wet, a convicted felon behind bars. I was jubilant. Justice had prevailed. At the age of eleven, I'd won my first trial and my first battle of good versus evil. I had joined the ranks of Mr. Gwynne and my Pop Pop Bellini, of school principals and police officers, of soldiers and superheroes. It was the best feeling I'd ever felt in my life, a glorious moment. I smiled smugly at Karen, who looked on without saying a word.

"Okay, who's next?" I said, examining each boy before settling on Wally Miller, the bully. I couldn't wait to convict him and have him thrown into the river. "Wally Miller," I said, "I charge you with kidnapping and murdering crayfish. How do you plead, guilty or not guilty?"

Wally strutted up to me. "Guilty," he sneered. "What are *you* going to do about it?"

I turned to the other boys for support, but they stood frozen. None of them was willing to challenge Wally Miller. I said nothing.

Wally laughed. "That's what I thought," he said. "You're nothing but a one-armed freak." He stepped forward and shoved me with both hands, knocking me to the ground, then turned and had a laugh with his buddies.

I wasn't about to let him get away with it. I scrambled back to my feet and charged after him. The other boys tried to warn him, but just as Wally turned around to face me, I bunched up my fist and hit him square in the mouth. He fell to his knees. A little trickle of blood oozed from a gash in his upper lip.

Wally was stunned. I was stunned. The other boys were stunned. And terrified. They had just witnessed a one-armed girl whip the bully of the Juniata River. They knew there would be hell to pay for each of them when Wally tried to restore his reputation. One by one, they quietly disappeared into the woods from which they had come. Wally rose slowly to his feet, wiped his mouth, and looked at the red smear on his hand.

"I'll get you back for this, Cuttler," he said.

I stood my ground defiantly with my fist clenched. He knew better than to mess with me anymore and walked away.

That left Karen, Lenny, and me. Apparently thinking Wally's defeat meant he was somehow exonerated, Lenny started stepping out of the river, but I stopped him.

"Get back in that water, Lenny Basilio," I warned him. "You've been sentenced to life."

Lenny stepped back obediently. He had just seen what I had done to Wally and wasn't going to try his luck.

I sat down beside Karen on a log. My knuckles ached from slamming into Wally's teeth. Karen and I didn't talk. What happened was too traumatic. We just looked at the river and Lenny.

After about five minutes passed, Lenny got bored and fidgety. He started skimming rocks across the water and kicking and splashing around idly. When these activities no longer entertained him, he began inching his way down the river, hoping I wouldn't see him. I ordered him back. He complied but turned right around and tried it again. Soon it turned into a sort of game. But when I ordered him back for the fourth time, he made a break for it. Unfortunately for Lenny, he slipped on the riverbank mud and gashed open his knee. I caught up with him and dragged him back into the water by his wrist. He tried to free himself, but my grip was too strong. I held him in place until he stopped squirming.

"How long are you going to keep him in the river?" Karen called to me from the riverbank.

"For the rest of his life," I said, tightening my grip on him. "He's got to pay for his crime. The crayfish deserve justice."

"Then you're going to have to stay there the rest of your life too," Karen said. "He's just going to keep trying to get out."

She was right, of course, but I was determined that Lenny serve out his sentence. I was wearing a fabric belt with a sliding loop buckle. I looked around for something to tie him to, but there were no tree branches close enough to the water. Then I got an idea. I took off the belt, lashed it around my arm and Lenny's, and cinched it tight with my teeth. Now we were bound together, prisoner and guard. He had no chance of escape. As long as I stayed in the river, Lenny would stay in the river. I looked back at Karen proudly. She shook her head, amused.

There we stood in the water, Lenny and me. He struggled every once in a while to get free, but it was no use. When he whimpered or protested, I told him to shut up. When he splashed or caused me to stumble, I elbowed him in the side. He would receive no more mercy than he had shown the crayfish. This went on for nearly half an hour, but it felt like all afternoon. It was getting late. We would normally be heading back home. Karen finally got up and said she was leaving.

"Wait," I said. "You can't go. You've got to stay here and keep me company."

"No thanks," Karen replied, climbing up the riverbank.

"But you've got to," I said. I was furious. She had betrayed me during the trial, and now she was doing it again.

"No, I don't," Karen replied. "I didn't do anything to the crayfish, and it wasn't my idea to put Lenny in the river. I'm going home."

"Well, what am I supposed to do?" I said. "Stay here all night with Lenny by myself?"

Lenny looked mortified.

"I guess so," Karen replied. "If you want to keep him in the river for the rest of his life. Have fun." She started walking away.

"Wait," I pleaded. "What am I supposed to do? I've got no choice. The crayfish deserve justice."

Karen stopped and gazed back at me in disbelief. I must have looked as miserable and pathetic as Lenny. Then she turned and waded out into the water. She seemed almost angelic coming toward us, her face glowing radiantly in the afternoon sun, her blue eyes sparkling from the reflection of the stream. When she reached us, she tugged on the belt that bound Lenny and me together.

"You can't bring the crayfish back, Brek," she said tenderly. "But you can set yourself free. It's not about Lenny anymore. It's about you. How long do you want to wait in the water?"

# 9

I inserted the golden key Luas had given me into the lock of the massive wooden doors leading into the Courtroom. Suddenly the doors and the entire train shed itself vanished, leaving me standing beside Luas in an immense space bounded only by energy. The walls were translucent and electric, and if they could be said to have had a color, glistened like water in a crystal decanter on a sterling silver tray. It was a room like no other, a room where time and space merged. A room in eternity.

At the opposite end of the Courtroom, the energy condensed itself into a triangular monolith several stories tall, seemingly working Einstein's theorem in reverse. The slab was both dark and luminescent, composed of what appeared to be the finest sapphire, with a triangular aperture near the top through which light entered but did not exit, allowing nothing of the interior of the slab to be seen. A semicircle of pale amber light radiated outward from the base of the monolith in a broad arc, and this light formed the floor itself. At the center of the floor stood a simple wooden chair, absurdly out of scale in substance and size. Behind this chair, but beyond the circle of light and exactly opposite the monolith, sat three more chairs. Luas ushered me toward them and insisted I take the one in the middle. He took the left chair and, after seating himself, placed his hands on his knees, closed his eyes, and said to me: "Tobias Bowles will be presenting the case of his father, Gerard."

A moment later, another person arrived, standing in the same spot where we had been standing, a golden key like mine still turning in his fingers. He was only a young boy, perhaps eight or nine years of age. His skin was dark and his features Middle Eastern, with soft brown eyes that seemed to have seen and understood too much for his years. He wore his hair long and un-kempt. A cream-colored robe draped from his shoulders to the floor. Luas rose to his feet when he saw him, looking disappointed.

"Oh, it's only you, Haissem," he said, scowling. "We were expecting Mr. Bowles . . . Well, here we are anyway. Haissem, this is Brek Cuttler, the newest lawyer on my staff. Brek, this is Haissem, the most senior presenter in all of Shemaya. I must say, Haissem, she's arrived not a moment too soon. We just lost Jared Schrieberg and now, it seems from your appearance, Mr. Bowles as well."

*Jared Schrieberg?* I thought. Odd. That was Bo's grandfather's name.

Haissem reached out to greet me with his left hand — a perceptive gesture, as most people reached by instinct for my right hand and were embarrassed to come up with an empty sleeve.

"Welcome to the Courtroom, Brek," he said, bowing politely, his voice high and pre-pubescent. "I remember sitting here to witness my first presentation. Abel presented the difficult case of his brother, Cain. That was long before your time though, Luas."

"Quite," Luas agreed.

"Not much has changed since then," Haissem sighed. "Luas keeps the docket moving even though the number of cases increases. We're fortunate to have you, Brek, and you're fortunate to have somebody like Luas as your mentor. There's no better presenter in all of Shemaya."

"Present company excepted," Luas said.

"Not at all," said Haissem. "I only handle

the easy cases."

"Few would consider Socrates and Judas to have been easy cases," Luas replied. "I'm just a clerk."

Haissem winked at me. "Don't let him fool you," he said. "Without Luas, there would be no Shemaya."

"Wait a minute," I said, bewildered. "Cain and Abel? Socrates and Judas? What are you talking about? What's the joke?"

Luas turned to me impatiently. "Do you believe theirs were clear cases about which there could be no doubt?" he said.

"I, I guess not . . ." I said. "I really have no idea, but my point is that you couldn't possibly have — Well, what happened to them, then? What was the verdict?"

Haissem patted Luas on the back. "I must enter my appearance and prepare myself," he said. "I trust you'll explain everything." Haissem reached again for my left hand, and for an instant his eyes seemed to focus on something inside me that was much larger than me. "We will meet again, Brek," he said. "You'll do well here, I'm certain of it." He walked toward the chair at the center of the Courtroom, and Luas motioned for us to take our seats.

"We present only the facts," he whispered as we sat down. "Our concern here is not

129

with verdicts."

"But if they were really put on trial, then surely you must know —"

"Nothing," Luas interrupted. "We know nothing about the outcomes. The Judge never speaks. One might speculate, of course. There are instances when a presenter feels the result should go one way more than another, but it is strictly forbidden. The consequences for a presenter who attempts to alter eternity last all of eternity. We must not seek to influence the result."

I watched him, trying to see through him, behind him, still unwilling to believe, still clinging to life as it used to be, searching for explanations for what was happening. Nothing made sense. "The surgery isn't going well, is it doctor?" I said. "You're making me worse. I'm becoming even more delusional."

"Nonsense," Luas replied. "Look, Haissem has taken his seat. You'll see things more clearly after he presents his case."

Haissem sat on the chair at the center of the Courtroom, adopting the same position as Luas, hands on knees, eyes closed, waiting. I kept my eyes open, watching. Suddenly, a powerful tremor rocked the triangular monolith, rippling its smooth surface. From the center of the monolith, from its

130

solid core, emerged a being like the one on the animated sculpture in the hallway, human in shape and size but without hair, face, or features, dressed in a charcoal gray cassock. Haissem maintained his position and the being stood before him for a moment, then returned to its dark home without a sound. When the tremor subsided, Haissem rose from the chair and, standing at the exact center of the Courtroom, raised his arms up from his sides in a broad arc. The energy of the walls and floor pulsed violently and surged toward him from all directions, seemingly compressing the space around him like an imploding star. The shock wave struck Haissem's body, instantly vaporizing him, leaving behind in the vacuum only his voice, detonating like a great cosmic explosion: "I PRESENT TOBIAS WILLIAM BOWLES . . . HE HAS CHOSEN!"

The Courtroom went dark. No light. No sound. No motion. Then the Courtroom vanished altogether.

What came next left me shaken to my core. I did not merely witness the trial of Toby Bowles's soul. Instead, by merging with his memories, I became Toby Bowles. I relived his life exactly as he had lived it. As had happened when I walked among the souls in the train shed, Brek Cuttler ceased to exist.

I find myself crossing a dirt road in a World War II military encampment. My body feels heavy, tired, anxious. My face feels thick and rough, covered with whiskers and grime. My mouth tastes unfamiliar, like a first kiss. My arms, two of them now, feel powerful but detached, as though I am operating a machine. There is an aggressiveness I have never felt before, a heightened wariness of my surroundings and other people. My thoughts and reactions are accelerated, more analytical; my emotions and ability to comprehend subtleties are dull and unused. I reek with body odors that seem both comfortable and unpleasant. My head aches from a hangover.

I am wearing a filthy green Army uniform and new black boots. This is my second pair of boots this month — a fact that I know implicitly but don't know how I know. I know too that I can have as many boots as I want, that there are enough boots at my disposal to outfit two armies. They're nice boots, shiny, black, and warm, but they can't be kept clean here in Saverne — another fact I know: the location of the encampment. The dust takes the shine off the boots as soon as you put them on, and there is nothing here but dust, darkening the sun and fading the colors. Everything is dust brown: the clothes, the tents, the once white requisition forms. In Saverne, the food tastes brown, the water washes brown, the stars sparkle brown, the air smells brown, and, when the dead arrive at the morgue here, they bleed brown onto the brown ground, ashes to ashes, brown to brown. I even dream in brown. The only thing not brown in Saverne is greed, which tints the eyes and fingertips a vibrant glossy hue of green.

Crossing the dirt road, I'm debating in my own mind whether to lowball the medical supply chief or give him a fair offer and make him think I'm doing him a favor by selling his extra supplies on the black market. But when I reach the middle of the dirt road, somebody yells, "Toby, look out!"

From the corner of my eye, I see an olive green Army truck racing toward me at breakneck speed, plowing a tantrum of brown dust into the air. The dust looks startled for a moment, as if it has just been awakened from a nap. I leap out of the way, spinning a pirouette in my new black boots and giving Davidson a thank-you slug in the shoulder for the warning.

"You gotta be more careful, Toby," he says. "You're gonna get yourself killed."

"Me, killed? No way," I tell him. "Not by no goddamned truck anyway. It'll take a French maid to do me in."

Davidson guards the entrance to a brown tent that was once olive green. Dirt blown from the road piles into drifts against the canvas, re-creating in miniature the blowing and drifting snow in the mountain passes to the south that make the Alps impenetrable at this time of year. Early winter cuts crisp and cold over the peaks and down into the French valleys, pruning the wounded and diseased from the battlefield and encampments, villages and cities. A mountaineer lucky enough to reach the summit of the Alps would see war on the horizon in all directions.

The tent is warmed by a well-stocked wood stove and insulated with boxes of medical supplies stacked from floor to ceiling with dusty red crosses painted on their sides. Each box is worth $200 on the French black market, making the tent into a bank vault. They form an aisle through to a desk at the center. A kerosene lantern hung on a tent pole produces a thin drizzle of light. Behind the desk sits a lean, powerful-looking black man. His left chest bears the name Collins and his shoulder the stripes of a corporal. We are of equal rank. He crushes the cigarette he's been smoking and lights another without offering me one.

"Scuttlebutt says Patton's crossing the Rhine near Ludwigshafen," I say. "Two Divisions are moving up from southern Italy to join the party. Price of boots and gloves just tripled."

Collins's mouth curls. "Where are they?" he asks.

"Keeping warm in a chateau."

"Don't be playin' no games wit' me, Bowles," he says. "I ain't got no time for it now."

My stomach churns a sour broth of hash and coffee up into the back of my throat. *I'm finally gonna get a piece of the action,* I keep telling myself. Just a piece of what everyone else has. *I didn't want to come here. I wanted to stay home and work on cars. That's all I ever wanted. I got a right to a little comfort, and I'll be damned if any black guy from Kentucky is gonna get more than me.* They assigned me to the quartermaster after I played up an asthma attack during basic. It beat carrying a rifle.

"Somebody's got to keep guys like you happy, and it might as well be me, right Collins?" I tell him. "What do you want, I

135

got it all: uniforms, tents, food, booze, utensils, tools, radios, movies, office supplies, sundries." It's all true. As a corporal in the quartermaster, I'm a walking department store and everybody's my best friend. As soon as the bees figure out where the clover is, they swarm to get it. Officers, GIs, locals — they're nicer to me than to the docs who cure their syphilis. They shake my hand and talk to me about me: Where'd I come from? Got a girl? Sure, good-lookin' guy like you's got a girl. Ten of 'em, and pretty too, I bet. They show me pictures of their girls, mothers, fathers, and kid brothers and sisters. I'm just a regular guy like you, they're all sayin', and us regular guys gotta stick together if we're gonna make it. Got any extra whiskey stashed back there? Helps me sleep better at night.

"You ain't got nothin' I want, Bowles," Collins says. "I'm the one who's got what you want. You're standing in my personal piggy bank, and my man Davidson out there, he's the guard. Now do you wanna sign for a loan, or do I tell Davidson to throw your ass out of here?"

I stand there for a minute, deciding whether to lowball him. I know Collins just came in with the Surgeon General's command. He's got no connections in the area, but he knows he's sitting on a fortune because medical supplies for the French population have become scarce and they'll pay almost anything to get them. I came in behind the invasion force and worked up some relationships with a few French doctors who have backers all the way south to Marseille. I decide to lowball him to see how he'll react.

"Twenty-five a box, unopened, and I'll throw in a crate of boots and gloves for every two medical."

"Davidson!" he hollers. "Get this lump of dog shit out of my office!"

"Look, Collins," I counter, backtracking a little. "You couldn't move this stuff if you set up a booth under the Eiffel Tower. I'll give you three boots and gloves for every two medical. I can't go any higher."

"One-fifty a box, Bowles, and you can keep your damn boots."

"Fifty."

"One-twenty-five."

"Seventy-five."

"Hundred."

"I got costs, Collins," I tell him. "No way you're comin' out ahead of me. Seventy-five, take it or leave it."

"I'll need a deposit."

"How much?"

"Thousand."

"What?"

"You ain't the only one interested, Bowles. You the third white guy been sniffin' round here today. One thousand in cash, final."

"I got five hundred on me," I say, reaching into my pocket. "I'll give you the rest tonight."

Collins thinks it over. "You know," he says, his thick lips parting into a toothy greedgreen smile, "I like you, Bowles. Get the rest here by eighteen hundred."

I give Collins the money and walk out of the tent doing the math in my head. I can move at least a hundred boxes a month. At two hundred bucks a box, that's twenty thousand gross, twelve-five net, minus grease money for the motor pool and perimeter patrol, maybe a thousand max. I just made eleven grand!

I nearly skip over to the enlisted club to grab a beer and celebrate. But on my way I see two men opening the rear panel of the truck that almost hit me, parked now about fifty yards away. They crawl up inside and begin unloading empty black body bags onto a folding litter, stacked twenty at a time. I stop to watch them. The guys in the morgue detail pretty much keep to themselves, and everyone else stays away from them. A guy will deny any belief in superstitions and yet walk out of his way to avoid getting anywhere near the morgue. I wonder whether the bags are new or whether they just reuse the old ones over and over again. It doesn't seem right reusing them, violates the privacy of the first guy and insults the second. They gave their lives, for chrissake. The least the Army can do is spring for new bags.

*Eleven grand . . . eleven . . . freakin' . . . grand!*

The body bags slap onto the litter like stacks of crisp, new script hitting a counter.

*Surplus, Toby. Just surplus,* I tell myself. *The stuff's just sitting there while some French kid dies because his doctor can't get enough sulfa and penicillin. A fellow ought to get paid when he puts himself on the line.*

Turning into the enlisted club I hear boots racing toward me from behind, pounding like hooves. Before I can turn to see what's going on I'm knocked to the ground. There's a sharp pain in my back. I try lifting my head, but it won't move. *Oh my God, they're shelling us and I've been hit!*

"Help!" I yell. "Help! Medic! I've been hit! I've been hit!"

The pain in my back increases, like a great weight is bearing down on me.

"Stop your damn yelling, Bowles," a voice says, close behind, just above me. "You're under arrest for theft."

Two MPs pull me off the ground and cuff my wrists behind my back. Over their shoulders, I see Collins in the door of the tent, shaking hands with another MP and handing him my money.

Haissem was sitting again on the chair at the center of the Courtroom. I felt the same sense of confusion and exhaustion that overwhelmed me after passing among the souls in the train station.

"Can you hear me now, Brek?" Luas said.

"Yes," I said, barely hearing him, as though he was far away. "What do you mean, 'now'?"

"I was talking to you during the presentation," he said. "When you didn't respond, I asked Haissem to stop."

"Oh . . ." I replied, lost, trying to separate my identity from Toby Bowles. "I'm sorry. It just seems so . . . real, like I'm remembering my own life."

"Yes, it is that way, isn't it?" Luas said. "When Haissem begins again, listen for my voice. At first you'll hear me speaking through the characters in the presentation, but what I say will seem out of context. If you fail to respond, I'll bring up the circumstances of your disfigurement again to bring you back. Unfortunately, it isn't possible to instruct you on how to separate yourself from the soul being presented. You must learn this by doing, which is one of the reasons for having you watch."

"What other reason is there?" I asked.

"To prepare you to present souls yourself," Luas said.

# 10

Luas nodded and Haissem continued the trial of Toby Bowles's soul. Again the Courtroom vanished and with it my identity as Brek Cuttler. I became Toby Bowles.

The war is over and I'm back at home now in New Jersey. I'm in the parish hall of my church during coffee hour after the service and seething with rage because my wife, Claire, has just told people that I don't make enough money to support her or my kids.

"How dare you tell them that!" I whisper to her through clenched teeth so no one else will hear.

"I don't know what you're talking about, Toby," she replies.

I glare at her before stomping out through the parish-hall doors, humiliated.

In the parking lot, Alan Bickel, one of the

parishioners, smiles at me and sticks out his hand.

"Mornin'," I grunt, brushing past him without shaking his hand or making eye contact.

I climb into our rusting 1949 Chevy Deluxe, slam the door behind me, start the engine, and light a cigarette, drawing the smoke deep into my lungs and holding it there with my rage until they both can be contained no longer. I still can't believe she said it. I exhale loudly, talking to myself, repeating what Claire said to Marion Hudson: "I'm sorry, Marion, but money's tight right now. We just haven't any extra for the building fund."

*How could she? To Paul and Marion Hudson? And there they go now, driving off in their new Cadillac. Every year a new car. From a dry-cleaning store? The guy must be running something on the side or cooking the books.* I bend down and pretend not to see them.

The rear door opens and my kids climb in, Tad and Todd, then Susan and Katie.

"Dibs on the window," Tad calls.

There's a big commotion and Tad starts crying.

"Dad, Todd hit me and Susan won't move. I called dibs first."

"Knock it off back there or I'll take off my

belt!" I yell. "For chrissake, Tad, you're the oldest. What are you, eleven now? And still cryin' all the time like you was a baby. If you don't like what Todd and Susan are doin', then give 'em one across the mouth. That's what I used to do to your uncle Mike when he crossed me. It's time you started actin' like a man, son, and I'm tellin' you right now you're playin' football come August. Period. I don't want to hear another word about it." I take another drag on my cigarette. "You're playin', right, Todd, old boy?"

"You bet, Dad," Todd says. "Mr. Dawson says he's startin' me at linebacker and quarterback."

Even though he's a full year younger, Todd stands two inches taller than his brother and weighs at least fifteen pounds more.

"Atta boy," I tell him.

Claire slides into the passenger seat beside me. "I really don't understand why you got so upset," she says.

I'm furious. I throw the cigarette out the window, slam the gear selector into first, and mash the accelerator before she can close the door. We roar out of the parking lot.

"Toby, for heaven's sake!" Claire screeches. "I haven't got the door closed and there's kids in the car!"

"No!" I holler over the engine. "There's a bunch of cryin' ingrates in this car and a woman who embarrasses her family in public and don't even have the sense to know it." My chest tightens and I feel the veins in my neck swelling. As usual, when I catch Claire doing something wrong, she refuses to respond. "You got nothin' to say?" I yell. "You ain't got no idea what I'm talkin' about?"

"The souls come into Shemaya Station just like you did," she says. "A presenter is assigned to meet with each postulant before the trial, then they wait in the train station until their case is called and a decision is made. Since they're not permitted to attend the trial, the presenter must acquire a complete understanding of the choices they've made during —"

"What the hell did you just say?" I ask.

"Do what you want, Toby!" Claire yells. "Every day it's something. I've broken one of the invisible rules in your invisible rule book. You're swearing in front of the kids on Sunday and driving like a maniac."

I explode. " 'Money's tight right now, Marion'? 'Toby can't take care of his family, Marion'? 'We barely make ends meet with his job on the railroad, Marion'? Don't think I haven't seen the way you look at Paul Hudson. But you know why I don't worry? Because there's no way Paul Hudson would give up what he's got for big, ugly thighs like yours."

Claire starts crying. "I hate you, Toby!" she screams. "I hate you! I want you out. Just get out and leave us alone."

"It's none of their damn business whether money's tight!" I yell. "It's nobody's business. You got that? Nobody's! Off they go in their big Caddy to their big country club. I'll bet they're Red too. There's Commies all over the place, Claire. They're after regular guys like me. That's why I ain't got a good job and never will. Marion Hudson's laughing at us and you don't even know it. Don't you get it? She knows we don't got extra. That's why she asked, to hear you say it. That's how they get their kicks. How can you be so stupid?"

"Mrs. Hudson's not like that, Daddy," says Susan from the backseat. "When I stay over with Penny, they always ask about you and Mommy and they're real nice."

"I don't want you kids over there again!" I holler. "Do you hear me? My God, Claire, they even do it to the kids. I can just hear it now: 'How's your mother and father, Susan? My, aren't your shoes old . . . and that dress.

What? They haven't taken you shopping in Manhattan? Such a shame.' And that Penny Hudson, I don't want her comin' over to our place anymore either. New bikes, new dresses. She's always got something new. She's a spoiled brat."

I can't control myself. Embarrassment, jealousy, and hatred pour out of me as if there's nothing else inside, as if I am nothing else. I want to give my kids and my wife new things. I want to be respected in the community. I want to live where the Hudsons live and eat where the Hudsons eat. I whip down Greenwood Avenue, barely stopping at the lights.

When we get home, I call Bob to see if he'll pick me up early — then I go upstairs and start throwing things in my duffel bag for the week: work lights, flares, two pairs of work pants, some T-shirts, and two pairs of work gloves. Claire stays downstairs with the kids, fixing them lunch, trying to keep them quiet. I take off my dress slacks, shirt, and tie and fold them neatly into the bottom of my bag along with a bottle of Aqua Velva. Sheila likes it when I dress up and wear cologne for her. She thinks I'm an important businessman. I don't have the heart to tell her the truth. I can't wait to see her. She's the only one who understands me. I zip the bag closed and put my Wolverines on top. Claire calls up from the kitchen.

"Do you want any lunch before you go?" Her voice is cold, emotionless. She's still upset but prides herself on not showing it in front of the kids. She knows damn well Bob's on his way over but asks anyway.

"No. Bob and I'll grab something on the way to Princeton Junction."

"When will you be back?"

"Not 'til Friday."

I carry my things down the stairs. "We're runnin' empty dump cars up to Scranton and full ones on through Altoona to Pittsburgh."

Katie toddles into the living room with a coloring book and crayon, her most prized possessions. She's just eighteen months old. "Daddy, what happened to your right arm?" she asks. "Did you do it because you were mad at your mommy and daddy?"

"Sure, I'll color with you, sweetie," I say, feeling miserable for having yelled and gotten everybody so upset. "Climb up here on my lap."

"Brek, do you hear me?"

"Luas?"

"Ah, there you are," he says. "Finally got through, good. I thought we lost you again."

My personality splits in two. Half of me

carries on a conversation with Toby Bowles's daughter, while the other half carries on a conversation with Luas. I exist simultaneously in two worlds and two lives.

"This is a circle, Katie. Can you say 'circle'?" She looks up at me with wide brown eyes and rosy cheeks, melting my heart.

"Cirsa."

"Concentrate on your memories," Luas says, "Bo, Sarah, your job."

I think of Sarah and her crayons. She's not much younger than Katie. I think of Bo, who has never yelled at me the way Toby did at Claire, and I think of my mom and dad. The distance between selves grows until two distinct lives emerge: mine, which has depth, substance, and nuance, and Toby Bowles's life, which I know well but only episodically. I feel his emotions and see through his eyes, but I finally understand now that he is not me even though he's someone I have experienced more intimately and completely than I've ever experienced another person before.

"So," Luas says, "what do you think of our Mr. Bowles?"

I can hear Luas but not see him. I see only the Bowleses' living room. It's as if Luas and I are commenting on a televised sporting event from the press box, but the field completely surrounds us like a gigantic IMAX screen. We are in the center of the action but apart from it, yet able to know one of the player's thoughts.

"I don't much care for —" I catch myself. "I thought we weren't allowed to make judgments about other souls."

"Well done," Luas says. "But a little too far. We're forbidden from making judgments, if you will, not observations. A lawyer may disapprove of the actions of his client but nonetheless remain an advocate for his client's rights. Wasn't that so with your client Alan Fleming? You disapproved of him failing to repay the bank loan but nevertheless you defended him."

I'm able now to watch the presentation of Toby Bowles's soul without confusing his life with mine. Although I am no longer inside his body, I somehow know all of his thoughts and feel all of his emotions, as though I am God looking into his mind.

Toby's friend Bob pulls up in front of the house and honks his horn. Toby wraps Katie in his arms and gives her a kiss. He hates saying good-bye, and it's worse now because of the awful way he's behaved. Claire, Susan, and Todd approach timidly. Toby wishes he could take it all back, but an apology would be empty and they wouldn't understand. He kisses Claire tenderly, and she responds with a lingering hug, at once absolving him of his crime and, at the same time, wounding him with the generosity of her forgiveness.

"I'll bring you all back something nice," he whispers remorsefully, still convinced material possessions are what they want from him. Todd and Susan give him hugs, but Tad stays in the kitchen playing walk-the-dog with his yo-yo, unwilling to forgive his father and muttering good-bye only after his mother orders him to say something. Toby doesn't know how to handle Tad anymore. "I'll bring him something special too," he mumbles to himself, "maybe the cap gun and holster set he's been wanting." Toby knows he's been hard on Tad, but it's been for his own good. Toby's father was the same way before he abandoned the family when Toby was eleven. At least Toby hasn't done that. The horn honks again. Bob's waiting. Toby waves, picks up his things, and walks out the door.

"Haissem is re-creating this?" I ask.

"Yes," Luas replies. "Remarkable, isn't it?"

Seven years later. Toby Bowles is now staggering under the weight of middle age. The

151

regrets of lost youth, the deterioration of his body, the fear of approaching death, the vain search for meaning and reaffirmation — all these things sour his life, making him restless and depressed. His hair has thinned and his worry lines have deepened.

He walks up to a small garden apartment in Morrisville, New Jersey, letting himself in with the key Bonnie Campbell leaves for him under a loose brick. The apartment is dark. He turns to lock the door as he's always careful to do, but Bonnie has been waiting and goes quickly for his ears, sending gusts of hot breath into the sensual pockets of his mind. His hand drops from the knob and they move quickly into her darkened bedroom before his eyes can adjust from the glare of the mid-afternoon sun.

Bonnie's robe falls to the shabby gold carpet, revealing a middle-aged body of creases and folds desirable to Toby only because the candlelight is forgiving — and because Bonnie's attraction to him refutes what he sees of himself in the mirror. The sheets are thrown back and their bodies embrace, fingers and lips uniting all that is opposite, other, forbidden. The delights are exquisite, suspending time. But bliss is fleeting, shattered suddenly by the distinct metal-on-metal click of the front doorknob cylinder. Toby bolts upright out of the bed, and Bonnie rolls beneath the covers, popping her head out the other side like a groundhog peering from its hole. A dark silhouette fills the doorway to the bedroom.

"Claire, honey?" Toby says in a voice trembling with remorse, shaken by the overwhelming surge of guilt that has been consuming him during his six-month affair with Bonnie Campbell. Yet he's almost relieved now that it will all finally be over and he'll be able to confess his crime and beg her forgiveness. The candles on the dresser flicker low in an unseen draft, then brighter in its wake, illuminating tears streaming down the intruder's face.

"That's not Claire!" Bonnie screams, pulling the covers up to her chin. "It's Tad!"

Bonnie Campbell had known Tad since he was a little boy. In fact, she had been close friends with Toby's wife, Tad's mother — Claire — making the humiliation of the encounter for Toby even more complete than if it were Claire herself. Bonnie owned the only pet shop in the small town, and as Tad grew older he purchased at least one of every creature she sold, climbing the evolutionary chain in step with his ability to care for the animals: an ant farm at first, then a fish, a lizard, some gerbils and hamsters, a rabbit, a cat, and, finally, a dog, a German shepherd. He even worked in her store after school. Tad knew her son, Josh, who was much younger. He knew her ex-husband, Joe. He had eaten many meals at their home.

Bonnie switches on the nightstand light, indignant and remorseless, full of pride for what she has accomplished, daring Tad to speak. But Tad does not see her. He sees only his father: naked, panting, stunned. Tears flood down Tad's face, but he says nothing. He turns and leaves the apartment without saying a word.

Toby's guilt and remorse vanish as quickly as they arose, replaced by rage and a sense of betrayal. He feels ashamed now, not for his own conduct but for his son's. He could understand why Claire would track him down, but Tad? His eighteen-year-old son? And to stand there crying the way Claire would have done? This embarrassment crowns all the other embarrassments and disappointments Tad has caused Toby over the years: his lack of interest in sports, his lack of friends, his weakness and inability to stand up for himself, his defense of his mother against Toby's abuse. Tad had judged Toby and turned on him at every opportunity, but now he had crossed the line.

Toby turns out the light and slides back into bed. He takes Bonnie now with a passion he has never before expressed, but not because he wants her. In fact, he finds her suddenly ugly and repulsive. Instead, he takes her to reestablish who is the father and who is the son, to reclaim his biological position as accuser and Tad's as accused, to reassert his authority to judge what is right and what is wrong, and who is right and who is wrong. And Toby vows to himself to have Bonnie Campbell more often now, and to boast proudly of it and rub Tad's nose in it — for Toby believes no conduct can be sinful if it is done in the open and to teach a lesson. He will dare Tad to say otherwise, dare him to tell his mother and risk destroying her life. And if that moment comes, Toby resolves not to deny it, because, in the end, it is Claire's fault that he has turned to another woman, not a weakness of his own.

Suddenly the Courtroom emerges into the foreground, displacing Bonnie Campbell's seedy apartment. The presentation is over and the lights come up. Haissem bows solemnly before the monolith, then walks over to join Luas and me.

"The trial is over," he says. "A verdict has been reached."

# 11

After the trial of Toby Bowles, I knew I no longer existed in the living world to which I had once belonged — your world, there on earth. Something momentous had happened to me, something so altering and absolute that reality itself was replaced by a new archetype of existence that could no longer be postponed or denied. It wasn't a matter of voluntarily accepting the fact of my death, any more than one voluntarily accepts the fact of one's life. It was more basic than that: a simple acknowledgment that this is what is now, and the other is no more.

Oddly enough, accepting my death wasn't terrifying. It was, in a way, liberating. I no longer had to rationalize the bizarre things happening around me and to me. I no longer had to search for a cure to an illness or an injury that did not exist. And, most important, I realized I no longer had to carry the many burdens of life. I no longer had to shower, brush my teeth, eat, sleep, exercise, work, or take care of my husband and daughter. In a very real sense, death is the ultimate vacation away from *everything*.

But death did nothing to ease the pain of losing Bo and Sarah. I missed her desperately. I longed and ached for her to my very core, and the pain of being separated from her was excruciating. Yet I didn't experience the agonized, gut-wrenching grief of a mother who has just lost her child. This is because even though I knew that *I* was dead, the fact that she wasn't with me in Shemaya meant that Sarah was still alive.

The thought that Sarah would lead a full and happy life helped ease the pain of facing my own death. On the day she was born, I knew, as every mother knows, that I would willingly sacrifice my life for hers. Realizing that I would not be part of Sarah's life stung me deeply. I wouldn't be there to celebrate her birthdays, watch her open Christmas and Hanukkah presents, do school projects with her, help her get ready for her first date, set up her dorm room, dance at her wedding, or be with her for the births of my grandchildren. But at least she would experience these things, the joys of life. And just as I had been reunited with my dead great-grandmother, one day Sarah and I would also be reunited. And also Bo, over whom I mourned like the loss of my own body, for we were joined as one.

So I veered between despair and hope over being separated from Sarah and Bo. But I also found myself experiencing unexpected, darker feelings of deep shame. I could not avoid the conclusion that I had failed my husband, my daughter, and myself. Death is, in the end, the ultimate failure in life, the condition we fear, fight, and avoid at all cost, that our every biological instinct and emotion abhors and resists. Even the words used to describe it are pejorative: you've either "lost" your life, as if you've somehow been careless and misplaced it, or your life has been "taken," "stolen," "forfeited," or "given up."

Yes, I was one of the losers now. The fact that all the people in history who had come before me were losers too — and that all the people who would come after me were losers in waiting — didn't make my death any less humiliating. I had abandoned my husband and child. Even worse, I had abandoned *myself* — Brek Cuttler: human being, mother, wife, daughter, granddaughter, friend, lawyer, neighbor, all no more. And I couldn't even remember how I died!

159

Did I commit suicide? Nothing could be more shameful than that. Is that why I couldn't remember, or wouldn't?

The more these thoughts haunted me and the more I began to think about everything I had lost, the more enraged I became. The injustice of dying after only thirty years of life galled me like nothing I had ever experienced before. It was a hot anger that burned hotter because I had no way to express the enormity of my loss. Nana listened patiently, but she could not, I thought, understand my condition, because, unlike me, she had died after having lived a full, complete life, raising her children to adulthood and seeing her grandchildren and even her great-grandchildren.

I also discovered that the afterlife, like life, is governed by a law of special relativity. My death felt not like the death of myself — in some sense I was still thinking, still experiencing something — but rather like the death of the billions of others on earth who remained alive but could no longer be seen. It was as if I was the lone survivor of a nuclear Armageddon. From my perspective in Shemaya, I had not been taken away from my family; my family had been taken away from me. I lost my entire world — the earth that had sheltered me, the waters that had nourished me, the sky that had inspired me, all vanished into a lyrical, haunted oblivion.

What finally broke me, though — the thing that drove me into the prolonged silence of grieving that replaces and becomes anger's surrogate — was not the gnawing despair of having lost everything, but the sarcastic resemblance of the afterlife to life itself. There was no release in my heaven, no salvation, no comfort, no "better place" to which I had gone after my death. There was, instead, only a perverse continuation of the discordant strands of my old life, freed of physical laws and boundaries, as if life and death were merely potential states of the same cynical mind. Where was the reward? Where was the eternal repose promised by the prophets? I had come full circle: the burdens of life had been replaced by the burdens of death. Paradise was, for me, being trained for a job at yet another law firm: Luas & Associates, Attorneys-at-Divine-Law.

The chilling trial of Toby Bowles had the incongruous effect of both deepening and lessening my own misery by showing me that things could actually be worse. Standing in the corridor outside the Courtroom after the trial, Haissem reported that only a fraction of Mr. Bowles's life had been presented and that a misleading portrait of his soul had been created. I was stunned, yet Haissem seemed perfectly content, and Luas was altogether indifferent. They seemed almost amused by my concern. I asked Haissem what evidence he would have offered in Mr. Bowles's defense if the trial had continued.

"Oh, many things," he said. "Toby Bowles actually lived a noble life."

"Really?" I said skeptically.

"Yes," Haissem insisted. "Would you like to see?"

"Sure," I said. "But how? The trial's already over."

Haissem turned toward Luas. "Do you have any objection to me presenting the rest of Toby Bowles's life?" he asked. "I think we have a few minutes before the next case begins."

"I think it's unnecessary," Luas replied, "but suit yourself."

"Very well," Haissem said.

Haissem used his golden key to reopen the doors to the Courtroom. We walked back in. Haissem retook his position at the center chair, raised his arms, and the Courtroom vanished.

What I saw next was an entirely different side of Toby Bowles, one I would never have imagined existed from the side that Haissem had presented earlier. For example, when Toby's train stopped at the Altoona rail yard, he changed into the Sunday clothes he had packed into his bag and hitchhiked up into the mountains to visit with his sister, Sheila, who lived in a beautiful private home for mentally disabled women on the shore of a small mountain lake. She lived at this home instead of the wretched public asylum to which she had been confined since a child, because every month of every year since the war, Toby Bowles paid the bills that allowed her to live there — even though he would never own a new car or a home as grand as Paul and Marion Hudson's.

Sometimes Toby and Sheila played together, walking through the rooms of the home on imaginary journeys she created. Toby would be her customer in a store selling only hugs, or the passenger on an airplane flying to the ends of rainbows. They would climb trees and relax in the clouds, or paddle across to the shore on the opposite side of the lake, which she thought was the most exotic place on earth. He was always patient with her, and Sheila would always take Toby up to her room before he left and show him the black-and-white photograph of their mama and papa with their forced smiles on the day she was born, holding their baby Sheila not too close because of the deformities in her face and limbs that are the clinical signs of Down syndrome.

I learned that Toby suffered many injustices during his life as well. He was eleven years old when Sheila was born and that black-and-white photograph was taken. It was the last photograph they had of their father, Gerard Bowles, who came home from the hospital that day with his face dark with disgrace and loathing. He told Toby that his mother had done something very wrong and that God had punished her for it and he must leave and never return. Toby was actually relieved by his father's departure at first because Gerard Bowles had been cruel to Toby and his mother, sometimes beating them with his belt while quoting passages from the Bible about sin and the purification of the soul.

But Toby soon learned what the loss of a father meant when his mother wouldn't stop crying and packed up their things to go live with his grandparents. This was when his new sister, Sheila, was taken away as a ward of the state. Lying in bed late at night, Toby worried for Sheila's and his father's safety. He prayed for their return and asked God to please forgive his mother for whatever she had done wrong to cause their family to split apart.

In his teenage years, Toby's unrequited longing and love for his father turned into hatred of the man who had never once written a letter to let them know he was still alive — or to ask if they were still alive. At his most violent moments, Toby fantasized about meeting his father on a street, introducing himself as his son, and pulling a revolver from a pocket and shooting him dead between the eyes. At other moments, when the possibilities of the future seemed expansive and bright, Toby imagined becoming a great success and one day being stopped on the street by his father as a beggar and shoving him aside without recognition or pity.

There were few times in Toby Bowles's life when he did not feel the pain of his father's abandonment. But Sheila became the beneficiary of this broken relationship, receiving the love Toby would have given his father. She desperately needed such a champion because her mother blamed Sheila for all that had gone so terribly wrong. When the time came, Ester Bowles gladly handed Sheila over to the state as though she were handing over a carrier of typhus. Toby became as protective of Sheila as he was of his own daughters. He would have gladly gone to jail or bankrupted himself to win her escape from the asylum. He nearly did both in extricating her. All the money he raised by stealing and selling supplies on the black market during the war went to Sheila, not for his own use — not even to feed and clothe his own young children.

The only other photograph in Sheila's room, next to her bed, was taken by the director of the home on the day Toby brought Sheila a terrier puppy she named Jack that went to heaven a year later when it crossed the road. Arm in arm, Sheila and Toby stand grinning for the camera with the furry bundle — proud sister and wealthy businessman from the big city (for who else, she thought, could afford such an extravagant gift?).

Sheila Bowles died in her sleep one year before Toby's affair with Bonnie Campbell began. Toby buried her on a brutal February morning in a small cemetery near the house by the lake, not far from the tiny wooden cross with the word "Jack" carved into its surface by her hands. In a voice breaking with grief and love across the windswept knoll, Toby handed his sister over to her Creator, and he told her Creator, his family, and the few mourners from the home, that the earth would never again be graced by such innocence.

"But God heard none of this!" I protested to Haissem, interrupting the presentation and momentarily restoring the Courtroom. "The moment of truth arrives for Toby Bowles, but his life unspools from bad to good instead of good to bad and he's hurled into hell without appeal . . . without a trace? What kind of God would conduct such a trial?"

"A just God," Luas replied. "The God of the Flood. Haissem presented the case through Mr. Bowles's own thoughts and actions. Could any of it be denied?"

"No," I conceded. "But only his sins were presented."

"Then only his sins were relevant," Luas answered, irritated by my challenge. "It was the Judge who ended the presentation, Brek, not Haissem. Who are we to weigh the gravity of Toby Bowles's offenses and determine what is just and unjust? I warned you earlier not to speculate."

"Wait, Luas," Haissem interjected. "It's appropriate that Brek is concerned. This shows that she takes her job seriously, which is exactly what we want. Understanding the mistakes and triumphs of Toby's life may help her when she enters the Courtroom on behalf of her first client." He turned to me. "There's more to the story. Would you like to see the rest?"

Luas wasn't willing to let it drop. "My point wasn't that the other parts of Toby's life are irrelevant," he said. "I only meant to say that justice is God's, not ours, and that justice will be done."

"I understand, Luas," Haissem said, curtly. "And my point is that justice has nothing to do with the trial of Toby Bowles at all."

Luas regarded Haissem suspiciously. "Then I respectfully disagree," he said.

Haissem ignored the comment and turned back to me. "Let me finish the presentation," he said. "You haven't even seen the most important part yet."

The Courtroom vanished again, and Haissem took us back to when Toby was a soldier in the war.

To avoid a court-martial for stealing medical supplies in Saverne, Toby was forced to leave the Quartermaster's Corps and "volunteer" for a frontline combat unit. Out of eight men initially assigned to his unit, all but one, Toby, were shot dead or drowned in the Elbe River in eastern Germany on the final push of the Allies to Berlin. Toby himself was hit in the leg while carrying his dying sergeant up the riverbank. He limped away, bleeding and stunned, and collapsed outside a small cabin in the woods near the burg of Kamenz.

When Toby awakened the next day, he found himself inside this cabin, delirious from loss of blood and an infection and surrounded by the family who lived there: a father, a mother, a teenage daughter, and two younger sons. They bandaged his wounds and gave him food and water, and he slept another twenty-four hours until he awoke again, this time to the sound of gunfire and shouting as the mother and children fled into a tunnel beneath the floorboards of the cabin and the father ran from the house with a shotgun.

Toby was strong enough to hobble along after the man to help. He had left his rifle behind at the river and had only his sidearm. They came to the edge of a clearing where they could see a very large house through the misty afternoon rain. They kneeled behind some bushes and watched as a platoon of soldiers with red stars on their sleeves drove the inhabitants from the house and out into the driveway: an elderly man, two middle-aged women, a teenage girl, two younger boys, and two younger girls, all dressed in party clothes.

The leader of the platoon barked a swift order in Russian, and the soldiers responded by quickly separating the old man and the young boys from the others and shooting them on the spot. When the women lunged toward the victims, they too were cut down in cold blood. Now only the teenage girl and the two younger girls remained standing. It all appeared to Toby as in a dream, through the fine mist, distorted by fever from the infection. Bodies dropping like shadows into darkness, continuing the savage nightmare that had begun for him earlier along the banks of the Elbe River. Suddenly, the man from the cabin, still kneeling beside Toby, jumped up and charged the platoon, firing his shotgun wildly into the air. The platoon returned the fire, killing him instantly and nearly killing Toby.

Toby started crawling back through the brush toward the cabin but realized that he would almost certainly be seen and that he would be leading the soldiers to the man's family. To save them and, perhaps, himself, he stood slowly with his hands over his head. He limped back out through the clearing, calling "American! American!" The grass was wet and the water soaked through his pants, stinging his wounds. All the while he was thinking not of himself but of Sheila and who would care for her now, and of his mother and how news of his death would plunge her deeper into despair, and of his father and how news of his death might haunt him with regret for the rest of his life.

Two Russian soldiers came forward cautiously with their guns raised, but as they neared Toby and saw his uniform, they lowered their weapons. *"Amerika! Amerika!"* they cheered, embracing him. But one of the soldiers saw the cabin in the distance and began advancing toward it. Toby knew the only hope for the family was for him to convince the soldiers that he had already taken the family as his prisoners.

He stumbled along behind the soldiers as fast as he could. When they reached the door, he slid past them, pulled out his sidearm, and motioned for them to stand back. One of the soldiers grabbed the pistol from Toby's hand, but Toby pushed the door open, yanked up the floorboards, and ordered the frightened family out of the tunnel. They were white and shaking fear. They glared at Toby for having betrayed them after they had saved his life. Toby

pointed at them and then himself and said
to the soldiers: "My prisoners! My prisoners!" He grabbed the mother and slammed
her violently against the wall, then the
daughter and the two boys. He pointed to a
medal on one of the Russians' chests and
then to his own chest, where a new medal
would be placed if he brought them in.

"My prisoners! My prisoners!" he said
again.

The Russians finally understood. They
smiled, slapped him on the back, and
returned his gun. Toby put the gun against
the temple of the mother, completing the
charade. The soldiers lowered their rifles
and laughed.

*"Amerika! Amerika!"* they said, shaking
their heads as they walked away.

When they had gone, Toby winked and
grinned at his captives and, to their astonishment, put his gun in his holster and gave
the mother a hug. When she realized that he
had saved their lives, she broke down in
tears.

But the celebration ended quickly when
the mother and her children realized that
the father hadn't returned. They wanted to
go out searching for him, but Toby re-
strained them and, using crude sign language to warn them of the dangers, con-

vinced them to stay.

Late the next day, after Toby first checked to be sure the Russians had left the area, he led the mother back to the clearing to retrieve the body of her dead husband. Despite the language barrier, he attempted to comfort her as best he could, pointing out the corpses of the people from the house in an attempt to explain that her husband had been brave to confront the soldiers and try to save their lives. The mother finally understood, and only then did she begin to comprehend just what Toby himself had done to spare her family the same fate.

Despite his wounds, Toby himself carried the lifeless body of the man back to the cabin and helped the boys dig a grave. The family's anguish overwhelmed him, and at times he cried with them because he too had lost a father, just as they had. But Toby wept also out of a desperate and mournful jealousy of these children, who had at least known their father and could bury him, and would remember him as a father who had loved them enough to sacrifice his life for them and others.

Although Toby couldn't understand their strange prayers, when the sons placed yarmulkes upon their heads and nobody made the sign of the cross, he realized these were Jewish prayers, spoken in Hebrew. For the first time, he realized that the family had not been hiding from the Russians, but from the Germans. He made the sign of the cross anyway, whispering a prayer for the dead man and for his own father, and for the entire world as well. Upon seeing Toby cross himself, the daughter, hysterical with grief, began wailing, "Amina! Amina! Amina!" over and over. She removed a small golden cross of her own from her pocket and made the sign on her own chest. Horrified, the mother reached over to slap her, but suddenly a deep and profound comprehension flashed across her face. She bowed her head and began to weep even more violently. Toby did not understand what had happened between the mother and daughter but helped them fill the grave.

The group began walking west toward Leipzig, where Toby hoped to find Allied troops. At Riesa, they came across an American infantry unit. With a small bribe, Toby was able to get the family all loaded onto a truck headed farther west into Allied territory. They rode together as far as Nuremberg, where they were taken to a field hospital and Toby finally received the medical care that saved his leg from amputation.

At the moment of their parting at the hospital, the mother was embarrassed because she had no way to repay Toby's generosity. But suddenly her eyes brightened. She whispered something to her daughter and made a gesture, asking a nurse nearby for a pen and a piece of paper. The nurse gave these to the mother, and she carefully copied Toby's last name from his shirt, B-O-W-L-E-S, on the paper. Then she spoke to Toby in German, saying: *"Mein erstes Enkelkind wird nach Ihnen benannt werden."* Toby obviously could not understand her, so she held the paper with his name on it against her daughter's womb and raised her index finger in the air as if to say "first." Then she held her arms as if she were cradling an infant and tucked the paper into her daughter's hand. Toby finally understood what she was trying to say. He hugged them both good bye and wished them farewell.

The hospital suddenly vanished and the Courtroom reappeared. I was astonished by what I had seen.

Luas led Haissem and me out of the Courtroom. Standing in the corridor while Luas closed and locked the Courtroom doors, Haissem said, "So you see, Brek, Toby Bowles did lead a noble life. It's all a matter of perspective."

"But what about the trial of his soul?" I said, alarmed by the gross injustice of the proceedings. "None of this evidence was presented during the trial. Obviously the verdict is unjust. Aren't you going to do something?"

"As I said before," Haissem replied, "justice has nothing to do with it."

"Again, I disagree," Luas interjected. "Justice has everything to do with it. Justice has been served. It is not our place to judge."

"But can't we file a motion for a mistrial or take an appeal?" I pleaded. "We can't just do nothing. If this verdict stands, the Final Judgment would be nothing but a sham. What kind of place is this? The accused isn't present for his trial, which takes place before a tribunal that nobody can see, attended by witnesses the accused can't confront, while being represented by a lawyer who is also his prosecutor, and the entire thing is ended by the judge before a defense can even be presented? Surely there can't be less due process in heaven than we have on earth."

Luas glared at me. "*Never* say anything like that again, Brek," he warned me. "This is the way of Divine Justice, not man's justice. We have no right to question it. God and justice are one."

Haissem touched my arm to calm me down. "I understand your concern, Brek," he said, "but you can be assured that the trial of Toby Bowles's soul was performed properly and that the correct outcome was reached. This will all become clearer to you after you've handled your first case. I must leave you now, but we will meet again. You're in good hands with Luas, despite our occasional disagreements."

Haissem and Luas bowed politely toward each other, and then Haissem walked away. After he had gone, Luas said to me: "He's the most senior presenter here, but I sometimes wonder whether his time has passed. The things he says sometimes are very dangerous."

# 12

My one solace in Shemaya was visiting the places that had been dear to me when I was alive. They were all there, exact replicas of my house, my town, my world. The only things missing were the people; it was like walking through an empty movie studio lot. These were lonely visits, but I found this loneliness, at first, to be a comfort. I needed to get away from Luas, the Courtroom, and Nana. I needed to get away from other souls' memories and other souls' lives. So I went home. But I didn't go there to grieve. I didn't dare look in Sarah's room or Bo's closet. I knew I would break down. I just wanted to be happy again.

So, trying to put my death behind me, the first thing I did when I got home was go shopping — my favorite pastime when I was alive. I decided that if God was going to strand me in this sadistic netherworld where everything reminded me of life's lost pleasures, I might as well indulge in some of those pleasures and enjoy myself a little.

I headed over to the local mall, and, boy, did I shop. This was, without exception, the greatest shopping trip I've ever had: no lines, no crowds, no pushy salespeople; I had the entire mall to myself, and, best of all, everything was marvelously, magnificently *free*. It was, in a way, heaven.

I replaced the black silk suit I'd been wearing since I arrived in Shemaya with a cute, insanely expensive wool miniskirt and top that I robbed from a startled mannequin. I plundered stock rooms, pried open display cases, and hauled my booty around on a merry train of rolling racks weighted down with four seasons' worth of apparel, shoes, accessories, makeup, and fine jewelry. I disrobed and tried on clothes right in the middle of sales floors rather than going back to the dressing rooms. If I didn't like something, I just tossed it over my shoulder and moved on. The only limit to my decadence was my ability to cart it all away. Like a looter after a hurricane, I backed my car up to the doors and crammed it full.

After an entire day of this, I dragged myself to the food court and helped myself to a double cheeseburger and milkshake, which spontaneously appeared at the counter, topping it all off with five white chocolate macadamia-nut cookies. I never felt full; only a lingering sense of decorum stopped me from consuming entire trays. Yes, heaven indeed.

By the time I returned home from my shopping spree, I was so exhausted that I left everything in the car and collapsed on the couch. To my delight, the television functioned normally and displayed any channel I selected as long as it was showing something prerecorded, like a movie or a sitcom. The live news, weather, and sports channels displayed only white static, which was fine by me. I dozed in and out, happily watching reruns of *M\*A\*S\*H* and *All in the Family,* but as evening came on, the weekend infomercials featuring gorgeous models demonstrating exercise equipment began having their guilt-inspiring effect on me (yes, even after death). I got up, dressed in the sleek new racer-back top and shorts I'd picked up at the mall, and went to the nearby gym for a workout to show them off.

Of course, the gym was empty and there was nobody there to show off to, which was rather disappointing because I thought I looked pretty hot for a one-armed girl who usually wore oversized T-shirts and baggy sweatpants during her workouts. Bo had been begging me for years to upgrade to new exercise clothes and would have loved the change. On the plus side, the fact that nobody was there meant no waiting for machines and no sweaty, smelly men grunting and ogling. It was like being rich and having my own personal health club. I climbed on a treadmill and tried to set the workout time for thirty minutes, but the digital timer, like all clocks in Shemaya, didn't work and I had to rely on the odometer. I started off at my normal pace and felt so good when I reached three miles that I continued on to six, then ten (more than I'd ever run), twenty, and so on until the indicator flashed that I'd run ninety-nine miles and was resetting itself back to zero. Ironically, being dead improved my endurance. I barely broke a sweat and my pulse remained in the perfect range the entire time. My muscle strength in death improved as well. With no effort at all I was able to lift the huge stacks of weights heaved around by the bodybuilders and football players.

I noticed I looked better dead than alive too. In the mirrors on the walls around the gym, my muscles were as taut and sculpted as an Olympic athlete's. My stomach and thighs were as tight and smooth as the day

when I turned eighteen. No evidence what-
soever that I'd delivered a baby only ten
months ago. Preening before the mirrors,
my body seemed more beautiful and fascinating to me than it had ever been before.
*What an exquisite and amazing creation,* I
thought. A fractured Renaissance sculpture
no less perfect for the amputation. It *was*
art, music, science, mystery. I wasn't given
two arms in Shemaya — probably because I
could think of myself only as an amputee —
but my body seemed all the more beautiful
for it. When I brushed against the cold steel
frame of an exercise bike, a shiver ran up
my spine, reconnecting me to the body I
saw in the mirror. In that moment, I regret-
ted how foolish I'd been during my life for
not having noticed all these amazing things
and what a gift I had been given. This body,
my body, just the way it was, had always
been holy, had always been mine, and had
always been as beautiful and precious as life
itself. *How could I not have known that?* I
wondered. *How could I have taken it for
granted for so long?*

I finished my workout perspiration- and
odor-free, no need for a shower. Nightfall
had come and I considered going to a
restaurant and then a movie by myself, but
I decided to spend the evening at home,

watching something on TV and eating pop-corn.

When I got back, I changed into my new silk pajamas. To my delight, a gigantic bowl of buttered popcorn and a tall soda sponta-neously appeared on the coffee table. I snuggled up under a blanket and put on the television. The 1950 film noir classic *D. O. A.* was playing on every channel — as though somebody wanted me to watch it, which was more than a little creepy. I hadn't seen it since my film class in college, but I liked it then and was content to see it again. It begins with an accountant named Frank Bigelow entering a police station to report a murder — his own. He was mysteriously poisoned and has only a few days to find out who killed him and why before he dies. The similarities between Bigelow's quest and my own became instantly obvious, which is probably why I subconsciously put the movie on all channels.

*Why did I die?* I wondered. *Had I been murdered? By whom? And, again, why?*

These questions quickly distracted me from the movie. I could wait no longer for answers. I decided right then and there that I would do everything I could to find out what happened to me. And I would begin by retracing my steps — the last steps I could remember of my life.

Still dressed in my pajamas, I left the house and roared off in my car toward the convenience store. Everything looked as I remembered it in my dreams: the road, the sky, the buildings. I pulled into the parking lot singing "Hot Tea and Bees Honey" as I had done that night with Sarah. The fall air was fresh and cool. I entered the store, walked to the back, grabbed a carton of milk from the refrigerator case, and turned down the aisle where Sarah had knocked the cupcakes onto the floor.

It's almost six-twenty,
says Teddy Bear,
Mama's coming home now,
she's almost right there.

Hot tea and bees honey,
for Mama and her baby;
Hot tea and bees honey,
for two we will share.

I stooped down to pick up the cupcakes.
This is where all my dreams had ended since arriving in Shemaya — hollow and questioning, like a failed coroner's inquest. Cause of death: *unknown.* But, strangely, this time there was no overpowering smell

of manure and mushrooms as there had been before. I walked up to the counter with the milk carton and waited, hoping recollection would be stimulated and there would be an answer. None came. I remembered nothing of my life beyond this moment. Frustrated and enraged, I threw the milk carton across the counter. It exploded white against the shelves stocked with cigarettes.

"What happened to me?" I screamed into the silence. *"What happened to me?"* I walked back out to my car in tears.

On the drive home, a car appeared in my rearview mirror — this was my first encounter with another car since Huntingdon when the traffic had backed up on the street and I thought I was going insane.

The car followed me at a normal distance for a few miles; but when we reached a long, deserted stretch of road with corn and hay fields on both sides, the high-beam headlights of the car behind started flashing and bursts from a red strobe light filled my rearview mirror, hurting my eyes. The red light came from low on the windshield, like an unmarked patrol car. I decided to pull over even though I knew it would be unoccupied. Sitting there on the side of the road with my car idling, admiring the authenticity of the virtual-reality game I seemed to be playing with myself, I remembered Bo warning me he'd recently seen a speed trap on this stretch of road.

Of course, no patrolman appeared at my window, but I decided to get out and go have a look. The engine of the police car was running but there was nobody inside. I opened the driver's door. It looked like the interior of a normal four-door sedan rather than a police car after all. There was no police radio or any of the other equipment you would expect; the only resemblance to a police car was the red strobe light on the dashboard, connected by a coil of black cord to the cigarette lighter. Glancing in back, I saw a videocassette tape on the floor and went around to the rear door to get it. But as I slid across the seat to reach the tape, the door slammed shut behind me and locked me inside. Then the shifter on the steering column mysteriously moved itself from park to drive and the car pulled back onto the road without a driver. Looking over my shoulder, I could see my own car following behind.

I laughed. It all could have been very spooky, terrifying even, but after you've accepted your own death, what more is there to be afraid of? I picked up the videocassette. Handwritten on the label were the words "What Happened?"

*Well, how appropriate,* I thought. *Maybe God speaks to souls on video and I would finally find out what happened to me.* But I would have to wait until I returned home to watch it.

I sat back and relaxed, as if I were on an amusement-park ride, curious to see where the car would take me.

We headed south for a few miles. There were no other cars on the road, and all the homes and businesses were dark. The seasons stopped cycling. It was autumn everywhere now. Colored leaves rained down on the windshield like drops of thick, wet paint. We turned off onto a side road at Ardenheim and up an old dirt logging road into the mountains. The headlights of both cars shut off. We traveled along, hitting ruts and splashing through mud puddles. The car I was riding in finally stopped in the middle of the road. My car following behind stopped as well, but then turned and backed itself off the logging road into a grove of pine trees, pushing beneath branches as it moved until it was covered with pine boughs and could no longer be seen in the moonlight. A moment later the videocassette suddenly vanished from my lap, as if it had been a mirage all along. The car I was riding in backed its way down the logging road in the direction from which we had come and drove out onto the highway, turning its lights back on.

*How strange,* I thought. But I had seen far stranger things in Shemaya — and I had nothing better to do — so I decided to play along.

The driverless sedan with me sitting in the backseat continued driving south through the night toward Harrisburg. This was the same route I took when traveling between Delaware and Huntingdon, and I began to suspect that Nana and Luas had somehow contrived all of this as a way of bringing me back home. The radio came on, switching itself between country music stations as the signals faded, proving to me that my mind was not in control of the car — I rarely listened to country music.

We passed Harrisburg and eventually Lancaster, finally turning off the main highway and heading into the rolling farmland of Chester County toward Delaware, just as I had suspected. But before crossing the state line, we turned off onto a winding secondary road, following this for several more miles until we turned again onto a smaller country lane. There were no streetlights or power lines now. The sky was coal black. The last uninhabited home passed from view miles ago, asleep in the cool harvest air pregnant with the scent of decaying leaves and apples. Finally, the pavement ended, and we were traveling on a gravel road descending a steep ravine through woods and turning onto a rutted dirt road leading through an open, overgrown field, then back into more woods and down an even steeper slope.

The road ended at a crumbling cinderblock building protruding from the ground like an ugly scab. Its windowless walls stood barely one-story tall and were pocked with black streaks of mold and a leprosy of flaking white paint. It resembled the shell of an abandoned industrial building and looked out of place in the country. I had the feeling I had been there before but no distinct recollection.

The gear selector moved itself to park, the engine shut off, and the doors unlocked. I got out of the car and walked up to the building, lit by the yellow glare of the headlights. The cloying stench of manure and mushrooms — the same odor I had smelled in the convenience store in my dreams — made the air heavy and difficult to breathe. Pulling open the worm-eaten door, I was fearful now even though I knew there could be nothing inside to harm me.

As I stepped inside, bright daylight erupted across the sky, a huge explosion, vaporizing the building, the car, the woods, and my own body.

Suddenly I found myself transported into the bedchamber of a great Roman palace — a structure more immense and splendid than even the Pantheon. White stone columns soared into the bowl of a fantastic marble dome overhead. Beneath it sat a glittering golden bed surrounded by divans covered in plush crimson fabric. Standing in front of this bed, bloated and nude, was Emperor Nero Claudius Caesar. At his feet, groaning and pleading for mercy, lay his wife, Poppaea, fully clothed and several months pregnant with his child. Her white gown was streaked red between her legs.

"You ungrateful whore!" Nero bellowed before driving his foot deep into Poppaea's abdomen. "I put Octavia's head on a platter for your amusement and this is how you repay me, by ridiculing me!" He kicked her again, more savagely, and this time her ribs gave way, cracking and breaking like twigs. Poppaea gasped for air, blood drooled from her mouth.

"Get out of my sight!" Nero yelled.

Then the Roman palace vanished just as suddenly as it had appeared. In its place emerged the Courtroom with Luas standing at its center. The faceless being from the monolith whispered something in his ear and then returned to its home inside the stone. I had no idea how I'd gotten from the cinder-block building in the woods to Nero's palace and then the Courtroom. The journey was seamless and bewildering. Luas walked over and spoke to me.

"Hello, Brek," he said. "I'm sorry you had to see that. How was your visit home?"

"Wait a minute," I said, puzzled by what I had just seen. "You just presented Nero? The Nero who supposedly fiddled while Rome burned?"

"Yes," Luas said. "Foul character, isn't he?"

"But he died two thousand years ago —"

"Yes, and I've been representing him ever since," Luas said. "The presentation usually ends here, or just after he has the boy Sporus castrated and takes him for his wife. When I return to the Courtroom the next day, I'm informed that a final decision on his fate still hasn't been reached and I must present his case again." Luas sighed. "This is my job, it seems, to try Nero's soul every day for eternity. Seems God isn't quite ready to make up his mind about this one."

"I don't understand," I said, disoriented and taken aback.

Luas escorted me out of the Courtroom and led me down the corridor toward the train shed. We continued our conversation as we walked.

"Didn't you say we only present the close cases?" I asked. "Nero's case seems pretty obvious."

"Yes, well, there are two sides to every story, aren't there? It may seem strange, but Nero did have some redeeming qualities — not unlike Toby Bowles. I never get to them during the presentation, of course, but he had them. Anyway, ours is not to wonder why. Nero is a postulant here, and we treat him like all the rest. Just be happy he isn't one of your clients."

Before reaching the train shed, Luas led me around a corner into a corridor I hadn't seen before, one so unfathomably long that I was unable to see the end of it. It seemed to stretch out into space, a hallway in a vast office building with literally thousands of identical offices lining both sides of the corridor, each with tall, slender wooden doors and transoms above them closed tight. Bright fluorescent lights bathed the walls in the uniform and compassionless glare of bureaucracy.

"What is this place?" I asked Luas.

"This is where we have our offices. As you can see, there are quite a few lawyers in Shemaya."

This startled and impressed me, but I was still struck by Nero's trial. "So Nero and Toby Bowles are treated the same way?" I said. "Nothing they did right their entire lives is heard in the Courtroom? What's the point of conducting a trial at all — if you can even call it that? Why not just send them straight to hell?"

"Ah, back to that again, are we?" Luas said. "Please try to understand, Brek, there is no Bill of Rights or anything like that in Shemaya. The procedural protections in which you placed such great faith as an attorney on earth are entirely unnecessary here. No lie can go unexposed in the Courtroom, and no truth can remain hidden. Justice is guaranteed as long as the presenters remain unbiased and do nothing to tip the scales."

"But how can there be justice if all sides of the case aren't presented?"

"Do I need to remind you," Luas answered in a reprimanding way, "that millions of people on earth, including Christ himself, have been tried, convicted, and punished unjustly? Surely God requires no lessons from us about fairness. Of course, justice has many dimensions, and we've been speaking only of fairness to the accused. You lost your arm when you were just a little girl, Nero Claudius turned Christians into tapers, and God once drowned nearly every living creature on earth. To know whether justice has been done, one must consider all of its aspects."

We somehow reached the end of the limitless corridor. Luas stopped us at the last office on the right. A small plaque on the door read "High Jurisconsult of Shemaya."

"Ah, here we are," Luas announced, opening the door. "The next phase of your training is about to begin."

# 13

There was a simple wooden desk in the office, two chairs behind the desk, a single guest chair in front, and two candles on top. No windows, papers, files, phones, pencils, or other office items. Luas closed the door and struck a match to light the candles.

"Please have a seat here beside me," he said. "We're going to interview a new postulant together and then watch the presentation. I will be your proctor. After this, you will be assigned your first client and conduct a trial on your own."

"Am I being forced to represent them?" I asked. "I mean, what if I refuse?"

"Forced?" Luas said. "Certainly not. The choice is yours, but it's a choice you have already made. That's why you're here. You will represent them because, like all lawyers, justice is what you crave most and you won't rest until you have it."

"There's no justice here," I said flatly. "At

least not the kind I crave."

Luas smiled condescendingly. "Perhaps you will introduce it to us then," he said.

I thought about this for a moment and, for the first time, considered the possibility that I just might be able to help these poor souls, that this might be the reason why I was brought to Shemaya, to fix a broken judicial system. Lawyers had a long and proud tradition of bringing about reform and restoring justice to the world. I had always dreamed of doing something truly significant and grand.

"Perhaps I will," I said. "Perhaps I will." Then I looked down and realized I was still wearing my pajamas from what was supposed to be a relaxing evening at home, watching a movie and eating popcorn.

"You needn't worry about your clothes," Luas said, noticing my embarrassment. "The postulants can't see us. But if you'd feel more comfortable, you may change into these." From a desk drawer he produced the black silk suit, blouse, and shoes I'd been wearing since I arrived in Shemaya — the ones I'd discarded at the mall during my shopping spree.

"How did you get these?" I asked, confused.

"I didn't get them," he said. "You did. Go

ahead, put them on. I'll step outside."

By telling me I got the clothes, Luas was trying to remind me that I was making all of this up — my physical appearance and his, that is, not Shemaya itself, which seemed to exist quite independently of me. Even so, I took the opportunity to dress in proper attire, out of respect for my profession if nothing else.

Luas returned to the office and seated himself beside me behind the desk, surrounded by darkness. The dim candles gave his face a dull orange color.

"Before I invite the postulant in," he said, "I must warn you that there is a grave danger in this meeting, one for which I have been trying to prepare you. More than Mr. Bowles, more than your parents, your husband, or even your own child, will you come to know the postulant we are about to meet. Only slightly better will you know yourself. To avoid losing your identity forever, you must employ the tactics I showed you earlier. No matter how difficult it might seem, you must continue to remind yourself of the circumstances of your disfigurement. Try to recall the smallest details: the smell of the air above the manure in the spreader, the sound of the flies buzzing over the heap, the puzzled look of the cows as they watched you and your grandfather spreading their excrement across the fields. The way the heavy, wet dung, produced by the first alfalfa of the season, clotted in the bin like plaster, jamming the tines.

"Your parents had told you they were taking you to your grandparents' farm to enjoy some time in the country, but you had heard the viciousness of their argument when your father revealed the arrangements, against your mother's wishes, to admit her into a treatment center for alcoholics and your mother retorted that he had been having an affair. All that held them together was you, and you were convinced that only a crisis would hold you all together now. You considered running away, but this would only separate you from them. You had already tried modulating your grades, but the good marks only gave them confidence of your adjustment and the bad just another source for blame. Behaving and misbehaving had the same weak effect, and crying worked only temporarily and could not be sustained. You had even contrived illnesses, but doctors confirmed your health and the proper functioning of your organs."

I could no longer bear the pain of hearing all this. "Enough!" I said. "Please, stop."

Luas ignored my pleas. "You did not plan

what to do next," he continued. "Your grandfather had warned you to stand clear as he worked his pitchfork through the pile. After finishing, he climbed down from the bin and back up onto the tractor, but he left the guard off the conveyor chain. You watched the chain hesitate for a moment under the load and then break free with a bang, whirring through the gears and cogs as the tractor engine roared and the manure flew. The thought struck you in that very moment, before he could disengage the power and replace the guard. You ran up and thrust your hand into the gears. You thought you'd only cut your finger or perhaps break it. But feeling no more than the return of a firm handshake at first, you watched in astonishment and disbelief as your forearm was ripped from your elbow and was hurled along the conveyor like a toy on an assembly line. You stood frozen for a moment, the way one does upon first seeing one's own reflection, watching yourself watch yourself, but not fully recognizing the image. In the moment before you lost consciousness, your body tingled — not with pain but with the brief exaltation that you had finally succeeded in reuniting your parents and all would soon be well."

"No more, Luas," I begged, sobbing.

"Please, stop."

"But there is more," Luas said callously. "So much more. This is the only way to separate yourself from the powerful memories of the postulants you will meet, and this is what must be done. Two years later, Brek, after your parents had divorced and the right sleeves of your clothes had been sewn shut, you took the witness stand in the Huntingdon County Courthouse, where you would one day practice law, and a young attorney named Bill Gwynne asked you to show the jury the mangled stump of your arm and tell them what happened. It was the most critical testimony in the case, to establish the liability of the manufacturer of the manure spreader and bestow upon you and your family a small fortune in recompense. The courtroom was silent, every moist eye focused on you. You had practiced your testimony so often with Mr. Gwynne that you actually believed what you were about to say. He had promised you justice. You faced the jury, and do you remember what you said?"

"Yes, yes," I cried, traumatized and ashamed. "I remember. There's no need for you to repeat it."

"Oh, but I must," Luas said. " 'I was standing on my toes,' you told the jury, 'trying to see what my grandfather was doing. I slipped on the wet grass and fell against the guard. I didn't hit it very hard, but the guard gave way and my arm got caught in the gears —' You became too emotional to go on. The memory of what happened next was too painful."

Luas's relentless recounting of the story was having the desired effect. He had me so deeply engrossed in the shame of my own memories that I couldn't possibly confuse my life with that of the postulant I was about to meet. I could see myself there on the witness stand, a ten-year-old girl again. The judge, robed in black, glares down at me from the bench, old and terrifying like God. The pinch-faced stenographer yawns as she taps her keys. My grandfather, pale with guilt and remorse, nervously fondles his pipe, aching for a smoke. My grandmother waves a roll of Life Savers at me for encouragement. My mother sits all by herself on the other side of the courtroom with her "I told you so" face, snarling at my father and grandparents. My father sucks on a Life Saver my grandmother insisted he take, and checks his watch. The defense lawyer from Pittsburgh, too slick and condescending for Huntingdon County, whispers to the vice president of the equipment manufacturer, a Texan who crosses his legs and strokes the brown suede of his cowboy boots.

To my right sits the jury who will decide the case: three farmers, a hairdresser, a housewife, and a truck mechanic. The farmers tug uncomfortably at the collars of their white dress shirts; the hairdresser, wearing too much makeup, cracks her gum; the housewife, wearing too little makeup, fusses with her hair; the truck mechanic bites his dirty fingernails, stealing glances at the hairdresser.

"It's okay, honey," Mr. Gwynne says. I know he's here to protect me, my knight in shining armor, gallant and handsome. I have a secret crush on him. "Take a moment to blow your nose; I know it's difficult with one hand, Brek. I'm sorry we have to do this, but the makers of the manure spreader here want their day in court, and they're entitled to it. Just a few more questions, okay? We need you to be brave now and tell the truth. Are you certain the guard was in place? I'm talking about the metal shield over the chain."

"Oh, yes, Mr. Gwynne, I'm certain."

"And you slipped and bumped into it?"

"Yes."

"And it gave way?"

"Yes."

"And your arm got caught in the chain."

"Yes. Gee, I'm sorry, Mr. Gwynne. I'm awfully sorry for all this. I should have been more careful."

"You have nothing to be sorry for, Brek," he reassures me. "We're the ones who are sorry for what happened to you. You've been very brave for us today, and we appreciate it."

In less than an hour, the jury returned a verdict against the manufacturer for $450,000. An expert hired by Mr. Gwynne testified that if the spreader had been designed properly, there would have been no need to remove the guard to fix the problem in the first place, meaning that my lie might not have made the difference after all. But that did not change the fact that I had lied, I had committed perjury.

One-third of the money went to Mr. Gwynne for his efforts; another third put me through an expensive Quaker boarding school, four years at a private liberal arts college, and three years at an Ivy League law school; the rest paid my medical bills with some left over for other expenses, including a semester abroad in Europe. Only my grandfather knew for certain I had lied about the guard, but we never spoke about it to each other. He testified that he couldn't remember whether he left it on or off, which made his testimony seem like only half a lie. I guess he was able to live with that.

But Luas wasn't finished with me yet: "Nobody in the courtroom that day knew," he said, "not your parents, not Bill Gwynne, not even your grandfather, that you deliberately put your hand into the machine. You told only one person, Karen Busfield, and that was twenty years after the trial. Do you remember?"

"Yes," I said. "I remember."

I couldn't help but remember. Karen Busfield, my best friend from my childhood, who was so gentle that she couldn't bring herself to punish boys who murdered crayfish, who went on to become an Episcopal priest, asked me to defend her in a criminal case for which she could receive the death penalty.

# 14

Karen Busfield's criminal case came back to me in Luas's office as if I were seeing a portion of my own life being replayed by Haissem in the Courtroom.

It's late at night; Bo and I have put Sarah to bed and fallen asleep ourselves. The telephone rings, startling me awake. My heart pounds as I fumble for the receiver, trying to comprehend what's happening, and fearing the worst because of the late hour.

"Yes? Hello?" I say groggily.

"Brek? Hi, it's me, Karen."

"Karen?" I say, trying to regain my bearings. I can't see the clock. "My God, what time is it? Are you okay?"

"It's two a.m.," she says. "I'm really sorry for calling you so late, but I'm in trouble. I need a lawyer."

The familiar sounds of a jail echo in the background, rough voices, the slamming of heavy steel doors.

"Where are you?"

"Fort Leavenworth," Karen replies.

"Leavenworth? What are you doing there, counseling inmates?"

"No," she says. "I am an inmate."

I can tell she isn't joking.

Bo rolls over. "What's going on?" he asks.

I cover the phone. "It's Karen," I whisper. "I think she's been arrested."

"What?"

"You're a military chaplain," I say to Karen. "What could you have possibly done?"

"I can't talk about that right now," she says.

"Okay," I say, understanding that the call is being monitored. "Can you at least tell me what they're charging you with?"

"Assault, criminal trespass, and . . ."

"And what?"

"Treason and espionage."

"*Treason and espionage?* Are you serious?" Bo's eyes widen.

"Yes, I'm serious."

I sit on the bed, dumbfounded.

"Brek, are you there?" Karen asks.

"Are you sure they said treason?" I ask.

"Yes," Karen replies.

"Okay, I'm coming," I say. "And I'm bringing Bill Gwynne with me."

"No, just you," Karen says.

"Treason is a big deal, Karen," I warn her. "I don't want to scare you, but it carries the death penalty. I'm bringing Bill with me — and maybe twenty other lawyers. Let me call the airlines. We'll be there as soon as we can."

"Just you, Brek, okay?" she pleads. I can tell she's on the verge of breaking down. "Please?"

"Okay, honey," I say. "Okay, I'll do whatever you want. For now. We can talk about it when I get there."

"Thanks," she says. "Don't rush. Take care of Sarah first. I'll be fine. I'm really sorry about this. How's she doing?"

"Sarah's okay," I say. "It's you who I'm worried about."

"I'm really sorry —"

"It's not a problem," I say. "This is what I do. Let me pack a bag. Do you need anything?"

"Just you," Karen says. She starts crying. I can hear a woman's voice giving her orders in the background. "They're saying I've got to hang up now," she sniffles.

"Everything will be all right," I assure her. "I'll be there as soon as I can. Stay strong. And, Karen, no matter what you do, *don't answer any questions,* okay? Tell them you're invoking your right to remain silent until you've spoken with your attorney."

"Okay. Thanks, Brek," she says. "I've got to go now. Bye."

I hang up the phone.

Bo is fully awake and sitting up. "They're charging an Air Force chaplain with treason and espionage?" he says. "You've got to be kidding. I hope you realize this is going to be front-page national news."

"I know," I say bleakly. "But you can't be the one to break the story. Karen called me as her lawyer. My conversation with her was confidential attorney-client communication. The fact that you happened to be sleeping beside me doesn't change that."

"But —"

"Promise me, Bo," I say. "This is serious. I understand why you'd want to be the first on a story like this, but there's no way you can report it or tip anybody else about it. I can't be Karen's lawyer if I have to worry that everything I say in my own home might wind up on the wires the next day."

"Okay," he says, disappointed. "But get ready. You're going to be facing a lot of other reporters — guys who won't be as nice as me. You'll be on television every day — maybe even more than I am."

"Great," I say. "Maybe I'll replace the

weather girl."

"Let's not get carried away."

"Can you take care of Sarah while I'm gone?"

"Sure, we'll manage. I'll call in a few favors."

I kiss him on the cheek. "Thanks," I say. "I'm going to need your help to get through this."

"You've got it, whatever you need." He kisses me on the forehead, then looks me in the eyes and grins. "Kick some U.S. attorney's butt and make us proud."

I hug him and head for the shower.

Later that morning, I fly to Kansas City, rent a car, and drive the rest of the way to Fort Leavenworth, arriving late in the afternoon. Two female guards escort Karen, dressed in orange prison coveralls and wearing handcuffs, into the small room with a table and two chairs reserved for attorney visits. Karen looks terrible — pale and gaunt with dark circles under puffy, red eyes, as though she hasn't slept or eaten in days. She takes the chair across from me and flashes me a weak smile. The guards leave the room and close and lock the door behind them so our conversation will be confidential, but they continue monitoring us through a window.

"Oh, sweetie," I say, fighting back tears and reaching out to touch her hand. One of the guards raps on the window and gestures toward a sign in the room that reads "No Physical Contact Permitted." Karen scowls at the guard, but I obey, putting my hand in my lap. We look at each other silently.

"I'm really sorry I dragged you all the way here," she says. "How was your flight?"

"Fine," I say, "no problems. How are you holding up? Are they treating you okay?"

She looks down and tugs on her coveralls. "They took my clerical collar."

"Don't worry," I say, "we'll get it back. I'm meeting with the U.S. attorney later this afternoon to see if I can get this cleared up, or at least negotiate a low bail. You're a priest with no criminal history; you're obviously not much of a threat or a flight risk." I glance at my watch. "We only have forty-five minutes. Tell me what happened."

Karen yawns and rubs her eyes. "They've been questioning me for two days. I haven't gotten any sleep."

"What?" I say, alarmed. "Questioning you for two days? Didn't they tell you that you had the right to a lawyer?"

"Yes," she says, "but I told them I didn't think I needed one."

210

"You didn't think you needed one!" I snap, more than a little cranky myself from having been awakened in the middle of the night to travel from Pennsylvania to Kansas. "They're charging you with treason and espionage and you didn't think you needed a lawyer? Why did you bother calling me, then?"

"Please don't yell at me," Karen says.

I take a deep breath. "I'm sorry," I say. "It's just that it makes it so much harder to defend you if you've been talking to them for two days already. Did you confess to anything?"

"Of course not . . . at least not that I'm aware of."

"That's exactly my point," I say. "Two days with no sleep, who knows what they had you saying. No more talking, okay?"

Karen nods obediently. "Okay, no more talking."

"Good, now tell me what happened."

She looks at me and then, fidgeting with her fingers, looks away.

"I can't help you unless you talk to me, Karen."

"I know."

I sit quietly, waiting, but she won't speak. I can tell she's completely humiliated. "Okay," I say, finally, "I'll tell you what. Let

211

me tell you something I've never told anybody before, something *I* did wrong once."

"You've never done anything wrong," Karen says.

"Yes, I have," I say. I tug on the empty right sleeve of my suit — the same black silk suit I was wearing when I arrived in Shemaya; I wore it that day because I knew I would need all the confidence I could get to meet the U. S. attorney. "Do you see this?" I say, showing her the empty sleeve. Then I proceed to tell her everything about how I had lost my arm, including my perjured testimony during the trial. When I finish, Karen smiles gratefully and compassionately — like a priest.

"You were only a child," she says, softly. "You've already been forgiven. Do you know that?"

"Yes," I say, "I know. And *you've* already been forgiven for whatever you've done too. Do you know that?"

She smiles again and wipes her eyes. "Yes, I guess I do."

"Now tell me what happened."

"Okay," she says, summoning her strength. "Well, since you're my lawyer, I guess I can tell you . . . I'm a chaplain to the missileers."

"The who?"

"The missileers — the airmen who man the nuclear missile silos. You know, the ones with their fingers on the buttons, ready to launch ICBMs to end the world when the president gives the command?"

"Really?" I'm impressed. "I thought you were just an ordinary base chaplain ministering to enlisted men and their families or something."

"I was. Do you remember about a year ago when I told you they were transferring me to Minot Air Force Base in North Dakota?"

"Yes."

"Well, Minot is one of the bases that has Minuteman intercontinental nuclear ballistic missiles on alert. Because of the sensitivity of what they do there and the special security clearances I had to receive, I wasn't allowed to tell anybody that part of my duties included serving as a chaplain to the missileers and their families on base. They don't want the Russians or North Koreans turning clergy into spies."

"Interesting," I say. "Okay, so what happened?"

"I'm against nuclear weapons," Karen says.

"That might be a problem," I reply. "But

it's not treason."

"Well," Karen says, "I guess I told some of the missileers that launching nuclear missiles is wrong and they should refuse to do it if they're ever ordered to."

I stop her. "Wait a minute. When you say 'wrong,' you mean wrong as in wrong unless we're attacked first, right?"

"No," Karen says, "even in retaliation."

"So if the Russians or North Koreans launch nuclear missiles at the United States, we're not supposed to respond?"

"We're supposed to forgive, Brek. We're not supposed to resist violence with violence."

"But that's what the military does, Karen," I say, incredulous. "They resist violence with violence. That's their line of work; it's their entire reason for being. Why did you become a military chaplain if you don't agree with what they do?"

Karen looks puzzled. "Would you ask why a doctor works in a hospital when she doesn't agree with sickness and disease? We go where we're needed most, Brek. Doctors go to hospitals because that's where the sick people are — and lawyers go to prisons to help people charged with crimes. Nobody needs more help in practicing nonviolence and forgiveness than the military — and nobody in the military needs to learn about it more than the people who can destroy the world in a fit of revenge-seeking."

I'm stunned — it's the crayfish trials all over again. "That's all very nice in theory," I say, "but the best way of deterring a nuclear attack is to make sure our enemies understand they'll suffer the same fate if they ever try it."

"But if we're attacked," Karen replies, "then, by definition, nuclear deterrence will have failed, so why bother to retaliate?"

"I don't follow you," I say.

"Let's say we're attacked by nuclear weapons this afternoon," Karen explains. "If that happens, it will be despite our threat of retaliation and mutually assured destruction. In other words, our threat of retaliation didn't work — it didn't deter the attack."

"I guess so . . ."

"So if it didn't deter the attack, then retaliating would be risking the destruction of the world to carry out an already failed strategy. It would be both illogical and immoral."

I scratch my head, trying to follow her logic. "Look," I say, annoyed, "I'm not here to debate national nuclear strategy. I'm here to defend you against a charge of treason and espionage. There's a right to free speech in this country — a right we protect, by the way, with nuclear missiles — and it means that you can say anything you want regardless of whether others agree, so I still don't understand what you did wrong and why you're here. Telling missileers not to launch their missiles might be a breach of your duties as an Air Force officer and get you a dishonorable discharge, but it's not treason. You didn't levy war against the United States or give aid and comfort to our enemies."

Karen glances at the guards and lowers her voice. "There's more to it than that," she says. "I went down into one of the missile silos."

"What? Did you break in?"

"No, one of the officers in my congregation, Sam — I mean Captain Thompson, one of the missileers — let me go with him and Brian, Captain Kurtz, during their shift in the MAF."

"What does that mean, MAF?"

"Missile Alert Facility, that's what they call the underground launch-control capsules. Each MAF controls ten Minuteman missiles."

"Was he allowed to take you there?"

"He got special permission. See, they're

normally two-person crews and they stay underground for twenty-four hours, but the Air Force has been studying whether three-person crews spelling each other over longer shifts would work better, so having me along wasn't entirely unusual. And I already had a high security clearance because I counsel them. I wanted to see what it's like down there so I could understand better. You have no idea how much stress they're under, sitting for hours on end with their fingers on the button. They've got questions and need somebody to talk to."

"I can imagine," I say, "but going into a MAF isn't treason either."

Karen holds her eyes on me. "They went on alert while we were down there. A satellite supposedly picked up what appeared to be the launch of two North Korean ICBMs. The protocol required Sam and Brian to have their missiles ready to launch within five minutes."

"Wow, did they ask you to leave?"

"Yes."

"And did you?"

"Not exactly, not right away. It's surreal down there, Brek. The MAF capsules are suspended on these huge shock absorbers, like egg yolks inside eggs, to help them withstand a nuclear blast. They rattle around a lot, so the first thing Sam and Brian are required to do is buckle themselves into their chairs. The entire place started rumbling and shaking when the huge steel blast doors over the missiles slid open. We could see them on the closed-circuit monitors. Within seconds, the tips of the missiles were pointing toward the sky."

"That sounds surreal all right," I say.

"It was."

"So, what happened next?"

Karen takes a deep breath and exhales. "Sam asked me to leave but I froze. They were within five minutes of killing millions of innocent people. The enormity of that was beyond comprehension. I was in a position to stop it and save them. Maybe God put me there to do just that. I had a moral obligation. I couldn't let it happen."

I shake my head.

"I'm not the criminal here," Karen says. "In any other context, I would have been a hero for saving those people, and Sam and Brian would have been arrested as terrorists for planning to detonate a weapon of mass destruction. But somehow in this crazy world, I'm the one who's prosecuted for trying to stop them? That's insane. It's like people are drugged or under a spell or something. They don't see the madness of it. Somebody's got to wake them up before it's too late."

Karen's eyes bore into me. "You understand, don't you?" she says. "Please tell me that at least you understand."

I don't understand, but I don't want to argue with her any further. "Okay, Karen," I relent, "I understand."

"I guess I need to wake you up too," Karen says. "That's okay. There's still time."

"Look," I say, "it really doesn't matter what I think, Karen. What matters is whether what you did down in that missile silo constitutes treason. So far, I'd say it doesn't. Is there more?"

"Yes," she says. "When I refused to leave, Sam picked up a phone on the console and called the SPs — the Air Force Security Police — to come down and escort me out. While he did that, Brian focused on his checklist for getting his nuclear warheads armed and his missiles ready to launch. They brainwash them well. He was completely detached and methodical about it, like he was doing nothing more than sitting on the floor in his living room, following instructions for assembling a piece of furniture. The fact that he was following instructions for killing millions of people didn't seem to bother him at all. It's theater of the absurd. If a future race populated the earth after a nuclear war and found a record of this, they wouldn't believe it. We willingly made ourselves extinct for the sake of getting justice. Incredible. I had to do something. The countdown to the end of the world had begun. We were only four minutes away."

"So what did you do?" I ask, half wincing, afraid she attacked them.

"I shook him," Karen replies.

"You said *shook* him, right? You didn't *shoot* him or anything, did you?"

"That's not funny, Brek," says Karen.

"I wasn't trying to be funny," I say. "I just want to be clear. What exactly do you mean by 'shook' him?"

"I grabbed him by the shoulders from behind and I shook him. I was trying to wake him up. That's what I've been telling you. They were in a trance. They all fall into some kind of trance when they go down into the MAFs. As soon as they get on the elevator, morality and rational thought get suspended. Somebody needs to wake them up."

"Did you hurt him?"

"Of course not," Karen says. "Look at me. I barely weigh one hundred pounds. Those guys are both over six feet. He didn't even feel me shaking him. It was like I wasn't there, Brek. He just kept going through his checklist, flipping switches, reconfirming launch codes, checking the gauges and monitors. A day earlier, he was playing with his two young children in the nursery of the base chapel, rolling on the floor with them, laughing and hugging them. Now he was a machine — a machine of death. It was chilling. I've never seen anything like it."

Karen looks at me grimly. "When I couldn't wake him up by shaking him," she continues, "I went around in front of him. I pushed his checklist out of the way and grabbed his wrist. 'Brian,' I said, staring him in the eyes. 'It's me, Karen. Wake up. You can't do this,' I said. 'You can't kill millions of people. Even if you survive, you'll never forgive yourself. They're people like you and me. They're mothers and fathers and little children like your children. They have families and dreams. Please, Brian,' I said, 'wake up.' "

Karen looks off into space, reliving the moment. The pain on her face is palpable. I think of Bo and Sarah, and of my mother and father and grandparents. My eyes start tearing up a little. I understand now. For a moment, I am awake.

"What did he do?" I say.

"It was terrible, Brek," Karen replies. "He shoved me, hard enough to knock me onto the floor. Then he unbuckled himself from his seat, pulled his service pistol from the holster under his arm — they're all required to carry them — and he stood over me, pointing his gun down at me with both hands. His eyes were wild. 'Get out of here!' he yelled at me. 'You're interfering with a nuclear missile installation! I'm authorized to use lethal force, Captain Busfield! Get the hell out of here right now or I'll kill you!' "

"Oh my God, Karen," I say.

"I looked over at Sam for help, but he didn't even turn his head. He just kept going through his checklist, getting his warheads and missiles ready. Before I could get up off the floor, two SPs burst through the door with their guns drawn. It was over. They handcuffed me and led me out. They kept me under guard on the surface for a few hours until a team of FBI and CIA agents arrived. They flew me here to Leavenworth that night, and they've been interrogating me ever since. They think I'm a spy or a double agent or something. More theater of the absurd. Obviously the entire thing was a false alarm and there was no North Korean missile launch, or we wouldn't be here having this conversation right now."

I look at Karen with my mouth gaping open in shock. "I'm glad he didn't shoot you."

Karen brushes back the hair from her face. "Me too," she says. "So, that's what happened. Will you take my case?"

My look of shock turns slowly into a grin of admiration. As crazy as it was, she had risked everything for her convictions. "Well," I say, "on the flight here I thought of at least twenty possibilities of what could have landed you in jail for treason, but none of them involved nuclear warheads. Like you said, doctors go to hospitals, lawyers go to prisons . . . and I guess priests go to missile silos."

"I guess so," Karen says proudly.

I'm silent for a moment. "But there's always the risk, isn't there," I say, "that we'll get too close and catch our patients' diseases?" I reach out and take Karen's hand, causing the prison guard to rap on the window again. I don't care. "Yes, Karen," I say. "Of course I'll take your case."

All this came back to me while sitting in Luas's office, waiting for the new postulant to arrive. Luas said nothing more. He had accomplished his goal of immersing me so thoroughly in the miasma of my own past that there could be no chance of me becoming lost in the life of another soul. Or so I thought.

Luas struck a match to light his pipe, adding a third flame to the darkened room. Suddenly the door opened and the faceless gray-robed being from the Courtroom appeared. In a subservient voice, it asked whether we were ready.

"Yes," Luas said, exhaling a cloud of smoke from his pipe. "I believe Ms. Cuttler is now prepared. Please send in Amina Rabun."

# 15

Amina Rabun's life passed before my eyes in an instant, ending sixty-seven years after it began in the quiet dawn of a day that looked like any other day. Our interview of Amina Rabun consisted only of sitting in her presence and receiving the record of her life. No questions were asked and no conversation took place. None was necessary. The memories of Amina Rabun came to us whole and complete unto themselves.

Even so, I caught only a few brief glimpses of her life at first, as I did with the other souls in the train shed. In a sense, meeting the soul of Amina Rabun in Luas's office was like picking up a novel and leafing through a few random pages. I lighted upon a moment, at the beginning, from her early childhood in Germany before the start of World War II, when her father held her in his arms on a tree swing during a warm summer evening and sang her favorite song.

Everything at that moment seemed so safe and peaceful, so fresh and promising for such a beautiful little girl and her loving father. But then I cheated and skipped ahead to the last page of the book to find that Amina Rabun died bitter and betrayed in the United States. How could everything have gone so disastrously wrong? And I found a meaningful passage somewhere in the middle of the story where our lives had briefly intersected — when she received the complaint I had drafted against her on behalf of Bo's mother, seeking reparations for the crimes perpetrated against the Schriebergs by the Rabuns during the war. That I had known this woman whose life would soon be judged in the Courtroom was chilling — not only because of the momentousness of the Final Judgment, but also because I knew her innermost thoughts, feelings, and memories.

As I said, these were only brief chapters, snapshots. I could not even begin to comprehend Amina Rabun's life, or the choices she had made, or the worlds in which she had lived and the people who populated them, until I read all the pages from beginning to end. This would take time. And Luas's effort to help me keep my life separate from hers had succeeded in making me far more interested in rereading chapters from the autobiography of my own life. I experienced no difficulty distinguishing myself from Amina Rabun, at least not at first. Our interview ended in what seemed simultaneously like a flash and a lifetime. Soon the being from the Courtroom re-appeared at the office door and ushered Amina Rabun's soul back to the great hall of the train shed, where it would wait with the other souls until her case was called.

Luas eyed me warily in the flickering candlelight of his office, trying to gauge how I had fared. "Who are you?" he asked.

"I'm Brek Abigail Cuttler," I said, proudly. "That wasn't so hard after all."

"Good, very good," Luas said. "Let's see if it stays that way. The risk of relapse among new presenters is high and can occur at any moment. It can be very disorienting and disconcerting. I want you to stay with your great-grandmother until we're certain you've adjusted fully to the burden of having another life resident inside your own."

"Okay," I replied, having nowhere else to go anyway. This was one of the advantages of Shemaya — no plans, no appointments.

Luas stood up behind the desk and blew out the candles. "I'll check in on you in a

227

few days to see how you're doing and discuss the case."

"Great," I said.

We left the office and began walking back through the impossibly long corridor. About midway down the hall, one of the office doors opened and a handsome young lawyer emerged wearing a dark blue suit and white shirt with a blue-and-gold-striped tie loosened at the neck, as though he had just finished his workday. His round wire-rim glasses seemed to require constant attention to keep from sliding down the steep slope of his nose. He didn't notice us and nearly backed into Luas while closing the door behind him.

"Careful there," Luas said, stepping wide to avoid a collision and coming to a stop. "Ah, Tim Shelly, meet Brek Cuttler."

Tim extended his right hand but, seeing I had no right hand to return the gesture, sheepishly retracted it, stepping with me the same awkward dance I had stepped with countless others during my life. He seemed perfectly nice, but I had a distinct uneasy feeling, as though I'd met him long ago and he wasn't who he now seemed to be.

"Brek here is our newest recruit," Luas said. "She just met her first postulant." Luas turned to me. "Tim hasn't been with us much longer than you, Brek. He's had a more difficult start of it, though. Came away from his first meeting with a postulant convinced he was a waitress at a diner. Wouldn't stop taking my breakfast order — poached eggs and toast, no butter, mind you, Tim. It wasn't until he made a pass at me that we achieved a full separation of personalities."

Tim seemed embarrassed but I found the story hilarious. It felt good to laugh again. It had been so long.

"You'd make a good catch, Luas," I said, joining in.

"Now, now," Luas said, "you mustn't tease me. Tim — or rather the postulant — was interested in me only because her boyfriend made conversation with a pretty woman at the other end of the counter and she was trying to make him jealous."

Tim nodded in agreement. "I really was lost. It took me a while to separate her memories from my own."

"Well," Luas said, "I must attend to some administrative matters. Tim knows the way out. Would you be so kind as to escort Ms. Cuttler?"

"Sure," Tim said.

"Splendid. She'll still need the blindfold before entering the hall."

"Understood."

"As I said, Brek," Luas cautioned, "I'll check in with you to see how you're doing. Sophia knows how to reach me if there are difficulties. Please make no effort to evaluate Ms. Rabun's case. There'll be opportunity for that later. Just get accustomed to her memories and emotions, both of which are quite powerful, as you well know. You should spend most of your time relaxing. Sophia will be with you. You're sure you're okay?"

"Yes . . . yes, I'm fine," I said.

"If she starts taking breakfast orders, we'll know who to blame," Tim said, gamely, getting in the last jab.

"Guilty as charged," Luas said, bowing in mock apology. "I must be off."

We watched him walk down the corridor and disappear into one of the offices.

"How long have you been here?" I asked, eager to learn about Tim's experience and everything he knew about Shemaya.

"I'm not sure exactly," he said.

"I know what you mean," I replied. "Where are all the clocks and calendars? That's been one of the most difficult parts of the transition for me."

We started walking toward the great hall.

"Have you done any presentations on your

own yet?" I asked.

"No, I've only watched," Tim answered. "Luas says the next one's on my own, though."

"Me too . . . after Amina Rabun. Are these all presenters' offices? There must be thousands of them."

"Yeah, I just got mine. There are a bunch of empties down at this end. Where are you staying?"

"With my great-grandmother, at her house — or what I remember of her house."

"Nice. I stayed in a tent with my dad when I first arrived. He and I used to go hunting in Canada, just the two of us. He died a couple of months before I got here."

"Sorry," I said. "Or maybe I shouldn't be . . . I guess you've got him back now."

Tim hesitated. "I guess," he said. "It was great seeing him at first, and he really helped me adjust, but he's gone again."

"Gone? Where did he go?"

"I don't know. One day he just told me I was ready to live here on my own, but that we'd see each other again someday. That's when I realized that we can live anywhere we want while we're here. You don't have to stay at your great-grandmother's."

"What do you mean, anywhere?"

"Well, anywhere you can imagine . . . Let's

see, so far I've lived at Eagle's Nest in Austria and Hitler's bunker in Berlin — I'm really into Nazi history." These seemed like odd choices. It made me think of Harlan Hurley and Die Elf and their endless fascination with all things Hitler. But maybe it was no stranger than Civil War reenactors living in canvas tents on weekends. Tim went on, "I've also stayed at the White House for a while, Graceland, West Point. I've flown bombers and fighter jets and driven tanks. I even took a trip on the Space Shuttle. If you can imagine it, you can do it."

"Wow," I said. "That's amazing. I thought you could only go to the places you've visited during your life. That's all I've been doing."

"No, anywhere you want. I'll show you when we get outside. You can't do it in here."

When we reached the train shed, Tim opened a bin near the doors, removed a blindfold, and tied the thick felt cloth over my eyes. Passing through the great hall, I peeked again at the souls. It was like walking through a library and randomly sampling paragraphs from the thousands of autobiographies cramming the shelves, each authored by a different hand but, like all autobiographies, revealing the same truths, suffering, and joys. I closed their covers when we reached the vestibule on the other side, neither confused nor weakened as I had been before.

Despite my uneasiness about Tim, for the first time since arriving in Shemaya I felt a flicker of hope rather than apprehension, the way a visit from a friend brightens the darkness of an extended illness. I flipped off the blindfold, and Tim and I virtually raced outside like two kids let out of school.

I could see the roof of Nana's house through the trees. The train shed somehow bordered the western boundary of Nana's property. The entrance into it was little more than a disturbance in the air between two maple trees that had been there since I was a child.

*Could the entrance to heaven have been so near all along?* I wondered.

But, of course, we were nowhere near Delaware or my Nana's home. It was all being made up spontaneously in my mind. I could even hear the sound of light traffic along the road.

"Nice place," Tim said, looking around. "Okay, so where do you want to go?"

"Um . . ."

"Just pick any place, you can see them all."

"Well, okay . . ." I couldn't think of anything on the spot, then *Gone With the Wind* popped into my mind for some reason. "Tara," I blurted, of all possible things.

"I've never been there," Tim said. "What would it look like?"

All at once we were there, standing on the wine-colored carpet sweeping through the foyer and up the grand staircase of the fictional plantation mansion. Crystal chandeliers tinkled softly in a gentle spring breeze that stroked the plush green velvet curtains of the parlor, carrying the sweet afternoon scents of magnolia, apple blossom, and fresh-cut lawn. With our heads turning, we walked out to the portico with its whitewashed columns, then along the sun-drenched veranda and back into the dining room with its sparkling tea service and glassware.

It didn't matter that Tara had been only a description in a novel or a set in a movie any more than it mattered to readers of the book or audiences in the theaters. Nor did it matter that I could not remember the exact details as they appeared in the book or on the screen. My mind instantly provided what I expected to see, feel, and smell. I was slightly out of breath when we reached the top of the stairs, and I felt a very real stab of pain when I banged my shin into the corner of a dry sink, proving that we were not wandering through a mere illusion. Everything was in its place, except Rhett and Scarlett, of course. I bounced on her bed, giggling like a little girl, intoxicated by the dream turned reality. Tim had never read the book nor seen the movie and did not share my enthusiasm, but I dragged him through each room anyway like a starstruck movie-studio guide: "This is where she shot that Union scoundrel," I squealed. "And this is where Rhett left her."

Back in the parlor, we stopped to examine a miniature ship in a bottle on the fireplace mantel. As quickly as my mind recognized the ship, my thoughts replaced the plantation with ocean and the mansion with the masts and hull of a sixteenth-century caravel on the high seas. There we were on the wooden deck, dressed in our business attire like a pair of farcical bareboat charterers. A huge wave caused the caravel to roll sharply to port in gusting winds, forcing us to claw our way on hands and knees toward the starboard rail through a drenching saltwater spray.

"Maybe you could warn me next time you're about to think about a ship!" Tim shouted. We fell off the crest of another wave, and the ship lurched to starboard, knocking him onto the deck. I had seen it coming and braced myself against the bulkhead.

He collected himself and rose wearily to his feet. "Think calm seas!"

I did and the seas quieted instantly, as if two gigantic hands had reached down from the heavens to tuck and smooth the immense sheet of ocean, snapping the surface flat as a pane of glass. The skies instantly cleared and the sun came out. Tim sat down on the deck and I joined him. We could see what looked like a small Caribbean island in the distance.

"My grandfather took me sailing on the Chesapeake Bay when I was a girl," I said. "Sometimes I'd fall asleep with him at the helm and dream I was one of the early explorers lost at sea."

A tropical breeze rocked the boat, cooling the warm touch of the sun. We floated adrift with only the far-off sound of gulls and the easy slap of water against the tired wooden hull breaking the silence. I was exhausted and stretched out on the sun-splashed deck, propping my head against a hatch cover.

I soon fell asleep in this paradise. In my dreams I returned to the Chesapeake Bay. I was on my Pop Pop Bellini's sailboat and he was teaching me to steer. The day was perfect, breezy, and warm. The sunburned skin of my grandfather's bare chest and shoulders added color to the spotless white fiberglass coaming around the cockpit of the boat. A weathered, old blue captain's hat shaded his eyes as they darted from the jib to a landmark on shore toward which he told me to aim to make the most efficient use of our tack. As soon as we sailed out of sight of the dock in Havre de Grace he allowed me to take off the life jacket my parents insisted that I wear because swimming with one arm is virtually impossible.

But my beautiful little dream about sailing with my grandfather suddenly turned into a nightmare — a nightmare that often awoke Amina Rabun, whose memories now lived inside me. Because I experienced Amina's memories as my own, I experienced the nightmare directly as though I were Amina.

In this nightmare, my little brother, Helmut, and I (Amina) are playing near the sandbox constructed by our father out of colored bricks behind our large house on our property at the edge of the forest outside Kamenz in eastern Germany. Papa's company employed many skilled masons, and he had them arrange the bricks on three sides of the box into patterns of ducks and flowers and extend the backside into a wide brick patio area, the opposite side of which had a large brick barbecue. Beds of roses, carnations, and begonias surrounded the two opposite ends of the sandbox, and our lush green lawn spread across the front.

Despite the obsessive state of tidiness in which our father maintains our patio and lawn, the sand in the box is excreting a putrid odor and I do not want to play in it. I tell Helmut he should stay away too, but he plunges in without concern. Soon his legs, hips, and torso are swallowed up, as if he is sinking in quicksand.

"Help, Amina! Help me!" he cries.

I reach in to grab him, but as I peer over the edge into the box I realize there is no sand. Instead, the arms of thousands of cadavers, tangled, blackened, and rotting, are swarming around like snakes inside the box, clutching at Helmut, pulling him down into an immense grave that extends deep into the earth, as if the box is situated over a portal into hell itself. I call out to Papa for help and pull as hard as I can to free Helmut, but I cannot overcome the strength of all these thousands of arms.

And then the nightmare ended. I awakened to find myself no longer on my grandfather's sailboat or the ship in the Caribbean. I was lying on the grass outside my Nana's house in Delaware, looking up at her and Tim Shelly, who were kneeling beside me.

"Brek, are you okay?" Nana asked.

I tried to comprehend what had happened. "I think so," I said.

Nana smiled and stroked my shoulder. "You remember your name. That's a good sign."

I sat up and looked around. "I just had the most terrifying dream," I said.

Nana comforted me. "You're safe now, child," she said. She turned to Tim. "Thank you for bringing her to me. I'll take care of her."

Tim stood up to leave. "No problem," he said. He stared down at me with a chilling expression on his face, on the verge of being heartless and cruel. I had the same uneasy feeling as when I first met him. I knew him from somewhere, but I couldn't remember where. "Thanks, Tim," I said.

He walked off through the trees toward the train station.

Nana sensed my apprehension. "Does he make you uncomfortable?" she asked.

I sat up and brushed the grass from my skirt. "Yes," I said. "I feel like I know him but he's pretending to be somebody else. I just can't remember who he is."

"It will come back to you when you're ready," Nana said. She helped me to my feet. "There is a reason you meet every postulant and every presenter in Shemaya. You must discover why you have been introduced to Toby Bowles, Amina Rabun, and Tim Shelly. The sooner you do this, the sooner you will adjust. And the sooner you will have an opportunity to leave."

# 16

Amina Rabun's brother, Helmut, died at the age of seven years and three months, but not in a sandbox. A five-hundred-pound bomb punched through the roof of the gymnasium at his school, killing everyone inside. The old men who had no children in school and could, therefore, examine the scene objectively, the way men do in their fascination with destruction, remarked how the debris was driven outward in a ring around the blast zone. This was not questioned by the hysterical mothers and fathers or the city elders and townspeople. We had all heard the bombers circling overhead and the crack of the antiaircraft guns. Helmut liked the pommel horse and the trampoline.

The bomb that hit the Dresdner Schule für Jungen at 0932 hours on 22 April 1943 instantly dissected and immolated the thirty-two little boys playing beneath it, scattering many times that number of arms, legs, and other body parts hundreds of yards from where they had last been assembled. The Nazi officials who took control of the scene collected these remains and divided them into roughly equal sheet-draped mounds, one for each family believed to have had a son in gym class that day. With solemn voices during the invocation, they proclaimed that the children had made the supreme sacrifice for *das Vaterland,* and we should all be very proud. Despite the dark hairs that curled around the edges of our little sheet, we cried and prayed over it as if it were our own little blond-headed Helmut. Mama swooned and had to be carried from the street and sedated for a week.

My nose itches. I reach to scratch it with my right hand, miss, reach again, and miss again, as if I am swatting a fly rather than part of my own anatomy. There is a throbbing, penetrating numbness in my arm. This is the phantom pain. The ghost of my forearm haunts me each night, deceiving me during sleep by reattaching itself to my body and performing the functions a forearm performs, like scratching itchy noses and swatting flies. Having set me up this way, it exacts its revenge for my carelessness around the manure spreader by vanishing just as my eyes open in the morning, so that I am forced to reexperience the terror of seeing a bandaged stump quivering above me like a broken tollgate on a windy day. The stump points indiscriminately at the eighty-seven squares of ceiling tile in my hospital room. I have counted them often and am certain of the number. The morning nurse, Nurse Debbie, comes in and eases the stump back down to my side, sending bolts of pain shrieking to my brain and from there to my vocal cords. She apologizes.

"Time for breakfast and more morphine," she says, calling me sweetie and fussing over me.

Luas and Nana are sitting at the foot of my bed. I do not know what they are doing here. Their mouths move, but I cannot hear them, so I ignore them. Globs of gray oatmeal dribble down my chin from a spoon held by fingers not yet accustomed to holding spoons. Nurse Debbie serves the narcotic after breakfast, injecting it directly into the intravenous tube that still replenishes the fluids I drained onto my grandfather's pickup-truck seats and the emergency room floor. The poppies submerge me into a warm, perfect, opiated sleep from which I always regret returning.

■ ■ ■ ■

At the suggestion of Pater Muschlitz, the parents of all the little boys killed at the school in Dresden agreed to bury their gruesome parcels in a mass grave as a sign of communal loss. All except my Papa.

"My son will have his own grave!" he raged, in denial of the fact that only God Himself could determine which sheet or sheets concealed Helmut. "He will not be buried like an animal! Like a common Jew! He will be buried in the family plot outside Kamenz!"

Papa ordered his staff to design a monument appropriate for the son of a wealthy industrialist, constructed, he insisted, of the gymnasium's broken concrete and twisted rods of steel so no one would forget the cowardice of his murderers.

"It must be bigger by threefold than all other monuments in the cemetery! It must be completed immediately!"

He permitted himself only two days to bury Helmut and grieve. Then he returned to Poland with the explanation that the war effort there had intensified despite our having conquered the country years earlier. "The Third Reich urgently requires the expert services of Jos. A. Rabun & Sons to assist in various matters of national security that cannot be discussed," he said. Papa had stopped smiling after his first trip to Poland. His eyes had turned darker and narrower, as if he were being haunted by someone or something.

In the half century since Großvater Rabun opened the doors of his small masonry shop near Kamenz, Jos. A. Rabun & Sons had swelled into the mighty *Körperschaft* that trenched modern Dresden's sewers, paved its streets, and erected its buildings. Our little family business became the premier civil-engineering and construction firm in all of Saxony province, providing for our needs very well. Because of this, its demands were never resented by the family. We had far more than most — ample food, beautiful clothes, sufficient funds with which to enjoy dining out, the opera, and even wartime travel abroad. We lived comfortably on my grandfather's estate with its large chalet-style house, riding stables, and gardens reflecting his love of the Alps. Other, less fortunate citizens of Deutschland had sacrificed so much more.

After Papa left for Poland, I met my best friend, Katerine Schrieberg, at our secret place on the estate — a hollow in the woods surrounded by a dense grove of pine trees and guarded by a thicket of briars and vines. She was nervous and pale as always, her fingers incessantly rubbing all the blessings that could possibly be extracted from the golden cross I had given her to present if she was ever stopped by the Nazis in the woods. I could see that my failure to appear during our last three scheduled meetings had made her very concerned. When I told her the sad news about Helmut, she cried as if it had been one of her own brothers, so much so that I found myself comforting her instead of she comforting me. Of course, she was fond of Helmut and felt sorry for me. But she wept also for herself and her family — for if the mighty Rabuns of Kamenz were no longer safe, where did that leave the weakened Schriebergs of Dresden? She asked if I would come back with her to her house, and I eagerly accepted the invitation, welcoming the opportunity to escape, for even a moment, the pall that had descended onto my life with the Allies' five-hundred-pound bomb.

The house in which the Schriebergs lived was not really a house at all. It was an abandoned hunting cabin built by my grandfather deep in the immense tract of forest that stretches from Kamenz all the way to the Czech border. Before taking up residence there, the Schriebergs lived in a beautiful townhouse in the finest section of Dresden and owned several theaters, two of which, in fact, had been constructed by Jos. A. Rabun & Sons. Katerine and I were very close. We had taken dance and violin lessons together since grade school, and her parents and mine held seats on the boards of many of the same civic and charitable organizations until the Nazis banned Jews from such positions.

But then, in 1942, the Schriebergs abruptly booked passage to Denmark after accepting the then generous but nevertheless insulting offer to sell their theaters, home, and belongings to my uncle Otto for 35,000 Reichsmarks in total, rather than allow the government to seize the properties for nothing. They had family in Denmark who had agreed to house them, but when news spread of Nazis rounding up fleeing Jews at the train stations and loading them onto boxcars headed for Poland, they changed their plans and decided to take their chances by staying and hiding. Katerine made contact with me and asked about the hunting cabin.

She and I had sometimes slept in the cabin on warm summer nights and talked about the boys we would marry. It had not been used by my family since the start of the war, so I agreed to allow the family to stay there, and soon began these discreet visits to our meeting place with baskets and sometimes small wagons loaded with food and supplies, always honoring their constant pleas not to tell anyone of their existence — not my mother, not Helmut, and most important, not my father or Uncle Otto. No one.

Katerine's father, Jared Schrieberg, and her younger brothers, Seth and Jacob, were industrious and immediately set to excavating a tunnel beneath the cabin through which to escape if anyone should approach. She told me they practiced their flight twice daily regardless of the weather and could silently vanish beneath the carefully re-installed floorboards within thirty seconds exactly. They came and left from this tunnel, did most of their cooking at night to avoid attracting attention to the smoke from their fires, and relieved themselves far away from the cabin to avoid even the scent of habitation. It was a miserable and demeaning existence. I felt sorry for them, but their precautions proved unnecessary. The very boldness of hiding on the property of an officer of the Waffen-SS (the organization into which my uncle Otto accepted a commission) made life there secure for them in the way that life for certain tropical fish is made safe by living among lethal sea anemone.

When Katerine told her parents the news about Helmut, tears filled their eyes and they said they would sit shivah for him, which they explained to me was the Jewish mourning ritual. In my youth and ignorance, I panicked. I did not want them confusing God with their Jewish prayers into mistakenly sending Helmut to the Jews' heaven. As politely as I could, I begged them not to do this. When they insisted, I grew furious. I had helped them at great personal risk and would not tolerate their interference in such matters. My grief for my brother and my hatred of his unseen murderers found an outlet in the Schriebergs, and I yelled at them in a voice more than loud enough to remind them upon whom they depended for their survival: *"Sagen Sie nicht jüdische Gebete für meinen Bruder!"*

The room fell silent. Katerine stared down at the floor, biting her lip as Frau Schrieberg dug her fingernails into Katerine's arm. Seth and Jacob looked to their father in horror, expecting him to punish my impertinence as he had so often done to them. But Herr Schrieberg only smiled coldly at me, revealing a flash of gold through his graying beard and mustache, unwittingly contorting his long, bulbous nose into the very caricature of a Jew mocked regularly in German newspapers of the day. As if surrendering a concealed weapon, he cautiously pulled the black yarmulke from the balding crown of his head and placed its flaccid shape before me on the battered plank table that served the family as dining area, desk, and altar. The Schriebergs would not offer prayers for my brother's soul. I glared back at the old man and thanked him with a healthy dose of teenage impudence, having for the first time cowed an adult. He had no option. I left without another word and ran quickly through the woods, regretting my resort to such tactics but intoxicated by exerting my will so forcefully and effectively against my elders. The Schriebergs' submission to my demands made me feel powerful and, for a moment, in control of the uncontrollable world around me. At least I didn't have to live like them, like animals.

The skin has miraculously knitted itself over the amputation and the bandages have been removed, but even so, I refuse to touch or even look at the stump of my right arm. It terrifies me. Dr. Farris, the psychologist assigned to all amputees at Children's Hospital, assures me this is perfectly normal.

"I've counseled many children in your situation, Brek," he says. "Victims of fire-crackers, car accidents, farm kids like you too. Most react the same way. They think that what remains of their arms and legs are monsters poised to take what's left of their bodies, but you must remember that this is the same arm you were born with. It's been terribly injured and it needs your love and compassion. You're all it's got. Can you do that?"

"I'll try, but it isn't fair," I cry.

Dr. Farris looks at his watch. "Oops, time's up for today. I'll see you next week, okay? I think you're doing great."

I find my mother reading a fashion magazine in the waiting room.

"Done?" she asks.

"Yep."

Luas is standing in the hallway outside Dr. Farris's office. My mother doesn't see him. He smiles and extends his left hand without first extending his right, pulling me with the gesture back into Nana's living room in Shemaya.

"Thank God you're back," Luas says. "Sophia and I were beginning to wonder whether you would ever return."

I look around the room, dazed and confused by the flood of images, emotions, and personalities rushing through me. Nana brings me a cup of tea, and I sit down on the sofa.

"You've been spending a lot of time with Ms. Rabun," Luas says. "She led an interesting life."

I slide my hand into the right sleeve of my bathrobe and trace the familiar contours of my arm: the shrunken, atrophied bundle of biceps; the rough, calcified tip of humerus jutting like coral beneath a puffy layer of flesh capping the bone.

"Yes, yes she did," I say.

"The Schriebergs lied, you know," Luas says.

"About what?"

"They sat shivah for Helmut."

# 17

Separating myself from Amina Rabun was one of the most difficult things I'd ever done in my life — or death. Amina Rabun's story became *my* story. Unfortunately, as with many plays, her story was a tragedy.

On the rainy afternoon of 23 April 1945, a Soviet scouting patrol advancing south toward Prague stumbled upon the Rabuns of Kamenz. It was the day of Amina Rabun's eighteenth-birthday celebration.

The Allies held Leipzig to the west and the Russians were massed along the Oder to the east, making the defeat of Germany inescapable. Amina's father, Friedrich, and her uncle Otto had already pulled back to Berlin with the retreating remnants of Hitler's forces. They advised their families against leaving Kamenz, however, reasoning that the Russians were interested only in Berlin, that the Americans would soon take Dresden, and that the armed forces of the latter were preferred to the former with respect to treatment of civilians. Privately, the Rabun brothers were also concerned for their affairs and property, which almost certainly would be looted if abandoned — if not by enemy soldiers then by their own German neighbors who had suffered such privation during Hitler's desperate last stand.

Unaware of the approaching Russian forces, Amina rose early that day to begin baking for the party, but not before Großvater Hetzel, who had risen even earlier to slaughter a pig to roast in a pit dug several paces from the long garage full of polished Daimler automobiles resting on thick wooden blocks because there was no fuel to run them. By noon, the sweet scent of pork, yams, cabbage, and fresh *Kuchen* teased everybody, especially Aunt Helena's four hungry children, two boys and two girls, who had been playing hide-and-seek all morning despite a soft rain and their mother's unwillingness, in anticipation of the feast, to prepare their usual hearty breakfasts.

Sensitive to the effect displays of prosperity could have during such lean times, only family members had been invited to the party, all of whom, save those living in the manor itself, conveyed their regrets due to lack of transportation to the country. It was thus agreed that leftovers would be delivered to the hungriest of Kamenz by anonymous do nation to the cathedral. Amina also planned secretly to smuggle a portion to the Schriebergs, who had enjoyed very little meat recently and, having long ago relinquished observance of kosher laws in their cabin, would happily accept scraps of pork.

All went merrily and well into the early afternoon, with everything and everyone cooperating except the weather. But even the rain that had been falling since morning was kind enough to resist becoming a downpour until just after Großvater Hetzel removed the pig from its pyre. Children and adults raced inside as much to stay dry as to enjoy the feast. They assembled in the formal dining room around a large table upon which had been arranged the finest place settings and two large hand-painted porcelain vases overflowing with bouquets of wildflowers freshly picked from the surrounding gardens. In the background, a phonograph whispered Kreisler and Bach into the air. Colorfully wrapped gifts were arranged near the seat of honor at the head of the table, including several packages for the birthday girl delivered by special SS courier from Berlin.

The anticipation continued to build until finally, with considerable ceremony, the grinning pig atop a tremendous silver platter made its debut to ravenous applause. The browned head and body of the beast remained intact, resting peacefully in a soft bed of garnishes as if it had fallen asleep there. Before carving into the meat, toasts of precisely aged Johannisberg Riesling were made first to the beautiful young Amina, then to the cooks of the feast, and finally to the safe return of Friedrich and Uncle Otto and a swift end to the war. Amid the happy conversation, laughter, and music, the revelers could not hear the Soviet scouting patrol approaching. They had no opportunity to defend themselves or flee.

The soldiers swiftly entered from three sides of the manor and herded everybody outside into the rain. After conducting a quick search to ensure they had everyone, they segregated Herr Hetzel and the young boys, ages six and twelve, from the group. Without warning or hesitation they shot them all on the spot before they could offer protest or prayer, as if this was simply a matter of routine for which the soldiers assumed everyone had been rehearsed. Amina's mother and aunt were shot next while running to their aid. Left standing, like statuary in a graveyard, were Amina Rabun and her stunned cousins, Bette and Barratte, ages eight and ten. The three girls' features were petrified into rigid sculptures of terror, waiting for the next bursts of gunfire that would join them with their fallen family members. The girls were spared such a fate, however.

Two gunshots were heard unexpectedly from the woods behind the house, from the direction where the Schriebergs lived in the cabin. The soldiers dropped to the ground and returned a fearsome barrage with their automatic weapons. Amina and her cousins stood motionless in the crossfire, afraid even to breathe. Then everything became silent. In the distance across the field, in the direction from which the two shots had been fired, Amina saw what appeared to be an American soldier holding his hands over his head as if he were surrendering. The Soviet commander directed two of his men to approach the soldier while the rest of the platoon held its position. Several minutes passed. Finally, Amina heard some Russian words shouted back from the woods and the commander gestured for his men to get up. After several more minutes, the two Russian soldiers returned, one of them carrying a simple double-barrel shotgun, the kind Amina had seen her father pack on hunting trips.

Laughing at the weakness of this threat, the soldiers presented their trophy to their commander. Soon the rest of the platoon joined in the laughter and cheering. But amid the backslapping and congratulations, as if the same idea had struck each of them at the same time, attentions were turned slowly toward Amina, Barratte, and Bette, who still had not moved.

The men looked hungrily from the girls to their commander and back to the girls. They began to cheer louder and louder, insisting that their request be granted. Amina could tell instantly what they wanted. The commander looked at the girls and then back at his men and shook his head in mocking disapproval. The cheering became even more frantic. Finally, like Pontius Pilate, the commander turned his back on the girls and wiped his hands. Amina, Barratte, and Bette were dragged into separate bedrooms of the manor and beaten and raped repeatedly throughout the night.

At dawn, the commander of the unit ordered his men to move on.

Amina staggered from the room in which she had been held captive, in search of her cousins. She found the older, Barratte, dazed, bruised, and bleeding but, thankfully, still alive. She already knew that the younger, Bette, was dead. When the drunken and gorged Russians had permitted Amina to use the toilet late during the night, she slipped briefly into Bette's room and found her naked body cold and blue, her face broken and bloodied almost beyond recognition because she would not obey their orders in Russian to stop crying. Even after that, Amina had heard men with Bette at least three times.

I cried so long for Amina Rabun and her family. I cried for her more than I had cried even for myself after I lost my arm. I lived each horrifying moment with her. I believed I would die in the agony of the soul of Amina Rabun, if dying from death were possible.

I spent long periods alone on Nana's front porch, mourning, convalescing, trying to make sense of what Amina Rabun had experienced during her life, and what I had experienced during my own. I searched for meaning within the endlessly conflicting seasons of Shemaya that struggled with one another for space in the cramped sky, like quadruplets in a womb. An entire year of days condensed into a single, dazzling moment of nature in rebellion against time. The apple tree I'd climbed as a child extended its limbs through all four seasons at once: some branches in blossom, some leafy, others tipped with ripe green apples, others in autumn and winter bare, like an unfinished painting. Always changing yet always the same. Endlessly, like human generations. Do trees mourn the loss of their springtime buds, or do they look forward to their arrival?

One day, Nana joined me on the porch. "You told me I had to discover why I was introduced to Amina Rabun, Toby Bowles, and Tim Shelly," I said.

"Yes," Nana replied. "Did you?"

"Katerine Schrieberg, Amina's best friend, became Bo's mother, my mother-in-law," I said.

"Yes."

"Amina saved Katerine from the Nazis. Without Amina, Bo would never have existed, I would never have known him, and Sarah would never have been born."

Nana nodded.

"Toby Bowles saved Katerine from the Russians. Without him, Bo would never have existed, I would never have known him, and Sarah would never have been born."

Nana nodded again.

"But I convinced Katerine to sue Amina and Barratte to recover her inheritance."

"Yes, you did," Nana said.

"I had no idea that Amina and Barratte had been raped by the soldiers or that the soldiers had murdered her family."

"No," Nana said. "You didn't know."

"And Amina didn't know that it was Katerine's father who fired the shots at the soldiers from the woods, or that he lost his life trying to save her and her family."

Nana nodded yet again. "People on earth often judge each other without having all of the facts," she said.

I thought about this for a moment. "But it happens here in Shemaya too," I said. "We can't read people's minds on earth, but everything is available here and still cases are decided on only half of the facts. Nothing's changed. I don't understand it. What's God's excuse?"

Nana patted my arm. "Only the Judge can answer that question," she said. "Maybe the facts of who did what and when become unimportant when judging a person's soul."

We sat together quietly for a moment, watching the merging seasons.

"Bo was named after Toby Bowles," I said. "Katerine lost the sheet of paper with his name on it but she remembered the sound of his last name — Bowles, Boaz — she almost got it right."

"Yes, she did. She almost got it right," Nana said.

"But I still don't know why I was introduced to Tim Shelly," I said. "I don't know how he fits into any of this, and I can't remember how I know him."

"You will when you're ready, child," Nana said. "You will when you're ready."

A few days later, Tim Shelly came to visit me. I was out walking along the Brandywine River behind Nana's house. I had created a row of snowmen on the riverbank in the alternating bands of winter. Portly and resolute, they watched over the river and me, keeping me company. Tim jumped out from behind one of them and scared me badly. I always walked alone.

"Don't worry, I won't hurt you," he said mockingly, as though he had exactly that intention. He reminded me at that moment of Wally Miller, the bully from my childhood who killed the crayfish and whom I had punched in the mouth after he knocked me to the ground. I thought that might have been how I knew him, that maybe he was using a different name.

"You're not Wally Miller, are you?" I asked.

"No," Tim said. "Who's he?" He seemed genuinely puzzled.

"Never mind," I said. "It doesn't matter."

I continued walking along the river and Tim followed me. He stopped acting menacing and started talking about his mother. He missed her terribly. He said she hadn't been well since his father died and he worried about how she was taking his own death. They were mushroom farmers, and they had lost their farm and only means of income after his father died. He said his mother was too old to find a job. Tim was all she had left, and now he was gone too. How would she survive?

We stopped walking in a band of spring, at a patch of wild daffodils where a large tree hung out over the river, defying gravity. Tim seemed vulnerable at that moment, like a lost little boy. I felt sorry for him.

"Do you ever wish you could see your husband and daughter again?" he asked.

"Always," I said. Tears welled up in my eyes, the way they did whenever I thought of Bo and Sarah. "I miss them so much that some days I can't even get out of bed," I said. "I have no photographs of them, no letters, nothing the way living people do. I'd give anything to see them again."

"I miss my mom a lot," Tim said. "My dad told me when I got here that we can't go back. We can't see the living or communicate with them."

"I know," I said. "My Nana told me the same thing."

Tim broke a few pieces of bark off the tree and threw them into the river. They floated away like tiny ships in the current.

"Are you all right?" I asked.

"Yeah, I'm fine."

But he looked nervous now, like he was hiding something.

"Are you sure?" I said.

"Yeah, it's just . . ."

"What?"

"It's just that I did. I saw her the other day. I saw my mother. I went back and visited the living."

## 18

"Shall I take you to them?"

Elymas appeared as Tim Shelly told me he would, during a moment of despair when going forward seemed no more possible than going back. That moment for me came on the rocking chair in Sarah's room. I had not been home since my last visit there to disprove my mortality had instead so thoroughly confirmed it. Home teased me the way a casino teases a gambler, luring the eyes and the mind into a world offering pleasure and hope but delivering only pain and disappointment. Tim too had gone back over and over to his family's mushroom farm, which was as deserted as Sarah's room. This made the sudden appearance of Elymas so startling and so welcome.

Elymas was older than Luas and much more poorly preserved. His withered body floated inside a pair of green plaid pants that piled at his ankles and gathered high around his chest, held there by a moldy brown belt. A food-stained yellow shirt sagged over his narrow shoulders, buttoned crookedly so that the left side of his body appeared higher than the right. He had a corncob face and relied for balance upon a cane with four tiny rubber feet at the bottom. He was completely blind. His eyes glowed glassy, white, and terrifying.

"Shall I take you to them?" he asked again, hovering in the doorway of Sarah's room, too vulnerable and frail to have made such an impossible, gigantic promise. A light breeze could have lifted his body like a scrap of paper and carried him off.

I had been crying, mourning the loss of my daughter and my life. "But they said it isn't possible —"

"You did not listen carefully," Elymas said. "They said it is not possible to direct the movement of consciousness from realm to realm. They said nothing about you interacting with it. Shall I take you to your husband and daughter?"

"But —"

The old man banged his cane fiercely against the floor. "Do not question me! Many wait for my services. You must tell me now whether you wish to see them."

"Yes, yes, desperately."

"Then open your mind to me, Brek Abigail Cuttler. Open your mind and you shall see them."

The old man's eyes dilated until they consumed his entire face from the inside out, and then they consumed me. I felt a sudden motion in the darkness of his eyes, as if I were being hurled through space. Two small points of light emerged in the distance from opposing directions, each emitting a soft, warm glow like the flames of two candles carried from opposite ends of a room, growing as I approached them. Suddenly the shapes of Sarah and Bo emerged, with our dog, Macy, barking at their feet! And around them an expanse of an azure sky, an outline of poplar and ash trees, a swing set, a slide, a jogging stroller. The playground near our home! I couldn't believe my eyes.

Sarah toddled toward me. I swept her into the air, pulling her close, burying my nose in her hair, drinking in her sweet scent. She wrapped herself around my neck and pressed her face against mine. My tears dripped down her cheeks. Then Bo's strong long arms enveloped us both. I felt his scratchy Saturday beard against my neck and smelled the clean sweat on his back from his long run through the town, the college to the playground. He wore his faded blue jogging shorts and a T-shirt with a large red "10" stenciled on the back. Macy whimpered and leaped into the air to get my attention.

"I miss you so much," Bo whispered. "Sometimes I don't think I can go on."

"I know," I whispered, "me too."

I turned my face to his. We kissed, looked into each other's eyes, and kissed again, longer and deeper. Sarah squirmed to free herself and return to the swing. Bo and I exchanged disappointed but happy smiles. He buckled her into the toddler seat, and we took positions in front and behind to push her, her face sailing within inches of ours as she squealed with delight. Bo had her dressed in my favorite denim jumper and sneakers, with her hair tied up into an adorable fountain on top of her head.

As Sarah flew through the air, I recognized my own features in her face — my dimpled chin and cheeks, my small nose and olive-shaped eyes — and behind them, an unbroken line of ancestors — of Bellinis, Cuttlers, Wolfsons, Schriebergs, and other family names long since forgotten, marching back in history and time, waiting there to step forward into the next generation. This little girl sustained their memories and kept alive their hopes and dreams. *And mine.*

Bo and I talked over Sarah's laughter and the squeaking chains of the swing. He said he had taken my death very hard and had just returned to work for the first time. They had stayed with his brother and sister-in-law at first. Then his mother visited for a few weeks to help out until he could get used to taking care of Sarah alone. He had put the house up for sale because the memories were too painful, and he was looking for a job at one of the New York television stations to be closer to his family. They were doing fine, though, he insisted. Work helped occupy his mind, and Sarah woke only twice during the night now looking for Mommy. He had the roof fixed and had gotten the garbage disposal running. Bill Gwynne from the firm had called to offer any help he could with settling my estate, which was kind of him. My parents called once or twice a week, but the conversations didn't last long and were filled with awkward gaps of silence. Karen came by to talk and left some books about grieving that sometimes helped.

I tried to assemble my thoughts. There was so much to say — not about what had happened to me since my death but about what I wanted for their future. Bo looked so strong and handsome standing there in his shorts and T-shirt, so determined and resilient, yet so wounded and vulnerable. I fell in love with him all over again, deeper than before. I wanted to tell him that, and tell Sarah how proud she should be of her daddy. I wanted to tell her how I wanted her to be like him. And like me. I wanted her to know me — who I had been, how I had become who I was, the experiences to treasure, the mistakes to avoid. I wanted her to live life to the fullest because I could not. But as I struggled to form these words, the color suddenly began bleaching from their faces and with it the green from the grass and the blue from the sky. They were fading from view.

"No! No!" I cried. "Bo! Sarah!"

"We love you!" Bo called back. "We love you forever . . ."

And then they were gone.

I was back in Sarah's room. Elymas stood in the doorway. I lunged at him.

"Take me back!" I pleaded with him. "Please, please, it's too soon. Please, take me back."

A toothless smile spread across the old man's face. "But of course," he said, patronizingly. "We'll go back, Brek Abigail Cuttler. In due time. In due time."

"No, take me back now!"

He turned toward the stairs. "That is not possible."

"Wait," I said. "Please, don't leave me."

He grunted for me to follow him. Using his cane to feel his way, he slowly climbed down the stairs. When we finally reached the bottom, he said: "Listen very carefully, Brek Cuttler. Whether you see your husband and daughter again is up to you. But know there are reasons you were told otherwise. Luas is concerned about your effectiveness as a presenter. He believes you should devote your efforts to the Courtroom, and he is concerned you will spend too much time with your family and that it may affect your work. Sophia is concerned that you will not be able to adjust to your death unless you let your loved ones go. It was easier for them to tell you contact is not possible. Do you understand?"

No, I did not understand. I was furious.

"I do not share their views," Elymas said. "I do not presume to determine what is best for others. The choice is yours, just as they too have been free to choose. I come only to present you with possibilities. I do not criticize your decisions. Now, I must be going."

"Wait, please. I want to see them again."

271

"Yes," Elymas said, "I'm certain you do. But you must understand that when Luas and Sophia learn of your decision they will be angry. They will deny that it is even possible and do everything in their power to convince you of this. They will tell you it is all an illusion, and they will slander me and claim I am nothing more than a sorcerer and a false prophet. They may even threaten your position as a presenter and insist that you leave Shemaya."

"I don't care," I said. "I just want to see my husband and my daughter."

The toothless smile flashed again across the old man's unseeing face. "We only visit them in their dreams," he said. "Take your time, Brek Cuttler. They will be there when you decide. Think about what I have told you."

Then Elymas banged his cane three times on the porch floor and he was gone.

■ ■ ■ ■

# PART III

■ ■ ■ ■

# 19

City Hall in Buffalo, New York, rises thirty-two stories from the eastern shore of Lake Erie, like a great art deco frigate making a port of call. So prominent is the thick spire at the top of the building that lake pilots, navigating their barges laden with Midwestern grain and ore, use it to reckon their courses from twenty miles out. Inside the sturdy office tower, however, a different form of reckoning takes place.

As if by some tasteless architectural joke, both the Marriage License Office and the chambers of the Divorce Court are located adjacent to each other on the third floor of the building, either making a commentary on the impermanence of marriage or, perhaps more benignly, affording one-stop convenience to people entering into and departing from life's most important voluntary relationship. The irony of this curious placement of governmental services is not lost on Amina Rabun Meinert while walking past the doors of the former, which she first visited with her fiancé four years earlier at the age of twenty-two, and now through the doors of the latter, where she intends to be rid of him. The crisp *clip-clip* of her heels echoing from the vaulted ceiling telegraphs news of her return and rouses the sleepy young clerk. He denies Amina entry into the courtroom because at that moment the court is sitting in closed session — something about abuse of a minor and confidentiality. He explains that the case of *Meinert v. Meinert* will not be called before ten-thirty. And, no, her attorney has not signed in yet.

"When the weather is nice," the clerk says, trying to be helpful, "folks go up to the observation deck to wait."

And the weather is indeed nice, surprisingly so for early March. A confused mass of warm southern air has raced up the coast, blessing cities as far north as Montreal with three consecutive sixty-degree days.

"Where is observation deck?" Amina asks in her broken English with a heavy German accent.

The clerk looks puzzled for a moment. "On the roof," he says, pointing upward. "You can see the lake from the top of the building. Take that elevator over there to the twenty-fifth floor and then walk up three floors to the deck."

"*Danke,*" she says. "I mean, thank you."

Amina tucks her handbag under her arm and walks back down the hall, past the Marriage License Office and into the restroom to check her makeup. The reflection is reassuring.

*George will be fine,* she tells herself. *He understands. You cannot be with him in that way, with any man in that way. You encouraged him to go to other women, which was generous. And you thanked him by giving him money to establish a business. You owe him nothing. You are doing the right thing.*

Amina touches up her lipstick.

*But you have seen him cry, and you did not know that men could cry.*

This plea comes from a different side of Amina Rabun, the Nurturing Amina who consoled Barratte with whispered lullabies after the Russian soldiers left the house in Kamenz. Nurturing Amina made only rare appearances and was always meek and supplicating. Survivor Amina — the dominant side of Amina — detested Nurturing Amina.

It was Survivor Amina who carried Barratte five miles to the hospital at Kamenz and then returned to the manor to bury her mother, grandfather, aunt, and cousins. One month later, Survivor Amina identified the bloodied bodies of her father and uncle in a Berlin morgue and buried them too. Survivor Amina also located her father's trusted advisor, Hanz Stössel, the Swiss lawyer who, at Amina's direction and in exchange for twenty percent, liquidated Jos. A. Rabun & Sons, A.G., and all the Rabun wealth — landholdings, equipment, automobiles, art collections, gold, and the Schriebergs' home and theaters — and moved the fortune to a secure Swiss bank account. It was Survivor Amina who later bribed the Russian officers into allowing her and Barratte to board a train pulled by a Soviet zone locomotive out of Berlin on May 13, 1949, the day after the blockade was lifted. And it was Survivor Amina, not Nurturing Amina, who seduced Captain George Meinert of the U.S. Army into a bed at the Hotel Heidelberg, and then onto an ocean liner with Barratte, and, ultimately, into the Marriage License Office on the third floor of City Hall in Buffalo, New York.

But now in the mirror where Amina applies her makeup appear the brown shoulders and arms of another man. He wears a helmet with the red star of the Russian army but he has no face. Amina Rabun knows this man well. She has been living unfaithfully with him for years, and he accompanies her wherever she goes. He is a jealous, harsh man, but she gave up trying to escape him long ago, and she has grown accustomed to his presence and his demands. She can deceive him, but only for short periods.

*Yes, you are doing the right thing,* says Survivor Amina. *You are doing the right thing for George and Barratte, for Bette and your mother, for your grandfather, your aunt, your father, and your uncle. For all the Hetzels and Rabuns. You will not betray them.*

From the observation deck atop City Hall, Amina Rabun looks out across the vast blinding expanse of white that is Lake Erie in late winter under a cloudless blue sky. The sudden thaw brought on by the warm front has caused the thick crust of ice and snow on the lake to heave, sending huge ice floes down the Niagara River into the massive concrete supports of the Peace Bridge between the United States and Canada. If the ice refuses to break up and move downriver soon, the Coast Guard will detonate explosive charges to clear the jam. Amina can see men with ropes cinched around their waists walking on the floating slabs, jabbing long poles into the crevices to set them free.

Two men stand on the observation deck opposite Amina, smoking cigarettes. The men's faces are in shadow, but the sun touches the top of the taller man's hat, turning it into a gray flannel torch. The men appear animated in their discussion. One of them points at a newspaper folded in half on the ledge. Amina draws closer.

"Good-bye, comrade," Amina hears the larger man say, flicking his cigarette over the rail.

Amina is startled by this term, *comrade*. It is a word used only by communists. Suddenly the rendezvous seems clandestine and dangerous. Perhaps she has stumbled across spies.

"Yeah, good riddance," says the smaller man.

They both laugh and turn inside for the elevator.

Amina picks up the newspaper. The date on the front page is March 6, 1953. It is the morning edition of the *Buffalo Courier-Express,* and the headline reads "Stalin Dead." A seemingly benign black-and-white photograph of the dictator looks up at Amina from the paper. She smiles at the news of his death. But her smile quickly fades when she learns the cause of death.

*A stroke in the middle of the night? For the leader of the troops who destroyed my family and my nation? It should have been a bullet. A thousand bullets. He should have died the slowest and most painful death in the history of the world. But the news is good just the same. Very good. And the air is crisp and warm, the sky blue, the sun bright, the day hopeful. Stalin's death is certain to emancipate me from the nightmares, and twenty-five stories below, a judge will soon emancipate me from the strains of a marriage of convenience.*

And here, Amina thinks, is an interesting coincidence. Two weeks earlier, George had asked her to attend Ash Wednesday services with him. She had said yes, but she still did not understand why she agreed. Could there be a connection to the death of evil and a change of fortune? Certainly one had been hoped for. Amina had not been inside a church since the funeral of her father, and not once with George, making him all the more bitter. George Meinert wanted all the trappings of a family, including his beautiful wife sitting in the pew beside him every Sunday in the church where he had been baptized. Amina denied him not only the physical intimacies of marriage but also these tiny morsels of relationship and respect.

Yet for some strange reason, on the Tuesday before Ash Wednesday, just two weeks before their divorce would become final, Amina relented. Perhaps in apology for the times her absence had caused George such pain? Perhaps to disprove his conviction that kneeling before an altar would somehow make her a different person and save their marriage? Or perhaps she had begun to forgive God for all that had gone wrong?

But Ash Wednesday had such a strange liturgy, the most primitive and ghoulish of all the Christian holy days. How bone-chilling she found it for a priest to whisper those terrifying words: "Remember that thou art dust, and to dust thou shalt return." And then, to be certain his grim message was not soon forgotten, to feel his thumb coated with the ashes of last year's palms smearing an ugly black cross upon her forehead as a badge of mortification.

Yet to Amina's surprise, a miracle of sorts had taken place during the service. She heard a far more subversive message that afternoon than she had ever heard in a church before.

"In ancient days," the priest had said during his homily, "Lent was observed as a time when notorious sinners and criminals who had been excluded from the church were reconciled with the congregation and God."

As the priest spoke these words, Amina believed she could actually hear the cries of all the penitents daring to ask for forgiveness, and the joyful weeping when open hands rather than fists were extended. At that instant, Amina Rabun Meinert wondered whether this is what Christianity offered the world — not sacred marks and secret words, but reconciliation.

On that Ash Wednesday in 1953, Amina Rabun Meinert accepted this impossible offer — on behalf of herself, yes, but, more important to her, on behalf of her father and uncle, whose sins committed during the war were unspeakable and who could not ask for forgiveness themselves. Indeed, on that miraculous Ash Wednesday, Amina Rabun sought forgiveness for all things done and left undone. And for this momentous act of contrition, she expected nothing less of God than an end to the punishment of her family. For she had long believed that the murders and rapes in Kamenz were a punishment for the sins of her father and uncle.

Now Amina looks again at the newspaper, and then out across the vast sparkling expanse of the lake. The fresh air and promise of the coming spring fill her lungs. She smiles inwardly. Yes, the death of Joseph Stalin was as fine a symbol of a new covenant with God as were the billions of tiny rainbows sealed into ice crystals across the frozen surface of Lake Erie.

# 20

When the High Jurisconsult of Shemaya deemed that I had spent sufficient time digesting the life of Amina Rabun, he summoned me back to his office in the infinite corridor. The hallway seemed even more cheerless and institutional than during my first visit — a sort of department of motor vehicles for souls. I figured Luas was the chief technocrat, although after everything I had seen so far in Shemaya, I began wondering whether the bureaucrat, or the bureaucracy itself, was corrupted.

I was furious with Luas for not informing me of Elymas and the possibility of seeing Bo and Sarah. He would know I had gone, of course, as he knew everything about me without me saying a word. I expected the scolding that Elymas had warned me would come, but instead Luas smiled benignly from across his desk and said: "So, how shall we present Ms. Rabun?"

We were both playing the same game of evasion. "Just as she is," I replied.

"Naturally," he said. He was dressed in the same sport coat, trousers, and open-collared shirt he had been wearing when he found me bleeding and naked in the train station. I wore blue jeans, a T-shirt, and sneakers — the outfit I typically had worn to my office on weekends to catch up on paperwork. He rocked back in his chair. Three thin ribbons of smoke rose into the stale air from the two candles on the desk and the pipe he held in his left hand. "But which part of her?" he asked. "We can't replay every moment of her life. That would serve no purpose. Our role as presenters is more selective. We must present the choices she made."

Choices. The same word Haissem had used in the Courtroom to begin the presentation of Toby Bowles: "He has chosen!" Chosen what? To wait in a train shed with thousands of other souls while bureaucrats work the algorithms of their eternities?

"What choices are those?" I asked.

"The choices Yahweh promised Noah we would make," Luas replied, gripping the pipe between his teeth and talking between them. He was obsessed with Noah and the Great Flood. All his metaphors eventually ended there.

"Did you get here by drowning?" I asked with a smirk.

"No. I was decapitated, actually."

I looked at him skeptically. "You seem to have a head," I said.

Luas smiled. "Yes, well, you put it there, so I suppose I do. But during my lifetime, I looked nothing like you now see me. There are no bodies in Shemaya, Brek, only thoughts. You're free to dress me up any way you like. When the thought of me as a combination of the mentors you respected during your life no longer serves you, my appearance will change." This reminder of the irrevocability of my death was painful. Most of the time, Shemaya seemed like life, a Disney World sort of place filled with wonder and surprises — and sometimes terrors, but, nevertheless, life. The idea that none of this was real — the candles, the desk, the office, the train station, even our bodies — was not only difficult to comprehend but still deeply upsetting to accept.

"How did it happen?" I asked, preferring to discuss Luas's death over my own. "I mean, how were you decapitated? Were you in an accident?"

Luas puffed thoughtfully on his pipe. "One must begin at the beginning to answer such a question. Why did Yahweh promise not to destroy the earth after having just destroyed it?"

Like I said, he was obsessed. "I think we went through all this when I got here," I reminded him.

"Did we . . . ? Oh, yes, you're right. Sorry. I've confused you with one of the other new presenters. Let's pick up where we left off, then. What if Noah had disobeyed?"

"Asked and answered, your honor," I said impatiently, invoking my courtroom training for protecting witnesses from badgering.

"He'd have been killed with the others," Luas said, answering his own question. "The price of disobedience was exceptionally high, don't you think?"

"Well, the death penalty *is* the ultimate punishment," I said. I was in a foul mood. I wanted him to know I was upset.

"But this was the ultimate death penalty, Brek. Not only Noah's life but the lives of his family and the entire human race. The animal kingdom as well. Disobedience meant the end of everything, not just the end of Noah. The stakes could not have been higher."

"You're all about choices," I said. "What choice did Noah have? Build an ark or everybody dies? People make him out to be some kind of hero for doing God's bidding. But he had the biggest gun in the world pressed against his head. Who wouldn't build an ark? He was just doing what anybody else would have done to save their own neck."

Luas placed his pipe in an ashtray on his desk and stood up.

"Precisely. Now we're getting somewhere," he said. "So, how shall we present Ms. Rabun?"

"Precisely *what*?" I asked.

"What's the first thing Noah did after the Flood?"

"I don't know."

"He made a burnt offering."

I shrugged. "If you say so."

"That's what the Bible says," Luas replied. "Why make a burnt offering?"

"I don't know, to give thanks?"

Luas began pacing the small room. "Correct, and what was it worth, this offering?"

"I guess what all offerings are worth."

"Really?" Luas said. "This man, Noah, had just witnessed the mass murder of millions of people and animals. As you said about building the ark, who wouldn't have been grateful for having been spared after all that? But look at it from God's perspective, Brek. What did God really want in all this?"

A good question. What did God really want? Why even bother with us? "Respect, I guess," I said finally. "Respect. Love. The same things everybody wants."

"Precisely. Now, is that what billowed up from Noah's burnt offering? Respect and love? Or was it something else. The stench of fear, perhaps? The fear of instant death and annihilation —"

"But —"

"Throughout history, the tendency has always been to read the story of the Great Flood from mankind's perspective, from the perspective of the accused: *man's* fall, *man's* destruction, *one man's* obedience, *one man's* deliverance, *one man's* thanksgiving, *mankind's* guaranteed survival. But perhaps the story is told not so we understand the condition of man, which we know all too well. Perhaps it is told so we understand the condition of *God.*

"Noah built the ark because the price of disobedience was intolerable. He offered the sacrifice because he wanted to appease God. He didn't do these things out of love for God. Not that we should criticize Noah . . . he did exactly what was his to do. But if we look more closely, we see that it was divinity itself, entangled in the greatest of all ironies, that cheapened the gestures, desecrating both Noah's obedience and sacrifice. The story of Noah is the story of God's need for man, Brek, not man's need for God. It also explains why, because of that divine need, the possibility of evil must be permitted to exist for there to be any possibility of love. It explains why a serpent inhabited the Garden at the beginning of time, and why it will continue to coil around our feet until the end of the age."

"I don't understand," I said.

"Look," Luas said, "what changed in those forty days was the very essence of God's relationship to man, not man's relationship to God. God changed *His* ways. We didn't change ours. Think about that. Humanity paid a terrible price but we won. Yahweh recognized the problem instantly, the moment the waters receded and the sacrificial fire was lit. By punishing man for disobeying and turning away, the Flood had destroyed love itself. It is essential that you understand this, Brek. For true love to exist, the option not to love must also exist. When love is demanded and extorted, it becomes fear, and fear is the opposite of love.

"So, Yahweh had a fateful *choice:* He

could accept the possibility of sin to achieve the greater prize of love, or He could endure the false praises of creatures too terrified to do anything else. He chose the former, gifting to humanity the freedom to choose. So critical is our understanding of this act that Yahweh selected the refraction of sunlight into the many colors of a rainbow as the eternal symbol of our freedom to follow many different paths. No matter how far we may stray, no matter how much it hurts — God or us."

Luas returned to his chair behind the desk.

"We are all heirs to that promise, Brek. All of us, including Amina Rabun. But that promise is both a gift and a curse. With the freedom to choose comes the responsibility for one's choices. The Courtroom is the place where those choices and responsibilities are reckoned. So, I ask you again: How shall we present the case of Amina Rabun?"

# 21

Elymas sits on the rocking chair in Sarah's room, pushing himself back and forth with his cane against the corner of her crib. He is expecting me. I have made my decision. I must see Bo and Sarah again. The old man's toothless smile appears when he hears me enter. I'm here to see my husband and daughter, but it feels shady, like a drug deal.

"Shall I take you?" Elymas asks.

"Yes."

His eyes widen and I disappear into them. I emerge this time in a quiet country cemetery on a sloping hillside bent in prayer against the wooded slope of the Bald Eagle Mountain. I have been here several times before. This is the cemetery near my grandfather's farm where the Cuttlers bury their dead. It is a pretty place. And sad. The sun this day burns warm and bright, but the graves do not taste the sun or feel its heat. A requiem of red oak trees enshrouds those who sleep here, the paper-thin membrane of chlorophyll demonstrating the easy dominance of darkness over light. But the shadows moving beneath the leaves appear to be of a different darkness and a different light. They flicker over the stones and dance across the grass without relation to the sway of the trees or the stirring of the small memorial flags.

At the end of a row of well-kept plots kneels a man in his fifties. His hair is thinning and his middle thickening. He resembles Bo's father, Aaron, when I was first introduced to him, pulling weeds from the garden behind their house. The man in the cemetery hears me rustle through the grass and rises to his feet. In his right hand he holds a small silver teacup and in his left a black yarmulke. The cup falls when he sees me, crashing onto a sterling silver tray placed at the base of a small, granite gravestone. I cannot see the name. The collision knocks over a silver teapot and two other cups, spilling their contents.

"Brek?"

"Bo?"

We race around the gravestones to hug each other.

"I knew you'd come today," he whispers.

I look at him. He appears hollowed out,

like he has aged decades, a faint shell of the man I once knew. "Are you sick?" I ask.

"No, why?"

"Because . . . because you don't look well. You look so different from when we met two days ago."

"Two days ago?"

"Yes, two days ago, at the playground with Sarah. Have you forgotten already?"

He holds me at arm's length. "That was fifteen years ago, Brek."

"No, it wasn't," I insist. "It was the day before yesterday. Remember? You had just finished your jog, and we put Sarah on the swing. You told me how you'd been staying with David and that things were starting to get back to normal. You were looking for a job in New York."

He looks at me as if I am crazy. "I remember," he says. "That was fifteen years ago, look —"

He walks back to the grave, pulls a copy of the *Centre Daily Times* from beneath the serving tray, and shows it to me. The headline reads "Killer Executed." The dateline reads "July 21, 2009."

Bo leads me to the trunk of a large oak tree at the end of the row of gravestones and we sit down together. He's wearing wrinkled slacks and a polo shirt that look as if he's slept in them. His face is covered with gray whiskers.

"I got the job in New York but lost it," he says dejectedly. "I haven't been able to keep a job for more than six months at a time ever since. No television station will touch me. They're afraid of people who tell the truth. Maybe I drank a little too much and missed a few deadlines. Television is a sham, Brek, and the news is a sham. It's all a game."

I can't believe how much he's changed. He's obviously paranoid, and he twitches involuntarily, like a drug addict or an alcoholic.

"I'm doing fine, though," he continues. "I'm a counselor at a homeless shelter now. They're letting me stay there while I get myself together. Good people. I run an AA meeting and keep an eye on things. I'm thinking about doing a documentary. I've been talking to some old friends at the station. People think the homeless are animals, but they're just like everybody else. They had normal lives once — then something went wrong."

Bo reaches out to hold my hand, but I pull it away.

"Have I changed that much?" he asks.

This isn't the Bo Wolfson I knew, the man

whom I fell in love with and father of my daughter, the brilliant, courageous reporter, the handsome anchor of the morning news who smiled down from billboards with Piper Jackson. "You've changed a lot," I say.

"I've missed you so much, Brek," Bo says. "When I heard they were executing that bastard Bowles this morning, I had to drive up here to see it. I was hoping he might make an apology, but nothing. No apology. No remorse. Nothing. None of his buddies from Die Elf had the guts to show up either. They've all crawled back under their rocks. But I loved watching him shake when they fried him. You saw it all, though. I knew you were there. I could feel you in the room."

"Who, Bo? Who are you talking about?"

"Ott Bowles. That's why you came back, isn't it? Because it's finally over and justice has been served? You can rest in peace now. And I'm gonna make a fresh start. Clean myself up; I'm not that old. Maybe I'll even get back into the news. I'd be a great producer. I've been talking to some old friends at the station —"

And then it occurs to me. Bo knows how I died. Of course. I should have asked him before but our visit was cut short. I can finally find out how I died!

I grab him by the shoulder and shake him

frantically. "Bo, was I murdered? Was I killed by Ott Bowles? Is that how I died?"

In the distance, I can see Elymas walking slowly toward us.

"It's time," he calls out in a dry, hacking voice. "It's time, Brek Abigail Cuttler. Come with me. It's time."

Bo closes his eyes and covers his ears. "No!" he shouts. "No, not the voices again!"

"Bo," I cry, "please, tell me how I died. I've got to know."

Elymas calls out again. "Come with me, Brek Cuttler. It's time."

I glance down at the newspaper on the ground beside Bo. If fifteen years have passed, then Sarah would be old enough to tell me how I died as well. Oh, how I long to see her. My heart leaps with hope. I shake Bo again. "Bo! Hurry! I have to go. Just tell me, where's Sarah?"

Bo opens his eyes and drops his hands. He glares at me in disbelief.

"What do you mean, where's Sarah?" he shouts.

"Where is she?" I plead. "Hurry, I need to see her."

Bo jumps up from the grass and starts running away, weaving through the gravestones with his hands gripping his head as if he's in pain. I chase after him.

"Wait! Wait, Bo!" I call. "What's wrong?"

"Why are you doing this?" he yells. "Please, please just leave me alone."

He makes a short loop around the graveyard, returning to the headstone and the upset tea service where I first found him. He falls to his knees, tears streaming down his cheeks.

Elymas is moving closer. "Come with me, Brek Cuttler," he commands. "It's time."

"Bo, please," I cry, "please, it's all right. Everything's all right. Just tell me, where's Sarah?"

He looks up at me in rage. "What do you mean, where's Sarah?" he screams. "Don't you know?"

He points at the tombstone. Engraved at the top is a crucifix superimposed over a Star of David. The sight of this heresy startles at first, but the symbols look somehow correct together, as if the perpendicular lines complete the thought of the interlocking triangles and are their natural conclusion when manipulated properly, like a Rubik's Cube. Engraved beneath them in large block letters across the polished surface are the words CUTTLER-WOLFSON. Beneath these, in smaller letters, is this:

BREK ABIGAIL
December 4, 1963 — October 17, 1994
*Mother*

SARAH ELIZABETH
December 13, 1993 — October 17, 1994
*Daughter*

*Hot tea and bees honey,*
*for two we will share . . .*

## 22

I found Nana Bellini in the garden behind her house, stooped low over a row of tomato vines sagging with ripe, red fruit. Her silver hair, pulled back in a bun, shimmered under the darkening skies of an approaching summer storm. She hummed a tune while filling a small basket with fresh produce, aware that I stood nearby in the cool spring air watching her. Reaching the middle of the row, she twisted off a huge beefsteak tomato, so large and swollen that its skin had split open exposing its tender pink meat inside. She held it up for me to see.

"Even vegetables suffer as much from abundance as from want," she observed. "Some, like this one, are bold and flashy, taking everything they can. Others sip only what they need, content to share with the community." She pulled apart a snarl of average-sized tomatoes and pointed to a stunted tomato vine off by itself in a patch of cracked, barren dirt. "And then there are the ascetics, joyfully suffering without any hope of bearing fruit themselves, secure in the knowledge that their sacrifice will make the soil richer next season and they'll become the fruit of future generations." She turned around to me. "The wise farmer values them all, equally. If one is favored over the other, the entire garden suffers."

I drew closer. I wasn't there to talk about gardening. "Why didn't you tell me Sarah was dead?" I asked. "Did you really think I wouldn't find out?"

Nana stopped picking and slid her arm through the hoop handle of the basket so that it swung from her elbow. Flecks of black soil clung to her wrinkled fingers and denim blue skirt. "There was nothing to tell, dear," she said. "You knew it all along. You didn't want to remember. You weren't ready."

I had nothing more to say to her. She had deceived me. I needed to find my daughter. Sarah had to be somewhere in Shemaya.

I ran off through the woods to the entrance of the train station. Flinging wide the doors, I shouted to the souls inside: "Run! Run now, while you still have the chance!"

But they didn't dare move. They watched me, unblinking eyeballs hovering in space, with the same suspicion my grandfather's cattle watched him when he was trying to do something for their own good. There was a time when they would have rushed through those doors, but that was when they still believed mortality was the fantasy. How very real it had become, and how very soon would the Final Judgment be passed upon their lives.

I had entered the train shed without a blindfold because I was searching for Sarah. This was a grim task. I could see in their memories how each had died. There were infants, children, and adults in every horrifying shape and condition, stricken by every conceivable cause of death, wasted away by starvation and disease, blistered and burned, gnawed and digested, shot through with holes, stabbed and sliced, blue from drowning, bloated from rotting, blown apart, hacked, crushed, broken, poisoned, suicides, murders, accidents, illnesses, old age, acts of God. But their stories no longer affected me. Only one story concerned me now. I searched everywhere for Sarah, but she was not among them. Although I wanted desperately to see her, like a parent searching a morgue after a calamity, I was relieved. And then terrified.

*What if her case had already been called?*

*What if she had already been judged and gone on without me?*

I ran from the train shed, frantic to find her. I could think of only one place left to look.

The golden key Luas had given me turned the lock, depositing me inside the Courtroom. There was no one, just God and me, alone, inside the Holy of Holies. He had taken my daughter. I had come to take her back. I was not as trusting as Abraham with Isaac. I moved to the presenter's chair and looked up at the sapphire monolith, searching the smooth surface for the slightest blemish that might indicate a hint of acknowledgment or compassion. When I found none, I asked meekly in my nakedness:

"May I see her? I gave her life."

God looked on, unblinking and unmoved, my existence too infinitesimally small to notice, my plea too insignificant to deserve a response.

"Where is she!" I screamed at the top of my lungs.

The answer came back as a deafening concussion of silence — the silence of God's love being withdrawn into the infinite vacuum of space, heard by the soul, not the ears, and mourned by the soul, not the heart. I looked around the Courtroom. Its walls pulsed with the purest energy of the universe while just outside, in the train shed, the walls were spattered with the innocent blood of humanity — the blood of those judged against unattainable standards by a Judge who, Himself, was guilty of the crime.

"Where is my daughter!" I screamed again. "Goddamn you! What have you done with her?"

God created all things.

God created evil.

God is all things.

God is evil.

God shall punish the wicked.

Therefore, God shall punish Godself.

I raised my arms as Haissem had done, and in unison with every man, woman, and child since the beginning of time, I spoke:

"I PRESENT GOD, CREATOR OF HEAVEN AND EARTH . . . *HE* HAS CHOSEN!"

The Courtroom shattered into a billion shafts of darkness.

I find myself in a beautiful garden paradise. My name is Eve.

I am creation, a first thought, a last, a beginning without end.

I am a before, an after, a space in between.
I am spirit, a single breath of God.
I am love.

"I am love! I am love!" the air sings. And the waters too, and the creatures that swim, creep, fly, and walk. The stones whisper "I am love" as they support the soil, which whispers "I am love" and supports the plants, which whisper "I am love" and support the creatures even as they raise their heads toward the sun, which whispers "I am love" and warms the Garden through which I tread.

Another like me walks in this Garden.

"We are love! We are love! We are love!" we sing. And we *are* love. Love given. Love unending. Love without condition. And the knowing we are all of this, and the knowing that this is All There Is.

And the Lord God formed man of the dust of the ground and breathed into his nostrils the breath of life; and man became a living soul.

And the Lord God planted a garden eastward in Eden; and there he put the man whom he had formed.

And out of the ground made the Lord God

to grow every tree that is pleasant to the sight, and good for food; the tree of life also in the midst of the garden, and the tree of knowledge of good and evil.

And the rib, which the Lord God had taken from the man, made he a woman, and brought her unto the man. And they were both naked, the man and his wife, and were not ashamed.

Now the serpent was more subtle than any beast of the field which the Lord God had made. And he said unto the woman, Yea, hath God said, Ye shall not eat of every tree of the garden?

And the woman said unto the serpent, We may eat of the fruit of the trees of the garden:

But of the fruit of the tree which is in the midst of the garden, God hath said, Ye shall not eat of it, neither shall ye touch it, lest ye die.

And the serpent said unto the woman, Ye shall not surely die:

For God doth know that in the day ye eat

thereof, then your eyes shall be opened, and ye shall be as gods, knowing good and evil.

The serpent coils upon a rock so I may see him more closely.

"That is the only way, then?" I ask him.

"Yes, it is the only way," he says. "You long for the experience of love. But Love itself may be had only by calling upon that which you are not, for you cannot experience that which is Love until you first know that which is Not Love. Therefore must you separate yourself from Love and enter the realm of Fear and Evil."

"But what is Fear? What is Evil?"

"All that you are not."

Adam and I eat of the fruit, and call upon all that we are not.

We hear God's voice. Adam rushes me among the trees to hide. We tremble and giggle. Our bodies touch the leaves and feel their chill, but also touch each other and feel our warmth. Adam is large, strong, and coarse. I am smaller, weaker, and soft. In seeing and touching him, who is so different, for the first time do I experience and feel myself. We long not to join with God, but to join with each other.

And then we are ordered to leave.

Adam presses his lips to mine. I melt in the taste of his mouth. Now this I whisper: "I love you! I love you! I love you!"

Now I find myself in the fields. They call me Cain, son of Adam.

The wind of the earth is hot and filled with dust. I shield my eyes as I jab a stick into the ground and pour seeds into the holes.

My mother has told me of a place close but far away, a beautiful place, lush and green, where there is always enough to eat and drink, where the wind is cool and clean. She told me she left this place to experience love and from that experience she produced me. She told me that when she created me, when she first laid her eyes on me, she felt what God felt when He created my father. She tells me I am created in God's perfect image because she and my father had been created so. But I do not see the resemblance.

Abel came after me. My mother and father say they love him as much as they love me, but they have always made his life easier than mine. He follows the herds, while I break the soil. He brings God the fatty cuts from his best lambs, while I can offer only the meager produce from my fields. God is more pleased with Abel's gifts than mine. I hate Abel.

"Why are you so angry?" God asks. "Are you not also perfect in my sight?"

"Because you love Abel and not me."

"That is not true, my son. And if you dwell on this, it will be your ruin. Even so, you may do as you wish."

Abel is weak and easily fooled. I tell him a lamb is injured and lead him into the fields. He does not see me unsheathe my knife. I come up behind him and slit his throat. I watch his blood spill onto the ground. He should not have taken God's love from me.

Justice is the sweetest fruit in the lands east of Eden.

The Courtroom reappears. I am no longer alone. Luas and Elymas are seated on the observer chairs.

"That was quite bold of you, putting God on trial," Luas says to me. "What was the verdict?"

"Guilty as charged," I say. I glare at him. "Where's my daughter? Where is Sarah?"

"You'll find out soon enough, Brek Cuttler," Elymas says. He waves for me to approach them. "Come sit with us. See how God's justice is done."

"Ha!" Luas says mockingly. "You haven't seen anything since the day I blinded you for your insolence, you old beggar."

"That is true," Elymas replies, "but justice too is blind, yet she sees more clearly than any of us. And you, Luas, were once blinded for your own wickedness, as I recall. When will you stop thinking you're better than me? Who's next on the docket?"

"Amina Rabun," Luas says. "Hanz Stössel will be presenting her case." He turns to me. "Pay close attention, Brek. You will be presenting your first client soon. This is the final phase of your training."

"And if I refuse?" I say.

Luas shakes his head dismissively. "Not possible."

Soon an older man enters the Courtroom, holding a golden key like mine. He is tall and seems exceptionally weak and frail, but he wears an elegant double-breasted suit in the European style. I recognize him instantly from Amina's memories as the Swiss lawyer to whom she had turned to liquidate her family's assets after the war. I know also from her memories that he died several years before Amina.

I am alarmed to learn that Hanz Stössel will be presenting Amina's case. Although he had been Amina's lawyer during her life, they did not part on good terms. In fact, Mr. Stössel blamed Amina for ruining his reputation and career and causing his ultimate demise. Amina would not have disagreed. To the contrary, she carried the guilt of Hanz Stössel's downfall and death with her for the rest of her life. Allowing him to present her case is an obvious conflict of interest. He will do everything he can to see that she is convicted. The unfairness of the trials in Shemaya becomes more obvious, and more appalling. But Luas smiles warmly, either oblivious to the conflict or complicit in it.

"Ah, hello, Hanz, please come in," Luas says. "We've been expecting you."

# 23

The presentation of Amina Rabun begins immediately, before I can protest the selection of Hanz Stössel as her counsel and make a motion for his disqualification.

The Courtroom vanishes, and in the same manner as the theater-like presentation of Toby Bowles, we are deposited into another scene from Amina Rabun's life. This particular scene is set inside the publisher's office of a small newspaper called *The Cheektowaga Register* in a suburb of Buffalo, New York. Amina sits behind the desk with the door closed, talking on the telephone. She is wearing a white linen blouse and a heather skirt. A table fan runs quietly in the background.

Amina occupies this office because Hanz Stössel himself had advised her that, as an immigrant and a single woman with no employable skills but considerable wealth, she should consider purchasing a business to occupy both her money and her mind. He recommended a florist's shop or perhaps a boutique, nothing too taxing or complicated; but Amina heard that the newspaper was being sold under financial duress and thought that owning a paper would be more interesting. She had intended to retain the publisher to continue running the operation, but soon found herself disagreeing with his editorial judgment and fired him. Rather than hire somebody new, she decided to learn the newspaper business and take over operations herself. It would be a fresh start for her life and perhaps help her integrate into her adopted homeland. Who was more respected in a community than the publisher of the local paper?

Amina shakes her head while speaking on the telephone. She threatens the newsprint salesman on the other end with cancellation of her contract if he fails to match the ten-percent discount offered by a competitor. The salesman, a French Canadian, struggles to understand the English words tangled in Amina Rabun's German accent.

During this conversation, there is a knock and the office door opens. A large man with black lacquered hair appears at the threshold. Behind him, the newsroom buzzes with ringing telephones and reporters busily talking and typing at their desks. The man standing in the doorway strikes an imposing presence, but he appears apprehensive, as though he knows he is about to encounter a foe even more formidable than himself. Dark wings of perspiration spread across his blue dress shirt, but this is not necessarily from nervousness. The temperature both inside and out is eighty-eight degrees with one hundred percent relative humidity — a meteorological constant of western New York in the summertime.

The man takes in a deep breath, puffing his cheeks into small pink balloons. With his right hand, he mops a soggy handkerchief across his smooth forehead. In his left hand, he holds a long cardboard cylinder, the type used by architects to carry blueprints. While waiting for Amina to finish her call, his blue eyes wander ahead into the office like a pair of bottle flies, coming to rest on a beautiful Tiffany lamp in the corner. They caress the colorful glass petals and measure their value, then fly off to a framed black-and-white photograph of Amina's parents on their wedding day and an engraved plaque naming *The Cheektowaga Register* the best small-town newspaper in New York in 1958. His eyes come to rest on a painting on the white wall behind Amina's desk.

This painting is an extraordinarily valuable work of art, more likely to be found hanging in a museum than a publisher's office. It is an original oil painting by the French Impressionist master Edgar Degas, and was a gift to Amina from a man, much like the man admiring it from the doorway, who also happened to find himself in the same predicament. Degas's subjects in the painting are a bristly-bearded father dressed in a light overcoat and black top hat enjoying a cigar as he strolls along the edge of a Parisian park with his two handsomely dressed daughters and their dog, all moving in opposite directions at once. When Amina enters the office each morning and sees the painting, she recalls strolling with her own father on Saturday mornings along Dresden's broad boulevards to the offices of Jos. A. Rabun & Sons, and then to a small café for lunch. Sometimes in the café she would meet Katerine Schrieberg and her father.

Against a wall in Amina's office adjacent to the Degas painting stands a polished walnut case filled with copies of four books of poetry published by Bette Press, the company Amina formed when she acquired the newspaper. She named the entity in honor of her young cousin who had been raped and murdered in Kamenz. The bindings of each of these four books bear in gold leaf the Bette Press colophon — a square imprint of a little girl eternally fixed in mid-swing beneath the thick branches of a poplar tree, her hair and dress rippled softly by a breeze. The original wood carving of this colophon, still stained with ink from the first run of cover pages, rests on top of the bookcase. It is the work of master printer Albrecht Bosch, who studied at the Bauhaus School before fleeing the Nazis to Chicago. Mr. Bosch convinced Amina to print books alongside her newspaper and to employ him as her production manager. The design of the colophon, inspired by an early photograph of Bette Rabun, did all the persuading that was necessary.

The newsprint salesman at the other end of the telephone finally grasps the meaning of Amina's words and concedes the ten-percent discount, all of which, he wishes her to know, will come out of his commission. She thanks him for the gesture but feels no gratitude or sympathy. *The Cheektowaga Register* is his largest client, and he has done very well for himself.

Amina places the handset into its cradle, smiles, lights a cigarette, and observes the man waiting at the door. She has not met him before but finds his apprehension familiar. Three others like him have passed through her office, each conveying the same sense of anxiety, each indebted to her but somehow indignant.

Ten days earlier, this man was named Gerhard Haber. Twelve years before that, he was SS-Einsatzgruppen colonel Gerhard Haber — a fact confided to Amina in a cable from Hanz Stössel, who asked if she would be willing to help another German family as she herself had once been helped. Since the fall of the Third Reich, the Habers had been on the run, living in considerable discomfort in the Paraná River valley in Argentina. The Nazi hunters had tracked them as far as South America.

"Completely false," Stössel assured her concerning the war-crimes allegations against Haber, the details of which she did not want to hear. Too much knowledge, she had learned, is dangerous.

Sitting in her office pondering Haber, Amina is unsure exactly why she accepts these risks, first in helping Jews in Kamenz and now Nazis in America. Perhaps she does it for the thrill of knowing secrets of life and death. Whatever the reason, she has come to blame both the Jews and the Nazis for what happened to her and her family in Kamenz, and she convinces herself that given the opportunity to do it all over, she would permit the Gestapo to load the Schriebergs onto the train to Auschwitz, and the Nazi hunters to take the Habers to Israel. But she does not have it to do over.

Hanz Stössel had asked Amina to provide Haber and his family with false passports and new identities in exchange for another artwork of great value. She agreed, and Haber was there now to collect the passports and tender his payment. It was an easy thing for Amina. She told Albrecht Bosch what to print and he did exactly that, without question, in exchange for her indulgence of his expensive appetite for more sophisticated printing equipment and additions to his typeface collections.

Amina did not consult with Haber in the selection of names. Having never given birth to a child, she took great pleasure in bestowing new identities upon the people sent to her by Mr. Stössel.

She taps the ashes from her cigarette. "Come in and close the door," she says to Haber.

Haber complies, and Amina retrieves a single passport from her drawer and examines it.

*Gerry Hanson is a nice name,* she thinks. *Faithful at least to the first consonant and*

*vowel of the original. And completely incon-*
*spicuous.*

She hands it over to Haber for his approval. His eyes light up as he examines the authentic-looking exit stamp from Buenos Aires, which appears over the talons and tail feathers of a perfectly reproduced American eagle. The document is flawless.

*"Danke,"* he says.

Amina raises her eyebrows.

"Sorry," Haber corrects himself, practicing his new language. "Pardon me. I meant to say, 'Thank you.'"

Amina gestures toward the guest chair and directs the table fan toward Haber — not out of concern for his comfort but to disperse the offensive scent of his perspiring body, which has suddenly overtaken the office. She retrieves four more passports from her desk and opens them. "Remind me again," Amina says. "What are the names and ages of your wife and children?"

Haber tenses as if he has suddenly forgotten, then regains control of himself. "Hanna, age thirty-nine; Franz, age fifteen; Glenda, age thirteen; Claudia, ten."

Amina examines each passport and slides it across the desk to Haber. "Hanna is now Helen," she says. "Franz is Frank, Glenda is Gladys, and Claudia is Cathy."

Haber appears disappointed. Amina frowns. "You don't like the names?" she asks.

Haber shakes his head. "No, they are acceptable," he says, not wanting to insult the woman who holds so much power over his fate. He examines the passport for his youngest daughter. "If I may," he says timidly, "the birth date on Claudia's — I mean, Cathy's — is off by several years. Given her young age, it might attract attention."

Amina takes the passport, examines it, scowls, and tosses it into her wastepaper basket. Haber becomes rigid, fearing that he has just ruined everything. But Amina does not vent her dissatisfaction upon him. She asks him for the correct birth date, scribbles it on a sheet of paper, and calls out to her secretary. The woman appears immediately with a steno pad. Amina is pleased by her efficiency in front of her guest.

"Alice," she says, handing her the slip of paper, "please take this to Albrecht in the print shop and tell him he must reprint the Cathy Hanson document with this birth date. He'll understand. Tell him I need a rush. It must be completed this afternoon." Amina does not explain the nature of the project, and Alice does not ask. She leaves and Haber relaxes slightly.

"Thank you," Haber says, carefully pronouncing the words.

"Welcome," Amina replies.

For a brief moment, Amina feels sorry for Haber, but she quickly dismisses this sentimentality and reverts into the shell of Survivor Amina.

"You have something for me?" she asks impatiently, looking at the cylinder in Haber's lap.

"Yes, of course," Haber says.

He stands the cylinder on end, removes the cap, and extracts a long roll of dingy canvas, producing a small cloud of black soot. He apologizes for the mess as he unrolls the painting, which despite charred edges is in otherwise good condition. It depicts a funeral procession under gray winter skies — a coffin being carried through a snow-covered churchyard into the shattered ruins of a Gothic chapel. The name at the bottom right corner of the work is Caspar David Friedrich.

Amina touches the canvas and smiles. She has long admired the nineteenth-century Romantics, but most especially Friedrich, who himself lived in Dresden. The private girls' school Amina attended in Kamenz, only a few blocks away from the boys' school in which Helmut was killed, saw to it, by Nazi decree, that she learned first and most about Germany's own great artists.

"Where did you get it?" she asks.

Haber hesitates. "It has been in my family," he says vaguely. His evasiveness reminds Amina of the accusations against him, and she decides not to press for more information.

"They say Friedrich was influenced by Runge, but I don't see it in his work," Amina says. "Do you?"

"I trust you are satisfied?" Haber replies eagerly, either ignoring or not understanding the question.

"Yes," Amina says, more coldly now and in the manner with which she dispatched the newsprint salesman. She exhales a cloud of cigarette smoke and places the passports back into her drawer. "I'm sure Hanz told you that I would require authentication. Someone from the Buffalo Academy of Fine Arts will look at it this afternoon. Assuming there is no problem, you may return at four-thirty for your passports."

Haber rises and forces a smile from his lips.

"Yes," he says, bowing his head slightly. "I will be here." He turns and walks out of the office. Amina closes the door behind him and phones the curator at the fine arts academy.

Amina's office disappears and the Courtroom reemerges into the foreground. Hanz Stössel is standing at the center. Luas, Elymas, and I sit in the chairs at the back.

"Do you still believe she is a victim?" Elymas asks me.

"Victim of what?" I ask.

Before Elymas can answer, the Courtroom disappears again and we are back in the office.

Amina props the canvas up on her credenza, leaning books against the corners to keep it erect. She steps back to imagine how it will look when framed. From this perspective, taking more time to observe the scene, the mourners in the painting appear to her as her own family must have appeared when carrying Helmut to his tomb beneath the twisted girders and broken concrete of the memorial her father had assembled for him from the debris of his school.

"Victim of injustice," Elymas says. I can hear his voice but we are still in the office.

Amina wipes tears from her eyes as the

memory of that terrible day envelops her. She has been so consumed with the horror of Kamenz all these years that she has rarely thought of poor Helmut. She succumbs to the unanswerable guilt of such neglect, and of having named the press for her cousin, Bette, instead of her own brother, or her own mother or father.

"The creature weeps," Elymas whispers. "You feel her anguish, Brek Cuttler. But where is the compassion of her Creator? Can you feel that touching her soul? Does the throne express even the slightest concern? One tender thought or word? Where is justice? When will the scales be balanced?"

Helmut's death was, in the final analysis, an accident. The Allied pilots could not have known their bombs would raze a school filled with children. They did not look Helmut in the eyes and execute him. That is why she has been willing to forgive them and, therefore, to forget. But not the Soviets. No, their crime was deliberate and their faces depraved. There can be no forgiveness for them. Ever.

This self-pitying does not last long. Amina, the Survivor, will not permit it. She rubs the mascara stains from her cheeks and blows her nose. She resolves to display *Cloister Cemetery in the Snow* in memory of her brother Helmut and to tell those who ask that it means this to her.

And then an idea strikes her.

Amina has been planning to publish an editorial on the anniversary of the death of Senator Joseph McCarthy. She had been an admirer of McCarthy, not only agreeing philosophically with his fanatical distrust of communists but also embracing his rabid patriotism as a means of deflecting attention from her own Nazi heritage. Embracing Joseph McCarthy made as much good business sense to Amina Rabun and *The Cheektowaga Register* in the 1950s as embracing Hitler made good business sense to her father and Jos. A. Rabun & Sons in the 1930s. But there was also a deeper emotional attraction to McCarthy, for he stood alone in Amina's mind as the only one who truly understood the evil of the Soviet Union and the suffering of its victims. These understandings became the germ of Amina's forthcoming editorial. She would explain in personal terms what the Rabuns of Kamenz had lost to the Red hordes — and she would bravely contrast that with what they lost to the Allied bombs. It would be a moving, convincing, wonderful editorial. A fitting tribute to Joseph McCarthy.

The light in the Courtroom flickers, signaling that the presentation of Amina Rabun is about to shift to another scene. I am worried by Stössel's selections for the presentation. He has omitted Amina's entire life in Germany and the sacrifices she made for the Schriebergs. As I suspected, he is presenting only the dark side of her life and character. She has no hope of being acquitted, no hope of absolution.

# 24

The final act in the presentation of Amina Rabun begins. It is winter, February 1974, and Amina is just returning from a three-week Caribbean vacation to her rundown, drafty mansion in Buffalo, built in the 1920s by a Great Lakes shipping baron. She is accompanied by Albrecht Bosch, who has enjoyed his second visit to the tropics as her companion.

Amina and Albrecht have become intimate friends but not lovers, for Amina is adamantly asexual and Albrecht adamantly homosexual. They learned these secrets about each other the day they first met, in a bright tavern in the Allentown section of the city on the second anniversary of Amina's divorce, which also happened to be the first anniversary of Albrecht's separation from the artist who convinced him to come to Buffalo from Chicago and then left him for a younger man.

Thus, it was a common nationality and a common fate that brought Amina and Albrecht together — but it was Bette Press that made them inseparable. Albrecht Bosch was in love with the printed word. He invited anyone who would listen into his magical world of typefaces and printing presses and, once there, would explain with an artist's passion how a simple serif can arouse anger or evoke serenity, and how paper texture and weight can be grave or lyrical, pompous or comforting. He introduced Amina to the ancient struggle between legibility and creativity that ties typography to tradition like no other art form and allows for only subtle innovation. And like Amina's early teachers of Romanticism, he appealed to her Germanic pride by reminding her that Johannes Gutenberg gifted the printing press to humanity. In the joyful marriage of paper and ink that followed, Amina and Albrecht experienced the harmony of opposites that had eluded their private lives.

The mansion is cold when the travelers arrive back from their journey to the tropics, infuriating Amina because she had left specific instructions for the housekeeper to turn up the heat two days before their return. Amina asks Albrecht to adjust the thermostat and light a fire in the study, then heads for the mail, which has been stacked neatly for her on the large mahogany dining room table. She scans through the envelopes quickly, searching for anything that looks important or interesting and setting aside the monotony of bills and solicitations. Two envelopes fit the former criteria: a large, beige square of heavy cotton-fiber bond addressed to "Ms. Amina Rabun and Guest," and a menacing business envelope with a return address of "Weinstein & Goldman, Attorneys-at-Law." She takes both envelopes into the kitchen, puts on a pot of water for tea, and opens the invitation first. To her delight, she reads that the prestigious Niagara Society has, for the first time, requested the favor of her presence at its annual Spring Ball — *the* social event in Buffalo each year.

"Albrecht!" she calls.

"What is it?" Albrecht coughs. His head is in the fireplace, which has filled with smoke. He has already gone through half a Sunday newspaper but still can't coax the wood to ignite.

"We're going to the Niagara Society Ball!" Amina sings. "Get your tuxedo pressed."

"Not if I die of asphyxiation first," Albrecht coughs.

The telephone rings as the water comes to a boil.

"Can you get that, Albrecht?" Amina asks. "The tea's on."

Albrecht happily abandons the fire and takes the call in the living room while Amina pours the bubbling water into a creamy Belleek teapot. She adds Earl Grey tea leaves to the infuser, sets a tray with two matching cups, and carries it into the study. After fixing herself a cup and settling into her favorite wingback chair, she opens the envelope from the law firm, finding the enclosed letter:

Dear Ms. Rabun:

I represent Mrs. Katerine Schrieberg-Wolfson in her capacity as Executrix of the Estate of Mr. and Mrs. Jared A. Schrieberg.

As you know, my client has written to you on several occasions concerning ownership of certain theaters and real property in Dresden acquired by your family from the decedents during the war for the sum of 35,000 Reichsmarks, equivalent at the time to approximately $22,000 U.S. You no doubt realize the purchase price was far below fair market value and the sale was made under duress and threat of seizure by the Nazi government and incarceration of the decedents in the Nazi death camps. Therefore the sale was, and is, invalid.

Mrs. Schrieberg-Wolfson, on behalf of the Estate, seeks rescission of the purchase contract and return of all property. In that connection, she has previously offered in writing to refund you the $22,000 plus interest from the date of the sale. You have not responded to Mrs. Schrieberg-Wolfson's offer and she has, therefore, retained me to take the necessary steps to rescind the contract and recover the property or its value.

My research has disclosed that your family no longer owns the property, it having been sold in 1949, at your personal direction, by Mr. Hanz Stössel, Esquire. My client has authorized me to accept the proceeds of that sale plus interest, minus the purchase price, in full payment and settlement of the Estate's claims. We believe fair market value of the property in today's dollars would equal at least $3,500,000 U.S. If such an agreement cannot be reached, we will be forced to initiate legal proceedings against you and your cousin, Miss Barratte Rabun, to invalidate the purchase and to recover the full value of the property. We believe the courts in this country and Germany will be sympathetic to these claims.

My client deeply regrets the need to resort to the courts, but is firm in her resolve. She shall forever be grateful to you for sheltering her family during the war, and has expressed as much in her letters to you. This is, however, a matter of the unfair acquisition of property by your family under extreme conditions. As a result of that action, my client and her surviving family were forced to live in relative poverty compared to the lifestyle which you and your family have enjoyed. Mrs. Schrieberg-Wolfson seeks no more than to right that wrong. She bears neither you nor Miss Barratte Rabun any ill will.

I am authorized to initiate legal proceedings if I receive no response from you to this letter. In light of your position as publisher of a newspaper, it would seem that the negative publicity surrounding such a case would prove very uncomfortable. In that regard, our investigators have learned that Otto Rabun was a member of the Waffen-SS and that your father's construction firm, from which much of your family's wealth emerged, was under contract to build the crematoria at Majdanek, Treblinka, and Oswiecim. Such extraordinary facts will be difficult to conceal from the public in litigation.

I look forward to your prompt response.

Very truly yours,
Robert Goldman, Esq.

"How dare she threaten me!" Amina fumes.

Amina had received prior letters from Katerine Schrieberg and thrown all of them away. While the Soviet soldiers murdered members of Amina's family and raped her and her cousins, the Schriebergs remained huddled in a Rabun hunting cabin nearby and did nothing, risked nothing. When she ran to them for help the next morning, they were gone. Now this, after all their cowardice, after all Amina had risked to protect them, Katerine Schrieberg repays her by threatening to ruin her? It is too much. She takes the letter to the hearth, ignites it, and places it into the fireplace on top of the charred newspaper, warming her hands by its flames.

"What's going on in there?" Albrecht calls

from the living room. "Barratte's on the phone, do you want to speak to her?"

Barratte on the phone? This news startles Amina even more than Mr. Goldman's letter because she has not spoken to Barratte in nearly ten years. The bond between cousins became strained when Amina fled Germany with Captain Meinert and took Barratte with them. Barratte despised the Americans for the death of her father in Berlin as much as she despised the Soviets for the deaths of her mother, sister, and brothers in Kamenz. Her resentment of Amina for forcing her to leave Germany and live in the land of her enemies only grew as she endured years of abuse and humiliation in Buffalo schools as the little orphaned "Kraut girl" whose parents and country got what they had coming. At the first opportunity after she turned eighteen, Barratte took control of her inheritance and left. After that, Amina heard from Barratte only occasionally and knew little about Barratte's life. The telephone call on that cold Saturday in February came to her as a complete shock.

"What does she want, Albrecht? Is everything okay?"

"Everything's wonderful!" Albrecht replies. "Barratte had a baby boy this morning! Seven pounds, five ounces! She named him Otto Rabun Bowles! You're a grandmother, or a great aunt, or something, Amina! Here, come speak to her!"

The Courtroom reappears. The faceless being from the monolith is standing at Hanz Stössel's side.

"A decision has been made," the being announces without emotion, in the hollow voice of a proctor calling time. The presentation of Amina Rabun is terminated before the essay on her life can be completed.

# 25

"We're going out tonight," Nana said to me.

It was late afternoon and we were in the study of her house. She was reading, of all things, the 1897 *Farmer's Almanac* — the year she was born. I was needlepointing a Christmas stocking for Sarah. We had never gone *out* before. I pulled the needle through the fabric.

"Where?" I asked.

I had started the stocking when I was pregnant with Sarah. It would have been finished in time for her second Christmas. I picked it up again when I went home to meet Elymas after the presentation of Amina Rabun. I wanted him to take me back to see Bo, but Elymas never came. Doing something for Sarah became my way of protesting her death. I decided to act as though she were still alive — that we were both still alive. I made bottles of formula for her every morning and ran her a bath. I washed her clothes and crib sheets. I drove to the day care and then to work, and back to the day care and then to the convenience store. Every place was vacant. I drove through ghost towns. The unmarked police car flashed its lights to pull me over, but I kept driving until it disappeared from the mirror. When the loneliness became too great, I returned to Nana's house and brought the stocking back with me to finish.

"It's a surprise," Nana said, her lips spreading into a smile. This was actually the first time we'd spoken since I came back. We had spent several days silently passing each other in the house.

"I don't think I can take any more surprises," I said.

"Elymas does have a flair for them," Nana replied. "It's part of his charm, I suppose. But I wouldn't trust everything he says and does."

I looked at her. "Should I trust you?"

"You should trust the truth, child."

I put down my needle. "And what is the truth, Nana?"

"The truth is what makes you feel calm and loved, nothing more than that."

"That's meaningless."

"No, it isn't. It's the only meaning. Truth

is never anger or fear. They're illusions, and Elymas traffics in them."

I picked up the needle again, looped the thread, and pushed it through the fabric. I was working on the toe of an angel blowing a trumpet.

"He told me you would call him a false prophet," I said.

"He also told you that I'd be upset, but I'm not. You're free to follow false prophets if you wish. They all expose themselves eventually. Truth is never far away."

"I saw Bo and Sarah with my own eyes. I held them in my arms."

"I know, dear, I know. And you sailed on a caravel and walked through Tara, and everything around you here seems so real. But it all disappears. Things and bodies are not real. They're symbols, and symbols are impermanent. Life is impermanent."

"Bo's life has been ruined."

"According to Elymas, it has. But who's to say? Can you trust Elymas? Can you trust your own memories? Would Bo be closer to the truth by working at a homeless shelter or sitting in front of a television camera?"

"What happened to her? What happened to me? What are you hiding?"

"I'm not hiding anything, child. It's you who doesn't see the truth all around you."

She closed the almanac and pushed herself up from the chair. "When you're ready to see it, you will. But it's time now for us to get ready."

"For what?"

"You'll need an evening gown."

That got my attention. "Where do you expect me to find one of those in Shemaya?"

She had the devious look of a grandparent teasing a child with a present. "In your closet."

I went upstairs and opened the closet in my mother's room. There were five different gowns — beautiful silks, satins, and crepes with matching stockings and shoes. I was thrilled. Nana stood at the door, watching me.

"They're beautiful," I said, holding each one in front of me. "Won't you tell me where we're going?"

"I can't," Nana said. "It's a surprise."

She sat on the bed as I tried on each gown, twirling past her. They all fit perfectly, but we most liked the black satin gown with straps and the low bodice that exposed my shoulders and back. I was actually enjoying myself.

We went through the same process in Nana's room, settling on a gown for her with more color and a high neckline. She

pulled two strands of pearls and two matching pairs of earrings from her jewelry box
and gave a set of each to me. Standing
before the mirror, we made a striking
couple, and neither of us needed hair-
brushes or makeup. Hair and complexions
are *always* perfect in Shemaya.

We left the house with the last of the four
suns from the four seasons dropping beneath the treetops. Nana led me out the
back door and through the woods on foot
to the entrance of the train station. There
were strange new sounds when we entered
the vestibule, mystical and resonant — the
sounds of water rushing and wind blowing,
of dolphins laughing and birds singing, of
children talking and parents sighing, of all
creation living and dying. It turned out to
be the sounds of a band. A handwritten note
on the doors read "Reception for New
Presenters." We walked in.

All the postulants were gone, and with
them the static discharge of their memories
and the sad, horrifying, but sometimes
beautiful, states of their deaths. On an
elevated stage, near the board showing arrivals but no departures, hovered four faceless minstrels like the being from the Courtroom, each dressed in a long gray cassock.
Two played violins, one a bass, and the

other a cello, all of which vibrated in colors: auroral greens, violets, and blues. Before the band milled a crowd of formally attired men, women, and children, some off by themselves enjoying the performance with a plate of hors d'oeuvres and a glass of champagne (or milk for the children), others gathered into small groups, talking and laughing.

Banquet tables had been erected in the four corners of the hall and piled high with pâtés, caviar, cheeses, fruits, and other delicacies, and next to these were bars fully stocked with wine, liquor, and other refreshments. A small army of faceless, gray-dressed creatures tended the tables and bars and collected the empty glasses and plates from the guests. A magnificent crystal chandelier and a constellation of lesser chandeliers bathed the room in a warm, sparkling light. I looked around, trying to gain my bearings. Luas emerged from the crowd, dressed handsomely in a single-breasted tuxedo.

"Welcome! Welcome!" he said, greeting us. "We've been waiting for you!" He gave each of us hugs, then turned and waved his arms over the crowd. "Grand, isn't it?"

"Yes," I shouted over the din.

"And all in your honor, my dear. You've

graduated with flying colors, and now you're ready for your first client. I must say, we've got an excellent group of new presenters. Time for a little play before the work begins. You both look wonderful."

"Thank you," I said. "But I really don't feel like I'm ready to graduate or represent anybody. I barely understand the process . . . and I don't think I agree with the results."

"Have no worries, Brek," Luas assured me. "Everyone's nervous the first time, you'll do just fine."

Nana winked at Luas. "Brek was very suspicious about tonight," she said. "She almost forced me to ruin the surprise."

"Was she now?" Luas said. "Ah, but she's an inquisitive one. That's what we love about her."

"Here's another question, then," I said. "What have you done with all the postulants? The hall was filled a few days ago."

"And a perceptive question as usual. Didn't I tell you, Sophia?" Luas said. "They're still here, actually. Come, I'll show you."

We walked out of the train shed and closed the doors. "Okay," he said, "now, open them again."

All at once the music was gone, along with the minstrels, food, tables, chandeliers, and beautiful guests. The postulants were back — thousands of intensely bright spheres filled with memories floating in the dim, sulfurous light of the train station.

"How can they be here?" I said to Luas.

"Creation is a matter of perspective and choice," Luas replied. "What one wishes to see becomes what one is able to see. You have never seen the subatomic particles pulsating in the furnishings of your living room, nor the minuscule particle of your living room in the pin-wheeling galaxies of the universe, but this does not mean subatomic particles and galaxies do not coexist. Your powers as a presenter are maturing, Brek. You are seeing more of what there is to see. You are seeing as if through microscope and telescope."

Walking among the spheres halfway across the train shed, I saw a man dressed in rags with bulging eyes and a shaved head. He glanced at me but quickly looked away. Following behind him was a young girl, also dressed in rags. She stared at me with haunted, defiant eyes. Her right arm was missing, and she reminded me of myself as a girl.

"Are they presenters?" I asked Luas. "They don't seem to be dressed for the party."

"No," Luas said. "They're souls like all the others, but you're only able to see a small portion of their memories at this time."

"Maybe I could represent the little girl. It looks like we have something in common," I said.

"That is not possible," Luas replied. "The girl already has a lawyer, and your first client has already been selected."

# 26

Back at the party, my new colleagues — the many honorable and long-standing members of the bar of the High Court of Shemaya — were eager to celebrate my graduation and share stories of their first presentations. Disturbingly, they all related tales of trials terminated before a defense could be made, and what seemed like eternities spent trying the same soul over and over again to the same conclusion.

Constantin, for example, an older man with blackened teeth and scars on his face, told me he presented the soul of a police officer whose duty and pleasure it had been to torture prisoners into making confessions. "He was a singularly cruel man," Constantin explained, "yet the Judge sees fit to end the presentation each day before I can inform the court of his fondness for abandoned animals found on the street, which he sheltered in his apartment."

Another presenter, Allee, a pregnant teenager with swollen cheeks and hands, presented the soul of a young man who left his girlfriend after impregnating her. "He risked his life to save a child from a fire that swept through his neighbors' house one day," she said. "I try to bring it up in the Courtroom, but we never seem to get to it. I guess God doesn't think it matters."

I lost Luas and Nana in the crowd and continued on alone to a banquet table. Talking to the other presenters made me feel nervous and uneasy and I wanted to be left alone. After helping myself to some food, I drifted off toward a stone sculpture in the corner of the room that I hadn't seen earlier. It was a perfectly smooth sphere as tall as me and resembled a globe of the earth. A miniature stone figurine of a woman with long hair and wearing a skirt stood on the surface of the sphere at the top with three miniature pairs of stone doors arrayed before her.

When I looked more closely at the figurine of the woman, the sculpture reconfigured itself, so that I was now seeing the three pairs of doors before me, as though I were now the figurine. Over the first pair of doors in front of me was a sign that said "Self," over the second, a sign that said "Others," and over the third, a sign that said "Spirit." All three pairs of doors had mirrored surfaces, and I could see my reflection in all of them, but the left and right doors of each pair reflected different images of me.

The left doors displayed the image of me I had always wanted to see: taller, with more pronounced cheekbones, fuller breasts, and two complete arms. This Brek Cuttler was witty and sophisticated, a loving mother, brilliant lawyer, devoted daughter, exquisite lover, competitive tennis player, accomplished violinist, and wonderful chef. She was the perfect specimen of a woman, envied for having a perfect career, perfect body, perfect mind, perfect husband, perfect children, and perfect home.

The right door of each pair reflected a far less glamorous image. This Brek Cuttler was rounder and plainer, with a blemished face, thin lips, small breasts, limp hair, and no right arm. Yet she seemed nobler and less frantic than her twin reflected in the other doors. This Brek Cuttler defined herself by everything the other Brek Cuttler was not: comforting rather than competitive, spiritual rather than intellectual, forgiving rather than condescending, complimentary rather than complimented, trusted rather than feared. She was perfectly defenseless and, thus, perfectly indestructible, dependent upon everything and therefore perfectly independent.

"Love me," pleaded the perfect Brek Cuttler reflected in the left doors of each of the three pairs with the signs above them. Behind her in the mirror assembled the trappings of her success — the awed glances of men and women, the beautiful clothes and home, the powerful friends and powerful titles, the luxurious vacations, the coveted invitations, the ruthless victories. Her peculiar little twin reflected in the right doors of each of the three pairs said only, "I am." Behind her assembled the trappings of her freedom — represented by the universe itself, from the smallest gnat to the brightest star, each perfect in its own way, and in its own time.

The magical sculpture divided my miniature avatar into three, and each of us stepped forward to make our choices between the three pairs of doors. We were greeted at the thresholds by parents, teachers, and friends: to the left they all pointed, and through the left doors we went, finding behind them three more sets of doors requiring the same choices. Receiving the same guidance, to the left we went, and to the left again, again, and again, as we had been taught and raised, eventually choosing on our own. The sculpture rotated slowly, like a boulder being pushed uphill, the doors opening and closing.

Suddenly the sculpture transformed itself back to the way it had been, a large sphere with me no longer part of it but standing by its side. Looking down upon its surface, I saw, as though viewing the earth from high altitude, a labyrinth of doors, paths, and choices crisscrossing the surface like so many rivers and highways.

A man's voice, deep but gentle, came from my right, startling me: "A traveler who sets out in one direction eventually returns to the place of his beginning, seeing it again for the first time."

I turned to find a strikingly exotic man standing beside me. He was thin and of middle height and middle age, shirtless and shoeless, with smooth, titian skin and dark, black eyes. He wore a rainbow-colored dhoti wrapped around his waist and legs in the style of a Hindu ascetic, and on his head was a skullcap made of small gold beads. His face was peaceful, unfathomable, like that of a Buddhist monk during meditation. He was beautiful.

"Oh, hello," I said, trying to recover from the shock of his appearance. "I didn't see you standing there . . ."

"Do you like it?" he asked.

"Yes," I said, "it's very interesting, although a little disturbing."

The sphere rotated, and my three virtual representatives disappeared around the far side.

"Time leads in only one direction from which there can be no deviation," the man said. "But there can be many present moments, depending on the choices one makes."

"How can there be many present moments?" I asked. "Isn't there only one present?"

"Yes," the man said, "but it contains everything that is possible. If any point on the surface where the figurine happens to stand represents the present moment, then stretching behind her from that point on the sphere is the past, and out in front of her lies the future. Now, suppose you were to draw a longitudinal line around the sphere from the present moment where she stands — like the equator on a globe. You would see that this line represents all possible places on the surface of the sphere where the traveler can stand and still be within the present moment. The doors represent the decisions she must make on where to stand along that line."

I was confused. "If that's what the sculptor was trying to say, I missed it," I said.

"I don't think that's all he was trying to say," the man replied. "We've accounted for only two dimensions of the sphere so far — time, represented by the rotation of the sphere, and place, represented by the surface of the sphere. We've described only a flat disk, I'm afraid — half a pancake."

"I didn't do well in geometry."

The man smiled.

"There must be a third dimension giving volume to the sphere and meaning to the dimensions of time and place. The meridian line I mentioned, representing the present moment, doesn't just float upon the surface. It also extends beneath the surface, through to the core of the sphere, giving the sphere its depth and shape. This dimension of depth represents the possible levels of understanding of the traveler at any given present moment — the levels of meaning of place and time. Her perception might be very basic and primitive, in which case her understanding of her time and place would be near the surface. Or she might possess a more complete understanding of her time and place and all its nuances, in which case her understanding would be very deep and near the core.

"Meaning is also a matter of choice, is it not? We may experience the same present reality in many different ways. Thus, although our traveler has no ability to choose her particular time — because that is determined by the rotation of the sphere — she has complete freedom to choose both her place in the present moment and its meaning and significance to her — her level of perception. In this way, she experiences reality in three dimensions from a potentially infinite number of locations along the line of the present moment, assigning to her reality a potentially infinite number of meanings corresponding to the depth of her perception."

The man was talking way over my head. I was there to celebrate becoming a presenter, not to engage in a philosophical exegesis of time, space, and perception. I scanned the crowd for Luas and Nana and a polite way out of the conversation.

"My name is Gautama," the man said, perceptively extending his left hand.

"Brek Cuttler," I said, smiling sheepishly, embarrassed at having been caught looking for an exit.

One of the faceless attendants arrived to retrieve my empty plate.

"Yes, I know who you are," Gautama said. "I hope I haven't bored you. I myself am far more interested in the smaller steps along the journey, but standing back on occasion to glimpse the whole can be useful. For instance, it explains the presence of the postulants here among us right now, and our mutual inability to see each other because of our chosen levels of perception."

"Maybe," I said, beginning to understand a little of what he was saying. "But does it explain why every presentation in the Courtroom is terminated before a defense can be presented? I assume this has been your experience as well?"

"I'm not a presenter," Gautama said. "I'm merely a sculptor . . . among other things."

"You sculpted this?" I asked, embarrassed.

"Yes, but I see it has made you uncomfortable."

"It's a little intimidating," I admitted.

"We're not comfortable making choices," Gautama replied. "We prefer others to make them for us. But choice is what makes everything run, you know. It is the energy that powers the universe. To create is simply to choose, to decide. Even the Ten Commandments are choices — ten choices each person must make at any instant in time that create who they are and who they will become, although they can be reduced to three, which is what I've tried to do here with my sphere."

"Three?"

"Yes. The first four Commandments are simply choices about the Holy One, are they not? Will we acknowledge God — or Spirit, or Truth, whatever language you wish to use — or will we worship material things and settle for the impermanent world? Will we invoke the power of God, the creative force, to harm or destroy others, or will we love them as ourselves? Will we set aside time to appreciate Creation and Truth, or will we consume all our time in pursuit of finite ends? The remaining six Commandments concern choices about others and self. Murder, theft, adultery, the way one relates to one's parents, family, and community — these reflect how one chooses to regard others. Whether one is envious, and whether one conceals the truth, are ultimately decisions about one's self."

"Interesting way of looking at it," I said.

Gautama turned toward the crowd.

"Your understanding of this, my daughter, is essential, for these are the choices that must be presented in the Courtroom. From these choices alone is the Final Judgment rendered and eternity decided. The Judge is demanding and thorough. Some might even say the Judge is unforgiving."

"But the presentations are never completed," I said. "Some might say the Judge is unjust."

"Ours is not to question such wisdom," Gautama replied. "But you might ask yourself how many times the same choices must be presented before the story is accurately told."

I considered this, and I considered Gautama. He was so very much unlike anybody else I had met in Shemaya. "Since I arrived here," I said, "I don't think I've met anybody, except my great-grandmother, who wasn't a presenter. You said you are a sculptor, among other things. What things are those?"

"I help postulants recognize themselves and their choices. That is why my sphere is located here in the train station."

We turned back to the sphere. "I still don't understand the reflections on the door," I said. "I saw two different versions of myself."

"Are not all choices based in personal desires?" Gautama replied. "And are not all desires reflections of who we are or wish to become? We could distill the three choices presented here by the three pairs of doors into one, and conclude that all things in life turn upon choices concerning Creation itself. We could distill this even further and conclude that all things turn upon Creation's choices about Creation itself. In other words, Brek, we are co-creators with God. At the highest level of reality on the sphere, at the pole from which we start and to which we will inevitably return, there is but one possible here and now. All the rest flows from it, and returns to it, in the course of Creation — in the course of making choices. We choose who we are or wish to become, but in the end we are only one thing, permanent and unchanging, no matter what choices we make. The journey around the sphere is a circle."

Tim Shelly suddenly staggered up between Gautama and me, reeking of alcohol. His eyes were glazed over and his bow tie undone.

"Hey, *great rock!*" he said, pointing to the sphere and slurring his words. Then he placed his hand on my shoulder and slid it down my back inappropriately. "Go get somebody else, Gautama," he said. "Brek's mine."

I stepped back from him, appalled.

"You seem to be enjoying the evening, my son," Gautama replied, seemingly unbothered by the remark or Tim's apparent drunken condition.

Tim grabbed me and tried to kiss me full on the lips.

"Tim, stop it!" I yelled, pushing him away. "What's gotten into you?"

"What's the matter, Brek? Too good for me?" he sneered.

"I believe it is time for you to go home, my son," Gautama said.

"Why?" Tim said, "so you can have her?" He winked at Gautama and gave him a jab in the shoulder. "I've been watching you . . . I know you older spiritual guys still got it in you."

Gautama smiled but said nothing, as if he were dealing with a misbehaving child.

"Problem is," Tim continued, "she thinks she's too good for you too. She only screws Jew boys. I happen to know that she likes them circumcised. Well, I say it's time for her to find out what a real man feels like. You wait your turn here, Gautama, and we'll see what she thinks. It won't take long." Tim lunged toward me and I screamed, but Gautama stepped in front of him and spun him around in the other direction.

"Good night, my daughter," he said to me,

leading Tim away by the arm. "Enjoy the rest of your evening."

# 27

I left the reception badly shaken. For the first time in Shemaya, I feared for my personal safety. But was there really anything to be afraid of? Can a human soul be raped — or harmed in any other way? Tim Shelly looked like a man with a man's body. I felt his hand on my back, on my body. But none of these things existed — and yet they did. And how was it possible for anti-Semitism to survive even after death? I wasn't Jewish, and I never told Tim that Bo was. How did he know, and why did it matter? None of it made sense.

There was something genuinely cold and malicious about the way Tim looked at me. What happened to the sweet guy who thought he was a waitress and camped out with his father — the guy who visited Tara with me, and sailed with me on the caravel, and worried about how his mother was taking his death? Maybe it was just the alcohol talking . . . but how can a human soul consume alcohol, let alone become intoxicated?

I walked down the long corridor of offices. A chill came over me when I reached Tim's office, but this was nothing compared to the stab of dread I felt when I saw my own name on the office door next to his, engraved on a brand-new plaque. "Brek Abigail Cuttler, Presenter."

The door was unlocked, and I went in. The office was identical to Luas's, with a small desk, two chairs, two candles on the desk, and no windows. I was not the first occupant: the two candles had been burned unevenly, their sides and brass holders clotted with polyps of wax. It was a claustrophobic little room, a confessional in a rundown cathedral. The air hung damp and heavy, laden with the sins of those who had exhaled their lives there. But it was mine. I lit the candles, closed the door, and settled in behind the desk to enjoy the privacy.

Then came a knock at the door.

Tim?

I slipped quietly around the desk and braced the guest chair against the door.

The knock came again, followed this time by a girl's voice, Asian-sounding and unfamiliar: "May I come in, please?"

"Who is it?" I said, wedging the guest chair more tightly into place with my foot.

"My name is Mi Lau. I knew your uncle Anthony. I saw you leave the reception."

"Anthony Bellini?" I said.

"Yes. May I come in?"

I pulled the guest chair away from the door and opened it. What I saw standing before me was so hideous and repulsive that I shrieked in horror and slammed the door shut again. A young girl stood in the doorway, her body burned almost beyond recognition and still smoldering, as if the flames had just been extinguished. Most of her skin was gone, exposing shattered fragments of bone and tissue seared like gristle fused to a grill. Her right eye was missing, leaving a horrible gouge in her face. Beneath the socket were two rows of broken teeth without lips, cheeks, or gums and an expanse of white jawbone somehow spared the blackening of the flames. The stench of burned flesh overpowered the hallway and, now, my office.

"Please excuse my appearance," the girl said through the door. "My death was not very pleasant. Nor, I can see, was yours."

I looked down and saw myself as Mi Lau had seen me — as I had seen myself when I arrived in Shemaya, naked with three holes in my chest and covered with blood. I opened the door again. Mi Lau and I stared at each other, sizing each other up like two monsters in a horror movie. We obviously could not communicate or even be in each other's presence if our wounds were all we could see, so we engaged in the same charade played by all the souls of Shemaya, agreeing to see in each other only the pleasant hologram reflections of life the way we wished it had been.

In this filtered and refracted light, Mi Lau suddenly became a beautiful, young teenage girl with yellow topaz skin, large brown eyes, and long, thick, dark hair. She was a child on the verge of becoming a young woman — fresh, radiant, and pure, and dressed in a pretty pink gown, making the gruesomeness of her death all the more cruel and difficult to reconcile.

"I am very sorry my appearance frightened you," she said. She spoke in the rhythmic, loose-guitar-string twang of Vietnamese, but I somehow understood her words in English, as if I were listening to a hidden interpreter.

"No, I'm the one who should apologize," I said. "I didn't expect anybody at the door and then, well . . . yes, you frightened me. Please, come in."

Mi Lau sat in the guest chair with her hands folded in her lap. I closed the door and returned to my place behind the desk.

"How do you know my uncle Anthony?" I asked. "He died before I was born."

"We met during the war," Mi Lau said, "and he is also one of my clients."

"My uncle is on trial here?" I asked. "Can I see him?"

"Yes, you can come see his trial. I present his case every day."

"The Judge ends it before you finish?"

"Yes, like the others."

"It doesn't make sense," I said. "Why bother having a trial?"

Mi Lau said nothing.

"How did you meet during the war?" I asked. "What was he like?"

"Your uncle came to my village with other American soldiers," Mi Lau said. "They were chasing the Viet Cong. The VC stayed with us. We had no choice. They were mostly just young boys. They left us alone and didn't harm us.

"When the Americans came, there were gunshots, and my family hid in a tunnel beneath our hut. Always my mother would go into the tunnel first, then my sister, me, and my father last. But the fighting caught us by surprise, and this time I was last. The tunnel was narrow, and we had to crawl on our stomachs. We could hear the machine guns and the Americans shouting, and the VC boys screaming. My sister and I covered our ears and trembled like frightened rabbits."

"It must have been horrible," I said.

"Yes. But the fighting did not last long. Soon all became quiet until a powerful explosion shook the ground. Dirt fell into my hair, and I was afraid the tunnel might collapse. My father said the American soldiers were blowing up the tunnels in our village and we must get out quickly. I crawled toward the entrance, and that is when I saw your uncle. He was kneeling over the hole, holding a grenade in his hand. I remember it clearly. A crucifix with the right arm broken off dangled from his neck. I remember thinking it looked like a small bird with a broken wing. I smiled up at him. I was so naive, I thought that Americans were there to help us, that they were our friends. But he didn't smile back. He looked at me with terrible, hateful eyes, and then he pulled the pin and dropped the grenade into the hole.

" 'No! No!' I screamed. 'We're down here!' The grenade rolled between my legs. It felt cold and smooth, like a river stone. I saw him turn his head and cover his ears. And then it exploded."

Mi Lau spoke without anger or emotion, as if she were describing nothing more than planting rice in a field. I lowered my head, too ashamed and distraught to look at her. "I'm so sorry," I said. "I didn't know."

"Thank you," Mi Lau said. "I know all about your family from presenting him. They seem like such nice people. It is funny. Your uncle was convinced you would be a boy before you were born, but he was so happy when he found out you were a girl."

"I was told he died a hero."

"Maybe he did," Mi Lau said, "but a hero is something that lives in other people's minds. After blowing up all the tunnels in our village, he went off with some of the other soldiers to smoke marijuana. He said to them with a laugh: 'The best thing about blowing up tunnels full of gooks in the morning is that they're already in their graves and you can spend the rest of the afternoon smoking dope.' Then an hour later, he wandered off by himself and shot himself in the head. That was heroic maybe, to take his own life so he could no longer take the lives of others."

It took me a long time to absorb what she had said.

"How can you represent him if he killed you and your family?" I asked. "I'm sorry about what he did, but how can he get a fair trial? I mean, naturally you would want him to be convicted — and maybe he should be. That's probably why he's still here."

Mi Lau's eyes narrowed and she straightened herself indignantly. "I present Anthony Bellini's life exactly as he lived it," she said. "I cannot change what he did, and I do not bias the presentation in any way. Luas monitors us closely and disciplines any presenter who attempts to influence the result."

"But how can you even face him after what he did to you?"

"He can't hurt me again," Mi Lau said. "And I feel better knowing justice is being done. All is confessed in the Courtroom . . . there are no lies. Some say Shemaya is where Jesus stayed for three days after his death, before ascending into heaven, presenting all the souls who have ever lived. I believe Shemaya is where the final battle is fought between good and evil. Evil must not be permitted to win. It must not be allowed to hide or disguise itself; it must be rooted out, and destroyed, and all those who perpetrate evil must be punished."

Mi Lau stood, and suddenly she was

transformed back into the girl whose body had been mutilated and blown apart by my uncle's grenade. "I must go now," she said. "Welcome to Shemaya. You will be serving God here. You will be serving justice."

# 28

I woke the next morning to the nutty-sweet aroma of Irish porridge. It was a delicious, familiar scent that I hadn't smelled since Grandma Cuttler made it for my grandfather and me on the farm. I went downstairs and found Nana Bellini in the kitchen, already dressed for the day. She gave me a kiss on the forehead and placed a steaming bowl of porridge before me at the kitchen table.

"You'll need your strength today," she said.

There was something different about her. Her eyes seemed distant and moist, almost melancholy. I hadn't seen her this way before.

"Thanks," I said, delighted with the breakfast. "Are you okay?"

"Yes," she said. "It's just that the time has come for me to go, and I'm sad we'll be apart."

"Go? What do you mean, go? Go where?"

"Just go, child, go on. You came here wounded and frightened, and there's still some pain and fear left in you, but it no longer controls you. You've recovered from the shock of death. That's why I was here, to help you. You're a presenter now. You need space to experience, to spread out your thoughts and look them over — space to study and understand. The next steps you take must be your own. You're ready, and I'm proud of you. We're all proud of you. You give us hope."

I was terrified. "Take me with you," I begged. "I don't want to be a presenter. There's no justice here. Uncle Anthony, Amina Rabun, Toby Bowles . . . they're all convicted before their presenters even enter the Courtroom. The same trials are held every day, and the same verdicts are issued. It's . . . it's hell, not heaven."

Nana went to the counter to get some coffee. "Maybe you were brought here to change all that. Maybe God needs you to fix it."

"But God created it, and God is the judge. He's the one who stops the trials before a defense can be made. Only He can fix it."

"That's not God's way," Nana said. "We all have free choice, Brek. You have a choice about the kind of presenter you want to be, just as you had a choice about the kind of person you wanted to be."

"I don't want to be a presenter at all."

Nana sat down next to me. "That choice was already made, child. You chose to come here. The question is not whether you will be a presenter, but what kind of presenter you will be. That is something you must decide for yourself. You'll feel differently after you meet your first client. The postulants need you, Brek. You mustn't abandon them."

"But you're abandoning me."

"That's not true. I've done all I can. The rest is up to you."

I didn't feel ready. I knew I was rooted in solid ground, that I had been planted there by her, this remarkable woman who had nursed me when I passed through my mother's womb, and who nursed me again when I passed through the womb of life.

"Where will you go?" I asked. "Will I be able to see you?"

"Oh, I couldn't describe it to you in a way you'd understand," Nana said. "What I can tell you, though, is that, like all places, I'm going to a place I choose and that I help to create. I don't know where it is, or what it will be like, but I do know that it is a thought to which I go — a thought I've been thinking that, like all thoughts cultivated and cared for, becomes manifest in a tiny corner of the universe so that it may be experienced. Creation transcends every-thing, child. A million-billion acts of choice become a million-billion acts of creation."

"But I already lost you once, Nana," I said. "I can't bear losing you again."

*"Shhhh,* child, *shhhh,"* she whispered. And then she gave me what I needed most — one last, brief, wonderful moment of child-hood. She held me close and pressed my face against the wrinkled skin of her cheek. She allowed me to hear the strong pumping of her heart and smell the sweet fragrance of her skin. In her embrace I felt safe again. And then she said, "Haven't you learned, child? Don't you see? Visit my garden when you have doubts. Learn from the plants that live and die there and yet live again. And remember, oh child, always remember that I was here to greet you when you thought I had gone so long, long ago. You didn't lose Bo and Sarah, Brek. And you will never lose me. Love can never be destroyed."

# 29

When Nana left Shemaya, so did I. I wanted nothing to do with the sordid proceedings of the Courtroom. I would have rather spent eternity alone than participate in them.

Although Tim Shelly had turned on me, he had done me a great favor by showing me that I had the power to go anywhere, anytime, by simply thinking about it. So, I decided to do just that, embarking upon my own Grand Tour of the earth, seeing and doing things no person had ever done, or could ever do, in a single lifetime. I needed a vacation, an escape from death.

I started off at a leisurely pace, recreating and sunbathing on some of the most exclusive beaches in the world: Barbados, the French Riviera, the Greek Islands, Tahiti, Dubai, and Rio de Janeiro. I lived the lifestyle of the rich and famous, sleeping in the most exclusive villas and resorts, sailing aboard the most luxurious yachts, flying on private helicopters and jets, arriving in the most expensive limousines, dining at the finest restaurants, drinking the most expensive champagnes, shopping at the most exquisite jewelers and boutiques, and winning — and losing — millions of dollars at the most exclusive casinos. It was a dream life, a heaven. I scuba dived the coral reefs of the Galápagos, climbed the highest mountains of every continent, trekked across the Sahara, sailed solo around the world, paddled a canoe the entire length of both the Amazon and the Nile, walked the Great Wall of China, visited the North and South Poles, and went on safari across the game lands of Africa.

All this was great fun — for a while. But I was alone everywhere I went — on the beaches, in the villas, on the planes, in the casinos. I had nobody to share my good fortune with or even to envy me from afar. I imagined that this must be how God felt before creating humanity. Could there be any greater sorrow in all the universe than having all of *this* and no one to share it with? As I traveled alone from one wonder of the world to another, from ocean to desert to mountain, I came to understand why God would have been willing to risk everything — even rejection, suffering, and war, as Luas had said — for the joy of hearing just one breathless human being say, "Oh *my God . . .* look at that!"

Yes, by taking this journey I had been able to avoid Tim Shelly, Mi Lau, Luas, Elymas, and what I considered to be the tragedy and injustice of the Courtroom, but I needed to share my experience of the afterlife as much as I had needed to share my experience of life itself. Like God, perhaps, I grew increasingly desperate for an *other,* a companion in my paradise.

In this way, I came slowly to understand why the serpent had told Eve that it is the risk of evil that makes life rich and the experience of contentment and joy even possible. I had returned, in a way, to the Garden of Eden and found it to be as wanting as Eve had found it; for in paradise, there is only perfection. Without its opposite, perfection cannot be understood or experienced, just as the light from a candle at the center of the sun cannot be understood or experienced until it is removed from the sun and placed into the darkness.

Strangely, at the end of my tour of all the riches of the earth, I was ready, again, to be cast out of paradise. Jesus was said to have experienced a similar moment after the devil offered him all the kingdoms of the world but Jesus turned them down, accepting the risk of suffering and death for the sake of experiencing love.

And so, as Gautama had said I would, I returned to the place of my journey's beginning, seeing it again for the first time. I returned ready now for my first client. But secretly I was hoping, as I had hoped every day since I arrived in Shemaya, that this would be the day I would be told it had all been a very strange and terrifying dream. And that it was time to wake up.

# 30

Luas didn't answer when I knocked on his office door. Instead, the being from the Courtroom appeared in the hallway to inform me that the High Jurisconsult was occupied and would see me after I had met with my first client. I was to go to my office and wait.

I did as I was told, and soon the being from the Courtroom arrived with a postulant, closing the door behind on the way out and leaving us alone in the office. I had decided beforehand to keep my back to the postulant and face the wall behind my desk. I wanted to postpone the exploration of my client's past and attempt first to communicate under present conditions, one fellow soul to another lost from a common home and left to a common fate. I would not lightly rob my clients of their memories, or demand that they wait in the other room while I negotiated eternity with their Creator. They would be given the opportunity to participate in their own defense, to explain on their own terms what had happened during their lives and why.

So there we sat for a moment, my first ecclesiastical client and I, together on the precipice of eternity.

"Are you afraid?" I asked.

"Yes," a male voice responded hesitantly.

"I understand," I said. "I will do everything I can to help you."

But I was afraid too. Every lawyer has doubts, and what was at stake in the Courtroom of Shemaya was far greater than in any courtroom on earth.

*How can I bear another's burdens when I cannot even bear my own? How dare I attempt to reconcile another's accounts when my own debts remain unpaid?*

"I don't think anybody can help me," he said. "I have done a terrible thing."

His voice was barely audible, resigned, without hope. I could not allow such despair to go unanswered, no matter what demons haunted me and no matter what he had done. Not only did his plea stir my compassion, but it made plain for me, as if there all along, that this was the call I had prepared my entire life to answer. This was the reason I had been chosen to defend souls at the

Final Judgment. It seemed at that moment as though the mystery of my own life, and afterlife, had been revealed unexpectedly in the suffering of another soul. I would devote myself to rescuing my clients from the pit of desolation and injustice. I would redeem them before the throne of God.

With the joy of this revelation, I could no longer keep my back toward the soul across from me. I yearned to see his face in the light of truth, and to learn everything I could about his life, both the good and the bad. I would bless, not judge, and do everything in my power to guarantee him every benefit and annihilate every doubt. I would speak out in the Courtroom with the partisan voice of an advocate and risk even my own punishment to win justice. I would never allow to happen to this soul what had happened to Toby Bowles, Amina Rabun, and my uncle Anthony.

These were the promises I made to myself when I turned to face my client — promises that, perhaps, I had made years ago, as a young girl, when a conveyor chain disfigured my body and reconfigured my life. I knew now that I had been brought to Shemaya to fulfill those sacred vows and, perhaps, to secure my own redemption.

But as I turned to greet this beautiful,

helpless soul upon whom I would lavish my devotion, my love, my eternity, I was met by a very different kind of face. It was the wicked face of a killer, not the innocent face of a victim.

*No . . . no, not him. Please . . . please, dear God, not him!*

But it was too late.

The man who murdered me had died and gone to Shemaya.

His soul now roamed inside me. And I held his fate in my hands.

■ ■ ■ ■

# PART IV

■ ■ ■ ■

## 31

Otto Rabun Bowles understood none of his tumultuous family history as he sat dazed on the sideline during halftime of the football game after being hit viciously for two quarters by children nearly twice his size. He pleaded with his father not to be sent back into the game. But his father, Tad Bowles, responded as his own father had responded to him as a boy, by belittling Ott for acting like a baby and ordering him out onto the field.

This is when Toby Bowles, Ott's grandfather, made his surprise appearance. Toby had been estranged from Tad for more than a decade. As a result, Ott had never seen him, and never would see him again. The old man and former perpetrator of such callousness climbed down from the bleachers to intervene on his grandson's behalf by asking Tad to give the boy a break. Ott was all bruises and wonderment at this fallen angel about whom he had heard such terrible things, but who bore such a remarkable resemblance to his own father. Toby suddenly seemed like his only friend in the world, and Ott loved him on contact.

But Tad became enraged. How dare his father show up uninvited, and how dare he criticize him? Harsh words were exchanged between the two men — words that should have been spoken fifteen years earlier when there was context in which to understand them and love left to heal them, but that landed now like hammers on the firing pins of revolvers. When Tad could bear no more and restrain himself no longer, he shoved the old man — hard enough to cause him to lose his balance and fall to the ground in front of Ott and the other spectators.

Ott's eyes narrowed into slits of hatred for his father. Stunned and embarrassed, Toby used the bleachers to support himself, got up, and walked away, never to be seen by Ott again. Four years later, Tad's mother, Claire, called to report that Toby had died of a heart attack. The opportunity for Ott to forge a bond with his paternal grandfather had come and gone.

And so it was that the lifetime of memories contained within the soul of the man who murdered me became a sort of Rosetta stone, enabling me slowly, painstakingly, to piece together the connections between his life, my life, and the lives of the souls I had met in Shemaya — as Nana had told me I must if I was ever to escape this place. Bizarrely, I needed Ott Bowles's memories to guide me through the afterlife, because I had been unwilling since arriving in Shemaya to access my own memories about my death, and Sarah's. And because even if I had remembered everything, I could not have possibly known how deeply interconnected my life had been to so many different people.

I was stunned to learn that Toby Bowles, the first soul I had seen tried in Shemaya, a man whom I had never met during my life, was responsible not only for the existence of my husband and, ultimately, my daughter — by saving my mother-in-law's life in Kamenz — but also for the existence of my own murderer — by being Ott Bowles's grandfather. Yet this was merely the first of many astonishing connections I discovered between my life and the life of Ott Bowles — connections that had brought us fatefully together in life and, now, death.

Ott Bowles's parents met in a nightclub in New Jersey where Ott's mother, Barratte

Rabun, age thirty-eight and still quite attractive, served drinks. Many years later, Barratte explained to her son that something in his father's sad brown eyes and embarrassed smile made her want to hold and protect him. At twenty-six years of age, he vaguely reminded her of her older brother, who had been executed by Russian soldiers in Kamenz. He seemed different from the other young men at the bar who, having finally been given a voice by the alcohol they consumed, had nothing to say but "Feed me," "Where's the bathroom?" and "Sleep with me."

Even so, Barratte's attraction to Tad Bowles began to fade when she became pregnant with Ott. In truth, until the morning she delivered Ott, she had viewed all men, including Tad, only as game to be hunted and collected, stalking them like a poacher and mounting their dumb, wondering heads on the paneled walls of her memory. After Ott's birth, men in general, and Tad in particular, were not worth even this to her. She had harvested what little the male of the species offered the world — that precious fertilizer they squandered so recklessly. Now young Ott became her finest trophy, her beginning and her end. Each contraction of her womb breathed new life into her long-dead family, whose existence depended upon her sacred labor. Not for one day during Ott's childhood would she allow him to forget that the survival of the Rabuns of Kamenz depended upon *him*. He was the irreplaceable link to all those who had come before, and to all those who would come after.

Ott readily accepted this responsibility, but his father, in no way a Rabun, was never let in on the important secret. Until the lawsuit Bill Gwynne and I filed against Amina and Barratte Rabun on behalf of my mother-in-law, Katerine Schrieberg-Wolfson. The startling revelations in the complaint about the Rabuns of Kamenz came as a complete shock to Tad Bowles. Barratte had told him only that most of the members of her family were killed during the war, that she inherited a modest sum, and that a cousin in Buffalo with whom she no longer had a relationship had helped her escape from Germany before the Soviets closed the Iron Curtain. That Barratte's father and uncle had been wealthy, that they had accumulated this wealth from the death camps and the extortion of Jews, that Barratte had been raped by Soviet soldiers and her family murdered, and that she had hidden such a history from him — all this left

Tad feeling both frightened and betrayed.

Yet the scare also had the effect of soothing Tad's wounded ego, for Barratte's lack of emotion in the marriage could now be explained by reasons other than his own inadequacies. He had married a fraud, and perhaps much worse, so it was he who pressed for a divorce even as he purchased his fourth new automobile in as many years with tainted Rabun money. Of course, Barratte would have divorced Tad eventually, just as Amina had divorced George Meinert. When Tad hinted that he might seek custody of Ott, however, she threatened to destroy him. He knew she could and agreed to give her custody. One week after Ott's twelfth birthday, Barratte packed their things and moved from their home beside Tad's insurance office in New Jersey to Amina's small mansion in Buffalo to face the allegations of the lawsuit and restore her family's name.

The lawsuit against Amina and Barratte Rabun was not initiated lightly by my mother-in-law. Out of profound gratitude for the risks that Amina had taken to protect her family during the war, Katerine Schrieberg-Wolfson had decided not to follow through on the threat made by her former lawyer, Robert Goldman, to sue Amina and Barratte at the time of Ott's birth, in 1974. But twelve years later, I, as a freshly minted lawyer married to Katerine's only son, Bo — who was a rightful heir to the Schrieberg fortune — convinced her to reconsider.

I argued that the Rabuns not only had stolen Katerine and her brothers' inheritance — which perhaps could be overlooked, because Amina had saved them from certain death — but also had stolen the inheritance of their children and grandchildren. Justice could not so easily overlook this wrong. These future generations were entitled to a share of the estate created by their ancestors — just as future generations of Rabuns were entitled to a share of the estate created by their ancestors.

I also pointed out to Katerine that we would not be harming Amina financially by seeking to recover the value of these assets. Amina was wealthy in her own right as an heiress to the Rabun fortune and as a successful newspaper publisher. Reparations for the Schrieberg assets would have little, if any, effect upon her lifestyle, which had been lavish in comparison with the way Katerine had been forced to live without a similar inheritance. And I assured her repeatedly that we would be suing Amina and Barratte Rabun in name only. It was Otto Rabun, Amina's uncle, who as a member of the Nazi SS had taken the Schrieberg's assets. We would carefully draft our complaint to identify him as the wrongdoer, not his niece or daughter. After further prodding and encouragement by Bo — to whom the prospect of receiving a sizable inheritance had increasing appeal — Katerine finally relented.

Bill Gwynne and I promptly initiated the lawsuit, naming both Amina and Barratte as defendants. Bill was a master, and I watched in awe, helping him behind the scenes. From a torrent of Hague Convention subpoenas, we obtained from German archives and private files copies of contracts signed by Amina's father for the construction of the crematoria at Auschwitz and Majdanek. Equally damning, we obtained a copy of a patent issued in 1941 to Amina's father for an improved crematorium design, first installed at Auschwitz, that utilized better airflow management, ash-removal conveyors, and new refractory materials to elevate temperatures and increase capacity. In the accompanying technical drawings, Amina recognized the shape of the brick sandbox built by her father for her and Helmut. This vulgar resemblance, and the photographs of thousands of cadavers in the camps, haunted Amina's dreams the rest of her life.

Although these documents bore no direct legal relevance to our claim for recoupment of the value of the Schriebergs' theaters and home, they made sensational copy for the press, immediately turning the case in our favor. We had carefully focused our allegations upon Otto Rabun as promised, but Amina and Barratte Rabun, as the living children of Nazis, became the target of public derision and outrage. Soon the publisher of the award-winning *Cheektowaga Register* was being tried in the media as a war criminal — and Jewish groups were calling for a boycott of her bloodstained newspaper and the bloodstained books of Bette Press.

Katerine was horrified, and furious with Bill and me for allowing this to happen. But there was no way to put the genie back in the bottle, and Bill was unapologetic. Things happen in the heat of battle, he explained, and there is sometimes collateral damage. Amina and Barratte could have at any time spared themselves public embarrassment by simply doing the right thing and offering to settle the case years ago when Mr. Goldman wrote his letter inviting a negotiated resolution. We had done everything we could to avoid embarrassing them.

The public attacks generated by the lawsuit stung Amina and Barratte deeply, but they also had the effect of drawing the cousins together after years of separation. The two women had been through far worse together during the war, and in facing this new common threat they found again the mutual love and trust for each other that had sustained them during those terrible days, weeks, and months after Kamenz. Plus, now there was Barratte's twelve-year-old son, Ott, to consider. Amina's refusal to bear children meant that he was the only hope for a future generation of Rabuns. As a sign of reconciliation, Barratte asked Amina to be Ott's godmother. She joyfully accepted, becoming Ott's Nonna Amina.

With the survival of the family at stake, the cousins held each other close and faced the storm. In interviews and editorials, they explained how Amina had saved the Schriebergs at great personal risk; how the purchase of the theaters had been for fair value at the time, giving the Schriebergs the money they desperately needed to survive; and how just a few hundred yards from where the Schriebergs lived under her protection, the Soviets raped Amina, Barratte, and Bette and murdered their family. But coming from the mouths of the accused, these stories did little to change public opinion. Amina and Barratte Rabun were tried and convicted not for wrongfully withholding the Schriebergs' money, about which no one in the public seemed concerned, but, symbolically, for perpetrating the Holocaust itself.

The final devastating blow to Amina and Barratte Rabun, however, did not come directly from the lawsuit filed by Bill Gwynne and me. It came instead from Amina's once loyal secretary, Alice Guiniere. Seeing her demanding employer now as a monster who needed to be stopped, Alice recounted to the local U.S. attorney a mysterious visit to her employer's office one day by a Mr. Gerry Hanson. Alice also produced the discarded U.S. passport bearing Mr. Hanson's daughter's new identity with the incorrect birth date, and galley proofs of four passports bearing his, his wife's, and his other children's new identities, collected from a waste bin in the print shop of Bette Press. She explained that she had retained these documents because something didn't seem right at the time.

An investigation was quickly launched and a grand jury handed down indictments.

Standing before a press conference, the U.S. attorney revealed Gerry Hanson's true identity as Gerhard Haber, an accused war criminal and international fugitive, and announced that Amina Rabun and Albrecht Bosch were being charged with obstruction of justice, harboring fugitives, and forging official documents, for which they each could be sentenced to thirty years imprisonment.

With all energies turned to the criminal defense, Amina's lawyer telephoned Bill Gwynne with an offer to settle the civil litigation. In light of everything that had befallen Amina, and everything that had happened in Kamenz, Katerine Schrieberg-Wolfson instructed us to accept the offer immediately and end the litigation — for forty percent of our original demand.

In Amina's final editorial as publisher of *The Cheektowaga Register* — a position from which she resigned on the day she was arrested — Amina pointed out that for assisting the Schriebergs in Germany in much the same manner that she had assisted the Habers in the United States, she could have been shot. "No good deed ever goes unpunished," the editorial concluded, "but whether a deed is good or bad appears to turn not on the nature or quality of the deed itself but rather the amount of hatred that exists for those who are its intended beneficiary."

The role of Amina Rabun as godmother had suited Ott well. She became the fairy godmother who could afford Ott the luxury to be who he wanted to be — and to love him without condition and guide him gently along the path of his dreams.

Nonna Amina encouraged Ott but never insisted. When he showed no interest in playing baseball, football, or hockey (a heresy in a city just one bridge-length from the Canadian border), she did not pressure or prod. When Ott showed an aptitude for music, Nonna Amina purchased for him a piano and retained the services of a private instructor. When he showed a fascination with birds, she erected for him a small aviary behind the garage of her house. Although he was a bit old for it, she read to him nightly, in German and English, and took him to museums, aquariums, amusement parks, and movies. She also brought him to her office at the newspaper on Saturday mornings, as her own father had done in Dresden. There, her friend Albrecht Bosch — who had moved out of the mansion after taking a new male lover — showed

Ott how to print books and cards, and how being "different" need not necessarily mean being lonely and unhappy.

Amina and Ott thus became best friends, and she shielded him from his mother's excesses. Consumed by the past and what might have been, Barratte insisted that Rabun men should make their living excavating dirt and pouring concrete, and have their fun hitting each other on fields and killing animals in the woods. Ott's inability to live up to that standard was a constant source of disappointment to her.

The criminal indictment of Nonna Amina exploded inside Ott's life like a bomb. In an instant, he lost his dearest companion and was forced to endure his family's humiliation alone in a school where, as in all schools, mercy is in short supply. What little compassion that remained at home in Barratte was depleted quickly by the ordeal of defending her cousin and operating the newspaper in her stead. Ott's only other potential source of support, his father, had remarried and was already expecting another child with his new wife. The time between visits to New Jersey grew longer and longer until there was nothing left but time.

Ott turned in on himself then, to a mostly

silent world narrowed to manageable proportions and insulated from causes, effects, and accusations. He emerged from this place only as necessary, to respond to his mother when her threats became real, to scribble answers to exam questions that demonstrated a grasp of concepts and numbers that went well beyond that of his classmates, to correspond weekly with Nonna Amina and visit her once each month at a prison for women near Rochester.

But imprisonment turned Nonna Amina into a different woman from the doting godmother whom Ott had adored. Devastated by the betrayals of Katerine Schrieberg, Alice Guiniere, and nearly everybody else in her life; disgraced by her father's Nazi past; despised by the public; scorned, jailed, and nearly bankrupted, Amina Rabun became bitter and morose, and began displaying the symptoms of clinical depression.

A small ray of hope for Amina, Barratte, and Ott appeared when the U.S. attorney offered Amina a plea bargain that would set her free in three years instead of thirty — on the weekend of her sixty-seventh birthday, to be exact. In exchange, she would be required to disclose everything she knew about the organization used by former Nazis to escape capture. This would mean handing over her close friend and advisor Hanz Stössel to the Israeli Nazi hunters.

The prospect of performing such an act of treachery appalled Amina. It was not that she believed Nazis were guiltless or deserving of special protection. Rather, Amina held the more radical belief that all people deserved compassion and somebody must start somewhere. For the sake of that naive idea, she had risked her life to help a Jewish family when they were being persecuted and, later, a Nazi family when their turn had come. Had she shown favoritism? But Amina Rabun had suffered a great deal in her life, far more than most. Spending the rest of her life in a prison was too much to ask, even to protect a dear friend to whom she owed everything. Ott was growing up quickly, and she wanted to enjoy time with him. She wanted to put her past behind her once and for all. She had paid enough of a price to protect others. It was time to protect herself. And so she accepted the plea bargain.

On the basis of Amina's grand jury testimony, Hanz Stössel was arrested while on vacation in London and extradited to Israel. He lost his home, his family, his law practice, and his fortune. He died of pneumonia in an Israeli jail cell less than a year later.

Although Hanz Stössel preceded Amina Rabun in death, he bided his time in Shemaya. When Amina finally died, Hanz Stössel was chosen to present her soul at the Final Judgment.

I had watched the trial of Amina Rabun with righteous indignation, incensed by the obvious conflict of interest and the fact that Hanz Stössel had presented only half of her case. But my reservations about the unfairness of the trials in Shemaya faded when I was assigned to represent the soul of Ott Bowles.

# 32

Among the many things I learned from rummaging around in my murderer's memories was that it was the perceived injustice of Nonna Amina's imprisonment that first caused him to embrace his family heritage. Strangely, surprisingly, I felt a momentary touch of empathy for him as I relived these moments of his life.

Ott Bowles's letters to Nonna Amina in the penitentiary quickly became interviews for the story of the redemption of the Rabuns of Kamenz that he was writing in his mind. He begged her to recount in the smallest detail the lives of their fallen family, beginning with Joseph Rabun, the patriarch and founder of the company that bore his name and that had been a source of such pride and, now, disgrace. Amina resisted Ott's inquiries at first, finding the memories too painful to explore. But Ott was persistent, and gradually Amina opened up, discovering that writing about her past was an effective therapy for the deep depression into which she had fallen.

Barratte, by contrast, was overjoyed by her son's sudden insatiable curiosity about his heritage, deeming it the first step in fulfilling his destiny to become the savior of the Rabuns. So enthusiastic was she, in fact, and so determined to encourage and assist him in any way, that for Ott's sixteenth birthday she arranged a ten-day trip to Germany, coinciding with the reunification of the country after the collapse of communist rule and thus allowing them the luxury of freely visiting Kamenz, Dresden, and Berlin.

They began their tour by paying their respects at the poorly maintained grave sites of the Rabuns in the churchyard outside Kamenz. Here they found Ott's grandmother, great-grandfather, aunt, and uncles who had been murdered by the Soviet soldiers, and here they stood in awe before the oversized monument to little Helmut Rabun, made from the mangled girders of his school destroyed by the Allies' bomb.

As heartrending as this visit was for Ott and his mother, it paled in comparison to the sheer agony, and terror, that overwhelmed Barratte when they reached the ruins of the once grand estate where the Rabuns had lived — and where such unspeakable atrocities had occurred. The anguish of his mother deeply affected Ott. He vowed at that moment to right the wrongs of the past and restore the dignity and glory of the Rabuns, for the first time openly accepting his mother's mission for him as his own.

Ott returned home from this excursion a different young man, having discovered the world to which he believed he truly belonged. Unfortunately, most of this world existed only in the past. The silent world into which Ott withdrew himself began filling with voices: the pleas of impoverished German workers after the humiliation of World War I in the 1920s, the empty hypotheses of German intellectuals and the broken promises of German politicians in the 1930s, the strategic decisions of field marshals and the brutal commands of concentration camp guards in the 1940s. While Ott's classmates raced home from school to watch television or go out to movies, Ott raced to the library to read more about the history of the German people. Like a man starved for food, he gobbled down Germanic texts, histories, biographies, and novels.

When written words alone were not enough to locate him in the world for which he longed, he began filling his bedroom with its objects: silvery family photographs from Kamenz, a brick from the sandbox built for Amina and Helmut by their father, brittle yellowed papers from the business records of Jos. A. Rabun & Sons. Soon the collection expanded to include memorabilia from the gigantic days of the Third Reich — a red flag with its mighty slashing crosses, maps of Europe depicting what was and what might have been, a highly coveted Hitler Youth armband and cap. When Ott's room overflowed with these and similar items, he freed the birds and enclosed the aviary, converting it into a small museum and shrine. Instead of going to libraries, he started attending gun shows, where word of a young, well-heeled collector interested in authentic German military gear and weaponry spread rapidly. Soon brokers and dealers were offering their wares, and Ott was arming a small platoon of Aryan mannequins with German bayonets, pistols, rifles, and even some disabled German submachine guns and grenades — all war booty brought home by American troops and sold to the highest bidder.

Barratte, driven by her own demons, had

no possibility of distinguishing family pride from what was becoming, for her son, a dangerous romantic fanaticism. She happily endowed Ott's hobby, and with it the revival of her early childhood, using the dwindling but still considerable resources of the Rabun family fortune. She also became an active participant with Ott, repairing torn military uniforms, taking Ott to World War II conventions and shows, purchasing rare items as gifts for him, and assuring gun dealers that his purchases were made with her complete consent and fully backed by her credit. Amina, also, to whom Ott presented the entire collection as a welcome-home gift upon her release from prison, could find nothing wrong with her godson's passion. "How many thousands of boys are fascinated with such things?" she reasoned. "And besides, was it not time to embrace the past and stop running from it?"

Ott's collection of German war memorabilia, and the notoriety of Amina Rabun, gave him a certain celebrity status as his high school graduation approached. With Amina's encouragement, he entertained occasional visitors to the mansion — normally just curious teens, but sometimes serious collectors and even museum curators looking to expand their collections. By means of these interactions, and with Nonna Amina's return, Ott emerged slowly from the fantasy world into which he had withdrawn.

It was during one of these encounters at the mansion that he met Tim Shelly — a stocky brute a year older than Ott with thin lips, pale blue eyes, and a wire brush of dark hair cut close to his scalp. Tim arrived at the mansion one afternoon with his father, Brian, who resembled his son in nearly every detail except age. They explained that they were passing through New York on their way home to their mushroom farm in Pennsylvania from a hunting trip in Canada. They had heard about Ott's collection and wanted to see it. They were willing to pay for admission.

Ott was apprehensive. Tim looked like the kind of kid who would have knocked him to the ground and kicked him in the side for fun. He tried to think of a quick excuse to say no and send them on their way, but his mind went blank and he reluctantly led them around back to the aviary. He soon learned he had nothing to worry about.

When Brian and Tim Shelly entered the gallery and saw the first display — a Nazi SS officer in full dress uniform — they became immediately solemn and reverential, as though they were entering the sanctuary of a church. Ott realized they were as fascinated with Nazi memorabilia as he was. With eyes wide and mouths agape, father and son pointed in fascination and whispered their amazement as Ott explained each item's significance and how it had been acquired.

Ott rewarded these gestures of respect by allowing Brian Shelly to handle his most prized possession — a Luger pistol bearing the initials "H.H." that was said to have been taken from Heinrich Himmler when he was captured by British troops. Brian bowed his head and cupped the gun in his large hands, like a supplicant receiving the holy sacrament. Then he said something completely unexpected: "I just want you to know, Ott, that we think what they did to your godmother Amina was a crime."

Ott's heart leaped. It was the first time a stranger had expressed any sympathy for what had happened.

"Lies," Brian said, operating the smooth action of the handgun with an expert flick of his wrist. "And it starts with the biggest lie of all . . . the lie of the Holocaust."

Brian pointed the pistol at his son and ordered him to raise his hands. Tim responded by quickly knocking the gun upward and in one powerful motion yanking it from his father's hand, reversing the weapon on him. Not to be outdone, Brian responded with equal speed and force by grabbing Tim's wrist, twisting it behind his back and freeing the gun, then placing Tim in a choke hold with the gun pressing against his temple. Ott was amazed, and amused.

"Okay," Tim gasped. "You win . . . this time."

Brian squeezed the trigger. The hammer hit the firing pin with a hollow click.

"No mercy," he scolded his son. "You should've finished me off when you had the chance. You hesitated. How many times have I told you?" He gave Tim a violent jerk that made him gag, then released him and smiled at Ott. "There were never any death camps," he said. "The Jews made it up to take control of Palestine, and they've been using it ever since to take control of the world. We're under attack and we don't even know it. If we don't wake up and do something about it, it'll be us in the Jews' death camps."

Ott could hardly believe his ears. His dream had been to exonerate his family by proving that Friedrich and Otto Rabun hadn't knowingly participated in the gassings, but here was Brian Shelly claiming that the gassings had never even taken place!

"How do you know the Holocaust was a lie?" Ott asked, fearful the answer wouldn't be convincing.

"A friend of mine has been working on a documentary about it. He says there's no evidence of any gas chambers. It was all a fraud created by the Jews to justify the State of Israel, and the Allies and Russians used it to demoralize and pacify the German people after the war. When the documentary is finished, he's going to expose the Jews for the liars they are."

Ott invited Brian and Tim to stay and have a German beer with him and tell him more about the documentary. They accepted the invitation, but Ott ended up doing most of the talking, thoroughly enjoying himself recounting for Brian and Tim how Jos. A. Rabun & Sons had built Dresden and, embellishing here and there, how his grandfather and great-uncle had helped Hitler build the Third Reich.

Brian and Tim hung on Ott's every word. They said they had never been so close to a genuine Nazi family. In their excitement, they even asked Ott to speak in the fierce syllables of German to make the conversation more authentic. As the beer flowed, Ott was more than happy to show off his skills, engaging in outright fabrication to impress his guests, saying: *"Mein Großvater, Otto Rabun, war Mitglied der SS und kannte Hitler gut. Er beriet mit Hitler auf Operationen in Osteuropa und empfing persönlich das Eiserne Kreuz von dem Führer."* And then back in English: "My grandfather, Otto Rabun, was a member of the SS and knew Hitler well. He consulted with Hitler on operations in eastern Europe and personally received the Iron Cross from the Führer."

This all greatly impressed Brian and Tim. They, in turn, revealed to Ott that they belonged to a secret, exclusive group in the United States that considered people like the Rabuns to be heroes and martyrs. A fellow like Ott, they told him, with Aryan breeding and blood, might be just the type of person who could become an important member of this group, a leader even.

Ott was flattered and astonished. No one had ever spoken to him like this before. Their words reached down to soothe all the injuries and injustices of his life. In the warmth of Brian and Tim Shelly's wide embrace, Ott opened his heart to receive and be received.

It was a glorious evening for Otto Rabun Bowles, one he would long remember. When Amina came down to say it was time to close up the house for the night, Brian and Tim greeted her like royalty and begged her to pose with them for pictures. Being in her bedclothes, Amina refused.

Walking them out to their car, Ott said to Brian, "You've got to tell me more about this group you keep talking about. The people who are going to fight back. How can I join?"

Brian extended his hand. "We're called Die Elf," he said. "And you just did."

# 33

At 12:01 a.m., two guards lace a foul-smelling leather mask around No. 44371's head and face. It is almost a comfort, this mask, because it holds, like a memory, the final impressions and breaths of other men whose names have become numbers, and, in this way, whispers to the next man to wear it that he is not alone. No. 44371 knows what to expect. In fact, he knows just about everything there is to know about the art of judicial electrocutions. More, possibly, than the executioner himself.

No. 44371 knows, for example, that the idea of electrocuting criminals originated in the city where he himself once lived — Buffalo, New York — from the creative mind of a dentist in the 1880s who began experimenting with the application of electricity to animals after witnessing the accidental death of a drunk man who had stumbled onto a live wire. No. 44371 also knows that the beloved inventor of the electric light-bulb, Thomas Edison, promoted the concept of electrocuting criminals as a means of winning control of the electric utility industry away from archrival George Westinghouse, by demonstrating the dangers of Westinghouse's alternating-current transmission system over Edison's own safer but inferior direct-current lines. So determined was Edison to sway public opinion against Westinghouse that he invited the press to witness the execution of a dozen innocent animals with a thousand-volt Westinghouse AC generator, coining the term "electrocution."

The next year, he successfully lobbied the New York legislature to use Westinghouse AC voltage in the first electric chair. No one, Edison gambled, would want AC voltage in their homes after that. Westinghouse did all he could to stop it, refusing to sell the generator to prison authorities and even funding judicial appeals for the first souls to be put to death by the device. He lost those appeals, and the condemned men lost their lives, but he did ultimately win control of the electric utility industry.

Yes, No. 44371 knows well the peculiar history of the electric chair, and now all of it flashes through his mind. He studied it long and hard until he reached the point where he could hear the word "chair" and not swallow so much and blink so often, anesthetizing himself to the fear of his own death by bathing himself in it. And so, he read with more than morbid curiosity the case of William Kemmler, who, by murdering his paramour in Buffalo, won the honor of being first to sit in Edison's chair. And this made No. 44371 wonder about the peculiar relationship the City of Buffalo bore to the dentist, the electric chair, Kemmler, and No. 44371's own life.

In the year 1890, the U.S. Supreme Court denied Bill Kemmler's petition for a writ of habeas corpus, ruling that death by electricity does not violate the Constitution's prohibition against cruel or unusual punishment. So sanctioned, the citizens of New York wasted no time in trying out their new toy. They fitted Kemmler with two electrodes, one on his head and the other at the base of his spine, and for seventeen seconds they passed a Westinghouse alternating current of 700 volts through his body. Witnesses reported seeing hideous spasms and convulsions and clouds of smoke and smelling burned clothing and flesh. They gave him a second dose, of 1,030 volts, lasting two minutes. A postmortem revealed that

Bill Kemmler's brain had been hardened to the consistency of well-done meat and the flesh surrounding his spine had been burned through. Among those in attendance that historic day at Auburn Prison was a disgusted George Westinghouse, who remarked on the way out: "They could have done better with an ax."

Techniques improved.

No. 44371 has been assured by the guards that he will receive a lethal jolt of 2,000 volts straight away, then two more of about 1,000 volts each for good measure, each lasting a minute in duration and spaced ten seconds apart. His body temperature will be raised in that time to over 138 degrees Fahrenheit — too hot to touch but not so hot that he will begin to smoke like poor Bill Kemmler. His chest will heave and his mouth will foam, his hair and skin will burn, he will probably release feces into his pants, and his eyeballs will probably burst from their sockets like a startled cartoon character — hence the snug fit of the stiff leather mask the guards have just placed over his face.

Yes, No. 44371 knows all there is to know, and now with the mask over his face it seems like he knows too much. He knows that despite more than one hundred years

414

of practice, perfection in the art of judicial "electro-cution" remains elusive. Thus, weighing heavily now on No. 44371's mind as they clamp the cold electrodes to his shaved legs is the botched execution in the year 1990 of Jesse Tafero in Florida. During the first two cycles, smoke and flames twelve inches long erupted from poor Jesse's head. A funeral director with some experience in these matters opined that the charred area on the top left side of his skull, about the size of a man's hand, was a third-degree burn. But Jesse was dead, sure enough.

The guards tug at the leather straps around No. 44371's chest and waist, and now he starts to blink faster and swallow harder.

At the beginning of the twenty-first century, when for humane reasons society no longer destroys even rabid dogs this way — and the electric chair in most states has already taken its place in the museum of horrors beside disembowelment, the rack, burning at the stake, the noose, and the guillotine — No. 44371 need not have faced execution in such a brutal manner. In fact, four years before his death sentence was issued, the governor of Pennsylvania signed a law making lethal injection the preferred method of execution in the commonwealth.

415

But death by "Old Sparky," as some referred to the chair, was the one condition No. 44371 had insisted upon in his agreement with the district attorney to plead guilty to two counts of kidnapping and two counts of first-degree murder, irrevocably waiving all his rights to appeal. When his lawyers refused to assist him in striking such a deal, he fired them on the spot.

"Maybe a lethal injection can dull society's conscience of what it plans to do to me," he boldly proclaimed to his fellow death-row inmates, "but I won't take 'em! I hope my body bursts into flames and burns the prison to the ground! I want history to remember what happened to me and the Rabuns of Kamenz! Did the martyrs in the Colosseum deny their faith? Did Christ himself? Would the world remember any of them today if they were dealt a dreamy death with the prick of a needle? When humanity nailed Jesus to a cross, it nailed itself to the cross. And when humanity electrocutes me in the chair, it will electrocute itself in the chair!"

Such was the courage — or the madness — of No. 44371.

The district attorney was more than happy to seek a special order from the court to accommodate No. 44371's unusual request.

Yet even with the guilty plea entered in the docket and the special order signed, fifteen years had passed because neither No. 44371 nor the district attorney considered the possibility of collateral appeals being filed by opponents of the use of the electric chair.

Now, at long last, all those appeals have been denied. The death warrant has been signed, Old Sparky has been removed from the museum of horrors and returned to the death chamber, the possibility of a stay of execution has passed, and No. 44371 is finally about to be granted his wish. But now *he* is having doubts.

After all those years of studying judicial electrocutions, No. 44371 cannot control his panic in these final, terrifying moments. The leather mask reeks with the vomit of dead men, the copper cap scratches into his naked scalp, the electrodes dig into his legs, and his waist and limbs are lashed too tightly against the rough wood. He imagines the current crashing into his skull, detonating his brain like a bomb before plunging down his spine and fusing his gut under the intense heat, imploding his bowels. He imagines it leaping from his legs like a crazed demon, carrying his soul down, down into the earth. Then nothing.

No. 44371 hears the heavy breathing of

417

the guards, heavier now than even his own breath. His lungs are afraid to breathe because the next breath might be their last.

"Mount Nittany," he mumbles despondently, trying to conjure his last glimpse of the mountain from his cell window before they removed him to the isolation chamber a day earlier. He had hoped that remembering this last view of the world would calm him in the final moments. And, yes, yes, the paper! It's still in his fingers, a single scrap of newsprint he has kept in his wallet for years.

But what did it say? The words! What were the words? No. 44371 has forgotten them already.

"Doug! Doug!" he cries out.

"I'm right here," says the guard, attempting to sound reassuring while trying to steady his own nerves and bear his own fear and guilt. In these final moments there is compassion between inmate and jailer. They've known each other for so long, but they know too there's a job to be done and each man must play his part. There are no hard feelings.

"Doug, I can't read it. Read it to me, Doug."

No. 44371, whose arms are strapped to the chair, is trying to wave the sheet with his fingers and nod his head in its direction, but he's strapped too tightly and can't move.

"Just a second," the guard says, turning toward the narrow slit in the wall behind which the executioner stands, blinking. "I think . . . Yeah, it looks like they're ready now," Doug says.

"Wait!" No. 44371 pleads. "Please, Doug. I can't remember the words. I haven't given you any trouble."

"Okay, okay," Doug says, "I've got to take it from you now, anyway." The guard retrieves the scrap and says to the executioner, "Just a second."

"Read it, Doug." No. 44371 whimpers. "Read it."

"Do you want me to read all of it?" the guard asks.

"No, just the underlined part," No. 44371 replies.

"Okay, here's what it says:

No good deed ever goes unpunished, but whether a deed is good or bad appears to turn not on the nature or quality of the deed itself but rather the amount of hatred that exists for those who are its intended beneficiary.

No. 44371 takes a deep breath and smiles

419

beneath his mask.

"Thanks, Doug," he says gratefully. "I remember now. You'll put it in my pocket when it's over, right, like you promised?"

"Sure, Ott," Doug replies, relieved now that the prisoner seems ready to accept his fate. "Sure, just like I promised."

# 34

In life and in death, Nana Bellini kept lush pots of pink and white vinca, impatiens, marigolds, ferns, and a dozen other varieties on the front porch of her house. She planted ivy and wisteria vines around the perimeter and allowed them to pull themselves up the balustrade like children at play. The flowers perfumed the air, attracting hummingbirds and bumblebees that tormented the cats napping in the shade. Like the garden behind the house, the front porch was its own little ecosystem and parable of life.

That all changed when Nana left Shemaya, leaving me alone to take care of the place. But by the time Luas had come to find me after my meeting with Ott Bowles, everything had withered and died. Only raw piles of dirt filled the pots now, littered with fragments of dried stems and roots. The banister sagged and swayed dangerously in gusts of wind created by the thunderhead that stalked the four seasons of the valley day and night like a homicidal lover. The windowpanes of the house were broken, and paint peeled from the mullions and frames. The place looked as if it hadn't been lived in for decades. There were no cats or birds, and there was no color, just a monochromatic frame. My Shemaya had turned to shades of gray.

I hadn't seen Luas or been out of the house since the day the spirit of Otto Bowles entered my office and infected my soul. I had staggered from my office in a daze, down the long corridor, through the great hall and the vestibule, through the woods, up the steps of the porch, into the house. There I stayed, behind closed doors, reliving his life again and again, horrified and fascinated. My body aged with the house. My hair turned gray, thin, and coarse. My face contracted into the frightened expression of an old woman, barely more than a skeleton with absurd knobs of bone protruding from my chin, jaws, and forehead. My lips shriveled and hardened like an earthworm baked in the sun, disappearing into the toothless hole of my mouth. I slept during the day and woke during the night aching all over, my joints brittle and inflamed with arthritis.

I knew it would be Luas when I heard the knock on the door. There had been no visitors during all those years. He would be coming to say I could no longer delay the presentation. Otto Bowles was waiting in the train shed for his case to be called, and God was waiting in the Courtroom to judge his soul.

Luas said nothing about the change in my appearance. He only smiled — that knowing grandfather's smile of his, the way he smiled at me when I arrived in Shemaya, as if to say: *Yes, my granddaughter, you have suffered, and it is difficult, but I would only be making it worse by noticing.* I offered him a seat on the porch. "How are you, Brek?" he asked.

"I'd pull the switch again," I answered. I spoke now in the quivering voice of an old woman, weak but defiant. "Until there was nothing left of him but ash."

The dark anvil of the thundercloud crossed the sky. I imagined how I would feel to be pulled hot from a fire and hammered against its flank.

"Nero Claudius committed suicide," Luas said. His face pinched as his hands groped through his pockets to find matches for his pipe. "Unlike Mr. Bowles, he cheated the

423

world of its opportunity for justice."

"So God has a sense of humor after all," I said. "Satan is a lawyer and carries a briefcase. What did we do to deserve all this?"

Luas struck a match. It flared bright orange in the shadows. The white smoke from his pipe bubbled over the sides, too weak to rise into the wind.

"I did cheer when they stoned Saint Stephen to death," Luas said, "so I guess I had it coming. But this isn't hell, Brek. The Judge must be certain of our fidelity and self-control. If we are impartial when presenting the souls we most despise, then the Judge can be certain we will present all postulants with dispassion. Our motives must be pure when we enter the Courtroom — we can show no favoritism or emotion. The judgment is Yahweh's. He alone determines how Otto Bowles and Nero Claudius spend eternity."

A blue bolt of lightning flashed across the valley, followed by a loud clap of thunder. A doe and her fawn, tiptoeing through the band of deep white snow covering the meadow, lifted their ears toward the sky, confused by the sound of thunder on such a cold day in their part of Shemaya.

*Oh, take care,* I wished the doe with all my heart, one mother to another. *It's not safe here. They're after your baby, and they're after you. Trust no one. Assume nothing. Run. Run!*

"I did everything I could to bring people to justice," Luas continued. "But then one day I found myself blinded by this idea of forgiveness. I don't know how it happened. Oh, it was quite a conversion; I started preaching it to the people and criticizing them for appealing to the law courts."

"You misled a lot of people," I said.

"Yes, I did," Luas agreed. "I realized that when I met Elymas. When he threatened me, I couldn't just turn the other cheek. I blinded him on the spot, just as I had been blinded. He still carries a grudge about it even though I've apologized a thousand times. I went back to the old law of an eye for an eye, Brek, and I can't tell you how good it felt. But by that point, it was too late. The Romans imprisoned me as an enemy of the state. But I wasn't about to give up without a fight the way Jesus did. I demanded my right to a trial as a Roman citizen. When it looked like I couldn't get a fair hearing, I appealed to Nero Claudius. He had a good reputation in those days. Nobody knew he would turn out to be such a sadist. You know the rest. Now Nero and I meet again here every day in the afterlife.

Even mighty emperors receive their just deserts."

The storm clouds cleared, revealing four moons in the nighttime sky: a quarter moon, a half-moon, a three-quarter moon, and a full moon, each set against the constellations appropriate to its season, hashing the sky into astronomical gibberish. The air cooled and I wrapped one of Nana's shawls closer around me for warmth. Bats flickered above the trees, chasing after insects. In the distance I could hear a great horned owl and a whip-poor-will, and the bark of a lonely dog — the sounds I'd heard many nights on that porch as a child.

"Ott Bowles can speak for himself in the Courtroom," I said. "He made his choices. He doesn't need a lawyer. He needs an executioner."

Luas tapped his pipe against the banister to empty it of ash. "Perhaps so," he said, "but it is justice that needs our help in the Courtroom, Brek, not Ott Bowles. Presenters supply the distance that makes justice possible for the accused and the Accuser, the created and the Creator. Lawyers are the many colors in the promise of the rainbow as it fades into the horizon of eternity."

"*I* am the Accuser, Luas," I corrected him.

"There's no need for a trial because I've already found him guilty. It's time for justice to be served."

# 35

I'm holding Sarah in my arm and waiting for a clerk to come to the counter of the convenience store. Sarah's getting fussy and heavy, and I'm getting impatient.

"Hello? Hello . . . ?"

"Just a minute . . ." a female voice calls from the stockroom.

The clerk finally pushes through the double-hinged doors. She's a young woman in her early twenties, overweight, with too much makeup and a too tight shirt. Flicking back her hair, she apologizes for the delay. She smiles at Sarah, extending two thick fingers and tugging at her tiny hand.

"How old are you?" she asks.

I lean in close to Sarah like a ventriloquist. "Say, I'm ten months."

"What a big girl," the clerk says. "I've got two little boys, one and three. They'd sure love to meet a pretty little girl like you. What's your name, honey?"

"Sarah," I answer for her again.

"Hey there, Sarah. 'Sara Smile.' That's one of my favorite songs. You're a cutie."

The clerk releases Sarah's hand and touches her nose. Sarah responds by reaching out and touching the clerk's nose, making us both laugh. I give Sarah a squeeze and a kiss on the cheek. The clerk pulls the milk toward the register.

"Will that be all today?"

"That's it."

"Bag?"

"Yes, thanks."

I pay and we walk back out to the car, picking up where we left off with the song that's been playing on the cassette: *It's almost six-twenty, says Teddy Bear, Mama's coming home now, she's almost right there. Hot tea and bees honey, for Mama and her baby* . . . Sarah allows me to buckle her into her car seat without fussing.

It's dark and I need to use my high beams on the way home. We pass a couple of other cars heading in the opposite direction, but otherwise the road is empty until a single car appears in my rearview mirror and begins following us.

Coming around a bend and picking up speed on a slight downgrade, we reach a long, deserted stretch of road with corn and hay fields on both sides. The high beams of the car behind us start flashing, and bursts from a red strobe light fill my rearview mirror, hurting my eyes. The red flashes come from low on the windshield. I can tell it's an unmarked patrol car. Bo had warned me he'd seen a speed trap on this stretch of road.

Determined to take advantage of my expensive legal training, I'm already planning my defense as I pull off onto the berm. The officer couldn't have clocked me with radar while following me from behind, so he must be relying on his speedometer. I decide to request a copy of the speedometer certification at the trial — they're usually expired, and it's an easy way to get out of a ticket if you know to ask. But even if I did go over the speed limit, it couldn't have been for long. They have to record it for at least a full one-tenth of a mile. I'll come back tomorrow and measure the distance from the bend in the road to the point where he started flashing to pull me over, which looks like less than a tenth of a mile to me.

By the time the officer opens the door of his car, I have all my insurance and registration documents in order. Sarah's starting to cry now that I've turned off the music, but this could be a blessing. Maybe he'll give me a break because of Sarah and my arm. I'm not above seeking sympathy.

Against the glare of the high beams I can see only the officer's silhouette in the mirror with his revolver bulging at his hip. He's short, thin, and slightly bowlegged — not the large, powerfully built patrolman you normally think of. I counsel myself to say nothing incriminating and roll down the window. Strangely he stops at the rear door and tries to pull it open.

"Up here, Officer," I say, always polite to the police, thinking he somehow mistook the rear door for the front.

He inserts his arm through my open window and around the pillar to unlock the back door, then climbs in and slams the door shut.

"What's the problem, Officer?" I ask innocently, believing there must be some good reason for his behavior. Maybe he's afraid of being hit by passing traffic if he stands at my door.

A young male voice answers calmly: "Do what I tell you, Mrs. Wolfson, and nobody'll get hurt."

*How does he know who I am?*

I look in the mirror and see a gun pointing at my head. The kid holding the gun appears to be in his late teens or early twenties, with soft, downy whiskers on his chin, pale skin, and thin, almost feminine lips. His head is shaved and he's wearing a camouflage Army shirt. I've never seen him before in my life.

"Get out of my car!" I yell, outraged that he has the nerve to do something like this, not yet fully comprehending the gun or the reality of the threat.

A savage smile darts across his face. He points the gun down toward Sarah. There's a loud crack and a bright orange muzzle flash. Time slows like a rock falling through water. I feel myself screaming but my ears are ringing because of the concussion.

"Sarah! Sarah!"

I try to reach back to her, but the kid slams the gun into the side of my face, knocking my head forward. The heat from the barrel stings my cheek, and the bitter scent of gunpowder fills my nose. From the corner of my eye I see the hammer cocked to fire again. It's an oddly shaped handgun, older, like something I've seen in World War II movies.

"Drive the car!" he orders. "Now!"

But I'm crazed with panic, and I'm still screaming, "Sarah! Sarah!" I force my head back against the gun, scraping the barrel across my cheek like a razor. I can see her now. There's no blood . . . and . . . yes, thank God . . . she's still crying! The shot must have gone through the seat beside her.

The kid slams the gun into my face again, producing a stabbing pain through my sinus and a thin trickle of blood from my nose.

"Drive!" he yells. "Now!" He rolls down the rear window and waves to the car behind us. The lights stop flashing, and it pulls out in front of us. "Follow him."

I try to move the gear selector, but I'm shaking so badly that the stump of my right arm slips off the lever. The kid reaches up and slaps it into place with a jolt, and I pull out onto the road. We drive to a stop sign and turn left onto Route 22. With each oncoming car, the kid presses the gun against my head, warning me not to do anything to alert them. I'm searching frantically for a police car, or a gas station where I can pull off for help. All the while, Sarah's screaming at the top of her lungs, terrified from the gunshot.

"Make her stop!" the kid shouts at me.

"Please, just let us go," I say, trying to reason with him. "You can have my car and my purse, whatever you want; just, please, let us go."

"This isn't about money," the kid says.

"Keep driving." He uses his free hand to cover Sarah's mouth, which only makes her cries louder.

"You're hurting her!" I shriek, hysterical that he's touched my baby. "There's a bottle in the diaper bag on the floor. Give her the bottle, and let her go."

The kid finds the bottle and holds it in Sarah's mouth. She drinks the stale formula left over from her afternoon feeding, cries out, drinks again, then finally begins to settle down.

Everything is happening so fast that I have no time to think. We turn off a side road at Ardenheim and up an old dirt logging road into the mountains. The car we're following shuts off its headlights, and I'm ordered to shut mine off too. We drive into the woods in darkness and stop. The driver of the car in front gets out. In the moonlight, I can see that he's about the same age as the kid in back but taller and more muscular. His head is shaved and he's wearing camouflage Army clothes as well. He's carrying a gun in one hand and a videocassette in the other. He opens my door and yanks me out of the car, wrenching my left arm. The kid in back climbs out with Sarah and hands her to me, then takes the videocassette from the bigger kid, gets in the driver's seat of my car, drops the videocassette in the rear footwell, and backs my car into a grove of pine trees until it's covered with boughs and can't be seen from the narrow dirt road. He reappears moments later and says to the bigger kid: "Okay, Tim, let's get going."

The bigger kid, whose name I now know is Tim, shoves me toward the other car.

"Please," I plead with them, "you've got my car and my money. Please, just leave us here. I won't tell anybody."

"Shut up," Tim says, ramming his gun into my back.

I begin to worry they're planning to kidnap and rape me.

"Please, please don't do this," I beg.

"I said, shut up!" Tim yells, slamming me against their car, crushing Sarah between me and the window. She starts crying again.

"I told you, Mrs. Wolfson," the smaller kid says, "if you do as you're told, nobody'll get hurt. Now get in the car."

"You still want me to drive, Ott?" Tim asks.

"Yeah."

Now I know the smaller kid's name and that he's the leader of the two.

I climb in back with Sarah on my lap and try to comfort her. Ott sits beside us, digging his gun into my ribs. Tim takes the driver's seat and backs the car down the logging road the way we came, switching on the headlights when we reach the highway. We head south to Route 522, then Route 322 east toward Harrisburg. Sarah calms with the motion of the car and me holding her close. I'm trying frantically to remember the next exits, and whether there are any police stations, and what I've heard about self-defense — how the worst thing you can do is to allow an attacker to drive away with you in a car. While cradling Sarah, I slip my hand around the door handle to be ready to leap out at the first opportunity for escape; if I were alone, I might have jumped while the car was moving, but I can't take that chance with Sarah.

The miles go by. Ott and Tim say nothing to each other, or me, as we drive. Their actions are disciplined, efficient, and well-rehearsed, suggesting this is not some last-second lark by a couple of teenage punks. I smell no alcohol on their breath and notice no slurring of their speech. Ott keeps checking to see if we're being followed. Eventually Tim turns the radio on low, switching between country music stations, and Sarah finally falls asleep. I'm thankful she has no idea what's happening to her. An uneasy peace descends upon the car. Ott relaxes slightly and sits a little less rigidly, but he's always on alert, jabbing the gun into my side whenever we slow down.

"I've got money in the bank," I whisper to him. "Lots of it. You can have it all, just let us go. If you stop now, you won't get in any trouble."

Ott says nothing. Five minutes pass, ten, and fifteen. We're on a four-lane highway, driving farther south toward Harrisburg.

"Why are you doing this?" I ask.

"Why?" Ott replies, incredulous, without taking his eyes off the road ahead. "Because Harlan Hurley was sentenced today. He got fifteen years because of your Jew husband, that's why."

"Harlan Hurley?"

"Yeah, don't you watch the news? Your Jew husband was there at the courthouse, gloating in front of his TV cameras."

Shaved heads, camouflage fatigues . . . I begin to understand.

"You're members of Die Elf, aren't you?" I ask, more terrified than ever. I want to tell him my name is Brek Cuttler, not Brek Wolfson, that I'm a Catholic, not a Jew, and Sarah isn't Jewish either because to be Jewish she has to have a Jewish mother. But telling him this would be betraying my husband and my own beliefs. It would be betraying God. I wonder in that moment what I would have done if I were being questioned by the Nazis. Would I tell them I wasn't a Jew to save myself and Sarah, and let them take Bo away?

A state-police car pulls around us to pass on the four-lane. I don't feel the gun in my ribs anymore and raise my hand to signal it. But Ott sees me and says, "Look, Mrs. Wolfson, your baby likes the new toy I gave her." I look down and see that he has slipped the muzzle of his gun into Sarah's hand. I abandon my attempt to alert the trooper.

"Why are you doing this?" I ask again as the police car drives off ahead in the distance. "The government won't release Hurley because you've kidnapped us, they don't negotiate criminal sentences with anybody."

"Because somebody's got to tell the truth," Ott says.

"About what?"

"About the Holocaust . . . about my family."

"Are you Harlan Hurley's son?"

"No. I'm Barratte Rabun's son. Amina Rabun's godson. Do you remember them, Mrs. Wolfson?"

*Oh my God, this is the kid Bo had told me about on the phone earlier in the day. This isn't about criminal sentences or making a political statement; it's about revenge.*

We pass by Harrisburg and eventually Lancaster, finally turning off the main highway and heading into the rolling farmland of Chester County toward Delaware. Fifteen minutes later, we're on a winding secondary road, rushing past signs with arrows pointing toward Kennett Square, Lenape, and Chadds Ford. The gnarled, old oak trees along the two-lane country road jeer at us, waving their limbs in the dancing shadows like the damned welcoming our entrance into hell. Leaves fall in eruptions of red, yellow, and orange flames as we hurl down the abyss. I'm nauseated with fear, and my mind is racing: *How long will it be before Bo calls the police? He'll expect us no later than eight, and he'll probably call work and the day care to track us down. Maybe he'll figure we've gone to the grocery store or the mall. Ten o'clock — nothing could keep us out that late. He'll check first with my parents, then the television station to see if they've heard about any accidents, and then he'll call the police. They'll take the information, but they'll probably treat it as a domestic dispute and wait and see. Who knows when they'll start looking for us, probably not until tomorrow.*

The turns quicken and the pavement

deteriorates. We're on a gravel road now, descending a steep ravine through woods and ending on a rutted dirt road leading through an open, overgrown field, and back into more woods, down an even steeper slope. There are no streetlights or power lines. The sky is coal black, without the hope of stars or the kind solace of the moon. The last home passed from view miles ago, asleep in the cool harvest air pregnant with the scent of decaying leaves and apples. I start to panic again.

*They're going to kill us! They've taken us out to the middle of nowhere to kill us!*

"Listen," I plead with him, "I'm sorry about what happened to your mother and godmother. I'll do anything I can to make it better. You've got to understand, it was the government, not us, who put her in jail. We had no control —"

Ott slams the gun so hard into my side that I lose my breath.

The dirt road ends at a crumbling, one-story cinder-block building protruding from the ground like an ugly scab with windowless walls pocked with black streaks of mold and a leprosy of flaking white paint. It resembles the shell of an abandoned industrial building and looks out of place in the country. The cloying stench of manure and mushrooms make the air heavy and difficult to breathe.

We pull to a stop about twenty yards away. With the headlights illuminating the building, Tim leaves the engine running, pulls his gun, and goes inside. Ott waits nervously in the car with me until Tim reappears at the door and waves all-clear. He disappears inside again.

Ott climbs out and orders Sarah and me out with him. Pretending to fix my suit jacket, I stall for time.

*This may be our only chance.*

Ott is standing at the end of the open rear door, his head turned over his shoulder, looking at the building. The engine is running, but he could easily stop me if I tried to climb over the seat.

*I have to get him away from the car.*

I gently place Sarah into the footwell, where she'll be safe. She stirs and looks up at me. Under the dome light on the ceiling, her eyes reflect back her love for me, as though she knows what I am about to do and she's thanking me for risking my life for her. She's trying to be so brave. I love her with all my heart. Tears fill my eyes.

I climb out of the car, shaking. Ott's waiting for me but still looking at the building. He's only a few inches taller than me, not nearly as intimidating as Tim. I decide what to do. I place my left hand on the door frame for balance and then, with all my strength, I thrust my knee up hard into his groin. He doesn't see it coming and instantly collapses to the ground with a sucking groan.

*It worked!*

I slam the rear door closed, jump into the driver's seat, and hit both locks with my elbow. As I reach around the steering wheel with my left hand to shift the gear selector into reverse, Tim comes running from the building at full speed, covering the ground so quickly that by the time I step on the accelerator, he's already even with my door and he's pointing his gun straight at me through the window. Time slows again, slicing the final moments of my life into small frames to be archived for the rest of eternity, decoupling memory from reality and reaching back to everything before — to the hands that bathed me when I was delivered from my mother's womb and hugged me as a young child, to my husband, my family, my friends, my daughter . . . to the moments and the memories that had become Brek Abigail Cuttler. But just as Tim is about to fire, Ott lunges up at him from the ground, causing his gun to bark harmlessly into the air.

*He saved my life!*

Perspective accelerates to real time, to the blur of adrenaline and the desire to live. The car roars backward, toward home and safety, toward all we had created. But I'm racing backward so quickly and the path is so narrow that I lose control and we careen into a tree with a terrible jolt. Sarah starts wailing. I slam the gearshift into drive and stomp again on the accelerator, steering straight for Ott, who is on his knees aiming his gun at us. He fires four shots. The car slows and becomes less responsive, and I realize he's shot out one of the front tires.

For a fraction of a second, I think of swerving to avoid hitting him, in gratitude for sparing my life earlier. But we are frozen in time, Ott Bowles and me, controlled by instinct and the will to survive. I accelerate straight for him. He rolls out of the way at the last second and the car plows into a manure pile.

Determined to win our freedom, I rap the selector into reverse again. But there's a loud explosion and the rear-door window shatters into a hailstorm of glass pellets. Ott is sticking through the rear window, his gun pointing down at Sarah in the footwell, both arms outstretched and locked, police style.

"Don't make me do this!" Ott yells at me. "Don't make me do this!" His chest is heaving, every muscle tensed.

"Do it!" Tim shouts from the other side of the car, his eyes wide and crazed, intoxicated by the violence. "Do it now!"

Ott hesitates, and in that moment of indecision I shut off the engine and hand Ott the keys over my shoulder.

"Take them," I say, my voice shaking, just above a whisper, desperate to calm him down. "Please. She's just a baby."

# 36

"So, how long have you been a member of Die Elf?" Ott Bowles asked the bearded, well-dressed, dark-haired man seated across from him at the small cocktail table. He asked this question while sipping a beer and following a baseball game playing on the television over the bar.

"I'm not exactly a member," the man said, exhaling smoke from a cigarette, uninterested in the game. "Die Elf supports what I'm doing, and I support what they're doing."

It was late afternoon on a bright summer day, and the bar was deserted. Ott was not yet of legal age to consume alcohol, but Trudy, the owner of the bar built at the foot of a mountain between Huntingdon and Altoona, served her customers without regard to age. She was a large woman with flaming red hair, and this afternoon she sat behind the bar, watching the game and waiting for customers. The man sitting across from Ott was plainly of legal age, but he sipped club soda through a straw.

"Yes!" Ott said, clenching his fist as a runner crossed home plate. "Bottom of the ninth, and the Pirates are coming back." He swallowed a gulp of beer and belched in the manner that he believed men interested in sports belched.

"Well, you've got to admit, Sam," Ott said, "there's some guys in Die Elf who are wound pretty tight. I'm more German than any of them, and I'm proud as hell of my heritage, but I think they carry the racist stuff too far. I've studied World War Two. That's what got Germany into trouble. If Hitler had been less extreme and kept his eye on the ball, the outcome of the war probably would have been totally different. Germany might be the big superpower today instead of the United States."

"It's possible," Sam said. "But it was also Hitler's eccentricities and excesses that got him as far as he did. Who knows, maybe he wasn't excessive enough. One person's extreme ideas are another person's revelation and call to revolution. Anyway, the members of Die Elf have been good to me. I owe them."

Ott picked up his beer and turned back to

446

the baseball game. He wished he hadn't brought up the subject. He enjoyed the camaraderie of Die Elf well enough, and the paramilitary training and the paintball war games they played — and certainly the way everybody treated him like royalty because of his family's past. But their rabid hatred of Jews and blacks just made them look like a bunch of dead-enders and lunatics. Sam's defense of them meant he was probably just as fanatical, which was disappointing because Ott was searching for somebody who saw things the way he did and thought maybe Sam, who had always seemed more reasonable than the others, could be the one. "Where are you from?" Ott asked, changing the subject.

"New York."

"I mean your family. What kind of name is Samar Mansour . . . French?"

"No, Palestinian actually," Sam said.

Ott examined Sam more closely. He could see the Arab face now, the thick black beard and dark skin. But where did those blue eyes come from? Ott had never known an Arab, and he couldn't imagine how the members of Die Elf would want to do anything to help one. They hated anybody who wasn't white and Christian. Maybe it was because Sam seemed more European

447

than Middle Eastern with his aloof attitude, articulate speech, and pressed blue cotton dress shirts and black pants — more like a Londoner or a Parisian, or perhaps even a Berliner. "When did your family come here?" Ott asked, looking back up at the baseball game.

"My father came over when he was about your age. He was one of the Palestinian refugees . . . his parents were killed by the Jews during the war in 1948."

Ott glanced at him, then back at the game.

"Most Palestinians stayed in the Middle East," Sam continued, "but after the war my father got a job carrying equipment for an American archaeologist on a dig in Jerusalem, a professor from over at Juniata College, actually. Mijares was his name. In any case, he was very wealthy, and very generous, and he liked my father. I guess he thought my dad was pretty smart, because he offered to send him to college here, all expenses paid. My father accepted. He attended Columbia University, married an American woman, and stayed. I was born in New York."

Sam waved for Trudy to bring them another round of drinks.

"Be right there, honey," she said, pulling two glasses from under the bar, grateful for something to do.

"Just another refugee story," Sam said to Ott. "Not very different from your family's."

Ott was thinking the same thing. He finished his beer, accidentally dribbling a little onto his T-shirt. "You know our story?" he asked, reaching across to another table for a bar napkin.

"I know all about your family," Sam said. "Brian Shelly told me a little, and I've done some research on the Rabuns. People don't realize it, but Germans and Arabs have a lot in common. *Das ist warum ich beginnen wollte, Sie zu kennen.*"

A look of surprise flashed across Ott's face. *"Sprechen Sie Deutsch?"*

*"Wenig."*

*"Wie viele Male sind Sie nach Deutschland gewesen?"*

*"Ich habe ein ungefähr Jahr dort verbracht."*

They stopped speaking in German when Trudy brought the drinks to the table.

"You boys want anything from the grill?" she asked. "I can fix you some burgers."

Sam shook his head. "You want anything, Ott?" he asked. "I'm buying."

"No, thanks," Ott said.

"You boys just let me know," Trudy replied, a little disappointed. She returned to her stool behind the bar to watch the game.

"Too bad about Brian, wasn't it?" Ott said.

"Yeah," Sam replied. "He was pretty young to have a heart attack. I guess you never know."

"The funeral was tough," Ott said. "Tim and his mom took it hard. On top of everything else, I guess Brian had all their property mortgaged to the hilt and had stopped paying his life insurance. Tim said they had to sell their house and their mushroom farm to pay off their debts. He's been staying with me for a while."

"He's lucky to have you as a friend," Sam replied. "It must have been hard on you too when you lost your godmother. She was a great woman. I admired her newspaper writing a lot. It wasn't that long ago, was it?"

Ott nodded uncomfortably, losing eye contact. "About a year now, I guess — less than a year after she got out of jail. Prison killed her." He looked out the window painfully, embarrassed for showing his emotions. "So what exactly are you doing for Die Elf?" he asked, changing the subject back again.

"I'm making a documentary on the Holocaust. I'm going to show that it was a hoax created by the Allies and the Jews."

The Pirates scored another run on the television. Sam looked up, but suddenly Ott was less interested in the game. "So *you're* the one?" Ott said. "Brian told me he knew somebody making a documentary about the Holocaust, but he wouldn't tell me anything more than that."

Sam turned from the television back to Ott, grinning like the player who had just scored the run. "It was a secret for a while," he said. "Only a few guys knew about it. Brian, Harlan Hurley. Harlan's been a big help in funding it."

"Really, the guy who works for the school district?" Ott said. "He always seems pretty quiet."

"The quiet ones often do the most," Sam said. "He's been taking money from the —" Sam caught himself. "Let's just say that he's been using some creative financing to help fund my work. It takes a lot of money to do a documentary right — equipment, camera crews, travel expenses, studio time. I just finished the editing, actually. It came out great. The more I learned about your background, the more I thought you might be interested in the project. That's why I wanted to meet with you today."

"Can I see it?" Ott asked eagerly.

"Sure, soon," Sam replied.

"Where did you learn to do documentaries?" Ott asked. "Are you a filmmaker?"

451

"No," Sam said. "This is my first documentary, but I learn fast and I had an experienced crew. I was finishing my Ph.D. in history at Juniata — as a recipient of the Mijares Fellowship actually. The documentary was supposed to be my dissertation, but the head of the history department is a Jew and, for obvious reasons, he wasn't too happy with my subject or my conclusions. He gave me the option of picking a new topic or leaving school without a degree. I left. Harlan and some of the others heard about it, and they've been funding the project for a few years now."

"Wow," Ott said. "I give you credit for taking on one of the most controversial issues in the world. But it's going to be tough convincing people the Holocaust was a hoax. Don't get me wrong . . . nothing would make me happier than finding out it was a lie, but I've seen the pictures and read the histories. I've been to some of the camps too. My family built the incinerators. There's a lot of evidence out there to disprove."

Sam frowned. "But you don't really believe your family, or your countrymen, would murder millions of their own people in cold blood, whether they were Jews or not, do you? It doesn't make any sense. The Germans weren't barbarians, they were

452

Europeans." He paused and carefully folded his cocktail napkin into a triangle, then again into a smaller triangle. "I'm a student of history, Ott," he said. "As a student of history, I've learned that the men who leave a mark on this world are the ones who turn black into white and white into black. It's along the border between opposites that we find the energy to create and to destroy." He suddenly crumpled the napkin as if illustrating his point. "Microscopic atoms split into world-changing bombs. Tectonic plates shift and new continents are formed. Politicians make peace into war and war into peace. Religions turn sinners into saints and saints into sinners. Have no doubt: Whether the actions of men are good or evil depends upon which quality we choose to see."

The beer was hitting Ott now, and he was beginning to enjoy himself. He felt a warm tingling in his lips and forehead. Sam didn't seem to be the extremist he had feared after all. He was actually quite rational, a man who used logic and reason.

Ott enjoyed philosophical discussions and the challenge of talking to educated people. He believed he could do well in college if given a chance. He was even thinking about attending, maybe a university in Germany.

He hadn't done much of anything in the year since he graduated from high school, except hang out at the mansion in Buffalo or at Die Elf's training compound in the woods near Huntingdon. Most of the members of Die Elf were just disgruntled local men, unemployed or underemployed. They drove pickup trucks, drank beer, loved guns, and hated Jews and blacks but couldn't tell you why. But they had taken Ott into their confidence and shown him how to use Die Elf's sophisticated satellite telephones, e-mail encryption technology, and remote computer servers that ensured secure communication with other white supremacist organizations around the country. Maybe, Ott thought, he would study computers in college. He liked the precision and unambiguousness of math; and computers, as nonjudgmental machines, gave him the unconditional acceptance he craved.

"Think about all the great men," Sam continued. "Einstein demonstrated that mass is energy and energy, mass — now that's turning black into white and white into black. Galileo demonstrated that the earth orbits the sun. Columbus demonstrated that the earth is round. In the entire history of the human race, of all the billions of people who have ever walked the planet, we remember only a few thousand at most. Why? Because these are the men who demolished prevailing beliefs and formed new worlds using contradiction as their chisel. That's why they're remembered . . . and that's how I want to be remembered."

"Pretty interesting," Ott replied. "I guess I agree with you, but that still doesn't prove the Holocaust was a hoax."

Sam glanced up at the television. "Two outs," he said, sipping his beer. Then he placed the glass on the table and looked directly into Ott's eyes. "Prove? What is proof? And who's asking?" He smiled. "I know you, Ott Bowles. I know what you want. I'm just like you."

Ott was both puzzled and intrigued.

"I'm not a racist or a religious zealot, and neither are you," Sam continued. "We're practical men with a practical problem. The simple reality is this: The reputations of the German people and your family were ruined, and the homes of the Palestinian people and my family were taken at almost the exact same time. Other than the timing, you might think that these two events are entirely unrelated. They happened to different groups of people in different parts of the world. But there is a single common

455

denominator."

"Obviously the Jews," Ott responded wearily. He began to worry again that Sam was like the others. "But I thought we just agreed that we're not racists."

"We're not," Sam said. "We're rational thinkers exploring whether our problems have similar causes and effects. Let's take Israel for a minute. Now, there was no Israel between the year 70 and 1948 — three years after the Allies won World War Two. But before the year 70, Israel existed. What was the basis for its existence back then?"

"I don't know," Ott said. "I'm not up on Israeli history."

"It's simple," Sam said. "The Jews told the world a fantastic, unbelievable story that, for a while, everybody accepted. They said that God personally promised Palestine to Abraham. No witnesses, no writing, no deed or anything. Just one man's claim that God came down from heaven and said the land was his and his descendants' because they were favored and chosen by God for special protection against their enemies. Amazingly, this story was compelling enough for the Jews to hold on to that land for about three thousand years. But then the Romans came along and said, 'You've got to be kidding! God didn't say anything to us about you living here!' So they booted the Jews out."

"I guess so," Ott said, turning back to the baseball game.

"It's true," Sam continued. "And for the next two thousand years, there was no Israel at all. Didn't exist. But then, in 1948, the Jews got the land back. How? What happened?"

Ott was no longer paying attention and didn't hear the question.

"Come on, Ott," Sam said, "how did the Jews get Israel back? What happened in 1948 to change two thousand years of history?"

"I don't know," Ott said, uninterested in the question.

"They told the world a new fantastic, unbelievable story. This time their story was about the Germans and the Rabuns, not about God."

This got Ott's attention. He stopped watching the game and turned back to Sam.

"The Holocaust," Sam said. "The early Jews made up a story that they were entitled to Palestine because God gave them special protection from their enemies. But then they lost the land to the Romans. After two thousand years of trying to get it back, they realized they needed to make up a new story. Now the Jews are very smart people. So what they did is come up with a story that's the exact opposite of the first one. This time, they say that they're entitled to Palestine because they've been singled out for extermination by their enemies, and God can't or won't protect them. It's genius, actually. Pure genius."

Ott sighed. "The problem with your analysis, Sam," he said, "is that they're telling the truth. They *were* singled out for extermination."

Sam shook his head disappointedly. "Don't you get it, man? It's all about *beliefs,* Ott, not truth. Whether the Holocaust actually happened or not doesn't matter any more than whether God actually made a promise to Abraham. Black into white, white into black. The question at the moment is, Where does the Jews' new story leave the German people and the Rabuns of Kamenz? Let me tell you where. It leaves you labeled as evil butchers, the devil incarnate, distrusted and despised. It leaves you with Holocaust museums sprouting up everywhere to teach every child every year from now into infinity just how vile and subhuman you are. And where does this story leave my people, the Palestinians, who were living on the land when the Allies took it from them and gave it to the Jews? We're even less than the Germans! We're not even worth recognizing as a people on this planet entitled to a home. We're refugees, vile and subhuman too. I told you. Germans and Arabs have a lot in common."

Ott was intrigued. For the first time in his life, he had met somebody like himself with a legitimate reason to be angry — somebody who had suffered just as much, if not more, than he had. "You're right!" he said. "You're absolutely right. So that's why your people are blowing themselves up in Israeli markets — because your land was taken from you?"

"No," Sam said, lighting a new cigarette and exhaling a cloud of smoke in disgust. "We do suicide bombings because we're stupid, uneducated, and don't know any better. That only hurts us, not the Jews. I've spent time in Lebanon training with these suicide bombers. They're crazy . . . but in their defense, that's what desperation does to people. Do you see Jews blowing themselves up? Or Germans? Or anybody else? Of course not. But the Jews have been working on taking back Palestine for two thousand years, while we've only been at it for fifty. Who knows? Maybe the Jews were launching suicide attacks against the Romans in the first century when they were desperate. It takes time to see reality and the path from here to there. History is as much a function of the present as the past, and it's more a function of emotion than fact. History and truth are what we want them to be, Ott. But that leaves us with a dilemma. How do we fix the situation?"

"I don't know," Ott said.

Sam winked. "I think the answer is staring us right in the face, Ott. We need to use the same tactics the Jews used. We need our own story. But it can't be just any story. It has to be a *big* story, a big beyond belief story — like a secret promise whispered by God, or a conspiracy to exterminate a group of people from the face of the earth. If you want to achieve a gigantic goal, you've got to have a gigantic story. What made the Jews' stories work so well is that they're epic in size, totally fantastic, and so incredibly unbelievable that nobody would dare tell them with a straight face unless they were in fact true."

"Wait a minute," Ott said, confused. "I thought you just said they were lies."

"No," Sam replied. "I said the truth is irrelevant. It's all about *beliefs*. The truth is what people believe it is. When everybody believed the story that God promised the Holy Land to Abraham, then that became the truth for them and the Jews lived there for thousands of years. When everybody stopped believing that story, it was no longer the truth and the Jews were evicted. Two thousand years pass and now, when everybody believes the story that the Germans tried to exterminate the Jews, that's the new truth and the Jews are allowed to live in Israel again. Are you with me? What's the next logical step?"

Ott thought about this for a moment. He didn't agree with Sam's careless handling of the truth, but his argument did have a certain logical appeal. "I guess the next step is that when everybody stops believing the Holocaust happened, the Jews will be evicted again?"

Sam smiled. "I told you that we think alike," he said.

"But how can you get everybody to stop believing the Holocaust happened when it actually did?"

A sinister grin flashed across Sam's face. "The same way the Jews got everybody to believe God promised them the Holy Land when that never happened."

Ott was even more confused now. "Which is?"

"With a story!" Sam shouted. "That's what I just got through explaining. The

Germans and the Palestinians need a big, fantastic, unbelievable story. New story, new belief, new truth."

"So what's the new story?"

"The best way to counter a conspiracy is with an even bigger conspiracy. The Jews' story is that there was a conspiracy in Germany to exterminate them. So what do we do? We say the exact opposite — that there was an even *bigger* conspiracy among the Allies to fabricate the Holocaust to demonize the Germans and take over the Middle East."

Ott shook his head. "Why would the Allies do that?"

"Because the Germans started two world wars that cost millions of lives, and the Allies needed to shame and pacify them so they would never even think about doing something like that again. And because the Allies wanted a friendly presence in the Middle East to secure the oil supplies that make Western civilization possible."

Ott was slowly becoming convinced. "I think I get it," he said. "But it still sounds pretty far-fetched."

"Of course it's far-fetched," Sam replied. "That's the genius of it. That's been the genius of the Jews' stories throughout the ages. The story has to be far-fetched to be believable. All you need to do is show that pulling off the conspiracy was possible. That's critical. With God's promise to Abraham, it was easy — just say that God spoke to Abraham in private. Does God talk to people privately? Maybe yes, maybe no, but most people in Moses' day thought it was possible. Same thing with the Holocaust. Was it possible that the Germans murdered millions of Jews? Sure. They built concentration camps, they had most of Europe under martial law, and it was a bloody war."

Ott glanced up at the game. "Struck out," he said with a groan. "They lost." He turned back to Sam. "But how could the Allies have fabricated the Holocaust? It's been one of the most thoroughly documented events in history."

"Easy," Sam said. "By definition, wars are about killing your enemies, right? Well, isn't it interesting that there was no such thing as a 'war crime' before World War Two? Before that, mass killing during wars was taken for granted. But after the Allies won World War Two, they did something that had never been done before. They invented this new concept of a war crime for certain 'special' types of killing. And then they categorized Germany's killing of Jews as war crimes and held trials — even though Germany slaughtered millions more Russians, and the Japanese slaughtered millions of Chinese, and the Allies firebombed German cities and dropped two nuclear bombs on Japan. None of those killings were war crimes, only Germany's killing of Jews was deemed unusual and deserving of extra punishment. Of course, Germany was in no position to defend itself, it had just been defeated. So, *could* the Allies have fabricated the Holocaust? Absolutely. They liberated the camps, they controlled the evidence, they conducted the war-crimes trials. Motive and opportunity, Ott. And there are plenty of alternative explanations for why large numbers of Jews died in concentration camps that don't involve deliberate gassing. So, do you see? If we want to solve our mutual problem of restoring the reputation of the Germans and the homeland of the Palestinians, then whether the Holocaust actually happened or not doesn't matter in the least. We just need people to start questioning their beliefs about it with a new story."

"Amazing," Ott said, completely in awe of Sam now, and increasingly intoxicated by the beer. "It's brilliant."

"Thank you," Sam replied, pleased by the

compliment.

"So, what's the next step?" Ott asked.

A confident smiled formed on Sam's bearded face. "There's no better way to tell a story than with a film. We live in a visual world, and seeing is believing. So, that's what I've done. I've made a documentary that tells the new story of the Germans and the Palestinians, a story that will change the course of history." Suddenly Sam's confidence disappeared. "If, that is, I can find the money to get it out to the public. It won't do any good if people don't see it. Distributing a film is extremely expensive."

Now a confident smile formed on Ott's face. "I've got money," he said, his speech slightly slurred from the alcohol. "My godmother left everything to my mother and me. She was pretty rich."

"Really?" Sam said, feigning surprise.

Ott puffed out his chest. "I don't like to talk about it, but I could probably buy and sell everybody in Die Elf. How much do you need? I want your documentary to be seen around the world."

Trudy, the barkeeper, changed the channel on the television, and now the Channel 10 *Evening News* was coming on, with its triumphant music and flashing montage of scenes from central Pennsylvania, ending with the camera zooming in on the handsome, graying anchorman.

"Good evening," he said in an authoritative baritone. "Football star O. J. Simpson is questioned in the slayings of his ex-wife and her friend, and President Clinton is set to announce a plan for national welfare reform . . . but the big story tonight on Action News is our exclusive undercover investigation with startling revelations that thousands of dollars of curriculum and textbook funds from the Snow Creek Area School District were diverted by the financial controller of the school district to a local white supremacist group in which he is a member."

"Oh my God," Sam said. "Can you turn this up?" he hollered to Trudy.

"Here with the story is Action News investigative reporter Bo Wolfson . . ."

Trudy increased the volume on the television, and the camera panned back to show Bo Wolfson sitting next to the anchorman.

"Thank you, Rob," he said, before turning to look directly into the camera. "Over the past six months, Action News has been conducting an undercover investigation into a secretive local white supremacist group known as Die Elf that has a paramilitary training camp near Huntingdon. During our investigation, we discovered that one of the prominent members of this group is Harlan Hurley. Mr. Hurley also happens to be the chief financial controller of the Snow Creek Area School District.

"Our investigation led us into the public books and records of the school district, where we found that over the past three years, nearly one hundred thousand dollars of taxpayer funds dedicated to the curriculum and textbook budget of the school district has been paid to a shell company called TechChildren, controlled by Die Elf. We've also learned that these funds were used to make a documentary claiming that the Holocaust, in which more than six million Jews were murdered by Nazis during World War Two, was a hoax. In an interview earlier today, we confronted Mr. Hurley with these allegations and undercover videotape of his attendance at a Die Elf meeting several months ago during which the documentary was discussed."

Sam and Ott looked at each other in disbelief as the screen filled with an image of the front of the Snow Creek High School, then the main office reception area, and finally Harlan Hurley. He was a large, balding middle-aged man with no chin, a slightly lazy eye, and pasty white skin, wearing an overstretched blue short-sleeve dress shirt and a red polka-dotted tie. He was seated at his desk with a wide grin on his face, apparently excited about his fifteen minutes of fame and having no idea of what was about to happen.

"Mr. Hurley," said Bo, after some preliminary questions, "are you familiar with a company called TechChildren?"

Hurley's lazy eye involuntarily shifted toward the ceiling, thinking, stalling. "Why, yes," he said, his smile forced now. "I believe I have heard of that company."

"What is TechChildren?"

"Well, I believe they create textbooks and other educational materials."

"Does the Snow Creek Area School District do business with TechChildren?"

"I'm not certain. You see, we do business with so many companies. You'd be better-off asking the curriculum director, Mrs. Biddle, that question. How else can I help you today, Mr. Wolfson? We're particularly pleased with the new budget the school board just passed." With this diversion, Hurley relaxed slightly and his original smile returned.

"You do sign all checks for the school district, correct?" Bo asked, unwilling to be distracted.

Hurley cleared his throat. "Yes, yes, of course. I'm the financial controller. I pay whomever I'm told to pay by the principal."

"Have you ever heard of an organization called Die Elf?"

Hurley's face crimsoned, but his smile remained, like somebody who has just accidentally walked into a post in front of a crowd and wants them to believe he intended to do it.

Back inside Trudy's bar, Sam Mansour watched the interview with increasing distress, seeing all his plans unravel before his eyes. "I don't believe this," he said to Ott. "I don't believe this."

"No, I can't say that I have heard of that," Hurley replied to Bo on the television. "Is that another textbook company?"

"No," said Bo. "Die Elf is a white supremacist group, Mr. Hurley. Are you sure you've never heard of it?"

"Absolutely not," Hurley snapped, his voice rising. "What does this have to do with the Snow Creek Area School District? I don't have time for this. What are you suggesting?"

The camera switched to Bo, who stared down Hurley with calm contempt, ready for the kill. "I'm suggesting, Mr. Hurley, that TechChildren is a front organization for a white supremacist group called Die Elf, that you have illegally diverted nearly one hundred thousand dollars in school district funds to that group, and that you, sir, are a white supremacist."

Hurley leered back at Bo. "Those are outrageous accusations, Mr. Wolfson! You are doing tremendous harm to the children of this school district by making them."

"So you deny these accusations?" Bo asked.

"Of course I deny them!"

"Very well. I have a videotape I'd like to show you, Mr. Hurley, and then I'd like to give you an opportunity to comment on it."

Bo gestured toward a small television monitor that had been placed on Mr. Hurley's desk. The screen flickered with a dimly lit videotape. Muffled voices could be heard from the speaker, as though the camera had been hidden inside a bag. Harlan Hurley could be seen sitting in a roomful of men, all focused on a single man at the front, pacing back and forth in front of a Nazi flag.

Watching inside Trudy's bar, Ott shook his head, relieved that he hadn't attended that particular meeting and that his face wasn't being broadcast around the world in association with Hurley and the rest of the group.

"My Aryan brothers," the man pacing at the front said. "Today is a great day! Today we are ready to educate the children and the people of this nation in the truth. Our very special Aryan brother from the Arab world, Samar Mansour, has just finished a documentary proving that the Holocaust was nothing but a Jew lie, as we knew all along."

Ott glanced over at Sam, watching with his mouth open. On the videotape on the television, Sam stood to accept the applause of Hurley and the other members of Die Elf and thank them for their support.

"It is time," Sam said to the gathering, "for Arabs and Aryans to join forces against their common enemy. This documentary is the first step in what I hope will be a long and successful collaboration. My contribution to the battle against the Jews will not be another suicide bombing like my brave Palestinian brothers, who are willing to sacrifice their own lives for the cause. No, I intend to demolish not just a few bricks of the State of Israel but the very foundation upon which it stands. No gas chambers, no Israel!"

The room erupted into applause.

Trudy, the bartender, looked from the television to Sam and back, slowly realizing that she was seeing the same man in both places.

"It's over," Sam said to Ott. "They're probably out looking for me right now. I've gotta go." He left twenty dollars on the table and walked out with Trudy looking after him.

Ott turned back to the television to see Harlan Hurley's face twisted into a shape as ugly as the swastika on the flag at the meeting. Hurley said to Bo: "Sometimes people got to stand up for what's right and fix what's wrong. One day you'll understand that I've been doing both, and the people of this school district will make me a god-damned hero. Now get the hell out of my office."

# 37

How bizarre it is for me to see life through a man's eyes. Through my murderer's eyes.

How bizarre to experience his moods and obsessions, his sorrows and joys. To see a baby and not ache to hold her but to see a beautiful woman and crave her with every nerve. How bizarre to be Ott Bowles as he shoots a bullet into the seat next to Sarah and to hear her screaming. To feel the intense, almost sexual gratification of exercising complete dominance and control over me and to see the terror in my eyes. To see the small movements of my head as I drive down the road, to feel the softness of my body through the gun in the backseat, to feel contempt for me and everything I stand for but, at the same time, to be physically attracted to me and to imagine what it would be like to make love to me. How bizarre to listen to me pleading for my daughter's life and my own and, for an instant, to feel sympathy for me and question whether I should have kidnapped a mother and her daughter. To count down the last days of my life on death row, to come to peace with my death, to contemplate and confront its presence, and then to be delivered into it, strapped into a chair, electrocuted.

How bizarre it was to see how incredibly insignificant Sarah and I were inside Ott Bowles's life, how little we really mattered. To Ott Bowles, Sarah and I were symbols, not human beings, a means to an end, nothing more than that.

And so, gazing back through my murderer's eyes, I could appreciate the logic of a kidnapping, because through those eyes I could see how all hope for the Rabuns of Kamenz vanished when my husband aired his tape of Harlan Hurley and Samar Mansour carving their initials into the tree of history with the crooked iron spikes of a swastika.

Those days had been so different for us, so magical and glorious. The story was picked up by the national networks, and we threw a party to celebrate. We never considered the impact of the story on Hurley, Mansour, or the other members of Die Elf, because they were symbols, not human beings, for us. They represented *our* unseen enemy: the bully around the corner, the false prophet in the pulpit, the subversive thought rotting the fabric of society. Like a little David, *my* Bo had slain the great beast, and we were proud. We had no idea that at the same time we were celebrating this wonderful victory, Samar Mansour was sealing a videocassette copy of his documentary into a padded mailing envelope with the following note:

Ott,
    The truth is what we want it to be.
    We may never see each other again.
    Plant the seeds.
Your friend,<br>Sam

By the next morning, the police have arrested Harlan Hurley on multiple counts of theft, mail and wire fraud, and racketeering. A manhunt for Samar Mansour ends with confirmation that he has fled the country, probably to Lebanon. Two days later, Ott receives the videocassette in Buffalo and inserts it into the tape player in his bedroom after his mother goes to sleep.

Sam Mansour's documentary is very well constructed and very well produced, just as he had promised. It begins with a grim, catatonic river of historic black-and-white photographs appearing and disappearing on the screen: men in Nazi uniforms, the frightened faces of women and children being loaded onto train cars, electrified fences around concentration camps, prison barracks, showers, mounds of decaying corpses, smokestacks, incinerators. The images flash by faster and faster, finally trailing off to a screen of black.

From this darkness emerges the mournful cry of an oboe. This is the first sound we hear on the documentary, playing a dirge to accompany the slow march across the screen of hundreds of titles of articles, books, and films about the Holocaust — every title Sam Mansour could find during his research. As the last of these scroll across the screen, the oboe is swallowed by the symphonic roar of Wagner's *Die Walküre,* and then the sneering face of Adolf Hitler consumes the screen. Finally, the title of the documentary appears in white letters superimposed over an aerial shot of Auschwitz, swooping down onto the reddish vein of rusting train tracks leading into the camp and the platform where millions of feet beat their last steps: *What Happened?*

Sam Mansour stands on this platform as

the camera zooms in. He is wearing the same black pants and blue shirt he had been wearing at Trudy's, the color of the shirt matching his eyes. His thick, dark hair is carefully combed, and he is waiting for us, the audience, to join him. His voice suits the role — educated, evocative, authoritative, believable. Ironically, he looks and sounds more like a rabbi than a Palestinian doctoral student attempting to disprove the Holocaust. Smiling, he introduces himself as Sam Mansour. He seems affable, unbiased, dispassionate. He asks the audience a very serious question: "What happened?"

He begins walking to the fateful showers. The camera follows. As he walks, he explains the purpose of the film and assures us that he has no agenda other than the truth. As his proofs unfold, he asks us to leap with him the many gaps in logic and evidence that must be leaped, but he keeps coming back to the "truth," always the truth, insisting on it, demanding that we believe he is acting in our best interest.

As a matter of cinematography, with the parabolic camera angles, haunting guard-tower lighting, and echo-chamber sound effects — as if everything is being spoken inside a concentration camp shower — the documentary is exceptionally good at creating the impression of actually being there during the dark days. Watching it for the first time in his bedroom, Ott is mesmerized. The filmmaker's skill, and Ott's own desperate desire to believe, help Ott to overlook the warnings implicit in Sam's pleas for trust and the baseless allegations of conspiracy and cover-up that strain reason as the documentary unfolds.

I can see now that only Ott's frantic race to vindicate the Rabuns of Kamenz by refashioning a new happy ending for Germany and the Jews could have led him to betray the carefully embalmed body of recorded Nazi history that he so gingerly and faithfully exhumed during the long years of Nonna Amina's imprisonment. I can see now that only under the craving for and influence of justice, this most intoxicating and dangerous of drugs, could Ott Bowles have been led to deny, as if life and death themselves are merely a matter of one's shifting whims and subjective fancies, the mass slaughter of 360,000 Jews at Chełmno, 250,000 at Sobibór, 600,000 at Bełzec, 360,000 at Majdanek, 700,000 at Treblinka, and 1,100,000 at Auschwitz. This is how Ott Bowles came to see within Sam Mansour's "documentary" — if it could even be loosely called this rather than a mere propagation of lies — exactly what he wanted to see: the vindication of his family unfolding before him like a sweet dream.

Bo had waited until after the interview of Harlan Hurley aired to tell me that the weekend nights he supposedly spent on call at the station were actually spent camped out in a rented pickup truck, in the woods outside Die Elf's compound, with a cell phone in his hand and one of my grandfather's shotguns across his lap, waiting for Bobby Wilson, his producer, to come out alive with the damning video — and ready to go in after him if necessary. I made him promise never to do anything that stupid again.

As a reward for the success of the investigation and the risks they had taken, the station promoted Bobby to senior producer and offered Bo the anchor position on the morning news, with the promise of moving him up to the noon and five o'clock time slots as soon as his desk skills improved. We were ecstatic. People at the grocery store and mall began stopping Bo for autographs. Suddenly I was the wife of a local celebrity. These were happy times: my law practice was growing, our daughter was thriving, and Bo's dream of becoming an anchorman at a major-market television station, or even on one of the national networks, looked more promising than ever.

During the confusion surrounding Hurley's arrest and Sam Mansour's flight from the country, Ott had the presence of mind to gather up the Die Elf backup computers, encryption codes, and passwords and store them in a safe location. The idea of kidnapping Sarah and me to force the networks to air the documentary came later. To his credit, he never planned to harm us. That was Tim Shelly's idea.

## 38

The building in the woods to which Ott Bowles and Tim Shelly drove Sarah and me that Friday night in October 1994 was the original mushroom house on the old Shelly farm near Kennett Square. It was built by Tim's great-grandfather Clifton Shelly in the 1930s, when most mushrooms were harvested in the wild and people were just learning how to grow them commercially.

Like his father and grandfather before him, Clifton Shelly was a dairy farmer. He began experimenting with mushroom farming when he saw the demand for the edible fungi far exceeding the supply provided by the trained gatherers who roamed humid forests with sacks, looking for mushrooms sprouting in the shaded compost beneath trees. To re-create and better control these conditions, he erected a windowless block building at the bottom of an isolated ravine, away from prying eyes and near a pond where water would be plentiful and ice could be harvested during the winter to cool the mushroom house in the summer. Soon he was producing sizable crops of the fungi and taking them to market, stunning grocers and mushroom gatherers alike with the volume and consistency he produced. As fungiculture techniques advanced and profits grew, he replaced his milking parlors and corncribs with mushroom houses and abandoned the original mushroom house at the bottom of the ravine because it was too small and remote for large-scale production.

Tim Shelly was certain that nobody knew of the existence of the old mushroom house — particularly not the large California-based agribusiness conglomerate that purchased his family's mushroom farm at auction after his father died. It was far removed from the rest of the buildings and secluded deep in the woods, now overgrown with heavy brush. He suggested it to Ott when Ott told him about his plan to kidnap Sarah and me. In such a remote location, Tim reasoned, there would be virtually no chance of detection, and with masonry walls and no windows, there would be virtually no chance of escape. Ott looked the building over and thought it would do, but to be certain he drove in and out at different hours of the day and night, and he even stayed for a few days in an outbuilding next to the mushroom house to see whether anyone would notice. No one did.

This outbuilding, which was basically an old wooden storage shed with a couple of windows, is where Ott and Tim stayed after the kidnapping. They stocked it in advance of our arrival with food for several weeks, plus a generator, two of Die Elf's computers, a satellite telephone, and several crates filled with assault rifles and ammunition taken from Die Elf's compound. They covered the car we arrived in with a tarp and shoveled mushroom soil over it so it couldn't be seen from the air. It was from near this outbuilding, and from one of these computers, that Ott sent an e-mail message to Bo when we arrived, attaching a digital photograph he had taken of Sarah and me in the mushroom house.

Ott made no attempt to conceal his identity — he wanted the world to know exactly who he was and why he was doing what he was doing. But he did use encryption software to conceal our location, routing his e-mail from server to server around the world, deleting the message headers and identification tags, and making it appear as though the transmissions originated from somewhere in India. Ott's only stated demand in the e-mail was to have Sam Mansour's documentary aired during prime time by a national television network. If that happened, he promised, Bo and the world would witness our safe return and Ott's voluntary surrender to the authorities. He explained in the e-mail that a videocassette copy of the documentary could be found in the rear footwell of my car, which was parked in a grove of pine trees just off the old logging road in Ardenheim. He made no demands for money or even for Hurley's release from prison. He asked only that the world consider the possibility that the Nazi gassings had been a fabrication, and that his family and the German people had been wrongly convicted of genocide. Since Bo was a television news reporter, this simple request shouldn't be too much. He gave Bo three days to make the necessary arrangements.

Ott made no express threat against our lives, and in his heart he never thought it would come to that. So convinced was he of the objective merits of the film that he believed the networks would jump at the chance to air it when they saw it. And he was perfectly content to serve time in jail for kidnapping in exchange. The thought of becoming a martyr for a cause gave his life a higher purpose and deeply appealed to him. He fully expected a reply message from Bo within hours with the airdate and time, and he had a portable television ready, from which he could watch the documentary when it aired and monitor news reports of our kidnapping.

Despite being kneed in the groin during my attempted escape, Ott was delighted with how well things had gone that first night. Sarah and I were locked away in the mushroom house, and an e-mail reply from Bo came within an hour, telling Ott he was doing everything possible to have the tape aired and begging him for our safe return. Two hours later, all the television news networks were carrying the story of our kidnapping, with photographs of Sarah and me, and photographs of Ott, Harlan Hurley, Tim Shelly, and Sam Mansour. The fact that Bo was a television news reporter and that I was an attorney — and that Sarah and I had been kidnapped by a white supremacist attempting to disprove the Holocaust — touched off a media firestorm. The prospect of a mysterious Holocaust documentary, an international manhunt for a fugitive Arab, and Ott's skillful use of computer technology to communicate while concealing our location made the story into a sensation. By the next morning, the television newscasts were featuring experts on neo-Nazi groups, the Holocaust, hostage negotiations, and the Internet, together with mediated debates among Christian, Jewish, and Islamic scholars and leaders brought together to confront the underlying pathology of groups like Die Elf. It was exactly the kind of international media attention Ott wanted.

The only thing that worried Ott in all this was how his mother, Barratte Rabun, was handling the news. She refused requests to be interviewed by the reporters staking out the mansion in Buffalo. But, to Ott's surprise, by Saturday afternoon some of the networks were airing balanced and even sensitive background reports about Barratte, Amina, and the Rabuns of Kamenz, explaining how Amina had saved the Schriebergs in Germany, how the Rabuns had been gunned down by Soviet troops and Amina and Barratte had been raped, and the litigation over the Schriebergs' theaters and property. Some commentators even began to create an almost sympathetic picture of why Ott might have kidnapped us for the sake of a Holocaust documentary, causing Ott to believe more deeply than ever that he had done the right thing.

All he wanted in the end was justice. He started comparing his actions to the courageous exploits of Amina herself in Germany — at an age not much younger than his. He even began viewing Sarah and me the way Amina had viewed the Schriebergs, "heroically" providing us with the necessities for our survival — water, food, baby formula, diapers — and an austere but safe shelter in the woods. Two vulnerable fish among lethal sea anemones. He asked himself, *Am I not protecting this woman and this child from those who would harm them? From men like Tim Shelly and the members of Die Elf who would one day hunt them down and murder them? Will they not be safer when the truth of the documentary is known?*

Sarah slept while I stayed awake, worrying during our first day of captivity in the squalid, stinking mushroom house. The only light came from small gaps and cracks around the door, and the only bathroom facility was a bucket in the far corner. I knew nothing about the documentary and was convinced we had been kidnapped as part of a plot to extort Harlan Hurley's release from prison. I assumed by now that the police and FBI agents would be searching everywhere; we just needed to hang on until they found us, and do nothing to provoke Ott and Tim any further. I prayed to God to deliver us from our enemies. And to smite them.

When Sarah woke, I fed and changed her and sang "Hot Tea and Bees Honey" to her over and over. I whispered stories to her about her daddy and her grandparents and great-grandparents, and even her great-great-grandmother, Nana Bellini. I hadn't thought of Nana Bellini in a long time, and her memory calmed me. We played patty-cake and cuddled in our sleeping bag. Sarah was so good and so brave. She didn't fuss or cry. I think she enjoyed the close contact and the darkness, which might in some way have reminded her of being inside my womb.

Ott and Tim took turns checking in on us. Like the subjects in the famous Stanford psychology experiment with college students assigned the roles of prisoners and guards, Tim Shelly reveled in the role of jailer. He shoved me around, barking orders and obscenities at us, throwing our food on the floor. He obviously held no firm convictions of his own. He acted only on what others told him, but he would die for those others

— for anyone to whom he could attach his childlike adoration in the vacuum created by his father's death and Harlan Hurley's arrest. He was a mercenary, not a martyr.

Ott understood this and took full advantage of it, playing on Tim's fantasies of battle and the camaraderie of men-at-arms. Ott needed Tim's help — his brawn and expert knowledge of weapons — to pull off his plan. To get it, he lied to Tim about almost everything. He told Tim they would hold us hostage until Harlan Hurley was freed from prison, and that the arrest and kidnapping would start the race war that white supremacist groups had been preparing for so long to fight. Tim would become a great soldier in that war, Ott predicted, a hero. And Ott promised Tim that if things went wrong, his family's contacts in Germany and elsewhere, who had helped SS colonel Gerhardt Haber and other Nazis, would assist in their escape to South America, where money would be waiting.

Tim believed Ott's every word and longed for his chance at glory. But by the second day of waiting for the real combat to begin, boredom set in. Tim had gotten into the habit of conducting hourly searches of the mushroom house with his flashlight, examining the walls and dirt floor to see if Sarah and I were tunneling an escape. He would end his inspection with a pat-down search of my body, demanding that I lean with my face and arm pressed against the wall and my legs spread wide. I still wore my black skirt and cream-colored blouse from work. My stockings had disintegrated on the rough surface of the floor, and I had long since abandoned them. With each pat down, Tim would linger a little longer around my crotch and breasts, then call me a slut or whore and walk out. I made no reply, worried it would only agitate him further.

Late during our third night in the mushroom house, Tim performed his usual examination of the walls and floor but at the end walked up to where Sarah and I were huddled in our sleeping bag and yanked her away from me. I fought to hold on to her, but he hit me in the mouth with his elbow, knocking my head against the block wall, then carried Sarah to the opposite end of the building and plopped her down in a corner. She whimpered softly for a moment and then became quiet again. I tried to get on my feet to go after her, still dizzy from my head hitting the wall, but Tim slammed me back down onto the sleeping bag. In the dim yellow glow of the flashlight, he began tearing off my clothes.

I screamed for Ott and tried scratching and biting Tim, but even if I had two good arms he would have easily overpowered me. He was a large man — I no longer thought of him as a kid — built strong and solid with a thick chest and arms. He slapped me across the face and told me to stop screaming. When I continued, he punched me several times until blood spurted from my nose and mouth and I fainted. When I regained consciousness, he was on top of me. He had my panties off and my bra pulled up, and his pants were off.

Ott normally slept for two or three hours at a time during the night and had just awoken to make his rounds. He was outside relieving himself when he heard my muffled moans coming from the mushroom house. Still half asleep, he had left his gun behind. When he came through the door and saw Tim writhing on top of me, he thought at first that he was dreaming the nightmare that had sometimes terrorized him, of seeing his mother, Aunt Bette, and Nonna Amina being brutalized in Kamenz.

Tim looked over his shoulder and laughed when he saw Ott standing in the doorway.

"She only screws Jew boys," he said. "She thinks she likes them circumcised, but it's time for her to find out what a real man is like. You wait your turn outside and we'll see what she thinks. It won't take long."

Ott went wild. He charged Tim and kicked him in the head with his heavy boot as if he were knocking a humping dog off a neighbor's leg. Tim was stunned for a second, but then he reacted like the male of any species when another tries to take his mate. He roared up from the floor, unleashing on Ott all those years of training for combat and the frustration of waiting so long for the opportunity. He beat Ott mercilessly, slamming his panicked body against the racks and walls inside the mushroom house as if he were a doll.

I rolled over onto my knees to get Sarah and run, but then I saw Tim's pants and holster piled in the corner. In his desire to destroy Ott Bowles with his bare hands, Tim had forgotten about his gun. My grandfather had taught me how to handle and fire guns on the farm. I knew how to chamber a bullet and remove the safety, although steadying the gun with one hand while firing was difficult for me and bullets often went astray.

I grabbed Tim's gun, rose to my feet, and fired a shot into the dirt beside me. The sound was deafening and immediately stopped Tim and Ott from fighting. They both turned toward me, astonished. Then, as Tim had done with his father in Ott's museum in Buffalo, he lunged at me. I leaped back and squeezed the trigger three times. Tim dropped facedown onto the floor at my feet. His body heaved once, and a trickle of blood oozed out into the mushroom soil beneath his chest. His bare buttocks glistened with sweat in the flashlight.

I stared down at his body, stunned and horrified. I had just killed a man. I had just killed a man who kidnapped my daughter and me, a man who was trying to rape me. I couldn't believe any of this was happening.

I pointed the gun at Ott, trembling violently, my finger on the trigger. I didn't know what to do. I just wanted him to leave. He seemed as stunned as me, and he just stood there, waiting, almost hoping, it seemed, for me to shoot him. But I couldn't do it. He had risked his life to stop Tim from raping me, and he had stopped Tim from shooting me when I tried to drive away. He had spared Sarah's life when he could have shot her through the window. Somehow, even though he had put us through all of this, I felt sorry for Ott Bowles and didn't want to hurt him.

"Why?" I screamed at the top of my lungs.

"Why? All this for what? For what?" I backed away toward Sarah with the gun still pointing at him.

Sarah had begun crying when Ott and Tim started fighting, but she became quiet after I fired the three shots at Tim. I turned from Ott and stumbled through the darkness to find her. She was still where Tim had placed her, curled up on her side. I bent down and picked her up. She was wet, as though she had been perspiring or had peed through her diaper. I just wanted to take her back home to her daddy and the life we had made, where we would all be safe again. Cradling her against me and holding the gun, I made my way back toward the door.

I kept my eyes on Ott the entire time, illuminated by the flashlight and the small amount of light from the nighttime sky. He watched me warily but passively, as though he had accepted the truce I had offered. But when I stepped through the threshold of the mushroom house door, he made a move toward us. I was ready for him and didn't hesitate this time. I fired the gun.

The bullet struck Ott in the leg, and he collapsed to the floor next to Tim. I watched him through the door for a moment, deciding whether to shoot again. But then I suddenly realized that Sarah wasn't squirming

494

or crying even though I had just fired a gun next to her, with the same arm that was holding her.

I kneeled down to see her in the flashlight. Now I understood why she had felt so wet. Her clothes were soaked through with blood and her tiny chest was ripped open. There was blood all over her beautiful cheeks and the creamy white perfection of her stomach. Her brown eyes were wide, staring out into nothing.

One of the three shots I fired at Tim Shelly had hit my baby, my Sarah.

I had killed my own daughter.

## 39

The skies open as if all of the heavens surrounding the earth are filled with water and the seal holding it back is suddenly punctured. I have never seen it rain so hard.

Through all this rain, Elymas and I scale the rock cliff of a shrinking island mountain, climbing higher and higher above a shoreline that only minutes earlier had been arid grassland and Mediterranean forest. The branches of olive, cypress, and pomegranate trees sway like seaweed fronds in the surf, collecting floating grasses, berries, wilted flower petals, pieces of dung, logs, pottery, and the distended carcasses of animals — the detritus of the earth over which these trees once reached toward the sun. And one might ask, what sun? For despite the noontime hour, only a hint of ultraviolet gloom passes onto the despairing planet below.

Elymas had found me walking through the woods on my way to the Courtroom to present the soul of Otto Rabun Bowles. "We have one more visit to make, Brek Abigail Cuttler," he said, "to meet others with an interest in the outcome of the case. Come with me, you will not be delayed long."

I assumed he would take me to see Bo and maybe my father and mother, but instead he opened the portal of his unseeing eyes upon the terrible flood of Cudi Dagh.

Lightning flashes and thunder cracks across the sky. Elymas is above me on the cliff. The water rises in feet, not inches, the waves below consuming the foothills and everything in their path.

"We're going to drown!" I call up to him on the cliff, rain streaming down my face.

"Do not worry, Brek Cuttler!" Elymas yells back down to me. "Cudi Dagh stands seven thousand feet. Noah found refuge here. Come along quickly."

Less than one-third of that altitude remains as we press our cheeks against the face of the mountain for the final ascent. Elymas uses his gnarled fingers like a mattock, thrusting them into the crevices. He loses his grip only once, but it costs him his four-footed cane, which clicks against the boulders on the way back down to the roiling seas below. I keep my distance, afraid he will take me with him if he falls. I am as old and worn now as Elymas, moving slowly and cautiously, gasping for air and stopping often. I climb the mountain like a crippled goat, using the stump of my right arm for balance, barely able to see my next steps through the cataracts clouding my eyes. My clothes dissolve in the downpour into a paste of thread and dye that curdle into the wrinkles of my skin.

At the summit, we find a monastery constructed of mud thatch and thickset timbers ringed by an annular rock garden sprinkled with chunks of sandstone and quartz and veined blocks of marble. Behind the small building, a narrow escarpment offers what in better weather would have been magnificent views of the lesser mountains and plains of Ararat. At the far end, a monument is chiseled into the gray basalt ridge. It is a carving of an immense wooden barge run aground in rough seas, waiting for salvage beneath the pensive wings of a raven and a dove. On the deck of the barge gathers a herd of animals fortunate enough to have escaped the floodwaters — pairs of lesser mammals and reptiles of every species. At the bow stand the humble figures of a man and a woman.

Elymas nudges me inside the monastery,

where we find a small chapel kept warm by a fire that burns without fuel inside a stone fireplace. A semicircle of crude wooden stools encircles the raised hearth, and between these and the flames stands a small rectangular table that serves the monks as both dining place and altar. At the center of this table sits an unusual bronze menorah, tarnished waxy black. A one-armed crucifix, like the one that hung from my uncle Anthony's neck, is attached to the trunk and lowest branches of the menorah. The King of the Jews bends his left arm upward along the broad curve of the branch in a gesture of sublime exaltation.

Elymas ushers me through an alcove past one of the monks' cells, furnished with a bed of wooden slats suspended by iron straps above the floor. We enter the kitchen, which contains a small preparation table, a cistern overflowing with rainwater, and three wooden bins filled with dried fruit and nuts, as if the monastery has been recently inhabited. When we return from the kitchen into the chapel, we find that all but one of the stools in the semicircle around the hearth are occupied by monks wearing brown hooded robes. They face away from us toward the altar with its strange menorah, and on their laps they cradle laptop computers into which they stare reverently with their backs bent as if in prayer. Halos of fluorescent light from the computer screens give them the appearance of saints posed in a medieval painting.

We walk around them to see their faces, and I am stunned to discover that the first monk is Karen Busfield, wearing her blue Air Force uniform beneath her brown robe. Around her neck hangs the white linen stole on which I had embroidered a gold alpha and omega and presented as a gift at her ordination. It is a simple, conservative vestment, lacking the colorful ecclesiastical designs she preferred, but it was the best I could do with one hand. She wore it the day she married Bo and me and again the day she baptized Sarah. But she tried to give it back the day Bill Gwynne and I advised her to accept the government's offer to drop the treason and espionage charges in exchange for an honorable discharge and time served. She would be required only to plead guilty to criminal trespass on government property and promise to keep what happened inside the missile silo confidential. I approach her and touch her shoulder: "Karen, it's me, Brek. What are you doing here?"

She looks up from her computer screen but doesn't recognize me in my old age. Her cheeks are powdered with the brine of dried tears. Outside, the storm rages on. The timbers of the monastery stiffen like the scourged back of a flagellant paying his penance. Karen closes her eyes and begins mumbling a chant underneath her breath.

Next to Karen sits my mother-in-law, Katerine Schrieberg-Wolfson, the second monk of Cudi Dagh. She clutches two photographs against the side of her computer. The first is a picture of Sarah, her granddaughter, and the second is a black-and-white photograph of her father, Bo's grandfather, standing in front of one of his theaters in Dresden. Katerine Schrieberg-Wolfson does not weep as she sits transfixed by her computer. She has witnessed too much sorrow in her life to weep anymore. She regrets only that she had never told Amina Rabun that it was her father, Jared Schrieberg, on that dark day in Kamenz, when God turned his face from Christian and Jew alike, who fired the shots from the woods that drew the soldiers' attention.

"Poor Amina!" she cries. "But is it not a blessing that she didn't live to witness her only heir come to this? Oh, but now my precious granddaughter and daughter-in-law are paying for our sins! When will it end?"

Katerine gives no indication of recognizing me either. Instead, she looks suspiciously at the monk seated to her left, Albrecht Bosch, who is typing madly on his keyboard with ink-stained fingers. Bosch weeps profusely, as a father weeps for a son, and he pleads in vain at the screen: "No! No! No!"

Albrecht Bosch thought he had understood Ott Bowles's suffering, and that, by sharing his own sorrows with Ott, had shown him the way. He had been there for Ott as a friend, as the father he would never be in place of the father who never was. From his stool in the monastery, Bosch sends another e-mail to Ott, pleading with him to surrender. But the time for Albrecht Bosch's final appeal has passed, leaving him alone again in a world that had never really welcomed him.

Sitting on the stools next to Bosch, Tad Bowles and Barratte Rabun follow the drama on their computers in disbelief, each concerned not for their son but for the difficulties that will be visited upon their own lives by his behavior. Tad's preoccupation is his reputation: "My name will be forever associated with a murderer!" he bellows.

Barratte Rabun too is consumed by names, but hers is a different complaint — she mourns an opportunity lost to resurrect a name rather than the urgent need to bury one. That name, Rabun, has now been soiled beyond all recognition, and dirtied with it is her dream of the family that lived so long ago breathing once again within the bodies of its children and grandchildren. She beseeches the heavens: "How? How could I have lost them again? Twice in the same lifetime!"

The computer in Barratte's lap, where once she cradled this precious dream filled with such hope, sends back a message that the dream is indeed lost forever. And that message confirms for Barratte Rabun what her cousin Amina had understood and explained long ago — that the mercy of God will never shed its light upon the Rabuns of Kamenz. Barratte closes her computer and throws it into the fire. She will not grant the unforgiving God of that perverse, meaningless relic on the altar table another moment of satisfaction.

The stool at the apex of the semicircle sits vacant. Next to it sits Harlan Hurley, wearing orange prison coveralls beneath his brown robe, smirking from ear to ear as if he is playing a computer game and winning with every move. Events have unfolded in ways even his grand dreams could not have predicted. The scandal of using school district funds to support Die Elf and the making of the documentary has shoved Hurley's fascist drama onto the front page of every major newspaper and into the lead segment of every news broadcast and talk show. Deluded supporters have flooded the airwaves with words of support and the mail with money.

Next to Hurley in the chapel sit my poor parents, eyes transfixed upon their computers in anguish and disbelief. They do not even notice me standing beside them. How can one begin to describe the agony of parents witnessing the murder of their own daughter and their own granddaughter? In their grief-stricken faces atop Cudi Dagh, I see the unfathomable joy of my first moments of life — the jubilant astonishment and wonder that rises up from the vulnerability of birth to declare again for a cynical world the existence of unconditional love. I could not bear the gift of that love as I grew older. I convinced myself I was not worthy of receiving it, even as I recognized it emanating from me with the birth of my own daughter. Yet here it is again, pouring forth from the shattered faces of my parents, flailing itself against the computer screens in a futile attempt to shield me from harm, to protect the dying object of an infinite grace.

The digital clocks at the bottom corners of the computer screens on the laps of the monks of Cudi Dagh all display 4:02:34 a.m., 10/17/94. The screens flicker brightly, as if they are bursting into flame, then they show me holding Sarah, bloodied and lifeless, in the dim light of the mushroom house. I am screaming without sound, as if in a silent movie. The gun drops from my fingers. Ott Bowles, with a bullet hole in his leg, slides across the floor toward it.

The computer screens cannot show what Ott Bowles is thinking at that moment, but I know. His soul is mine now, and we are forever one. He is thinking about Amina, Barratte, and the Rabuns of Kamenz. He is thinking about the Schriebergs and how they have been ungrateful. He is thinking about the world and how it has been merciless. He is thinking about Harlan Hurley and Sam Mansour and how my husband has destroyed them. He is thinking about Tim Shelly and how I have killed him and my own child. He is thinking about how he rushed forward to help us out of the mushroom house but how I shot him down in cold blood. He is thinking about how unjust and unfair life has been.

Most of all, Otto Rabun Bowles is thinking about justice.

He knows now the documentary will never be aired, and that he will be forever misunderstood, blamed, and convicted for Tim's and Sarah's deaths. The Rabuns have always been misunderstood, blamed, convicted for things they did not do.

The computer screens on the laps of the monks finally show what I have been unable to accept from the moment of my arrival in Shemaya. Ott Bowles raises the gun and fires three silent shots into my chest. I slump over on top of Sarah. Moments later, police officers storm the mushroom house. They had been able to tràce his e-mails after all.

# 40

The giant fist of the storm pounds the roof of the monastery of Cudi Dagh, demanding that the gilty appear for sentencing. When the storm is not appeased, the mountain itself begins to quake, and the sea overtakes the summit, bursting through the door of the monastery. The one-armed Savior on the menorah breaks free from his nails and tumbles head over heels into the water, but none of the monks dare to retrieve him — and it might be that none of them care — for he alone would spare the condemned, and there is no room left in the monastery of Cudi Dagh for forgiveness.

"Find him!" I scream, but I am not searching for the fallen Savior. I am hunting for the sinner, Otto Rabun Bowles, and I burn with the desire to become the instrument of his torture and be within earshot of his shrieks. The thunderclap of electricity that too gently ended his life is only the beginning of what I have planned for him.

Harlan Hurley leaps from his stool in a blind panic, believing it is his soul the storm hounds; and perhaps it is, for when he reaches the door of the monastery he is vaporized instantly by a bolt of lightning, leaving behind only the shape of his silhouette burned into the wood. Barratte Rabun, Albrecht Bosch, and Katerine Schrieberg-Wolfson look after him in horror but decide to follow him through the same door, believing that the storm is now satisfied. They too are disintegrated immediately by three more bolts of lightning.

The water is now up to my knees, and, for the first time, I see Bo and my Grandpa Cuttler sitting in a corner of the monastery, oblivious to the waters rising around them, staring at a single computer held between them. Grandpa Cuttler doesn't understand computers and is perplexed by what is now a blank screen. Together they press the keys, trying desperately to restart the machine.

After photographing the crime scene at the mushroom house, the coroner took Sarah and me to the morgue. Bo called Karen and asked her to be there with him when he identified our bodies. She was the logical choice. Even though Bo was Jewish, Karen had baptized Sarah just six months earlier over the beautiful silver font at Old Swedes' Church. Confident that beautiful morning that Christ himself had claimed Sarah as his own, Karen lifted her high for the congregation to witness the blessed miracle of faith and water, and beaming with a mother's own pride — because Bo and I had asked Karen to be Sarah's godmother — she carried her new goddaughter up into the pulpit with her to deliver the sermon. Sarah listened without a sound, as if she yearned to understand.

Karen prayed hard for Christ to be with Bo and her in the morgue that day when the coroner pulled back the sheets. She prayed for him to reclaim the child he had accepted so recently and the woman, wife, mother, and friend who had been taken away. She anointed our heads with holy oil and pleaded for our souls.

But Christ did not come, at least not in a form Karen could recognize. She howled in anguish: "Where are you? Damn you, where are you?"

A raging torrent of water fills the monastery. Cudi Dagh is being swallowed whole by the flood. Bo, my grandfather, and my parents flee in terror, but Bo sees the one-armed

Christ figurine bobbing in the water and looks back at Karen.

"There's your Savior, Priest!" he laughs maniacally. "Justice nailed him to the cross, and now justice is setting him free!"

Karen splashes after the broken Christ in the same way we chased after crayfish in the Little Juniata River. She lunges, but he escapes through her fingers, disappearing beneath the water.

"I can't find him!" she cries. "I can't find him!" Twice more she sees him, and twice more he slips through her fingers as the waters rise, carrying him out into the storm.

Karen is the last monk to leave the monastery. On her way out she pulls off both the white stole I gave her and her winged Air Force insignia. She throws them into the fire on top of the charred remains of Barratte Rabun's computer, which is still burning.

Karen does not look back to see the rising waters quench the flames and carry the stole and the insignia out of the hearth unharmed. They float freely together for a moment, like a dove and a raven in search of dry land. The stole spots the long branches of the menorah first, then the insignia comes, and together they cling to the branches until the waters engulf the menorah too. At the last second, as the menorah disappears beneath a whirlpool of water, the stole and the insignia take flight again, searching the waters for a sign of compassion.

The water is chest deep now. Elymas grabs my hand.

"We must reach the ark," he shouts, "before it is too late!"

Suddenly, Elymas and I are standing on the deck of a great wooden ark in near-total darkness. The storm lashes the boat, and we are being tossed about on high waves. But Elymas insists we must stay on deck and not seek shelter below.

I hear the anxious sounds of animals beneath my feet — the cacophony of an entire zoo assembled under one roof. Each time the ark pitches, the cries of the animals grow louder, but I begin to hear other cries too: awful, relentless shrieks and moans come from outside the ship, rising above the wind and thunder, overcoming the sounds of the animals. These are the most chilling, terrifying sounds I have ever heard.

"What is it?" I ask.

Elymas points a gnarled finger overboard, and the clouds lift just enough for the sun's weak rays to illuminate the churning sea all the way to the horizon. Across all that distance, as far as I can see in every direction, the waters are covered with a slick of bloated bodies, human and animal. Each wave brings them crashing and grinding into the hull of the ark. Those humans still alive on this sea of horror are using the dead as rafts, clinging to the cadavers of their mothers and fathers, sons and daughters, calling out for mercy and forgiveness in languages I have never heard. The stench of decaying flesh is overwhelming, causing me to retch.

A deck hatch opens, and up through it climbs an old man, weathered, gray-bearded, and harried, followed by a young man and his wife. They look out upon the carnage spread across the sea and are horrified.

"Hurry! Hurry!" the young man yells. "We must rescue them, as many as we can! We cannot allow them to drown!"

The young man and woman begin running around the deck gathering ropes, but the old man orders them to stop.

"No!" he commands. "They have chosen, and for their choices they have been sentenced. Only we have been found righteous. Only we shall be saved."

The young man's wife falls to her knees at

the old man's feet.

"Oh, please, Father, please, let us help them!" she begs. "We cannot bear their suffering. Surely they are people born as you and I, who have done wrong and right as you and I. Surely you see that. You alone, Father, were chosen as righteous, and the righteous, Father, must take pity upon the wretched. Our ship is large and we could save hundreds, thousands. Please, Father, we must try!"

"Take her away from me!" the old man orders. "Take her out of my sight at once or I will throw her over with the others. I do not hear their cries. The time for weeping is past."

The son glares at his father with hatred but immediately obeys and leads his wife back down into the bowels of the ship. The old man looks out again upon the sea and then up at the heavens. Rain lashes his face so that it appears as if he might be weeping. But then he too turns back down through the hatch, sealing it tight behind him. Like a linen shroud soaked with sweet oils and spices, the clouds descend onto the sea, compressing the putrid air into the waves and muffling the groans and screams.

The grinding of flesh and bone against the hull of the ark continued for one hundred fifty days.

And then the waters receded.

Elymas and I were there when Noah sent forth the raven and the dove, and we were there when the dove returned with an olive branch. Noah and his family were the only people to board the ark, and they were the only people to disembark when it ran aground on Ararat. No one from the sea was saved.

Noah built an altar and made a sacrifice to Yahweh that day, and on that day Yahweh was well pleased. Yahweh blessed Noah and his sons, telling them to repopulate the earth. When Yahweh smelled the burning flesh of Noah's sacrifice, he promised never to flood the earth again. As a reminder of that covenant, rainbows appeared in the clouds.

After seeing all this, Elymas turned to me and said:

"Luas accused Noah of being a coward, but now you know the truth, Brek Cuttler. When lesser men would have faltered, Noah made no excuses for humanity. The story is not about love, it is about justice."

And then, all at once, I was back in the woods behind Nana's house, on my way to Shemaya Station. Elymas was gone. I was a young woman again, dressed in my black silk suit covered with baby-formula stains that turn to blood. I was on my way to the Courtroom to present the case of No. 44371.

# 41

No. 44371 sits on the same bench where I found myself when I first arrived at Shemaya Station. It is as if no time has passed. My blood is still tacky on the floor, turning red the bottoms of No. 44371's white-soled prison sneakers.

He looks just as I imagined he would after the executioner sent 4,000 volts of electricity crashing through his body. His scalp is bald and raw where it has not been charred into black flake and ash by the electrode. His skin and face are the color of stale milk. Abrasions cover his wrists and ankles. His eyes bulge from their sockets, and his trousers are soiled. He holds an object in his hands, but when he sees me, he hides it and looks down at the floor, hoping it will open up and devour him. No. 44371 knows that today is the day he will face his eternity.

Next to No. 44371, at the opposite end of the bench, sits a young girl who also stares at the floor. She looks familiar, like a young Amina Rabun playing with her brother in the sandbox, or a young Katerine Schrieberg walking with her father to the café in Dresden, or a young Sheila Bowles playing with a doll on her bed at the sanatorium. This girl is like all little girls — innocent, preoccupied, dreaming — but she sits naked on the bench, pale and emaciated like death.

*What could she have done to be brought to this place?*

As if in reply to my thought, she looks up at me and says: "God punishes children for the sins of their parents."

A low rumbling sound echoes through the great hall, a sound like a train entering the station. I turn from the little girl to see Gautama, the sculptor of the sphere from the cocktail party. He is dressed in the same rainbow-colored dhoti wrapped around his waist and legs, and he is rolling his magical stone sphere among the postulants. He smiles at them like a peddler trying to sell his wares, but they pay him no attention even as the sphere nears them and flashes the patterns of their lives across its surface, mapping their journeys to now.

Gautama stops his sphere in front of No. 44371. It sands itself smooth before erupting into the grotesque rash of Otto Bowles's life, crisscrossing the sphere like a ball of yarn — here a young boy embarrassed and enraged, unable to forgive his father for striking his grandfather at the football game, there a man firing three bullets into my chest and demanding death by electric chair. In his arrogance, sitting here on the bench beneath the dome of rusted girders and trusses, which from far above Shemaya Station might appear to be a manhole cover in some forsaken back alley of the universe, No. 44371 does not notice his life carved into the sphere, or think about the necessity of sewers to carry off the effluent of Creation. He stares stubbornly into the floor, daring it to rise up and seize him. I do not hear the cry of his soul as I did during the naive moment of compassion in my office before facing him. I hear nothing at all. I make a note to include his insolence in my presentation.

"Greetings, my daughter," Gautama says to me.

The surface of the sphere changes as I approach it, reproducing the pattern of my own life's choices. I had seen only glimpses of them at the cocktail party, between the pairs of doors, but now they are displayed in great detail, like a road map on a globe. The trail begins with my birth at the top of the sphere and the earliest injustice of being forced from my mother's womb, separated forever from her shelter and protection. The doors open next onto Nana's funeral and the injustice of being slapped by my mother — the mother who had created and loved me — for crying when I was forced to kiss Nana's corpse. The sphere shows the nights when my mother was too drunk or depressed to care for me, and her vicious fights with my father, who was too selfish and preoccupied to notice. Through another set of doors, I am thrusting my right hand into the conveyor chain, offering myself as a sacrifice to my parents. And there, through yet another pair, I am an amputee, crying amidst a group of children who have tucked their arms inside their jackets and circled me with their sleeves flapping in the wind. Father O'Brien tells me justice is for God later, but Bill Gwynne tells me it is for us now, and I testify that the chain guard was in place but failed when I stumbled into it. Boys torture crayfish in buckets, and I put them on trial, deciding that day to become a lawyer because justice is the only salvation.

The sphere rotates. Here I am, worrying with my grandfather about fuel prices and recession during the 1970s, and reading from my other grandfather's treatises about equity and law. My father announces he is remarrying, and my mother celebrates this, and another anniversary of my uncle Anthony's death in Vietnam, with a bottle of gin. I am not asked to the school prom — the boys are too afraid of me, and I of them.

The sphere rotates again, and I am in law school now, meeting my first client on an internship at the welfare clinic, promising that I will find justice for her and her eight children who have not eaten in three days. I overwhelm the bureaucrats with legal papers and easily win the case. There I am later, an intern at the Philadelphia district attorney's office, meeting my first victims of crime and promising justice for them too. I outprepare the overworked public defender and easily win the conviction. During the summers, I work at large corporate law firms with granite conference tables and expensive artwork on the walls. We promise the president of a chemical company we'll do everything possible to defeat the class-action lawsuit brought by the heirs of those who died after being exposed to his company's pesticides. My legal research for the case is thorough and creative, and the partners of the firm are so impressed that they offer me a full-time position, but I turn it down.

The sphere rotates again. Bo is in my bed asking me to marry him. I say yes, filled with joy and love. Our wedding is beautiful, a fantasy come true.

We move to Huntingdon. I convince my mother-in-law to sue Amina and Barratte Rabun for her inheritance. I know now how to acquire and control justice, to make it do my bidding and to savor its many pleasures.

The sphere rotates a final time. An average day of life together with my husband. I am scolding Bo because he has left his clothes all over the floor again. He does this all the time, even though I've reminded him. I attack him like a hostile witness on the stand. He has no defense. He just sits there in his shorts and T-shirt, looking confused. When he fails to apologize or concede the seriousness of his crime, I bring him to justice too. I am unwilling to allow even errant socks and underwear to pass unpunished for fear that injustice will tighten its grip around my life and my world. I bare my teeth and clench my fists. I throw things around the room, seething with irrational and unjustifiable rage. Then the sphere inches forward and shows me in my law office, writing a brief to help Alan Fleming escape repaying his debts on a legal technicality.

The sphere has come almost full circle now, displaying the final two choices of my life. The first is my decision not to shoot Ott Bowles in the mushroom house, choosing the door on the right. The second is my change of heart, my decision to shoot him as he steps toward me, choosing the door on the left. With that decision, the circle is closed and the sphere has returned to the place of my beginning, to the place of unconditional love before I was separated from my mother's womb.

Gautama rolls the sphere slightly toward No. 44371, and it superimposes his choices over mine. Somehow we have taken similar paths. Our ending in the mushroom house seems almost mathematically certain, the inevitable result of a series of parallel equations and geometric principles. We spent our lives protecting ourselves from the unbearable pain of injustice. We spent our lives renouncing the inconceivable possibility of forgiveness.

The girl on the bench stirs. She is interested in the sphere and reaches out with her right hand to touch it but cannot because there is only a stump ending at the elbow. I remember her now: I had seen her in the great hall during the cocktail party, when Luas showed me the postulants among the shadows. I was unable to see inside her soul then, and, for some reason, the surface of the sphere reveals nothing more of her now.

The sphere erases itself again. Two pairs of doors appear. They look like miniatures of the doors to the Courtroom. Above one pair is the word "Justice" and above the other the word "Forgiveness."

"Noah once stood before these doors," Gautama says. "And Jesus of Nazareth too was humbled by them. Now your time has come, my daughter."

The girl looks from Gautama to me, retracting the stump of her arm.

"You saw Yahweh butcher them," Gautama continues. "Mothers, fathers, babies. You sailed with Noah upon the sea of horror, you smelled their rotting bodies and heard their pathetic cries."

"Yes," I say.

"And when the waters receded and the sun returned, you saw Noah look up at the Murderer. You saw Him with your own eyes, my daughter, and yet, you still do not see."

"I saw Divine Justice unfurled in rainbows," I respond in my defense.

"Rainbows are not the colors of justice, my daughter. They are the colors of forgiveness."

"God forgave no one."

"That is true, my daughter. But Noah forgave God, and the colors of God's joy burst through the clouds. Thousands of years later, on one dark and terrible afternoon, the people tortured and murdered God. God forgave the people that day, and the colors of our joy burst through on Easter morning. Love is shown to be unconditional, my daughter, only when it embraces that which is least deserving of love. What you do not yet understand is that justice is the exact opposite of all that love is and all that you are. The longer you pursue it, the farther you run from the place you wish to be. The Kingdom of God can be entered only by the path of forgiveness."

No. 44371 rises from the bench and walks across the train station, leaving behind the young girl and the object he had been holding in his hands.

"But love is justice," I say to Gautama.

"It is not so, my daughter," Gautama replies. "Cain murdered Abel for justice. God flooded the earth for justice. The people crucified Jesus of Nazareth for justice. Terror and murder are the way of justice, not the way of love. Every war waged, and every harm inflicted, has been for the sake of justice. Soldiers kill because they believe their cause is just. Assailants attack because they believe they have just cause. Justice drives the abusive spouse, the angry parent, the screaming child, the feuding neighbor, the outraged nation. He who seeks justice is harmed, not healed, because to obtain justice one must do that which is unjust. God experienced perfect justice when He flooded the earth and destroyed the possibility of evil, but the price of achieving perfect justice was unbearable. All creation was destroyed, and God was separated from all that God loved and all that could love God in return. This is why the story is told, my daughter. It is a warning, not an invitation. Rainbows contain God's covenant never to seek justice again."

"But not to seek justice is to allow others to harm us, to become victims."

"No, my daughter. Not to seek justice is to love those who harm us and become victors. Love is not passive or submissive. It is the determined application of opposite force to hatred and fear, demanding the highest effort and skill. The warrior who fights back with weapons is honored and celebrated, but what bravery is there in meeting gun with gun? True bravery is displayed in meeting gun with arms wide open, refusing to submit to hatred and fear, even under pain of death. It is true that an assailant may fear retribution and stop his attack, but it is just as true that he may ignore the threat of retribution and continue the onslaught. Has justice prevented the crime? We are all born with the freedom to choose. The wise man who chooses love over justice controls himself. Extending unconditional love, he ends his suffering and reenters the Garden from which he came. Reuniting with his Creator, he knows, at last, what it means to be God."

I reach down and pick up the object Ott Bowles left on the bench. It is the small figurine of the one-armed Christ that fell from the menorah on Cudi Dagh. The young girl stirs and reaches out timidly with her left hand. I allow her to have it. She takes it and walks across the train shed to Luas, who has just entered and is seating himself on a bench next to a new presenter who has just arrived at the station and is sitting all alone, looking perplexed. I had not seen him there earlier. The girl offers Luas the figurine, but he waves her away and she wanders off. Luas smiles at the new presenter the way he smiled at me when I first arrived, as if to say: *Yes, my son, I see. I see what you are afraid to see, but I will pretend not to have noticed.*

# 42

The man on the bench tries to deny and conceal his wounds, as I had done when I first arrived, but I am a presenter now, and I can see them, and with them I see the last moments of his life.

The man's name is Elon Kaluzhsky. His abdomen is torn open, and pieces of his face and forehead are missing, along with both arms and legs. Twenty minutes before he arrived at Shemaya Station, when his body was still whole, he kissed his beautiful wife and three beautiful children good-bye for the day and walked the two blocks from their apartment on a quiet street in Haifa to the bus stop. Rosh Hashanah would begin at sundown that evening, and Elon Kaluzhsky was thinking about the festive meal they would share. He loved dates, and as he walked down the street he contemplated the Rosh Hashanah prayer that must be said before eating them: "May it be your will, G-d, that our enemies be finished."

With this thought fresh in his mind, Elon took the last available seat on the Number 35 express bus, which would bring him to the downtown offices of the profitable Israeli export business where he maintained the accounts. He was full of goodwill this morning and offered a pleasant hello to the oddly overdressed man seated next to him, wearing a long overcoat on an eighty-five-degree day. The greeting was not returned, but even this did not spoil Elon's happy mood. He smiled kindly at the elderly couple sitting across the aisle from him and at the pretty, young secretary next to them. Farther down the aisle sat several businessmen reading newspapers, a group of high school students, and a young mother cradling her infant son.

The express bus gathered speed and the buildings of Haifa flashed by. In the middle of the journey, in the middle of a street, the overdressed man stood calmly, braced himself against a support pole for standing passengers, and from beneath his long coat pulled an automatic assault rifle. Without uttering a word, he opened fire on the passengers, sweeping the bus in an arc. Brass shell casings rained down, and a fine spray of blood filled the air as bodies collapsed onto the floor, including the elderly couple, the secretary, the businessmen, the high school students, and the young mother cradling her now mortally wounded infant son.

Elon Kaluzhsky, who had been thinking about dates and their meaning, was an athletic man and reacted bravely. He tackled the man with the gun and pinned him to the floor.

"You Arab bastard!" he screamed at him in Hebrew. "You son of a bitch!"

The man spat in Elon's face and said, *"La ilaha illa 'llah."* And then he detonated the suicide bomb strapped to his waist.

Luas embraces Elon, who has just recognized that his own blood is flowing through the gaping wound in his abdomen and is now sobbing uncontrollably on the bench. Luas leads him away, to what Elon believes is the house outside Moscow where he was raised, to be cared for there by a tender spirit he believes is the soul of his mother, who died ten years earlier of cancer. Elon does not notice on the way out of the train shed that seated on the next bench over is the Arab man who blew himself and Elon down the tracks into Shemaya Station. I can see the last moments of this man's life too, and I recognize his face and his thoughts. Samar Mansour was not thinking about passengers or dates when he boarded the Number 35 express bus in Haifa. He did not even see the faces of those around him. He saw only Israeli soldiers firing bullets into the bodies of Palestinian children.

It had been hot the day before in Ramallah, and the customers in the café had become irritable from the heat, from the humiliating Israeli checkpoints, and from being penned into their neighborhoods like animals. When Samar Mansour heard the gunshots, he raced up the blockaded alley and into the line of fire to see if he could help. Children who had been throwing stones at the Israeli soldiers were running back down the alley toward him, but when he arrived he saw three boys lying in pools of blood on the ground. The Israeli soldiers aimed their guns into the crowd from the walls and rooftops. Samar lifted one of the injured boys and carried him to an arriving ambulance. The boy had a leg wound and was not hurt badly. Samar tried to comfort him.

Other men arrived at the same ambulance, carrying the other two injured boys. Samar heard a woman wailing behind them, "Hanni! Hanni!" as she tried to reach one of the boys. Samar could tell instantly the little boy was dead. Military ammunition does unspeakable violence to a child's small body.

Something changed in Samar Mansour at that moment. He thought of his father, orphaned by the Israelis and forced to carry the bags of an American archaeologist to survive. He thought of his Holocaust documentary, which had changed nothing at all, and of his theories, which had liberated no one. He thought of the little boy, Hanni, whose life in Ramallah had been full of misery, and of Hanni's mother, who would never forget the horrifying image of her son that day.

Luas returns to the train shed after leaving Elon Kaluzhsky with his mother and sits down on the bench next to Samar.

"Welcome to Shemaya," he says. "My name is Luas."

Like Elon, Samar tries to conceal and deny his wounds, but there is not much left of him to conceal, actually, just a head and some torn pieces of flesh and bone plopped in a grotesque pile on the bench. But in Samar's imagination, he is whole. Luas smiles at him, as if to say: *Yes, my son, I see. I see what you are afraid to see, but I will pretend*

531

*not to have noticed.*

Across Shemaya Station, Gautama rolls his stone sphere forward, toward a muscular young man sitting all alone on a bench. I recognize this young man as Tim Shelly. He is covered with sweat and has no pants, exactly as I had last seen him in the mushroom house. The surface of the sphere changes, but I cannot look.

"The choice is yours, my daughter," Gautama calls out to me. "You are standing before the doors, as all people who have come before you and all who will come after. Which door will you choose?"

# 43

I do not remember anymore.

Were my eyes blue like the sky or brown like fresh-tilled earth?

Did my hair curl into giggles around my chin or drape over my shoulders in a frown? Was my skin light or dark? Was my body heavy or lean? Did I wear tailored silks or rough cotton and flax?

I do not remember. I remember that I was a woman, which is more than mere recollection of womb and bosom. And for a moment, I remembered all my moments in linear time, which began with womb and bosom and ended there too. But these are fading away now, discarded ballast from a ship emerged from the storm.

I remember unlocking the doors and entering the Courtroom to present the soul of Otto Rabun Bowles. I was met there by the being from the monolith but denied passage to the presenter's chair.

"This way," the being said, pointing to the monolith itself.

A fissure opened in the sapphire wall. Once inside, I climbed several flights of stairs to the triangular aperture at the top through which light enters but does not exit. I came to a small balcony from which I could see the glistening amber floor of the Courtroom below. Looking out, I could see other Courtrooms, thousands of them, with thousands of sapphire monoliths rising up like chimney stacks across a city skyline, extending to the horizon and beyond.

In one of the Courtrooms close to mine, Mi Lau, the Vietnamese girl, stood at the presenter's chair and, extending her arms, announced:

"I PRESENT ANTHONY BELLINI . . . HE HAS CHOSEN!"

The energy from the walls of her Courtroom surged through her, washing into the Courtroom a dirt tunnel beneath a village, Mi Lau's family, my uncle Anthony, a grenade, and a horrific explosion. The being from the monolith ended the presentation when Uncle Anthony put a gun to his own head and squeezed the trigger. But God did not pass judgment upon Anthony Bellini's soul from the balcony of the monolith. God had not even been there to watch. The balcony was empty.

In another Courtroom nearby stood Hanz Stössel declaring:

"I PRESENT AMINA RABUN . . . SHE HAS CHOSEN!"

I had seen this presentation before and knew the ending. Again the balcony was empty. No one heard Hanz Stössel's cries for justice from his Israeli prison cell.

In yet another Courtroom, young Bette Rabun raised her arms and screamed:

"I PRESENT VASILY PETROV . . . HE HAS CHOSEN!"

The Courtroom turned into little Bette's bedroom in Kamenz, where a Soviet soldier named Vasily held her arms down while one of his comrades beat and raped her in the darkness. No one stood on the balcony of the monolith to witness the crime or to convict the prisoner.

In another Courtroom, Elon Kaluzhsky raised his arms and cried:

"I PRESENT SAMAR MANSOUR . . . HE HAS CHOSEN!"

Into his Courtroom roared the Number 35 express bus, the sounds of gunfire, and the concussion of a bomb. Again, the balcony in the monolith was vacant. No one saw the last terrible moments of Elon Kaluzhsky's life.

From a Courtroom behind me came Luas's voice:

"I PRESENT NERO CLAUDIUS CAESAR . . . HE HAS CHOSEN!"

I turned to see Luas being brought in chains before Nero. At the emperor's instruction, a Roman soldier raised his sword and decapitated him. Luas's bald and bloodied head rolled within an inch of the emperor's foot. He kicked it away, then motioned for the mess to be cleaned. The being from the monolith ended the presentation, and Luas walked back out of the Courtroom. No one watched from the balcony, and no one condemned Nero for his crime.

Moments later, Luas appeared inside my Courtroom, accompanied by Samar Mansour. They took their places on the observer chairs. Samar Mansour looked around the Courtroom in fascination and awe, as I did on my first visit.

"Brek Cuttler will be presenting the case of Otto Bowles," Luas whispered.

"I'm up here!" I called down to Luas, but he couldn't hear me.

Then Haissem entered the Courtroom, the young boy who had presented the soul of Toby Bowles. Luas was visibly disappointed, as he had been when Toby failed to appear to present the case of his father.

"Oh, it's only you, Haissem," Luas said, frowning. "We were expecting Ms. Cuttler . . . Well, here we are anyway. Haissem, this is Samar Mansour, the newest lawyer on my staff. Samar, this is Haissem, the most senior presenter in Shemaya. I must say, Haissem, that Samar has arrived not a moment too soon. We just lost Amina Rabun and now, it seems, Ms. Cuttler."

"Welcome to the Courtroom, Samar," Haissem said, bowing politely. "I once sat here to witness my first presentation. Abel presented the difficult case of his brother Cain. That was long before your time though, Luas."

"Quite," Luas said.

"Little has changed since then," Haissem said. "Luas keeps the docket moving, even though the number of cases increases. We're fortunate to have you, Samar, and you're fortunate to have Luas as your mentor. There's no better presenter in all of Shemaya."

"Present company excepted," Luas replied.

"Not at all," said Haissem. "I handle the easy cases."

"Few would consider Socrates and Judas easy cases," Luas said. "I'm just a clerk."

Haissem winked at Samar. "Don't let him fool you," he said. "Without Luas there would be no Shemaya." He took Samar's hand. "I must enter my appearance now and prepare myself. We will meet again, Samar, after your first case. You'll do well here. I'm certain of it."

Haissem moved to the center of the Courtroom. The being from the monolith emerged and whispered something to him, then returned. Haissem stood, raised his arms in a graceful arc, and in a voice much louder than the other presenters, almost an explosion, he said:

"I PRESENT BREK ABIGAIL CUT-TLER . . . SHE HAS CHOSEN!"

I remember hearing the sounds of water rushing and wind blowing, of dolphins laughing and birds singing, of children talking and parents sighing, of stars and galaxies living and dying . . . the sounds of the earth breathing, if you could have heard it from the other side of the universe. I remember hearing God in those sounds, crying out for forgiveness from Cudi Dagh, and I remember hearing humanity in those sounds, crying out for forgiveness from Golgotha. And there too in the music was the ineffable joy of Noah, reaching up from the littoral to forgive his Father, and above that the ineffable joy of God, reaching down from the cross to forgive His children. And somewhere still, more faint, but it was there, I heard the cry of Otto Rabun Bowles, and with it the song of another soul, so joyous it could be heard above all these sounds, singing three words over and over:

"I AM LOVE! I AM LOVE! I AM LOVE!"

It was the song of unconditional love — the song of Eve returning home to the Garden after such a long and terrifying journey. The song grew louder as the presentation of my life continued, and in this song I heard Divine perfection, because in it I heard all of Creation: my birth into the world was in that song as was my mother's first embrace. Flowers were there, and music, sun, and rain. Mountains and oceans were there, and books, sculptures, and paintings. Boyfriends and girlfriends were there, and brothers and sisters on porch swings, children at play in sandboxes, and a young man running to the defense of a woman. Horses, sailboats, and babies were there, apple trees and cattle too, and mothers nurturing their young. Bread, water, and wine were there. Eyes and ears, skin and hair, lips and arms and legs. Water was there, and blankets, sunsets, moons and stars, work and play, heroes and heroines. The generations were in that song, and generosity and selflessness too. And love was there. But fear was there too. A parent's abusiveness and a child's selfishness, a dishonest lawyer and her dishonest client, an adulterer and his lover, a soldier and his gun, a death chamber and an incinerator, racists, liars, drunks, rapists, and thieves. Boys who tortured crayfish were in this song, as were the God who slaughtered His own children and the children who slaughtered their own God.

The being from the monolith joined me on the balcony and asked if I had reached a verdict or wished to see more evidence. I said that I had seen enough. It returned to the floor of the Courtroom and ended the presentation. Luas and Samar Mansour left the Courtroom, but Haissem stayed behind.

He entered the monolith, and I could hear him climbing the stairs, but the soul who appeared on the balcony to greet me was not Haissem, the little boy. It was Nana Bellini. And she was holding Sarah!

I raced to her and took her into my arm. My precious baby, my beautiful child. She was perfect, complete, unharmed. Exactly as I remembered her when I picked her up at the day care, dressed in her sweatpants and sweatshirt, smiling wide at me with a sticky brown ring of Nilla Wafer around her mouth, her hair dark and full of curls like her daddy's.

Through my tears, squeezing Sarah close, I could see the Courtroom below filling with souls. Tobias Bowles was there, and Jared Schrieberg, and Amina Rabun, all radiant and beautiful. Behind them came Claire Bowles, and Sheila Bowles, and between them Bonnie Campbell. Henry Collins was there, and Helmut Rabun, and Amina's mother and father, uncle, grandfather, and cousins. My uncle Anthony was there, and behind him, Mi Lau's family. And then the crowd parted, as if to allow someone very important to pass. A young man carrying a tray made his way through the opening.

He entered the monolith and climbed the stairs, but he hesitated at the top when he saw Sarah and me. I didn't recognize him at first. He looked so different with all that hair and his eyes so clear and blue. Sarah smiled, and he came closer. He knelt and placed the tray before us. It was a silver tray with a silver teapot and three silver cups.

"Hot tea and bees honey," Ott Bowles said, his eyes filling with tears, "for three we will share."

# AUTHOR'S NOTE

I grew up on a farm in central Pennsylvania, but my folks weren't farmers. My father was an insurance agent and my mother a home-maker. Since we didn't earn our living from the land, I wasn't accepted by the neighbor-ing farm kids. Years of escalating bullying, harassment, and intimidation followed. One night, this culminated with a group of them staging an attack on my home and shooting and killing one of our dogs while she was asleep in her pen — our sweet little beagle named Paula that we had raised from a puppy. The police did nothing. A week later, after another nighttime attack when they blew up our mailbox, I went chasing after them in a blind rage with a loaded .32 caliber revolver in my car. I cornered them against a barn. When they got out of their truck in the darkness with the high beams of my car focused on them, I grabbed the revolver from the passenger seat.

At that moment, I imagined how good I would feel to finally get justice, gunning them down after all they had put me through. I had seen it many times in the movies and on television — the victimized hero finally gets his revenge. I had suffered so much abuse and humiliation at their hands. And now they had gone and killed an innocent creature. If they would shoot my dog, maybe I was next? It was time to stop them and make them pay. They deserved what was coming to them. I opened the door.

But at the very last second, in a startling moment of unexpected clarity, I thought of everything I would be giving up if I pulled the trigger — and everything I would be taking from them too. In the blink of an eye, I was required to make a calculation of guilt and punishment, of violence and peace, of past, present, and future, and of whether to take another human life. I was the judge, jury, and executioner. It could have gone either way. But somehow, miraculously, despite all of the pain I had endured, I realized at that moment that the price of getting revenge was just too high. I took my hand off the gun and drove home. It was a fateful decision that would shape the rest of my life.

Soon thereafter, I decided I wanted to become a lawyer — so I could get justice against the people who wronged me, and others, legitimately, without having to pay a price for it — in fact, while actually *getting paid* for it. Or so I thought.

I worked hard and graduated from an Ivy League law school. I did an internship with the Philadelphia District Attorney's Office and a judicial clerkship with a federal trial court judge. After that, I joined a prestigious law firm where I practiced civil litigation and earned a handsome salary.

I became very good at litigating and winning cases. I overwhelmed and destroyed my opponents with legal research, depositions, interrogatories, and motions — the cunning weaponry of the civil litigator. Each victory brought for my clients and me a thrill. But something unexpected happened. Over time, I began to realize that each of these victories had come at an enormous cost to both my clients and me. To get the justice we so desperately craved, we had to devote virtually all of our energy and waking moments to devising new and better ways of inflicting suffering upon the other side until they either surrendered or were defeated. Strangely, this meant enduring the same suffering ourselves — because we became the instruments of their suffering. My clients and I were forced to relive, obsess over, and amplify the original wrong that had started the conflict in the first place — whether it was a personal injury, an illness, family strife, a criminal act, a governmental prosecution, or a business dispute. Some cases lasted years, meaning that we were, in effect, re victimizing ourselves over and over again, digging at the old wound, keeping it alive and raw. Amazingly, I, as the lawyer, was actually paid a small fortune to do this to my clients — and myself. Yet despite the money, and the victories, I was actually *less* happy with my life — and so were my clients. After the initial "high" of winning wore off, we were left feeling worse but wanting even more. In the midst of all this, I began asking myself: Am I winning battles here but losing a much greater war? How can this be?

My grandfather was a devout Brethren pastor. I was raised Episcopalian and considered becoming an Episcopal priest myself. I have since gone on to study the world's major religions and have become a member of the Religious Society of Friends (Quakers). So I began to look to my spiritual training for answers. Jesus teaches in the Sermon on the Mount that when we are wronged, we should not seek justice but should instead turn the other cheek and forgive. The Buddha has a similar message. I had never understood this injunction. When people hurt me, I instinctively want to hurt them back. They should pay for their crime, and I don't feel better until they do. That is what justice and the courts are all about, and that is what Moses set forth in the laws upon which most Western and Middle Eastern justice systems are based: "An eye for an eye, and a tooth for a tooth." But here was Jesus saying the exact opposite. He seemed to be saying that you are better off just driving away, like I did that night with the farm kids. And by implication, he also seemed to be saying that the legal profession and the entire justice system are fundamentally flawed. This created a personal dilemma for me professionally and spiritually, but it is also a dilemma with which every human being must wrestle. In this world, we will inevitably feel wronged countless times and in countless ways during our lives. What is the path to restoring our happiness and peace when this happens: seeking justice or offering forgiveness?

This is the fundamental conflict that plays out in *The Trial of Fallen Angels.* I wanted to examine this question under the most

extreme circumstances I could imagine —
during the afterlife in the courtroom at the
Final Judgment, where the stakes are all of
eternity and where God Himself is called
upon to answer for the ultimate act of
justice, the Great Flood. What would it be
like to be a lawyer who represents souls in
this celestial courtroom? What would it be
like to be a soul who must face this Judge
— and confront all the fateful choices made
during a lifetime? And what if a lawyer in
this place was asked to represent the soul of
his or her own murderer at the Final Judgment? Would there be any room left for the
inconceivable possibility of forgiveness?

While exploring these fundamental questions of the human condition, I wanted to
write a novel that would at the same time
be a thrilling, page-turning story. As I wrote
the book and discovered the unexpected
answers to these questions, I was astonished.
And transformed.

# ACKNOWLEDGMENTS

It is with deep humility that my name appears on the cover of this book. In many ways, the history of this book goes back thousands of years, and it is the work of thousands of authors. I am better referred to as a scribe.

But even scribes are the beneficiaries of indispensable assistance that makes their work possible. In my case, this begins with my extraordinarily generous wife, Christine, who labored beside me on this project as an unremittingly steadfast supporter and an unrelentingly demanding editor for more than a decade. Her gifts to me and the world leave me speechless and in awe. My daughter, Alexandra, was less than a year old when I began writing this book but during the process became old enough and talented enough as a writer to edit it like a professional. She will be more than a mere scribe very soon. My son, Adam, has not yet reached that age of maturity, but he is old enough to have borne the burden of a father obsessed with a dream. For bearing that burden so well and with such patience, humor, cheerfulness, and love, I extend to him my gratitude and my hope that he chases his dreams, because sometimes dreams come true. Others who fit into this category of inspirers, boosters, nourishers, and bearers include my mother, Faye Kimmel, my brother and sister-in-law, Martin and Sherri Kimmel, and my cousins Myers Kimmel and Sielke Caparelli and her husband, David.

I received crucial early reassurance and incisive editing from my high school friend turned outstanding high school English teacher, Stephen Everhart. I received crucial ongoing encouragement and equally incisive editing from my encyclopedic and multitalented father-in-law, Louis Savelli. This book has benefited greatly from his intellectual prowess and sensitivity.

Finally, but in every bit first, I shower highest praise and appreciation on the dedicated professionals who took risks and devoted their skills to bringing this work to a wider audience. Sam Pinkus was the first literary agent to become an advocate for this book, followed several years later by the immensely talented Matt Bialer. Publishing giant Larry Kirshbaum later took up the mantle, not only as a literary agent but also as a penetrating editor and sage who brought unexpected nuance and focus to the work. The book is now in the capable hands of Jay Mandel and wonderfully enthusiastic film agent Jerry Kalajian. Globetrotters Lance Fitzgerald and Tom Dussel have secured the publication of the book in other lands and languages, while erudite and intrepid copy editor Mark Birkey has greatly improved the readability of the English text (any errors that remain are solely mine). Editorial assistant Liz Stein makes everything happen, and Lisa Amoroso and Chris Welch provided fantastic designs for the cover and interior of the book. And an unidentified but highly appreciated team of artists, salespeople, distributors, booksellers, website designers, readers, and social networkers will perform the miraculous.

With the exception of those whom I may have forgotten and from whom I beg forgiveness, there is one person left to thank. When publisher and editor Amy Einhorn at Amy Einhorn Books first read the manuscript, she said to me: "I don't normally publish spiritual novels, but if I did, I would publish this one." I can think of no higher compliment for this book. Or for its publisher. Amy took a hugely courageous leap of faith to publish something from beyond this world. In her brilliant editing, she contributed portions of her soul. She is one of the heroes in publishing. I will be forever grateful.

# ABOUT THE AUTHOR

**James Kimmel, Jr.,** is the author of *Suing for Peace: A Guide for Resolving Life's Conflicts.* He received a doctorate in jurisprudence from the University of Pennsylvania and is a lawyer who focuses on the intersection of law and spirituality and on helping individuals with mental illness and addictions in the criminal justice system. A member of the Religious Society of Friends (Quakers), he lives in Pennsylvania with his wife and their two children. This is his first novel.